THE CHRONICLES OF THE WOLF

Then the man raised his hand, the girl ducked, the truck flashed its high beams at me again and then it was backing out of the spot and then they were gone. Leaving an empty space between broken white lines of teeth on the pavement.

I had already let the curtain fall back.

I was glad I had already written today. I didn't want to write more. I didn't want to find a way to add a touch of hope to something like this. Something I didn't want to put into the book's pages.

Still, I made sure I just observed the young hooker and her pimp. Light could never truly exist unless darkness surrounded it, and I guess I felt the same way about hope. That people should see a little of the bad of the world, in order for hope to mean anything.

But I did promise myself to just observe. To never write of the lost face of the girl. The twisted face of the young man. I promised myself to just observe this, remember it, carry it, and never write about it. Never report it back to the wolf.

There was no need to hasten along what didn't need hastening.

BOOKS BY CHRIS J. CRANFORD

THE FERGUS GRIMM SAGA

Ghost Town

Recon Team Four

City of the Dead

An Ethereal End

Crown of Bones

Storm of Souls

City of Second Chances

The Crosse Series

The Deadening Wake

The Reality Thief

The Black Horizon

Finn Gallagher

The Chronicles of the Wolf

THE CHRONICLES OF THE WOLF

CHRIS J. CRANFORD

Forged Iron Press

ACKNOWLEDGEMENTS

Purpose.

I think about it a lot. Life is hard. It's not particularly fair. And how, in the middle of grinding away at life, can any of us find real purpose?

I believe in working hard. Helping those you love. Then helping those around us. If each of us could carry that small purpose, we could make the world a little better.place. We could rise like the tide and in that way raise others we never see with us.

It's why Fenrir—my latest tattoo—was important to me. The carrying of a purpose.

Getting this tattoo was a great experience. Not just because of the people, but because I got to see something I believe in: A group of people be a part of the community around them, reach out and inspire local children with art, use their art to inspire others, and make the world around them a little better.

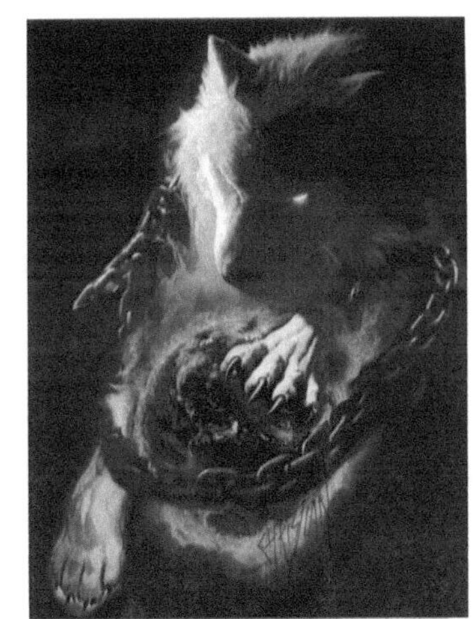

It's what life should be about.

There's good people in Time-warp Tattoo. Good people who love what they do, and use it to help others. Stop by the shop if you're visiting Orlando. Get a tattoo. Have it mean something to you. It's a cool experience, and worth the trip.

Appreciate not just the tattoo of purpose, Christian—appreciate the inspiration as well. And for getting Fenrir right. Carrying a purpose is the greatest of weights, but also the greatest of rewards.

THEN

The third entry of Finn Gallagher, Chronicler of the Wolf, into Sogur Endalok.
Dated March 11th, 2011

I closed the book and left it on the table, having finished writing what I was going to write for this day, in this moment. Observations of what was around me, the people, the families. Gatherings of the feel of the place, the good and the bad of it. I had soaked it all in and then put it on the pages, which was the reason I had been sent here, to Sendai. In Japan.

The chair I sat in was small, too small for a person my size. A sandy-haired American tourist taller than the Japanese men and women here. The hard back and flat bottom were uncomfortable, and my knees were wedged against the underneath of the table, but I was still in some relaxed state. Some warm glow of peace and enjoyment.

I couldn't tell you why I had been sent to watch the Doll Festival; it had been... interesting, to say the least. The display of fancy, imperial dolls in the city center, on their tiered stands, with the traditional robes of the emperor and empress and the rest of the court. More of the same dolls everywhere in the town, on smaller tiers in shop windows, sometimes a singular, fancy doll carried by a girl or her mother.

The display of those dolls was gone now, a week after the festival, even if little girls still ran around with other dolls now, older things of cloth and canvas, rabbits and kittens with human-like faces, and teddy bears. Running around and laughing with the laughs of child-like innocence that could warm anyone's heart.

I had done a little research while I was here. Most of the older dolls, the fancy ones that looked like royalty, those had been passed down from mother to daughter for generations. For centuries. Who knew how old one of those dolls might be? They were passed on with the hope they would protect the little girls from harm, perhaps along with a mother's wish for her daughter, that she have a peaceful and prosperous life.

Part of the experience of it had been nice. It had been, well, human. Watching families, Japanese men and women, walk around in groups. It hadn't felt like Christmas, not really, not to me, but the feeling that tingled inside of me was something along that vein. It was a festival that spoke of happiness and joy, of celebration and family, and while part of that had sunk into me, I couldn't for the life of me understand why he had sent me here to watch all of it.

To watch the festival. To observe the families here. To chronicle everything for the book.

Sendai was much different than my last job. I hadn't been working for the wolf long, not in comparison to those before me. I had just come from a stint in Gaza. There had been a lot of shooting, the Israelis and Hamas and even a few Egyptians. And while I was sure there was a history there, that the fighting came from something carved deeply inside all the parties, to me it had been nothing more than one group not wanting another to have a lot of weapons, and the other groups thinking the first group should mind its own business. It was a little crazy, there had been a lot of blood, and my observations had been both quick and scattered. I had been afraid for my life through most of it, and happy to get away from there as soon as I had.

This—in Sendai, here and now—was relaxing. Nice. Almost a vacation. There were no bullets flying around me. No dead bodies lying around a corner. No man with a scar down the side of his cheek staring at me, a pistol in his hand, his head tilting left and right as if to a pendulum, as if there was a decision to be made, if the man could just stop there for a moment and come to it.

I pulled myself from that memory. I found myself looking down upon the industrial district in Sendai, gazing over the dark waters along in the harbor, the large ships drifting in and out, all the smaller craft scurrying around the larger boats like water spiders across the surface of a pond. To my right were piers, docks, fisheries, and vessels with nets hanging from either side of them bobbing up and down in the low-lapping waves in the harbor. All of the ships came with sounds, the toots of horns of the smaller ships, and the longer bellows of the larger.

Peaceful, the image said to me. And that's what I had written into the book. Everything was peaceful to witness. Relaxing to observe. A pleasure to scribe into the book. A blend of old and new, with the industrial district down below and the traditional-style Japanese buildings around me. The flat, square buildings around the harbor, and the buildings right down the street with their sweeping curved roofs and upturned eaves I remembered mostly from old samurai flicks.

It all had been peaceful, and nice, if a little chilly. There was a bite to the air today that the warm sun above worked to balance out. The breeze blew softly and—even this far away from the harbor—

brought a mix of salt to me, salt with an undercurrent of fish. The thick, briny scent of the catch of today, and yesterday, with a hint of spoilage underneath, of fish perhaps too long out of water.

It was spring, or close enough, this early in March. The grass was lush and green, and the hills held a promise of spring in the closed blossoms along their slopes. Closed now, closed against the chill, I was sure. In a few more weeks I would see nothing but pink and red and white blooms everywhere, from all the cherry and plum trees flowering the landscape.

It was peaceful. Nice. It was pleasant, even. Relaxing.

Which made me wonder, even more, why Fenrir had sent me here.

Certainly the wolf didn't think I needed a vacation, after Gaza. Certainly he didn't have to keep track of vacation time or holidays or sick time, or anything like that. What I did wasn't nine-to-five, I didn't get nights or weekends off. It wasn't like this was a job to be hired for, that he offered things like retirement, a dental plan, or a 401(k).

The wolf had given me a life. And that, for me, was payment enough. I understood the terms of our deal and what I had agreed to. Fenrir had saved my life, he had healed me when nothing else would have, when no one else could have, and in return I had pledged my service to him. As weird as his terms had sounded, I had agreed to go where he sent me, observe the actions of the people there, and write those actions in the book.

Definitely weird, right? Such a small request, a tiny thing to pay for a life saved.

And the request had fallen along the scope of who I had been in my life, before. I had been a writer before the tumor had started baking in my brain. Well, I had called myself a writer. I had been writing, I had felt the call, I had woken every day trying to write, and in the ten years I had been writing I had one short story published, a little thing called *Reagen's Journey*, about a little girl lost in an alien world.

Then the tumor had struck. The cancer had dug into my brain, it had burrowed deeply behind my left eye and began its assassination of the cells there. Slowly at first, one by one, and then in grand sweeping strokes of its tumorous knife, the cancer had killed the dream, and there was no need for me to tell anyone of my desire to write, anymore.

Long story short from there, the wolf had found me. Found me through his own doctor, the doctor helping to keep Fenrir alive, Dr. Berley. It turned out the wolf had need of someone like me, and was willing to heal me for my service. Heal me, and keep me alive.

That healing, that moment had led to where I was now. Had led to a few jobs before this one, jobs I had many questions of, and of which the wolf answered little. The two of us were still getting used to each other; he gruffly responded to the few things I asked, in short chuffs and hot, exasperated breaths, and I danced around those chuffs and kept wondering.

There were a few things I knew. The wolf was still chained by Gleipnir. That made it hard for him to get around. Hard to get around and see what was happening in the world. Which made it hard for Fenrir to decide when he had to release Ragnarok.

Yeah, he still held onto that. The final battle, the call of the cleansing, seemed to burn within the wolf. He seemed to hold on to it with the tight-fisted clench of the greatest scrooge, the wealthiest miser, and at the same time look for the proper time to let the end of the world go. Which is why Fenrir looked for more information. Information I provided, by going around and writing down my observations, of people in times and places the wolf chose.

Like here. And now. I wanted to ask Fenrir why he didn't just let Ragnarok go. Let the end of the world happen. There was a part of me, a growing part, that needed to know the why of it.

I didn't know him well enough to ask. And I couldn't guess at the answer. There was only a sense I had, a sense that the ending needed to happen at a specific time and place, both of which the wolf needed to choose, and for that he needed information.

Looking around at the leftover remnants of the Doll Festival, I didn't know what information the wolf would gather here. Either for, or against Ragnarok. This place I had been sent to, it seemed to have been chosen without a real purpose. As if the wolf had picked it for me from a whim.

Purpose.

That was a funny word. I guess maybe I was stuck with figuring out mine, in this new life I had. Before, as the writer I told others I was, my purpose had been to write something that mattered. *Words* that mattered.

Maybe all writers felt that way, when they put pen to paper. I know I had. I know I still did.

And, in some small way, maybe I was still figuring that purpose out. Maybe I was still trying to write something that mattered. After all, if what I wrote down in these pages, if these words I wrote in Gaza or Sendai led to Fenrir releasing Ragnarok, well, then maybe I was writing *the thing* that mattered most.

Even if no one else would read this book. Even if this story wouldn't end up behind the windows of any bookstore in the world, I was writing down words that mattered. And so I could take a small comfort in my role here, a small comfort in being a part of this, of the new life Fenrir had granted me.

I couldn't know what might cause the wolf to release Ragnarok. To start the final battle. To begin the end of the world, the end of everything. The weight was heavy in my fingers, each time I picked up the pen, trying to decide what to include and what not after observing everything around me.

Try to keep that in mind next time you have to do a book report.

Of course, of course in the beginning I had tried shading my reports. Even in places like Gaza, which was of course, Gaza. With all the shooting and the armies and the dead bodies and the scar-faced guy holding a gun on me... well, it was hard to color something like that with positivity or glowing recommendations of the human spirit. I couldn't write each and every human there fired their guns with regretful faces, that in the end they sadly stood looking upon the dead bodies of people they wanted to call brothers and sisters, because none of that was true.

And reporting the facts sometimes was worse. The death toll. The number of women and children dead. The bomb-torn bodies. The acrid scent of burning tires after a car had exploded next to a restaurant. The look of the tire there, half-melted on the street, with part of an arm laying alongside it, fingers splayed out and stuck to hot rubber.

The facts were usually damning. Even when I tried coloring them in as good a light as I could. I had soon given up, the wolf could always tell. He always knew, he could discern the difference, no matter how I tried. No matter how careful I scrawled the words into the book, with or without bias, the wolf knew.

Maybe it was his experience, from all the scribes who had come before me. Those who had written in the book before me. The men and women who had written all the chapters before I had set pen to the pages.

I called it the book; I would always call it the book. I wasn't going to call it by its real name. I rarely looked at the Nordic runes almost carved into the top, a bunch of things that looked like half-drawn stick people, triangle-topped flags, circles with dots and a few different-sized square blocks, those etched words with even a deeper meaning carved into them

Sogur Endalok.

I won't say what those words mean. I won't tell you its title, I will never write them down in any page, or have them in any thought. I called it the book, I would always call it the book, because I didn't want to think about where its story might lead. Giving the book its real name would give it a purpose, and purposes always had endings, and I didn't want to think where this book's ending might lead.

I fingered the book now. It was hard not to, when it was out. It felt like a hardback, the front and back cover made of something stern, but it was protected with an odd dust jacket. Something that felt like leather, just thinner. More supple. Tight over the hard-backed front and back of the book.

Like the book, the dust jacket was more than a dust jacket. A tree ran along the spine of it, the trunk thicker than the book was wide, its branches spreading out over the front and back of the book, branches that seemed to number in the thousands.

Yggdrasil. That I would name.

The tree felt more real than not. Rubbing my hand over the supple leather-like surface of the dust jacket, I could almost feel the bark, rough along my palm. I could almost feel every branch brush its way over my fingertips. If I looked closer, which I rarely did, I could see a pair of ravens on one of the branches, though never the same branch. There would be a squirrel, scurrying its way up or down the tree. Sometimes I would see an eagle near the tree's top, sometimes a hawk on the beak of the eagle.

Sometimes I might see snakes. At least, I thought they were snakes. Maybe they were just the roots of the tree.

And sometimes, though I rarely looked this close anymore, I would see the dead man. What appeared to be a corpse, hanging from a thick branch of the tree. If I stared too long I thought I could see his body, drifting back and forth under that branch, as if a wind gently rocked him…

I pulled my gaze away.

The book would do that to you. It would do that to anyone. It had likely done that to every chronicler before me, every man and woman Fenrir had pulled into his service. However many of those that had been. The pages, if I dared to go back and look through them, numbered in the thousands. In the hundreds of thousands.

The book was without a beginning or an end. At least, it had no end at this very moment, which I was thankful for. And, as much as I had flipped back through it, trying to find the very beginning, I hadn't found its very first words. The languages had changed, from modern English to old English to Latin, from Latin to a variety of older languages, to Nordic runes themselves. There were smatterings of other languages, there had been the flowing script of a Spanish Chronicler, there had been oddly ordered Chinese writing in places, I had even caught hieroglyphics, once, on a random flip-through.

Languages throughout our history. Languages of our history. Everything in our past was in this book. And hopefully, everything into our future.

At least into and past mine. I had taken service to the wolf because it had saved my life. There were other attractions to the job, sure. A perk or two. I would live much longer than other humans. I could heal from most injuries, though a bullet to my head would kill me the same as choking on a piece of steak.

I wasn't immortal, but I was close. After the death of a dream, after a bout with cancer, close was good enough for me. Even if it meant writing stories that might lead to the end of my world.

So I sat there, ruminating about things. Thinking about my recent pledge to the wolf. Thinking about Gaza, and the bloodshed there. The things humans would do to other humans in the name of belief, or the desire for power. I could understand why Fenrir would send me there, I could understand him wanting to see the worst humanity had to offer, even if—after thousands upon thousands upon thousands of years—he hadn't seen enough yet to call the cleansing.

I just couldn't understand why he had sent me here.

I remembered him, back in his ice-cold cavern, the darkness surrounding the huge beast. I could remember the moment where—when he told me where to go next, after Gaza—I had blurted out why?

The chuff of the wolf. The hot, warm breath of the chuckle brushing across my face, bringing its moist scent of old meat.

"You go where I tell you, do you not?" Fenrir had asked me, mildly. If the rumbling stampede of his voice could be called mild.

"Of course, Lord Fenrir," I said quickly.

Another chuff. The wolf did not like to be called lord, or god, or anything else. He was simply Fenrir, I had been told that, and yet it was hard for me to not add an honorific, when standing in front of a god.

I corrected myself. Shivering in the icy cavern. I never could wear enough to stay warm, that deep under the earth. "Fenrir."

Another blow of his hot breath. Harder this time. Perhaps a warning.

"Then go to Sendai, Chronicler," the wolf said. "Go, enjoy yourself. Perhaps after this, you will understand."

And so here I was. Enjoying myself. Musing about the book I would not name, and all the Chroniclers before me. Watching all the families walk around, even if the Doll Festival was over, and had been over for a few days. Watching all the little girls still walk around, tiny things holding tiny dolls, keeping the dolls tight to their chests, hugging them as they walked around, hugging them tightly, so that all the rabbits and kittens and teddy bears would swing gently side-to-side underneath their arms, Raggedy-Ann like, as the girls ran from spot to spot along the harbor.

I smiled and closed my eyes, my hand on the book. Feeling

warm, even in the tiny chill of early March. Feeling a small thing glow inside of me, even if the branches of Yggdrasil lay under my palm.

A blaring beeping sound cut through the glow. Like the loudest car alarm a person could hear. A raging sound that cut through the smile of my thoughts, the glow of my reflection, had me yank open my eyes.

It was like an air-raid siren, just instead of that steady windup call of incoming aircraft, it was something that beat insistently against my ears. Loud and shrill-like. A screeching, clanging thing. The clanging was followed by a voice. Urgent sounding, even if the voice was prerecorded. And in Japanese.

I had no idea what the voice was saying.

And I didn't really get a chance to ask anyone.

In that same moment the ground started shaking around me. It shook like a giant had grabbed Sendai and shook the town. It shook as if the giant had picked up the entire island of Japan in both hands and shook it. Sendai, the town, the ground around me vibrated as if the giant was full of an old anger, as if he had woken up, had too much caffeine, and raged.

I grabbed the book, quickly, and in a motion that wasn't quite practiced slid it into its satchel, a brown thing that just seemed to fit the book, with a darker brown strap that currently hung around my opposite shoulder. I slid the book in and flipped the flap of the satchel over, covering the book.

And that was all I had time for. The ground was vibrating and bouncing enough that I fell out of my chair, fell to my knees, my hands against the sidewalk just trying to stay in place. The cement tore into my palms, and I watched the table of the restaurant I was sitting at dance away from me, over shaking ground. I watched the table dance even as my chair toppled over behind me.

The little girls, the families that had been walking around

together, were now running. Everyone was running, running up from the harbor, running past me in small groups and larger crowds. I had frozen a bit, noticing everything, observing it. Like any writer might, but especially a Chronicler.

The families streamed by. Fathers pulling mothers, mothers pulling sons and daughters. They streamed by in flashes of color, in sounds of screams and yells, Japanese words that I couldn't understand and could barely even distinguish with the clanging of the alarm. They streamed by, hand pulling hand, past me and up the street.

There a group of people stood. Outside what looked to be a large, firmly built building. Maybe a temple or a school, or some government building. It was a square, flat block of a thing among the sweeping roofs around it. The building—hopefully a shelter— lay a few blocks down, the crowds and people were hard to distinguish, but the people there held a pair of doors open and seemed to be waving at everyone around to *run*.

That seemed like a great idea. The earth kept bouncing, kept vibrating, though the vibrations seemed less now. As if the earth-moving giant had worked out a lot of his anger in the quick, violent shakes of moments ago.

The clanging of the alarm kept clanging. The words of the Japanese prerecorded voice kept saying whatever it was saying around the alarm. I pushed myself up. Both my palms were raw and bleeding, just a bit. My legs felt rubbery against the ground, but I took a step.

And kept standing. The earth trembled, a bit. Once or twice. I tested a second step and started heading down the street. Towards the square block of a building with people waving me on. Waving everyone on. I walked and started up in a light jog, and got about halfway there when I heard the cry.

I looked back. Down from the restaurant was a little piece of landscape. A tiny park, a green hill of lush grass that would be even greener when March turned into April, and which held the bare branches of cherry trees. There was a little girl there, crying and looking around, sitting with her small legs looking around.

I paused there, watching. I couldn't see anyone else around. There was no mother rushing over to pick up her daughter. No father there.

Perhaps they had run. Maybe the earthquake had scared them. Maybe a piece of ceiling had fallen and knocked them on their head, maybe they had fallen from a pier below the small park into the harbor water.

Whatever it was, the little girl was alone.

I looked back at the men shouting. Their arms waving at everyone. Pulling them in to whatever building they stood before. Waving me on.

They couldn't see the girl. They couldn't hear her, with the clanging alarm and prerecorded voice everywhere in Sendai. I was lucky enough to have heard her.

I took off in a stumbling run towards the girl. I picked up speed running to the harbor. She was trying to push herself up, she couldn't have been more than four or five. The earth shook again and she tumbled down and fell. The park had a little slope to it, she fell and rolled a bit further away from me, just a few feet, coming to a stop when the aftershock finished.

I cursed and ran faster, though my running was more staggering, as aftershocks happened almost sporadically, shifting the earth under my steps. I fell once more myself. It wasn't an easy run, the ground kept moving, it almost blurred when it shook, but I finally got there. Got to the little girl.

She lay there, crying. A teddy bear next to her. She was crying and a tiny arm had grabbed the arm of the teddy bear and I had never been more happy to pick something up and hold it in my arms. I fell to my knees and picked her up, folding the little girl into my chest, feeling the teddy bear between her warm body and mine.

The little girl felt small, small and warm. She cried, loud against my ears, but all I felt was relief. I kept her wrapped in my arms and staggered up, thinking to head back to the shelter. The earth moved again, once, as if it had finished with me. Finished with Sendai. As if it had done everything it wanted to.

I didn't look at the town around me. It hadn't been long, but I noticed without noticing the destructions. The small craft tossed alongside the piers. The roofs collapsed around me. Electric wires dancing alongside fallen poles.

I didn't look at any of that, though I noticed. I was a writer. I was a Chronicler, it's what I did. Which is why I felt it, before I saw it. Which is why I stood there, the little girl in my arms, and slowly looked back. Out to sea. And I saw it, the thing that had suddenly caused the rippling up and down my spine. That had stirred the deepest fear, dark in the underneath well-like depths of my brain.

A wave.

Not a wave, but the wave. Something that towered over the horizon. A wall of water rolling in from the ocean. A wall that rose, higher and higher, as the wave neared Sendai. A wave that, for all its size, moved at some inhuman pace.

Not a wave. Not even the wave. But a tsunami.

I held the girl tightly in my arms and looked for the shelter again. It seemed too far now, up the street. I didn't think I'd make it, part of me knew I would never make it, but still I ran. I hugged the girl tight to my chest and ran.

I ran not looking back.

I ran feeling the wave behind me, swelling larger and larger in the ocean behind me.

I ran, my feet pounding the pavement, staggeringly I ran, feeling the power of the tsunami behind me in the rushing thunder of it. In the loud crashing of the water, like I was standing right next to Niagara Falls.

I ran, holding the girl tightly to my chest and, though I had met a god and knew they existed, did something I rarely had done before. Something I hadn't done even in the depths of my madness, when the cancer was eating my brain from the inside out.

I prayed.

I got to the top of the little park. I ran down the street. The shelter was there now, but the people were gone. The doors were shut. I ran, feeling the wave grow larger behind me, seeing the shadow of it swell before me and engulf everything, hearing the rushing thunder grow louder and louder, feeling each strike of my feet pounding the street, holding the little girl tight against my chest, her legs swinging back and forth as I ran with everything I had.

Somewhere along that run was when the tsunami hit.

I had known I wasn't going to make it. I had known it the first moment I had turned and seen the wave. I don't know why I had run in the direction I had, in the general panicky way of fleeing, of flight, from something you can't hope to escape. I don't know why I had decided to run in the particular direction I did, why I hadn't looked for some closer place to hide. Why I hadn't hoped to find some miracle that would save me and the girl.

Maybe because there really had been no place.

Maybe because there had been no other hope.

Maybe because—in that flash of an instant of me seeing the tsunami and understanding what was going to happen, with that little girl huddled against my chest, her teddy bear between us, with her legs dangling from my arms and mine hugged around her small form, I wished for nothing more than to be back in front of that scar-faced man in Gaza, begging him to pull the trigger.

I don't know if I had actually died. I can tell you what I can remember. I can at least write that.

Something had hit my back with the force of a locomotive. It had picked me up and tossed me forward, into the row of buildings there, the traditional homes with the sweeping rooflines and turned-up eaves. I had tried to turn in the middle of the force and take the smacking force of it on my back. I had screamed and found cold salt water rushing down my throat. I was surrounded by it, I was surrounded by it and holding onto the little girl with everything I could. With everything I had.

It wasn't enough.

And I had no idea when I lost her. When the rapid hand of the tsunami had clawed the little girl away from me. But it had. There would always be that moment, the cracking slap of my back against the wall of the building, the cold chilly salt water surrounding me, surrounding us, the salt water pouring down my throat as I screamed and tried to hold on to the little girl, as her form was torn away from me, torn away in a wash of current I could never stand up to, never understand.

That water tossed me around. It was dark and I was sightless. It pounded me against stone and wood and whatever else swam in those currents with me. It pounded me and drowned me and tugged me deeper. I couldn't swim or hope to move or protect myself, and eventually, it all just ended for me with darkness.

Then a gentle, dawn-like awareness. The awareness that comes with light upon closed eyelids. An awareness that came with stabbing pains and aches of broken ribs, of a split gash on my temple, of warm blood spilling down my cheek and the gentle coughs of someone who had thrown up, over and over, but still had that moist feel of water deep in their lungs.

I retched, one more time. Felt that rattling wetness in my lungs still. Then opened my eyes. I was laying against the side of a building. I didn't recognize where. I lay a little to one side, leaning and feeling the strap of the satchel stretch against my neck, my elbow holding me against the street there.

The city around me was gone. The industrial district, the boats, large and small, the traditional homes with the samurai-flick roofs were all gone. In its place were broken timbers, blocks of stone, torn girders of steel. Boats lay everywhere, there was a fisherman's vessel right across from me, upside down on the broken carcass of a building, the fisher nets spread out to the side like empty wings.

I had no idea how long I had been there. How long I had been out. All I knew was that I had lost the little girl. That for one moment I had felt her, felt her warm body against my chest, felt her in my arms—and then a moment later she had been just torn away. Torn away, no matter my strength, no matter how hard I had tried holding on. Her body had slipped away from my arms, the water had stolen her, and I had this last memory, this memory I was sure would never go away, this moment where her tiny fingers rested at the slightest edge of mine, where my fingers had grasped so hard for hers...

And then, gone.

And then, blackness.

I looked at my hand. It was still clenched in a fist. I forced it open. A torn-off paw of a teddy bear lay there. I looked at it and cried, and cried, and cried.

I sobbed while people began walking around. I cried while they walked past me, looking for their own lost loved ones, for their destroyed homes, for other survivors. I cried and at some point pulled out the book and sat there, writing all this in too.

I sat there, writing about the sorrowful cries of an old woman walking up and down the street, alone. Calling out in a broken voice, before moving on and doing the same. Watching her fall once, fall down and cry and never move to get back up.

I wrote about the joyful family walking past, the father and mother, the daughter and son, all seemingly together and whole, and almost ashamed to be so. They walked by in a quiet happiness, a huddled happiness, a soft glow from them they tried to hide from others.

I wrote about all the men and women that worked long into the day, long past the day, digging into collapsed homes, digging out body after body, sadly never stopping, but piling up the bodies down the street in some vain hope to find one that moved. About the one man who came over with a hot cup of something, pulling the old woman to a seat, putting his arm around her even though she didn't know him, and sat there saying things I couldn't understand.

I wrote about a teenage girl that walked by me and stopped, watching me for a long moment. A girl with a look in her eyes, an aged look that would only get older as she grew. A knowing look, as she saw the teddy bear's paw still tightly clenched in the grip of my hand.

I wrote all those things. Understanding more than I had the day before. Understanding that an ending wouldn't be an ending, unless it was sad.

I wrote all those things, and more, in the book with no name. Coloring none of it. Shading not a word. Just wanting it to be a part of the story, to exist as a tale long after I was gone, to have someone, somewhere, always remember the tight warm feeling of a little girl held protectively to their chest. To read these words, remember this feeling, and to never want to let her go.

I came to the end of my story. One of many I had written now. Thousands of meaningless words scrawled on page after never-ending page. Observations I brought back to the wolf, things I had once attributed great importance to, and yet now, after a decade... I had begun to wonder.

The book felt heavy in my hands. Thick, yet also light. Oddly easy to carry for all its weight. The firm, leather-like jacket cover soft and cool against my palms. I flipped the last page, a page too thick to be paper, even if its crisp light edge curled against the side of my finger. As I flipped I moved my bookmark, something I had fashioned from the tiny paw of an old teddy bear, the paw mostly flat now, its stuffing removed, rough thread stitches sealing the bottom of its brown, fuzzy arm.

The next page was blank. There was always a next page, and it was always blank. Just like there were thousands of stories before the blank page, stories written by hands different from mine. Written in thick, bold strokes. Written in a light cursive hand. Written in weak scrawls.

There had been many writers before me. Other writers than Finn Gallagher. Scribe after scribe over the centuries. Chroniclers of other times, other places. All coming back here with their tales, with what they had observed, with what they had seen.

I folded the book shut, perhaps a little quickly. A little hard. The muffled whump echoed softly through the dark cave I sat in, like a single clap of gloved hands. The whump disappeared into the blackness before returning to me, a hollow sound for all its likeness. A faint stir of air brushed my cheek, cold, from the gentle *whop whop whop* of a large fan buried in a ventilation shaft far above me.

I shivered. It was cold in here, it was always cold this deep under the mountain. Cold and dark, smelling faintly of minerals and damp fur. In this day, in this moment, the cave felt colder than usual. Darker than usual. The lights were off; lately they were always off, the fluorescent lights hanging throughout the cave. The only light I had was a tiny bit from the window's glass behind me, a light that cast most of the deep metamorphic rock into a true blackness, a darkness one could never see on the Earth's surface.

Only here could one see the difference between light and dark. Only here could one see blackness as the absence of light. Only here could I sit and make my report to the creature I had bound myself to. Only here could I stare into the true darkness, the darkness outlined by a briefest edge of light, and watch dark shadows blend into one another, dark shadows moving among the truest blackness, so I couldn't truly see what moved, and what didn't.

A chuff sounded. Perhaps a chortle, echoing hollowly away, like the closing whump of my book. There was nothing after the chuff, so that the whopping of the fan was only interrupted by the thick, powerful breaths of the creature hidden right in front of me. Deep breaths from a thick, cavernous chest.

The current of air brushed over my face again; I shivered, again. I could never wear enough clothes here, never put on enough layers.

I had made my first report in jeans and a T-shirt; I had since learned to dress more appropriately. In what they call layers. Long johns under my jeans, a flannel shirt over my T-shirt. All of that finished with a fur-lined winter coat, boots, thick socks. And none of that seemed to be able to hold back the cold of the cavern, layers and thick coat liners never seemed to be able to hold in enough heat. The air always was too chill, and where the iciness of the air didn't steal the heat from me, the stone seemed to leech it out.

The creature took another deep breath, letting it out slowly, a long breath that came out as a long puff of moist steam. It was a breath that—even seeing it—I felt more than heard, I felt more than saw. It was a breath that came as a low rumble, one that reminded me of a stampede of bulls. A breath that blew over me, one I wasn't thankful for, for all its warmth, because it brought the scent of old meat.

"Is that all?" he asked, in his voice of rumbling stampedes.

"Yes." I had found it better, over the years, to answer his questions simply. To report on where I had been, what I had seen. To read the story of the place I had visited, to give the creature the facts. It was the price of my bond to the creature, it was what he had asked, and what I had promised. Such a small thing, I had thought at that time, for a long life.

For a life at all.

I had questions, after my first read. Questions that raised the creature's ire. Perhaps the same questions those before me had, perhaps questions he had tired of hearing. So, after reading the story, simple answers sufficed. I had learned not to give him something he might pick apart, something that might get us to one of our... debates, would put the world kindly. Especially when...

The creature stirred. Even in the blackest shadows of the deep earth I saw him move. Felt him move, as small vibrations running along the rock underneath me. The long length of body shifted, the dark fur covering his skin parted as he moved, tiny flashes of electric blue traced back and forth. Not all over his body, just in places, small trails of blue lightning darting back and forth underneath the creature's fur, electric pulses running from a metallic plate here, a circuit board-like thing there,

The voice rumbled. "Truly?"

Truly? I tried to hide my expression. No. Athens had been odd. Just like Portland had been odd before it. I had spent weeks there, noting what I had seen. Writing it all down, trying to keep my style clean and bare, knowing that somehow I always seemed to capture some opinion in my words, the creature always heard it, as hard as I tried.

There had been the almost abandoned stores and shops and restaurants in Greece, the windows boarded up, the doors locked. The blue masks, almost paper-like in their thinness, fluttering across empty streets. There had been groups of people with masks, other groups without. All of them huddled separately, small groups of people, there had been the isolated almost back-stabbing feel of a city where every neighbor looked at the person next to them from the side of their eyes, where each and every person only trusted the people closest to them.

And maybe, not even those people.

I had written all that down, but I hadn't written what had struck me most. That had been a young man, walking back alone down the street. He had passed me with one of those cheap plastic bags you get at a pharmacy. It was obvious he wasn't feeling well, his head down, his mask on, his hand flicking up to adjust it, his other hand tight around the neck of the plastic bag.

I would never know where he was going. Or why he chose to go out at that time and get that bag from a pharmacy. But I saw him though, just like I saw other people watching him. People across the street, standing singly, sometimes together. People with masks, people without.

Each of them stared at the young man with distrust, with mocking, with some emotion like hate underneath. Hate and anger and a wild loose rage that perhaps had no real origin, but just existed on its own.

It made me sad, thinking about that young man now. Sick in a time where sickness was the most scarlet of letters. Sick, and likely alone. Trudging out for who knew what reason into a world that surely would hate every step he took. Maybe he had been alone in his apartment, alone with no one to pick up any medicine for them, alone with no doctor wanting to see them, alone and getting sick and fighting the fear of going out into this world we lived in today.

The image stuck with me, the bent-over steps of the young man and his bag of medicine, walking alone in the world we lived in today. Walking alone and getting aloner, getting aloner and getting worse, until finally he had decided he had needed something: aspirin, ibuprofen, decongestant, whatever it was he clutched in his bag. Getting those meds, whatever square edges of it poked into that plastic bag, and then walking back under the mocking stares of some, the condemning stares of others.

I didn't know how to help the young man. I didn't know what the right answer was. I just knew it was a worse world today, than yesterday.

Athens had been a city once that had thrived with tourists. Where the people there welcomed newcomers with open arms. Now there were sides. There were groups. And then some nameless emotion hung in the air, something I couldn't name, not really, but something that felt like a lot like *blame*. Maybe more than just blame, something that felt like accusation, fear, hate, all those emotions tied together in what I felt there. All that tied together with a feeling of rebuke, with a hint of *how dare you* and the tiniest touch of evil, like the sharpest point of a knife resting on my spine.

If I had really written what I felt, I would have said something was on the horizon. Something was coming, something was being birthed, something dark and foreboding. There was a cold, barren feeling of a storm brewing.

I had felt those things, but I hadn't written them. Not about the young man, and everything I had felt watching him. I had penned the events I had observed. The things I had witnessed. I had kept my writing free of emotion and just covered the actions of what I had seen, because actions always revealed the truth. Actions were palpable, real things that might once have been the news, before the news had become something... different.

I had written clean. I had written the actions. I had kept my emotions out of it, and yet there was no real surprise, to the creature or me, when I hesitated at his question. Even with my one-word responses. Even with trying to keep my answers short.

The beast chuckled, a weird sound coming from his long, canine jaws. It was deep and throaty, it rumbled from his large belly. It was a chuckle reflected in the beast's eyes, open now that he was done listening, the twin yellow irises each larger than my head.

Big eyes, better to see things with...

The line just popped into my head. But I didn't laugh. One never laughed in front of Fenrir. The great wolf. The god who would bring Ragnarok one day.

And also, my master.

"You still think humans can be saved," Fenrir told me.

Did I?

Thinking about the young man, sometimes even I questioned what I believed. But even then, Fenrir knew. He knew the small flicker I held deep within myself, that there was a group of us who wanted better. Who wanted to help those they could. That strived to improve the world we all lived in, despite what they faced.

It was why I had started writing, after all. That belief. That hope that I could inspire someone to be that kind of person.

I hid my face from the wolf, staring at the cover of the book I held in my lap. The silhouette there of a large tree, the trunk along the spine of the book, its leafless branches spreading across the cover. A circle at the top of the spine of the book, a carved circle of a large serpent swallowing its own tail.

Everything was dark on the book. Everything was black. Shadows, silhouettes, reflections of things that exist in the real world. Outlines of what might have been. What could be.

I looked at it without looking. Something about the tree bothered me. Peering too close brought in a level of detail that just couldn't exist. The branches couldn't really go on endlessly, as if they numbered in the thousands. Surely there wasn't a shadow of a squirrel there, running along the bark. Surely there wasn't an outline of an eagle, always somewhere near the top of the tree, with a hawk sometimes perched on its beak.

Surely, if I looked closely, as I had done once, I wouldn't find the image of a man swaying softly in some hidden breeze, hanging from a rope...

I swallowed and looked away. There were no safe places here in the darkness. Nothing I could face but the book and the wolf. Maybe that was the point. My hand grasped the spine of the book, the cover was soft, pliable, a soft feeling almost like leather... and not.

The wolf waited, seeming to see all things. Understand each and every thought I had. Every motion I performed. He waited, and I knew he would wait until I answered.

He had all the time in the world, after all. I knew it, and he knew it. Especially, since he was the god who would end it. He knew he had all the time in the world, and he knew I believed some of the world should still be saved. He knew it; I knew it.

And both us knew, together, the day where they might need to be saved was closing in.

I finally answered. I finally admitted it. Like I always did. "I do."

The chuckle again, and yet not. More of a cough, a sharp bark. "You are not the first."

The wolf had told me that, many times. I wasn't the first to think so, that this world could be saved. I wasn't the first person to go out in the world and chronicle what was happening there, bring that news back to Fenrir. I wasn't the first.

But I might be the last.

"You are not the first," Fenrir repeated, his tone… *musing?* "Though you are perhaps the most persistent."

He shifted again. The wolf. In the blackness one of his great haunches moved, as if his leg was restless, or ached, the movement bringing the sound of claws scratching stone. Again I saw the bright sparks of blue electricity running over bare wires, between metallic plates and what looked to be electronic modules.

Fenrir had lived a long time. Even gods age. And, towards the end, maybe even gods needed a bit of help to last another century. Another decade. Another day.

The thought had me wondering, like it always did. Why did Fenrir hang on? Why did the wolf send me out into the world, repeatedly, to bring him back stories of what was happening. What did he glean from my words, as careful as I might craft him?

Why did Fenrir wait to release Ragnarok?

The rumble came, stronger. Angrier. As if from a place of pain. Saying the words the wolf had told me most often. "Ragnarok will happen. Everything, everyone, all: gods, beasts, men, *all* will fall, one day."

I took a chance. "I understand, Fenrir." The wolf did not like to be called a god, or a lord, or a king. The wolf did not speak to me as a god, he was Fenrir, and Fenrir was enough for him. "I just don't understand why. Why not try to save those who can be saved? Why not try to help those who might need help? If Ragnarok has to happen, why not make the next world better?"

We had had this argument many times. Maybe the wolf had had them in his past with the others before me, it was likely enough to have happened. Maybe the others had been happy enough with their long lives and, knowing their place in history, were happy enough not to ask the questions I did.

There had been many before me, though perhaps there wouldn't be many after. I had written enough to know when a story was drawing to its close. I knew when an ending was circling around in the pages ahead of me. I knew when a story was reaching its peak, and I knew when the moment was coming, where a story reached its crest and broke, washing away from the reader.

I certainly felt that, now. In the words I wrote. In the thickness of the book, the many pages before mine. The few blank pages after.

"Do you understand why a tree sprouts?" The wolf asked. His eyes piercing yellow lanterns in the dark. "Why the Earth circles the Sun? Why, when you thirst, you look for water and lap it up?"

Questions he had asked me the time before. Questions I answered, now, having thought about them. "The tree grows so that it can spread its seeds. Gravity holds the Earth to the Sun. And I drink water when I am thirsty to replenish what I've lost."

The wolf let out a snort; a hot wash of air hit me, bringing again its scent of meat long eaten. "Surface answers, my Chronicler. You speak to me of things on the surface, look past the skin and dig into the meat. Why is it, that water placates your thirst? Out of all the worlds you could be born to, why this Earth?

Circling this Sun? Why does the tree have to grow before spreading its seed?"

Like other times and other questions, I had answered these unsatisfactory. The wolf dug for something in me, and I was unsure what. I was even unsure of the *why*.

I shrugged.

"Exactly," Fenrir breathed, almost a pant. As if some emotion had been stirred in the wolf, an emotion that both angered him and exhausted him. His great lips long and black and mottled a bit with age. "The cleansing is not for you to question. Ragnarok is not for someone to decide. There will be no decisions of who lives or dies. There will be no *guidance* to the next world. No preparing. No saving."

He had said these words to me many times. In different ways. Being who I was, I had written them down. And still, still I could not find the answer the wolf searched for.

"You want to save *some*, Chronicler," The wolf coughed, a laugh, a snort, I could not tell. "Who would you save? Who deserves to live? What gives you that power? What gives you that right?"

What gave me the right?

Nothing, truly. Nothing gave me the right. But I saw the end coming, I could feel it. And when the end comes a man could face it, or he could turn away. He could face it and save what he could, or he could huddle up and hide and let the end take him.

"It is all or nothing, human," The wolf said, as if reading my thoughts. "It is always all or nothing."

I didn't want the end to come. I didn't want it to take me. It had happened before, and I hadn't been ready then, just like I wasn't ready now. I would fight now, like I had then. I would save *something*. It couldn't be all or nothing, it just couldn't be. Something had to remain.

"You don't know, Chronicler," the beast said. "You don't know, you can't begin to understand, the forces out there. The gods, those who want Ragnarok to happen. Those who don't. Those who want to prevent the end of the world and those who embrace it, they all play it like the game, *all* of them, no matter that they change the game on whims and fancies. No matter that the game changes while they play."

A deep, indignant breath. A snort. "They play it like I am some chip on the board, and all the while I wait. I wait, and I watch, until it is time for me to pounce." His voice had grown both angry and deadly at the same time, full of that quiet rage that comes when vengeance was long in the planning. "It is what the great hunters do best."

This was the first time he had spoken to me of other gods, aside from the very beginning. That I should be careful of those out in the world, careful of the lies, perhaps even careful in the truths, because some of the greatest lies were threaded with the hardest truths. That there would be those who wanted to sway me, one way or the other.

That other gods would try to find Fenrir, through me. They would try to sway me to their side. And if they failed, they would kill me.

It had happened in the past. At least, I had assumed so. There were reasons other hands had written in the book before mine.

Yet, for all his warning, I had met no other god. I was still relatively new in Fenrir's service, ten years now, so maybe that was expected. There had been no Thor bringing his hammer to an argument. No lightning bolts from Odin. There had been no lies from Loki. I had met none of them, none that I recognized, at least. There was just the world, and me reporting on it, and that had been all.

Maybe the other gods needed time to figure out who I was. That I was the new scribe in Fenrir's side. There were billions of people in the world, after all. It would be hard to single out one. Maybe there was a grace period, between the death of the scribe before me and the beginning of my service.

Maybe I was just too small a piece on the board, to play.

"Do you know the difference between gods and men, Chronicler?" The wolf's voice was still tinged with anger, it still rumbled with dreamed-of vengeance, and perhaps something more.

I held myself still. This, this was new. A new question. A new direction. Something Fenrir had never asked me before, his voice edged with some other emotion, something sharp and hot and yet, resigned. Something that cut, and felt perhaps a little broken.

The emotions of the wolf were always powerful. They would wash over me in waves, and leave something of themself behind. Sometimes angry. Sometimes glee. Sometimes salt, like an ocean had washed over me, leaving little bits of salt on my skin.

Did I know the difference? Other than the obvious? Gods were immortal, humans weren't. Gods had powers, humans didn't. I could answer any of those, but instead I shook my head.

In times of great emotion, especially with the wolf, simple is always better.

"There is none," Fenrir said, his words still colored with that pained edge, still sharp and yet somehow worn at the same time. As if deep inside the wolf, anger warred with acceptance. As if he warred still with pain, with age, with the fate he had been tasked with. "Gods can be just as petty as your kind, and twice as cruel."

His muzzle shook, violent and quick and brief, like he was letting his thoughts go. Letting go of the emotion buried deep within him. The motion reminded me of the twitch of a dog's head, as if a flea had buzzed near his ears.

Perhaps I should expect his words. Odin had trapped Fenrir, after all. Trapped and bound him with Gleipnir. Bound up the wolf and his Ragnarok with the thinnest of strands. And while the wolf never spoke of the All-Father, and though I never had seen the most powerful of the Norse gods, I knew enmity when I felt it. Deserved, or not.

"The end comes, Chronicler. Scribe. The end comes, whether humans are good, whether humans are evil," Fenrir stated, his voice firm. Resolute. "It will be all or none, and there will be none to save, because Ragnarok is a cleansing. Ragnarok will come, like the sprouting of a tree, like the circling of the sun, like your thirst... the cleansing will come and It. Will. Not. Be. Stopped."

His last words had been punctuated with heavy pants. His breath now came hot and heavy, each pant a deep exhale. The cavern flooded with the wolf's breath: the warm, moist scent of old meat.

I tried to breathe myself, in small amounts. Watching Fenrir. The wolf spoke to me more now. More than he had in the beginning. Perhaps he sensed the end as much as I did. Perhaps, even as he questioned my ignorance of Ragnarok, he still wanted some small understanding of his part in it. Perhaps that was the Chronicler's real purpose. As if the wolf wanted, needed someone to understand his purpose. As if nearing the end, he found that was something he needed.

If he thought about it at all. Why does a god need understanding? I let out a snort of my own. Knowing I had a better chance of figuring out why a tree sprouts.

His leg moved again. Claws raked the stone. A flash of something thin trailed from his hind leg, a silk-like thread there. Something that danced briefly with light, illuminating tiny figures etched into the thread, runes. I thought of the power there, in that tiny thread dancing with runes, of something so thin that held back a destructive force so large...

The wolf let out a moan, a sound I had never heard before. It was long and low and full of something I would call mournful. It was a call, a crying aloud of pain and loneliness and a long, long time carrying the heaviest of burdens.

The cave woke up around me. Beeps echoed along the walls as computer screens lit up from a large bank of them along the wall by the wolf. Beeps like a heart rate monitor, slow beeps of a large heart pounding heavily inside its chest. The screens illuminated the darkness, threw back a bit of the shadows, showing me the true size of the great wolf.

Fenrir lay before me on the stone. Great in size, as large as a house. He lay on a bed of old hide, something from an age long past, his dark fur threaded with white. His large frame sunken, as if the bones had once carried something much greater than the beast in front of me. Much greater in size and strength.

Feelings warred within me. The deepest desire I held, that of a Ragnarok that never came. A world ending which never came to be. That fear warred with some other emotion, something deep in my chest. Something that had me want to reach out to the wolf and hold that great being, hug him to me and hold him and feel his pain, feel his body shudder, put an arm underneath his great shoulder and carry part of his burden…

The wolf howled then. Howled like a great wolf of old, tilting his head up and howling in page and rage and defiance, tilting his head up until his nose touched the bottom of the cavern's roof. He howled long and low and let out all the pain that racked him, all the aches that came with age, the bone-cracking torture of carrying the heaviest of burdens, the stabbing sharpness of the wound that never seemed healed, the thing with plated metal overtop of it, along his haunch.

The howl went on forever. The sound reverberated in my skull; I ducked my head into my arms, still holding the book, protecting my ears against the howl. Feeling all Fenrir's great pain in that long, mournful, rage-filled cry.

Then it ended.

The cavern echoed in a hollow silence. In the absence of the howl. Fenrir lay before me. His head down on his hide, his jowls spreading across a pillow there, something the size of a king bed to me. He blinked, his eyes looked hazy, as if the wolf was looking back at another time and place.

His mouth barely moved. His words—for the wolf—came out in a whisper. There was a hint of a pup to them, something innocent and young. "I remember the sun," he whispered, such a tiny sound from the wolf, tiny and small and lost in memory. His lips curved, gently, just a small peeling back of his thick, mottled lips. "I remember the smell of the daises, of frolicking in the fields. Of rolling in the grass and the warmth on my belly…"

Something tingled along my back. I had never seen this side of Fenrir. His words brought an image in my mind, something unbidden and not of my imagination. Something from the wolf. A tiny pup in a field the size of an ocean. Daisies spread across the field, daises of all colors: white-petalled, yellow, red; all the flowers open to the brightest yellow sun hanging in the bluest of skies. The pup leapt and jumped in the field, rolled among the flowers, sniffed at one in particular, his long tail waggling. He looked back once, as if wanting me to follow…

Something in me ached. I turned away from Fenrir, turned away from the image that had suddenly burned itself so strongly in my mind, imprinted itself in my brain, as if stamped there forever. And then—right then—an alarm trilled through the cavern. It was shrill and loud and brought with it a red strobing light that probed through the dark chambers. The light spun, illuminating the walls in a glistening crimson.

A couple of people in white coats broke through a door behind me. The only entrance in and out. Doctors, scientists, they were both and more. The younger of them went right to the bank of computers, flipping a small keyboard down from under one of the screens and pushing a few buttons. In moments the siren went quiet, and the red strobing light blinked off.

The second man came to me. An older man with thick red hair, red hair lined with gray. Black-rimmed glasses framed a lined face, and a stethoscope hung loosely around his neck. An identification badge hung from the pocket over his heart, the badge having his name—Berley—and his picture, which looked much the same as the man himself in this moment: thin lips, a little upside-down at their edges. Eyes that were tired, worried; his hair a mess as if he had just awoke. A man of a size with me, perhaps a little taller, if not wider in the shoulders, someone I knew, having been here before. A doctor, a scientist, an engineer, Berley was all three and perhaps more.

He placed his hand on my shoulder, ready to usher me out. Berley's eyes were red-shot behind his glasses, as if he had spent most of his time awake. As if he had drank a hundred cups of coffee. As if the machines keeping Fenrir alive were no longer enough, and the wolf needed constant care. He pushed me towards the door —

Fenrir stopped us. His voice low and gruff. Full of a phlegmy-like gurgling. "Skald."

He had never called me that before. It was a lost word of a lost people.

I paused.

Berley's hand paused too. We both waited, until the deep, gurgling voice continued.

"It is time."

A thrill of fear ran through me. Time for what? For the cleansing? For Ragnarok? Was it too late now, too late to save anything?

I was more afraid than I could say, so afraid my heart thudded in my chest, my breaths of the chilly cavern air came quickly, brief exhales of fog in front of my face. Afraid, almost trembling in my fear, but finally I took a peek.

The wolf lay there in his bed. The technician off to wolf's side, at the bank of computers, typing furiously, the little clicks tapping smaller echoes through the cave. They came with smaller beeps and other lights and motions, the sound of a pump churning; a thin plastic tube illuminated with a pale blue light, the liquid flowing from a small machine next to the computers to the backside of the wolf.

There were a few beeps. Loud in the cabin. Some more of the fluid moved, and the wolf let out another low moan. The kind of low moan, an exhale of relief, as if morphine had been injected in the wolf, bringing with it the cool sensation that washed away pain, for the briefest of moments.

Pain always came back. I knew that as well as the wolf did.

"It is time, Skald," the wolf said, again. Barely holding his head up, his voice breaking between that phlegmy gruffness and a forced whisper.

I'm sure my fear echoed in my voice. I could hear the trembles return to me from the darkness of the cave. "Time?"

"Time," the wolf echoed, the whisper not as forced now. The morphine easing the wolf into the sleep. The wolf fighting the morphine, befuddled.

Time. Time was in some ways forever. In other ways it was always finite. It could run on and on, and it could end for any of us in a moment.

The thudding of my heart, the quick breaths, the exhales of fog, they all remained with the worry. With the fear. My thoughts oddly enough on answers, about why the tree sprouts, why the Earth circles the sun, why water quenches my thirst.

I worried about the cleansing, and if I could stop it. If I *should* stop it. I worried about Ragnarok, and if and when it happens, if my only job would be to record it.

All or none.

Could I just stand by and record it? Could I just watch it all happen? When perhaps I could save some small part of this world?

Fenrir's great muzzle sank lower into his pillow, his great yellow eyes blinked once, twice, slow openings and closings of the lids. His lips, when they moved, did so in small motions. Slow, sleepy, muttering motions.

His words—when he spoke next—surprised me. They were not about Ragnarok. At last, I hoped not. I hoped not yet. The wolf spoke not of sprouts or sun or thirst, none of the things that ran like mad in the background of my mind.

At least, he didn't speak of those things, right now. "Time for you to go," the wolf rumbled, sleepily. Finally. "Go to New Orleans, and find my daughter."

CHAPTER TWO

Honestly, I didn't know where to begin.

Well, that wasn't true. I could feel where to begin in the light pressure hanging against my hip. The feel of the book there, the weight I could feel without looking to see.

Like every time I left the cave, I took a moment to take in everything around me, everything I could see from the side of the mountain I stood upon. One of many mountains, the angled peaks of the Adirondacks circling around from where I perched, high up on my own hillside. One dark blue peak spread across the next, the side of one mountain blending into the shadowy side of the next, as far as the eye could see.

It was always breathtaking. The air chill, I breathed in its fresh scent, a cool pureness of the forest with a hint of pine from the tall spruce surrounding me. It was cold out, just the chill of fall though, not the icy cold depths from the wolf's cave, so all of a sudden I felt warm in comparison. Too warm, in my layers upon layers, too warm under my fur-lined winter coat.

I had gotten here early, in the middle of the night. Now the sun rose in the east. I faced it; the yellow orb rose there in a brilliant yellow-orange, the glow coloring the horizon behind puffy white clouds. The sky was a deep, rich blue. The kind of blue that promised a beautiful day.

I wondered about that.

The ground was firm, the lightly marked trail packed as if many feet had walked it, and the earth felt solid under mine. This late in the fall everything around me felt new and beautiful and fresh, even as one season ended another would begin; I took another deep breath of the cool air, the scent of pine was thick from the spruce trees hiding the entrance to the wolf's lair, tall trees with thick green-needled branches. The air felt good, clean, and I unzipped my winter coat. Feeling almost warm enough to sweat.

Funny, this deep into the season, to be taking clothes off.

I ran my hands through my long, sandy hair. Relishing the feel of it through my fingers, the smooth strands. Firm. Thick. Not too long ago it had been sparse and thin; my dark gray eyes—so gray they would waver into blue, depending on how I felt—cloudy and weak. I stood there enjoying the feeling of it, the feeling of being alive, seeing the mountains around me, the sun high above, inhaling deep breaths of the fresh mountain air with the hint of pine in it.

The thin, scattered trail led down from where I stood. I knew from the past where it led. I knew as I walked down it the spruce trees would thicken, then morph into taller hardwoods, the smooth trunks of maple and paler beech trees, some birch. I knew the slope would be steep for a while, I knew I would feel the slight tug of gravity pulling me further down the hill, forcing me to walk slower than I wanted. I knew at some point a stream would meander its way near the trail, and that I would walk comfortably next to it, listening to the water gurgle its way down the mountainside. I knew that I would finally get to my car, and from there, drive to a motel in a little town about thirty minutes from here.

I stood there, knowing all that, the memory of the many times I had walked this path, this trail. To me the motions would be like driving on autopilot. Like driving the same road so many times I couldn't remember the journey of it. I knew if I started walking it would be like pushing a switch, I would ignore the fresh pine, the changing trees, the gurgling stream, and all of a sudden be at my car.

But I didn't flip the switch yet. I stood there, staring at the dark-angled mountains ringing me and the yellow-orange sun spread radiant wings across the horizon. The peaks, the sun, all seeming to be at the same height as where I was. I stood there, breathing the cold air, tasting the hint of pine, and thought about at how I had come to be in the spot I was now.

I thought about things like Ragnarok and old gods. I wondered about them, about Ragnarok. About the imminent feel of endings. It hadn't been too long ago that these things had been old tales to me. It hadn't been so long ago that I had dreamed of writing about them, instead of living among them.

I had been a writer once. Not a great one, but, like all writers, I had dreamed of being great. Of having placed words on a page that *mattered*.

Had I also dreamed of having a bestseller? Sure. All writers had that dream, too. Well, most writers. But at the core of all of us, the writers who truly loved to write, there was something deep inside all of us: a call to write a story, a paragraph, a sentence or even a word that struck a reader in such a way that they would remember it forever. That it would color their thoughts. That it would mark them, change them, alter their journey through life. Forever.

Yeah, I had had that dream. I had it from a young age. I had gotten in trouble, once or twice, writing on the walls of my house as a kid. I had worn pencil after pencil to their nubs, scribbling in spiral notebooks, notebooks that would fall apart in tatters and leave little pieces of fringe stuck in their metal rings. I had later learned how to type, and had filled the cheap memory of the electronic typewriter in class with words, in class after class.

The dream had burned in me. Burned for a long time. Burned brightly, day and night. I played sports, football, basketball, and then went home to write. I bailed hay in the summers after school, and went home to write, my hands rubbed raw from the thick twine wrapping the hay, rubbed raw even through the cheap farmer's gloves.

I ignored those that told me I needed a real job. I went to college, got a degree in writing. Found out that wasn't really my thing. That the creative side of me needed more freedom than what Strunk and White gave me. That outlines and peer reviews only weighed me down. That what I wrote came from my inside, and my inside would not be tied to the structure of an outline, nor how others felt my story should go.

I just wanted to write. Write stories. There was an inner child to me that wanted to play, a creative part that wanted to build worlds, make up characters, have them fall in love and triumph over evils.

So I let it. I wrote the way I wanted to write. I had some middling success.

Well, I had one success. A short story published in Asimov's. Something less than four thousand words, something I had submitted without any real thought about getting published. Back then I had just written stories and sent them in, without any real expectation.

Then I had been excited, getting the letter that *Asimov's* had accepted the story. *Reagen's Journey*. I still remember the check, the way the four hundred dollars had looked typed across the face of it, the bold four followed by the hard-pressed zeroes.

For the longest time I didn't cash it. I did what all writers probably did with the first story or poem they published. I framed the check. Put it inside a cheap little black-framed thing from Walmart on my wall.

And I kept writing. Thinking that the bestsellers were next. The novels I had written would surely get picked up, some agent or editor would see them, one thing would lead to another, and then all of a sudden people would be reading everything I had written. Would be demanding more.

But the bestsellers didn't come. *Asimov's*, *Analog*, *Lightspeed*, they all sent me some nice rejection letters. Other magazines followed. There was some interest, maybe some promises, a few reach-backs here and there. An agent or two always wanted the rights to something, rights I didn't want to give up. In the end I self-published what I could. I'd scraped together money for a cover, for someone to proofread my work, thinking, always thinking, of writing that one thing that mattered. Of having just one reader be struck with something I had written.

Somewhere in the middle of all that, I started having headaches. I thought it was just stress at first. It could have been stress. After all, a writer who had only earned four hundred dollars for his work —and that check uncashed—had to have other jobs. My days were twenty hours long, full of tending bars or serving coffees or even other odd jobs, the kind of career suited for those who majored in Creative Writing. Sleep came infrequently, between the jobs and the burning desire to write, I lived mostly on caffeine and the fumes of caffeine, slept when I could, and less and less as the years passed.

Why wouldn't my head hurt? I'd always pop a few Tylenol and move along; the headaches seemed normal to me. Especially with all of that. But then the couple of Tylenol grew to six or eight at a time. Three or four times a day. I'd mix them with Advil. And then, the pain began to center behind my left eye.

Then I might have begun to worry. But, like all writers, like all humans in general, we can really ignore things when we want to.

We can push worry aside until tomorrow. We can ignore the signs and just get through the day, keep going to work. I could keep pouring the coffees and mixing the drinks and writing in the spare moments I was able. Always focused on the dream.

But the headaches wouldn't go away. They wouldn't wait until tomorrow. They grew worse. Quickly. I started having trouble seeing out of the eye. I had chalked it up to being too tired, my diet, a million things until the moment I was making a latte, to when I had slipped the cup under where I thought the steam wand of the expresso machine was, with my depth perception just a tad off.

The hot steam had scalded my arm. Had left a nice streak of red there, and painful blisters along my wrist.

Still, I kept trying to work. And still, the headache got worse. I started to blink in that eye a lot. I rubbed that eye, a lot. I was careful, sliding the cup under the steamer, feeling more than seeing the cup slide under the nozzle.

Then, the worst. My right arm started tingling. Started feeling numb on occasion, like I had slept on it funny, just in the middle of the day. My fingers there responded… sluggishly. When I typed up my stories in the evenings, my index finger was a split-second later than normal, so that the word *that*—more often than not—ended up *htat*.

More words got the same treatment, more of my fingers slowed down, more of the numbness spread down from my fingers into my hand, then my arm. Slowly at first, and then faster. Until there was a numbness all along my forearm, so that pinching it felt like another person's skin. I was right-handed, so I just learned to do everything with my left hand. Pouring coffees, driving, writing.

Still, the numbness got so I couldn't feel my skin, no matter how hard I poked it, couldn't move my fingers on my left hand, until my eye throbbed with pain the tingling on my arm went away and there was nothing, there was no arm, no hand, it was like nothing was there at all and finally, finally, I went to the doctor.

The diagnosis wasn't good. It never is, on the things we ignore, on the things we put off. Something inside us knows that the news is bad, we *know*, and in that knowing we avoid. Thinking if we never hear the news, it would never be real.

The doctor told me there was a large tumor in my brain, right behind my left eye. Pushing on my brain. Killing the cells there. A pregnant, cancerous thing. I remember seeing the scan of the tumor and swallowing at the large, white, bulbous thing swelling in my skull. Seeing the thin edges of it stretching deep into my brain, wondering which of its needle-like tendrils had killed my arm, and which of them were killing me. Seeing the color of my eyes, a steel-like gray, darken into something flaked with hate and rage. Seeing my hair at the time, sandy and thick, fall out with treatment after treatment and become something straggly and thin. Seeing my body, tall and strong, grow thin and wasted.

Bars and coffee shops didn't have the best medical plans. The four hundred dollar check was the first thing I cashed, but you can imagine that didn't cover much. It didn't take long until I was out of work, out of money, and dying in a hospital bed. In some cot with a mattress that had thinned after months of me lying there, cold no matter how many thin blankets the nurses put on top of me. No matter how hot they warmed those blankets.

Cold, so cold, and yet burning with a fever. Burning with a life wasted. Burning up, used up, no matter how much medicine the doctors pumped into me. Where I had lost weight, and—when I was lucid enough—swung at nurses with my good arm, screaming in anger, at a life wasted. Screaming with rage that things should matter, that I should matter, that I was going to write something that *mattered*, that this couldn't be happening to me, because I had life left to me.

I had mentioned I understood the wolf's pain. I did, at least, as much as I could. The two of us had the same feel to us, of pain that never left. That only grew. Of great waves of pain that could wear down the hardest of rocks…

I had a great anger back then. And those were the things I could remember, when I wasn't drugged out of my mind. Pounding my weak fist into the arm of a nurse, her eyes holding the greatest sadness above her mask, her irises holding a deep sorry in a deeper color of ivy. I pounded my fist against her arm, weakly and ineffectively and with a little shame in the recall of it, just because she had told me to keep my chin up, that tomorrow would be a brighter day.

And then there were the times I wasn't as lucid. When I wasn't drugged deeply against the pain, well, I thought it was the tiniest of mercies I couldn't remember what I had done or said in those moments. I think I would have been ashamed. I think I would still be.

I had read a lot of stories as a kid, and watched a lot of movies. My mom had been an English teacher, well she worked a lot of jobs, being a single parent, and a substitute English teacher had been one of those. She had loved books, really loved them, so she had taken me to a lot of libraries as a kid. And the occasional bookstore.

I mean, internet was barely a thing at the time, and books, especially libraries, were the easiest form of escapes. I fell in love with books, maybe because my mom had loved them so, and I had found my own escapes. In armloads of fantasy books, with visit upon visit to the local library. In all the rows of all the shelves of science fiction. In all the stories of all the gods and heroes and powers, of universes and worlds far away in space and time.

I had loved all the books, reading them even up until today, books and comics and all the short story collections. *Exile's Gate*, *Fire Dancer*, *Heroes Die*. Faded, destroyed worlds like in *Lord*

Foul's Bane. Later I had caught movies, and even those had fed my imagination, with monsters coming into the world, like *Pacific Rim*. With horrors that would eat you alive, like *Aliens*. Even *Star Wars*, that ragtag group in the first movie taking on the Death Star on nothing but hope and a prayer. With all of those books and comics and things, all those movies, the *Edges of Tomorrows*, the tales about heroes sacrificing themselves in a fight about a universe and winning.

Heroes people knew. Heroes people might never know. In worlds unimaginable.

Imagination wasn't helping me now. The books, the stories, the ones about heroes defeating the evil in front of them, none of those were helping me from my hospital bed. I was in a different story, a tragedy, something where the hero would never live to see what life he could have had. What life he might have left behind. If he had left it any better, for his living it.

I knew I would never see another movie, I would never read another book, and I would certainly never write anything like them now.

I know I had screamed then. I know I had railed against everything. I remember swinging my arm at one nurse, someone with her mask on, with hair tightly bound under her cap, her eyes soft and sad as she backed out of the room.

I know I had screamed, and I had railed, and I had *raged*. I had raged against the world. My mother had raised me Catholic, I had grown up Christian in my faith, loosely, I knew without knowing I had taken the Lord's name in vain during those last days. It probably won't surprise you to know that I cursed him, cursed all the gods, cursed everything in my madness.

Imagine my surprise, then, when one answered back.

In the last few weeks of me holding on, of me raging and cursing, Doctor Berley found me. He waited until one of those lucid moments, in between the times of me raging and swinging an arm frail and wasted, with flaps of skin hanging from it. He told me he could fix me, in no uncertain terms. He told me he could not only heal me, but that I could live a long, fruitful life. A much longer life than I thought. A much longer life than any human thought. A life that could matter.

Sure, I was skeptical at first. In the not-so-lucid times I might have thought I was dreaming. But Berley was kind, patient, and stayed by my side until I saw I had nothing left to lose. No other options. That death would be coming for me, its cold, boneless hand reaching around the corner there ahead of me, and if I wanted to live another minute, another day, another year, I had to try *something*.

There came the final day. Where I knew I had no other option. Where I knew I had a day or two or three, at most. Where I was as lucid as I was ever going to be. Where I understood that life had given me this, and I could take that moment and leave the hospital and go with Berley, or I could stay in the hospital bed, under the layers of thin blankets that never warmed me, no matter how many times the nurses heated them, and waste away into death.

You probably know what happened next. The good doctor brought me here. To this very mountain. Where the wolf first got his promise from me. He took the oath before anything else, and I never regretted giving it, not even now.

Fenrir did his thing. The god thing. I didn't feel anything at first, but then Berley operated on me. He removed the tumor, and it wasn't much later I had been healed. It didn't take months of rehab, or years of recovery, but just a few short days.

A miracle, I had thought at the time. Thankful, and grateful. And a bit in wonder, at this world I had dreamed of as a kid, when I had read all their stories. That the Norse gods were real, and alive, in my world. That I was a part of them now, and their story, a story no one knew. A story of today.

Now, I realized the albatross they had hung around my neck. The weight of its strap on my shoulder. Though I still was thankful, and grateful. An albatross is a lot better than a grave.

You might think I'm a bit candid about all this. That it's easy to accept that the Norse gods exist in our world, in this day and time, without any of us knowing about them. You might wonder how easy it was to believe, when Berley had found me, and brought me back to the wolf's cave.

There was probably more truth to all of it that I'm not telling you. More truths I'm not telling you. There was the sad truth of the state of my mind, my body, when they had wheeled me into the cavern in a wheelchair. Barely lucid and ranting.

There was a missing truth, a truth that I had never met any god. I had never met any god, anywhere. So why not, if offered the chance at the end of a pain-wracked existence, believe in the one that was going to heal you?

A missing truth, sure. Missing because I hadn't met Thor yet. Or any other Norse god, that I was aware of. But, seeing as how the wolf was the reason I was alive today, it was a missing truth I was okay not really digging deeper into.

And then there's the final truth. One all of us will face, one day. The sad truth that once we are at death's door, most of us will believe in anything. Be okay with anything, any fiction, any fantasy. We'll accept all of it, if it means living another moment of your life. To matter another day.

Hell, at the time I would have happily accepted a leprechaun at the other end of some rainbow, dancing around in his little green archer outfit granting me a few extra days of life and a bowl of Lucky Charms, and telling me both were magically delicious.

I'd have eaten them right up.

During the days I had been healing, I had asked Berley how he had found me. The doctor had told me he had caught my short story in Asimov's, and had always remembered it. Something about the story, how it made him smile. Walk a little taller.

He told me he liked to keep tabs on writers, especially the ones he liked, and perhaps you can understand why. Chroniclers never lived forever, not even in the best of times. We might not be immortal, though we could live a long time plenty of things out in the world could kill us. A bullet. Stepping in front of a bus. Choking on a thick piece of gristle in a piece of steak.

There was always a need for a scribe, and writers seemed to make the best ones. Maybe it was an eye for detail, for looking at the world around us and gathering it all in. Maybe it was the dream. Either way, their Chronicler had died, and once Berley had discovered I was on my deathbed, he had come to me.

I guess, in a weird way, I had written one thing that mattered to someone.

The thing was, who had my story mattered more to? The man who had read it, down in operations, with an old cup of coffee from an ombred carafe and a slow, steady heart rate monitor beeping in the cavern next to him? The aging wolf and his Ragnarok? Or me?

The mountain air didn't seem so pure, anymore. Maybe I had gotten used to it, standing there, my breaths deep and even and no longer smelling the pine. My eyes no longer seeing the dark blue-black peaks of the Adirondacks, spreading to the horizon. My skin no longer feeling the early morning warmth of the sun, rising in the east.

It was time. I flicked on autopilot and started my walk down the mountainside. The invisible albatross pulled me downward. I fought it just like I fought gravity, leaning back, forcing each step to be slow and careful. Everything happening like driving a car along a road for the thousandth time, with me noticing things but never remembering them, not noticing gravity pulling me down faster and faster, nor my subtle resistance to it. Not hearing the gurgling stream or observing the change in the forest, as the thick green spruce became dotted with maples.

Perhaps if I hadn't been in those thoughts, in autopilot, I might have felt that tingly sensation along my spine, that sense we all have of being watched. I might even have caught who was watching me. I might have sensed a purpose, a reason, even in that moment, and whoever or whatever might have been watching me, perhaps I could have intuited the meaning behind the watching.

But the thoughts had been strong that morning. The autopilot was real. I rode it all the way down to my car. Walked up to it, a blue rental sedan of four doors that smelled like cigarettes, for all the policy of the rental company. I keyed the fob, heard without hearing the beep-beep of the alarm, noticed without noticing the flash of the sedan's lights.

And got in. Sat in my rental car that smelled like old ash, started the weak four-cylinder up, and headed down the road to the town with my motel. Noticing without noticing the curves of the road, my hand lightly moving the wheel to the rhythm of the blacktop. Thinking all the thoughts I had been thinking, those thoughts riding undercurrents of worry and wonder, about how I might find a daughter the world didn't know existed, during a time when the world might be ending.

CHAPTER THREE

The town was one of the small mountain towns you find anywhere. The road I drove on split it in two. There was a small general store, with all the things a person might need if all of a sudden there was a heavy snow and no one could go anywhere for a week or two. Necessities. There was a hardware store, a tiny garage with a spray-painted sign above it. *Larry's Garage.* Simple and clean, although there was an old minivan out front, with Delaware tags, and a man and a woman in front of the garage yelling at each other.

They were waiting for the garage to open. The minivan had one of those smaller donut tires on the back, and it was covered in dust. There looked to be a child's seat in the middle. The woman was wide and tall and had a phone held next to her ear and still was shouting at a thinner, shorter guy, who was screaming right back. The shouting match was loud and I could almost understand them through the closed windows of the car.

I didn't roll down the windows. Part of me was sad. This town had always seemed quiet to me. Full of quiet, good people. The minivan didn't belong, but maybe that was just the way of the world today. Maybe there was just this slow creep of screaming and yelling, of people pointing at others, of accusers searching for anyone or anything to accuse, right or wrong. Maybe it was unstoppable, that the world ·was just slowly tipping over into its own Ragnarok.

Of course, that brought a shiver and thoughts of the cavern. Of Fenrir. So I pushed those thoughts away and drove on. A further bit down there was a nice enough diner, a two-story building of whitish walls, the diner downstairs and a smaller place upstairs, both facing a lake.

It had been a long enough journey to the wolf's cave from Athens. After finishing up in Greece. I hadn't had a chance to eat anything, and then had gotten my rental car and come here. Occasionally eating the old, hard candy bars and the stale cinnamon rolls, still sticky in their hard plastic wraps, that all gas stations had. All the diners and fast-food places had been closed last night, I was hungry now, and I pulled the sedan in to grab a bite.

I had eaten here before. Enough that the people working the diner recognized me, even if the customers didn't. I walked in, the tiny door ringing a bell, letting the world know someone was hungry. The smell of fried potatoes, heavy on salt and pepper and garlic, filled the air, mixed with spicy scent of crispy sausage and scrambled eggs and the sweet syrupy smell of pancakes.

The diner was mostly empty. There were a couple of old fellas in a booth to my left, both with orange hats on and thick coats, as if they were eating before going out hunting. Or maybe they had just gotten back. One of the fellas, a guy with a grizzled white beard and a weathered face, raised a cup of coffee to me and nodded.

Maybe some of the customers recognized me as well.

The waitress was behind the counter a long white thing in the middle of the dinner, with round cushioned stools in front of it, the cushions a faded, worn red, and the stools standing in a line like soldiers at attention. I remembered the waitress, she did me as well. She motioned to the counter, I shook my head and took one of the booths, also white, also with faded red cushions on flat bench-like seats. I was going to eat, but I was going to do some reading as well.

Might as well get a start on it.

The waitress—I thought her name was Linda, or something like that—brought me a black coffee and took my order. I usually got an omelet and some toast, Linda talked me into trying the new thing on the menu, some potato hash thing with a spicy Cajun gravy. She said the hash was heavenly, and the new cook was good.

There was no music in the early morning. No television playing. Just the sizzling of sausage on a grill, the small muttering talk of the new cook—a younger girl than the older lady I remembered—and the waitress. I noticed all this, all the sounds, the two men talking, the clinks of forks and knives against plates, the circling sound of a spoon stirring a cup of coffee, I noticed all of that and turned back to my own cup.

I used to like the fancy stuff. All the cream and sugar and flavors. It was a writer's thing, after all, to have a fancy latte and sit around in a bookstore. Now I drank the coffee black, and I couldn't tell you for the life of me why I had made the switch, it's just how I drank it now. The white cup was hot in my hand, hot and heavy, almost like the coffee itself: thick and black and hot. Thick enough that it felt like soup, and hot enough to maybe fully warm me from my trip from the cave.

Maybe.

The car's heater had warmed up enough that I had shrugged out of my winter coat during the short trip. The long johns weren't something I could shrug out of, so I still had those on underneath my jeans and T-shirt, and being prepared I had a smaller jacket in the car I could wear. Knowing the difference between the cold of the wolf's cavern and the regular cold of the fall in the Adirondacks.

I rubbed my face. The jacket smelled like old cigarettes, and I regretted leaving it in the car. The smell of ash was light on my coat's sleeve, so that it was something I just caught in the middle of smelling the coffee, or with a deep breath of the sausage and potatoes of the diner, or rubbing the sleep from my face. Just a small thing, but man it bothered me when I caught it.

Some people rarely, if ever, thought of others. Of how what they did impacted those around them. How the footprint they left might trip those that followed.

Maybe it was those kinds of observations that made me a good Chronicler. The little things. Tiny scents and sights I caught, when other people might just shrug and move on.

Either way, the smell bothered me, as light as it was. The thought of someone smoking in a car that they shouldn't smoke in bothered me. The thought of someone not just breaking a rule, it wasn't that, but doing something without regard for their fellow man. Or woman. Part of me hoped we could all be a little better, each time I took a breath of stale, old cigarette. I ended up taking the jacket off, bundling it into the side of the booth.

The potato hash was good. Spicy. The potatoes were square and crisp and colored a deep brown along their faces. The gravy was thick and peppery and a held hint of Cajun heat. A Creole heat that lingered on the tongue. I gobbled them up, mixing some of the hash with my eggs, and felt a little better after the meal.

I pushed the plates back. Cleaned the table with a few swipes of my paper napkin, then slid the book out of the satchel. Like before, the leather of the bag seemed to just fit the book, but it came out easily. Like before, the book felt heavy, like it held more meaning than I could fathom, but it was light in my hand. The supple cover feeling almost like leather in my palm, though I knew it wasn't that.

The book made a heavy thumping sound on the table. The spine sometimes felt rough in my hand, like there was real bark there. I tried to ignore the feeling, ignore the cover. A Chronicler could get lost staring at the tree. The branches, even though they looked like many, could all of a sudden spread into the thousands, millions. Like the worst case of blurry vision. There was the squirrel, running along the trunk, and there, there was the man with the noose around his neck —

The door jingled then. I looked up, saw a young woman, or an old-enough girl, walk in. Tall for a girl, with long legs and dark red hair tied back in a simple ponytail. Wearing tight jeans that hugged athletic hips, and a dark gray winter coat. Maybe wool, or fleece, and tied around her waist with a tightly-cinched belt. Her cheeks were red with the cold outside, as if she had been running, and her green eyes appeared to flicker with some joke she wasn't about to tell anyone.

She winked at me. It caught me by surprise. I put a hand over the book, the Chronicles, for some reason. My fingers touched the paw of the teddy bear, and flashes of memories flooded me, memories of a time I wanted to always remember and yet always forget.

Then the new girl waved to Linda, back behind the counter, as if they knew each other. She ended up taking a seat on one of the faded red stools there, talking to the waitress, getting a cup of coffee. The two chatted, in voices that were low and loud, laughing one good time.

I watched them for a moment. Wondering. Worried. Maybe it was just nerves, maybe it was the wolf there at the end, in the cavern. Talking about gods and games, how the game changed, and how the gods might change it.

Like I said, I had never met another god, other than Fenrir. I guess I could have and not known. But I thought I would have. After all, if another god was seeking me out, it was because of my connection to the Norse god of Ragnarok, and that god would either want something from me or want to kill me.

I thought at least I would be able to tell one of those two things.

Of course, then I was surprised again, too lost in thought. Again. A man had walked in, tall, dark, with dark hair and dark eyes. Wearing jeans and a jean jacket. He looked at the cook in the back a long moment before glancing my way. He cocked his head at the book, staring at the shadowy silhouette of Yggdrasil.

"Norse?" he asked. "Mythology?"

"Close enough," I said, keeping my hands on the cover. My fingers hiding the paw.

"I don't recognize it," the man said, still intense. His eyes looking at the spine, and only seeing more tree. The tree and the tiny serpent circle on the top. "Or the author."

"You wouldn't," I said. I found myself thinking I had sat too close to the door. Something the wolf had introduced worry, fear in me. Too many people walking in could see me, see the book.

The man grunted, as if wanting to ask me more. Then his name was called, I missed it, and he headed to the counter, giving a slight wave to the cook, taking a seat a couple of stools down from the new girl. The cook brought him a cup of coffee, which he held in both hands, his elbows on the counter and talking back and forth with the slim girl.

It started to feel too busy here. I recognized a feeling, that of being watched. Of being around those who *watched*. It was the writer in me, my subconscious, seeing things I didn't see, noticing things I hadn't noticed, putting it all together and then dancing along my spine with the knowledge.

I glanced outside. The mountain lake was off to my left, the waters dark and shimmering under the early morning sun. The tall hardwoods, the maples and the birch, shadowy in the gloom of a new day, the burning oranges and yellows and reds of their leaves muted.

Anything, I guessed, could be watching me from there. From anywhere. I grabbed my satchel in one and the book in another. Ready to put it away; I could study it later. Time enough when I got back to my motel.

The new girl slid into my booth, with her long legs and tightly cinched coat. She had brought a cup of coffee, topped off and steaming, and held it in both hands, much like the guy at the counter. Her eyes twinkled at me, flashes of emerald. "Hey there," she said. Her voice twinkled too. It was light, mellow, with a hint of south to it, some kind of drawl I felt was southern but might not be. "New in town?"

My hands had paused, holding the satchel, holding the book, the spine facing the girl. "Just passing through."

Her head tilted a bit. As if she was parsing that information, digesting it, turning it around in her head to look at it from different angles. As little as it was. "This town doesn't get a lot of visitors."

There was an odd feel to the girl. As if she was measuring me, maybe. There was that kind of interest, at least. Measuring, with a hint of wonder.

I glanced outside again, the girl's glance following me. The lake remained flat, as if holding a thousand mysteries underneath it. The muted leaves of the hardwoods shook a little, in a sudden breeze. A pair of black birds—crows?... I thought them too large, maybe the vultures around the area, that seemed to fit the mood better—fluttered on the branch of the nearest maple, flapping their wings, pecking at each other, and I imagined muttering to themselves. Everything was mysterious and dark and both dying and yet new at the same time. "It probably should."

"Beautiful, right?" she agreed. "I love it here."

"It's nice enough." I looked back at her, caught her smile widening. As if she had caught something.

"Emma-mae," she said, reaching a hand over. I was a little slow, but took it briefly. Her palm was warm from the coffee, firm but also soft, reminding me a little of the soft cover over the hard back of the book.

"Odd enough name," I said. To say something, even if—as soon as I said the words—I realized they were a little, let's say unfriendly.

She took it well. As if she had run across all kinds. Her smile widened, flashing even, white teeth. And she sat there, waiting, until I realized I hadn't offered my name.

"Finn," I finally said.

"Finn?" She tested the name. A tongue flicked out, quickly, running across her lower lip, and Emma-mae leaned forward across the table. The movement was subtle, a slow lean in, something that made me more aware of how near she was with the motion of it.

I wanted to lean back a bit. As if her bubble, the bubble of who she was, the force of the person she walked around as, as if that bubble pressed slowly against mine. "As in Huckleberry."

Her laugh was delightful. Not loud, but a sound full of smiles and the feel of sunshine warming your skin, of joy that warmed a person from the inside. It was nice and welcoming, something that connected me with her, just like her question. "Truly?"

I nodded. It wasn't a usual name, Finn. But my mother had lived near the Mississippi, and she had been an English teacher, well… a substitute English teacher, and two plus two usually equaled four.

"Finn isn't your first name?"

I rolled my eyes in a way that told her it was.

Her laugh happened again. Loud but not pitched that way, something she did to share it, not broadcasting it through the room, but sharing it with me. Her lean got a little closer, and true to my earlier thoughts I leaned just a little bit away. Even if the scent of her, the subtle scent of jasmine blooming in the night, had me wanting to stay close.

"Do you talk much, Huckleberry Finn?"

I guess I used to, back before the time I understood Norse gods were real, and walked the Earth. Most writers, we couldn't shut up when you got us started. But since my time working for the wolf, I had pulled back some. A little. I felt more outside the world, than in it.

I shrugged, a little. "Usually. I guess."

Her smile was delicious. Captivating. It curved just enough across her face, her lips a deep pink, a pale red, and the smile drew my eyes away from her gaze, deep and thoughtful. "You have an interesting…quirk."

Her mind was quick. I was used to more of a slow introspection, as a Chronicler. Her zigging and zagging had me pause. "I do?"

And she laughed again, loudly. Rolling her eyes. Getting a joke I didn't. Zigging from the zag we had just zigged to. Drawing her first word out. "Annnddddd, *of course*, you just broke it."

Her laugh was infectious, and I found myself, if not laughing, at least grinning. And wondering what quirk she had caught in me. I know I had changed some, from the writer I had been, the writer before the cancer, the writer before the wolf.

I wasn't the same person now, but I hoped some part of that person still remained. Some of that person's dream still remained. I hoped it hadn't been so long that I couldn't recognize that writer, anymore.

I felt pinned by her gaze. There was something in Emma-mae that seemed to see me. The new me, the older one, I didn't know. Just something that recognized me, in a way. Recognized the person walking around writing down stories that might bring about the end of the world. Recognized that me, and a different me.

I couldn't tell you why I thought that. I didn't know, and I wasn't sure it mattered, but there was a part of me that liked it. That liked our connection, as brief as it was. There was something in her eyes, or her smile, some connection with me that lightened the feel of the morning, that lightened the worry I had been carrying since leaving the cave.

"I'll confess a little something in return, Finn," something in her eyes telling me she wanted to say Huckleberry, but had decided against it. Perhaps for me. "My mother wanted Ella-mae, my dad's mother was Emma…" She lifted a shoulder as if saying, *what can you do?*

Our eyes met, then. We each took a breath, our chests expanding, just a bit. The scent of bitter coffee and the sweet scent of pancakes and fried potatoes mixing in some way with the night jasmine.

A moment of silence followed. The pause two strangers have where they realize there's a deeper connection between them, than either had known the moment before. Her chest swelled, then let go, as Emma-mae stared at me, her gaze light and twinkling and yet carrying some undercurrent, something mysterious and arresting and a who are *you*?

I took a second breath, and found it short. Found like there might not be enough air in the diner. And I found that, curious.

I hadn't been nervous around a woman in a long time.

It was odd to feel that now.

It was perhaps odder to feel a similar nervousness from her.

Sometimes the briefest meetings are like that. Chance encounters. A person in a small town, in the middle of nowhere. I had observed it in other places, in other people. A connection that hits you like a thunderbolt and leaves you wanting to draw a deeper breath. That leaves your heart pounding a little harder, your hands a little more clammy, your lungs feeling like they just needed a little more oxygen.

The two of us broke our gaze. Maybe it was the scent of coffee. Maybe it was the scent of breakfast. Because it sure wasn't the scent of night jasmine, when Emma-mae looked down at my plates. "You should try the pancakes here sometime, instead of the hash. Those things are the real breakfast of champions."

It was lighthearted, and maybe a little fake. Another zag from the zig. A deflection, from the heavy connected feeling of the moment before.

Still, I went with it. As nervous as Emma-mae, maybe. There was something to her I enjoyed being around, a connection I thought we both felt. It was nice to sit and enjoy just being with her, without having it mean more.

Even I had tried the hash on a suggestion, and now I wanted to defend it. Even if the hash had been spicy and filling in all the ways a breakfast should be. Even if it was warming in a way I felt like I needed, coming from that icy den. Even if the hash had given me a little hope, with where I had been and with what I had learned.

Even if I liked pancakes, too.

"It was good." I smiled, finding my eyebrows raising up, playfully. My eyes twinkling just a bit. "Filling. Delicious and hearty."

Odd, to find a part of me looking at Emma-mae and seeing her twenty years from now. The two of us, here together. Her with pancakes; me with hash. The two of us always ordering the same thing, always rationalizing which one was better, always talking about how filling and hearty the hash was, always talking about the pancakes being the breakfast of champions.

I could see this going on forever between us. The waking up together. The fun arguments each morning. The secret knowledge Emma-mae carried, the knowledge that I actually liked pancakes but always ordered the hash. Just for this moment.

It was funny, where my thoughts had gone in those split seconds. Funny how a part of me had been imagining her and me arguing this silly point forever, pancakes or hash. Funny how chance meetings could take a mind wandering some lost trail.

Emma-mae's eyes twinkled. They were here and somewhere else at the same time. Maybe in her own imagination. Maybe her own future, one where she was the champion of pancake stacks the world over. Maybe with her face on a bottle of syrup.

The heavy connection of moments ago seemed to recede, slightly, between us. The connection still there, but colored in pancakes and hash. Lightened. Her breath rose and fell, exhaling softly, and her eyes looked at me again, softly, curious. She motioned to my hands, now empty, as if they still held the book. "You like to write?"

Ah, zigging and zagging, how fast you go. "What?"

"Write." The arresting gaze was gone, and the smile was back on her face, light and carefree. "That book, it looked like one of those journals people carry around. The ones with the leather covers you see in the bookstores. Just..." She opened her hands, one holding the coffee cup, as if measuring the distance between them. "Larger."

Something tinged my subconscious then. A little thing. The need to keep what I was doing quiet. The worry about drawing attention to myself, about some other god finding me. Crazy, I know, but a worry, all the same.

"I used to," I said. Which wasn't a lie. I had liked to write at one point, and maybe I still did. Maybe one day I'd sit down and try writing a real book again. Maybe I'd throw a short story or two into the submission grinder. But now, now what I wrote about, it wasn't something one liked to write. "I mean, with a name like Finn, and an English teacher for a mother, you'd think that was something I was destined for."

She smiled at the joke, even if she knew that was something I had said to other people many times. Something I said almost by rote. She smiled, understanding that sometimes you have to say things that way, in order to cover up the real reasons.

"Huh," she said, tilting her head again. Taking a sip of coffee. The steam drifted up from the cup and circled briefly there in front of her nose, something sharp and pert, before fading away. She sat the mug down, still leaning forward, still intent. "Publish anything?"

"One thing, yeah."

The curiosity seemed to grow. "Have I read it?"

"You read *Asimov's*?"

"Occasionally."

"Years ago," I said. "*Reagen's Journey*."

"Huh," she said again, not a sound of question, but more of the sound of thought. Of searching a memory. The cup of coffee forgotten in one hand, the index finger of her other tracing little circles on the table. Her head tilted, in that motion we all have of finding something in our minds we had been looking for. "A young girl, alien world?"

I was surprised she had read it. Hell, I was surprised she remembered it. My own coffee sat undrunk next to me. One hand curled around the cup, the steam above the darkness wispy and faint, as if drifting away. Fading from the world. I felt, oddly enough, embarrassed. "Yeah."

"It wasn't bad," she said, and then, quickly, as if realizing how that might sound, "It was different. The journey, trying to get home. Trying to figure out the alien world. Trying to figure out her place in it. Only, in the end—"

"It was her world," I finished, then shrugged my own *what can you do?* shrug. A similar one to Emma-mae's, earlier.

I couldn't tell you why I felt embarrassed, only that it was the one thing I had ever published. The one thing that had mattered enough that someone else had wanted to publish it. At one point, that story had meant the world to me.

It had mattered. But it also had been a dream. A hope. And now, now the words came with the experience of a man who had dreams once, and understood now the difference between dreams and hopes and reality. "Feels a little silly to say it aloud."

Her eyes softened. Her hand, the one that had been drawing the circles, reached out and grabbed the back of my hand, the hand circling the cup. She squeezed it, gently, yet firmly. "The hard truths often are," Emma-mae said, then letting go. "So what are you writing now?"

Her hand had been soft, and warm. Comforting, in a way that I already missed it.

"I'm not," I said. "I'm not really writing anything." Then I covered the lie, a bit. "At least, not stories."

"Huh," she said a third time. As if a little surprised, and a little sad. As if she had really liked my short story, and was surprised to find I had stopped. "You should. You really should."

My grin grew more... wryer. More a smile of embarrassment than anything that could be attributed to happiness or joy. As if I was a boy, in class, being congratulated by the teacher for something we both knew could have been better.

A flush spread over my cheeks, and I felt a little warm. It had just been a short story, a short story written a long time ago when I had been more hopeful about life, about words that mattered, about lives that mattered, and nothing I had ever written since had come to anywhere near the same level of notoriety. Nothing had felt the same, that was certain. Not before the cancer, and not after. "It's just a story."

Her smile disappeared, the twinkle in her eyes too, and her head shook a little bit, left and right. "Stories are never just stories."

There was another moment of silence. Another observation by the two of us, of some bond between us. Something that tied us together, stirred the blood, drummed in my chest. I got the feeling as much as I could feel it, Emma-mae was even more aware of the connection. The quiet went on, until I thought even she could hear the beating of my heart, until her head had tilted and she had looked at something and had decided —

Something clattered behind the kitchen counter. Linda laughed and clapped her hands, dancing a bit there. The cook had bent down to pick up a large metal ladle, shaking her head, the dark guy chuckling and pointing something else out there. The cook's smile was rueful, she looked at her hand and her ladle as if wondering how one had fallen from the other, even while Linda was grabbing a towel to help clean up whatever it was that had spilled behind the counter.

Moments, right?

Moments I observed, moments of other lives, moments I might later write down in my journal. Happy observations of people connecting, of small bonds between a cook and a waitress and a man in a diner. Observations countering all the other things I had seen and copied down: an angry man and woman shoving through a crowd of people in a train station in Greece, a group of people with signs and masks, other groups, huddled together, faces open and sad and perhaps a little lost. Two groups of people, circles of men and women standing apart from the other, and yet forever bound together in their oppositeness.

I blinked, still looking at the counter. I was surprised to see Emma-mae standing now, standing next to the booth, her coffee almost forgotten in her hand. She was looking at me, at my face, as if seeing the very things I was thinking. Her head slightly tilted, again, as if that information too she was turning and looking at from all angles.

Our eyes caught. Her smile flashed again, breaking the moment. Maybe I wasn't the only one with a quirk. And maybe, just maybe, I was turning and looking at things at other angles too. We seemed to be stuck in a loop, observing each other, feeling, looking and turning and thinking…

Her smile turned a little, if not sad, or worried, something along those lines. Maybe it was unease. "You like to say things in threes," she said.

"What?"

"Your quirk," Emma-mae explained. As if she really had been in my head. "You like to say things in threes." Her eyebrows lowered just a bit, as if in thought. Or concern. That same sense of unease, disquiet. "You want to be careful about that."

I smiled then, a real smile. As much as I had been before a god, a real god in this world. As much as I had been in front of Fenrir and felt his power, as much as me living was an example of his power, I didn't believe much in magic. At least, not the superstitious sort. Not in the powers of threes, throwing salt over the shoulder, knocking on wood.

I felt the bond between us weaken a bit with the knowledge. Just a bit, and the thought saddened me. There was a real connection between us, something I wouldn't chase after, being who I was, but still it was sad to feel this solid connection with someone else, this tight thread between Emma and I, thin just a little. "Why?"

Her eyes remained uneasy, or worried, or maybe she was sad, too. Maybe sad, and for different reasons. Emma-mae shrugged, another one of those *what can you do?* shrugs, which, oddly enough, I realized was the third one we had shared in our short conversation. "Just something I've noticed… there's a real power in threes."

CHAPTER FOUR

Emma-mae left after that. Her walk different now. Slower. Thoughtful. Meandering a bit, perhaps sad. The bell on the door quietly *tinked* her exit with a single strike of its metal side, as if even the bell had been subdued. Her coffee, when she placed it on the counter, had barely made a sound. It had been placed there, softly, over the top of a crisp twenty-dollar bill.

A lot of tip for a coffee. The bill sat there now, folded under the cup, a corner of muted green bill hanging there in the air between the counter and the cup, lacking the white vibrancy of either. A tiny piece of a quiet forest between sharp-edged clouds of white.

I sat there, wondered. Lost a bit in thought. Linda came over, I thanked her for the breakfast suggestion and told her to give my compliments to the chef. Feeling odd to say something like that in a diner, a little greasy spoon place in a small town. She smiled in a way that said she understood, and I got the feeling I wasn't the first person to say those words here.

I left some money, including a nice tip, and headed back to the car. The sun was higher now, but the outside still held the bite of fall, and I started the sedan and sat there a bit. Giving the car a moment to heat back up, to get ready for its journey, waiting a bit for the air blowing out of the vents to be something other than lukewarm, trying not to smell the stale bit of smoke that seemed to be a part of the car.

And trying not to think of the Rule of Threes.

You might think it strange, working for Fenrir, but I wasn't superstitious. I didn't believe in things like throwing salt over my shoulder, like knocking on wood, like wishing upon a star.

Still, I avoided thinking about the Fates. About the Rule of Three. Because thinking about them brought a deeper awareness. Those rules existed everywhere, in everything, they were woven into parts of our lives that—on the surface—we weren't aware of. We could never be aware of.

Perhaps I had first really became aware of the rules in writing, in how to set up a joke. There had been the three acts of a play, I mean, why just three? Why is it important that we humans *need* a build-up, a climax, a catharsis?

I had sat back and wondered about that a lot. Wondered about myself, as a young kid, flipping through a picture book. Something large with a red cover, a picture of three bears walking through the woods like humans, coming home to a little girl with golden locks. There were other picture books, things I had toddled into the library with my mother and walked out with, pictures of three little pigs building homes of stone and wood and straw, with a big wolf outside.

Yeah, that one struck close to home.

All those stories as a kid, those and more. So many I had read as a kid. Of being Aladdin and rubbing the oil lamp with my sleeve, of being granted three wishes. I had laughed at the goats in *The Three*

Billy Goats Gruff. I had read *Rumpelstiltskin* and hell, I could barely write the name, much less say it three times.

The rules of three were everywhere.

So I avoided looking at them.

Because I knew, better than most, we all had a past, present, and future. I understood the world had had a very long past, and that I lived in its present. And I understood, to the very core of my being, that the world's future was much shorter than it should be.

And that thought, of all of them, was the closest tied to the writer I had been. About the writer I had been, and the one I was now. About Fenrir saving me, and the why of it.

About what I might be meant for.

The rules of three were everywhere. Especially in stories. Especially in writing. Which had me wondering if I could really write something now that mattered. If I could not only write something that mattered, *do* something that mattered as well.

Could something like destiny be the reason the wolf had saved me? Me, out of all the other writers? I mean, I had been just a struggling writer. A struggling writer from a poor background, with nothing but a wish and a dream and a pen.

That was the question I feared to look at, with every fiber of my being.

It was the thing I avoided most.

Because if the rules of three were real, if Fenrir was real, then the Fates were real. They were tied up in my life just like everyone else's. They were known everywhere, by everyone, by many different names. By things I felt and knew intimately, by creation, preservation, and destruction. By the maiden and the mother and the crone. By names like the Spinner and the Allotter and the Unturning.

In all of those stories I knew them. I felt them. I was consumed by them.

The past. The present. The future.

In my story they were known as Urd, Verdandi, and Skald.

Goosebumps ran along my skin, even now, thinking about them. Thinking about the Fates. About my fate. I saw the tree, everyday on the book jacket. I saw Yggdrasil and knew the tree was real. I saw the silhouette of Odin and watched him sway, in his search for knowledge. For the wisdom of the runes.

I knew the tree existed, and that it had roots. I knew the roots went to other worlds, to the land of the giants, to the land of gods, to the land of humans. And I knew one root in particular went to the home of the Fates. To the Well of Urd.

So while I wasn't superstitious, I won't say something dark and foreboding didn't run along my spine along that particular thought. Saying their names in my mind, like I was calling the Fates themselves. My life was too real to me now to have anything else happen.

No amount of throwing salt or knocking on wood would have stopped the cancer from eating into my brain. And I knew it was superstitious to knock on wood, even if you did it three times. But it wasn't superstitious to avoid thinking of things like destiny and fate. Because the Fates existed, if Fenrir did.

Maybe all that doesn't make sense. That I could see gods and still not believe in superstitious little things that came with the thoughts of them. I can just say it made sense to me. That I could believe in the things I see, the things I did, the things I wrote down with my pen about the world. I could write and want the world to be a better place. And somehow, somehow I thought I could blend those two things together.

So that's what I focused on. Writing about the things of this world. Maybe hiding what I could from Fenrir. Maybe blending the bad things with a touch of hope. Trying to find a way to save the world from the future it seemed to slowly plod towards, much like the tortoise and the hare.

I didn't focus on things like Fates. About things like Odin going to the Well of Urd. About the presence of Urd and Verdandi and Skuld. Of the tapestry of life being weaved, and the threads of the world being snipped short.

And there it was.

The real reason why I wasn't really superstitious.

I mean, why be superstitious when you knew what the ending was going to be? Why look for the writing of the book when you already had read the last sentence? Why knock on wood, throw salt, carry a rabbit's foot when none of those things would stop that book from being written, from the penning of the final chapter, from the flip of the last page?

All I could do was hope. Keep reading, keep writing, and hope. See if I could find a way for the world to keep spinning. Find a way to save some of it. Something of it.

Fenrir was old, dying. I saw it. He saw it. Berley knew it. Whatever science had kept the god alive, whatever technology tried to heal the wound on his haunch, that kept his heart beating and his lungs taking fistfuls of that chill cavern air, perhaps that's why he was looking for his daughter. To say goodbye.

He had held out a long time. Long enough, perhaps, to his mind. It hit me then, like a fist to the face. A question I hadn't ever asked, because I had never seen it. I had only asked why we didn't try to save those we could. I had always fought with Fenrir about that.

I had never, not once, asked him why he held Ragnarok at bay. Why he carried the burden for so long. Why he appeared to watch and wait, why he sent chroniclers out and listened to their observations.

Thinking of it, I could see the reason, maybe a little. My reports, through the years. How I had observed actions, written them down, passed them on. How those actions had become less and less those of a person helping an elderly grandmother cross a busy street, and more the crossing of a car across lanes of traffic to make a turn at a stoplight the moment after the light turned from yellow to red.

Fenrir had been looking for a reason to keep Ragnarok at bay.

Maybe he no longer found one.

The thought shook me out of my reverie. I found the car idling, waiting for me, the heat blowing out from the vents and inside of the cabin almost sauna-hot.

There was still a part of me that wanted to find the Fates. The place with all the answers. Maybe they could tell me more about the wolf. More about what he carried, and why he still carried it. Maybe they could help me find Fenrir's daughter.

And yet, the stories of the three Norns usually didn't end well. A person knowing more than they should didn't mean they would make wise decisions with that knowledge. And a person looking for reasons for why the world is ending, or why the ending is being kept at bay, maybe that knowledge would be more than that person would be willing to bargain for.

Especially if the knowledge would always end at the end of the world.

I took a moment, then, wondering. About things like the end of the world. Why there had to be an end, why it even existed. Why there was this great dark ending waiting for all of us. Why it loomed over everything, why it loomed so large most people couldn't even see it.

They just raced towards it, oblivious. Their faces tucked into phones. Their foot heavy on the gas pedal. Their frowns for the bills they open, for bank accounts too small, for the interest raise on a credit card they could never pay off. Never seeing the great end to everything that waited for us all, the cliff they all drove towards, as fast as they could go.

Had I ever known that ending existed? Maybe. Maybe that's why there was something inside me that wanted to write. That wanted to write words that mattered. That wanted to have a little hope I could do something, to keep that darkness at bay.

So, thinking that, I sat and wrote in the book. Wrote the words of the day. Understanding that the words I wrote may be more than just reports. I pulled the book out of its satchel, untucked the golden pen from inside its spine, a long, thin utensil with Nordic symbols scrawled down the side of it.

I pulled the book out and wrote about a little diner in the middle of a small town. Of a laughing waitress clapping her hands, of a pretty cook, perhaps a touch embarrassed. Of a dark-haired man leaning forward and talking, of a connection of three people who had no idea who they were in the largest scheme of things, but in their little bubble of a world, were happy. Were happy around each other, and that kind of happiness *radiated* against the dark gloom settling over the world.

I took longer and wrote about pancakes and hash. Of meeting someone and having that connection. Having that connection lead to hope. And that hope leading to years wanted, years desired, where a person might get up and order hash for decades, even though they liked pancakes.

I never wrote Emma-mae's name down. A part of me held back, there. I think maybe because it might have made the dream more real to me.

I finished writing, and closed the book. The muffled whump was familiar. Each time I closed it, it was an echo of things from the past. A reverberation that carried forward. Forward with my thoughts of the Fates and the Rule of Three.

I looked around the parking lot of the diner. I hadn't seen what car or truck Emma-mae had come in on. I hadn't watched her leave either.

Part of me wanted to find her, to have that person I connected with, of having those years of coming here together. There was something she brought out in me, some way of seeing life that I had been missing. Something I had missed, in my years chronicling. Of telling the stories of humans fated to die.

If I had to say it, I felt hope there. I mean, I always carried it, I wanted to write something that mattered, I wanted to write something that would save someone. I hoped, doing what I did now, that I could be that person. And something in that meeting had me feel like I could be. Something in Emma-mae herself, perhaps.

The opportunity had been missed, though. I fought the desire to go back inside the diner and ask Linda, or the dark-haired man, or the chef where I might find her. Where Emma-mae lived. I was sure, as nice as they seemed to be, and as much as Linda remembered me and as their little group radiated, they wouldn't want to hand out someone's address to a mostly-complete stranger.

The car shuddered a moment, the way cars did when perhaps there was a spot of water in the fuel. Or a filter had clogged up with something, briefly. Maybe it was just telling me to stop sitting here and *go*.

I could get behind that. The motel was a few hours from here. Far enough to keep anyone who might follow me from easily finding Fenrir's lair. I kept my foot lightly on the brake and swung the transmission from park to drive, hearing the motor settling down, ready to pounce. Feeling the engine engage.

The diner sat before me. I gave a last glance to that rental room above it. One day, if there were many days left, I'd have to rent that thing instead of driving a few more hours to my motel. Maybe on the last day, the last report I knew I'd turn in, maybe it'd be nice to take that room. To enjoy the radiance of a happy, small group of people in the middle of nowhere. To wake to a nice breakfast of cajon hash browns or sweet syrupy pancakes and stare out over the glimmering flat waters of a mountain lake, surrounded by the burning leaves of fall.

One day it'd be nice to just sit there and take it all in, and let everything else go.

CHAPTER FIVE

The motel itself hadn't been too far from the diner. A small two-story thing on the side of the mountain road, pale yellow walls covered in cauliflower-shaped splotches of old dirt and grime. It stretched straight down back from the office, a brown door with a brass handle every thirty feet, with a large front window hiding the room behind dark, closed curtains. Parking spaces lined the motel, with old faded white lines stretching out, like broken teeth poked out of an old, yellow gum.

I parked and got a small bag out of its trunk, a small backpack with some toiletries, then opened the door. The motel room was like a million other motel rooms I'd been in. Small. Square. With enough room for an old oak-stained dresser, a queen-sized bed, and a tiny square desk made of the same wood as the dresser between the bed and the far wall. There was just enough room to get to the desk, if you kind of waddled sideways between the bed and the dresser to get to that side.

There was a television on the dresser, a small, older flat-screen television. The bedspread was a pale cream with blue lines running through it. A color that didn't clash with the orangish-tan walls, from a blanket that was too thin for the cold of the room, a cold that seemed to come from the mountains outside. The carpet in the room was a dark brown, something that would hide all kinds of hair, all kinds of dirt and grime, all kinds of sin. Something shaggy and deep and hard enough to vacuum, so that the scent of all the previous occupants blended into something like freshly dug earth and the thick scent of pine cleaner.

The lamp on the desk didn't have one of HD blue bulbs; the canvas lampshade threw a yellow circle on the desk over the top of the open book. The chair in front of it was square and wooden and hard, with no cushion, and my lower back had started to ache for as long as I had been sitting.

I had been searching it a long time. Reading bits and pieces of stories of writer after writer. Flipping through the book like someone might flip through an encyclopedia or dictionary or thesaurus. Carefully placing the paw when I moved too far, and hoping that I would just suddenly open the book to the right page, hoping it would just magically appear the next time I flipped back a couple of chapters before with a sigh, turning page after page from there.

It was odd, no matter how far back I flipped, or how far forward, the thickness of the book, the number of pages before me seemed to be about the same. Somewhere between four and five hundred. I could flip back through centuries of writers, or I could go right to my latest entry, and there still seemed to be a couple of hundred pages on either side of the page I was looking at.

The oddest thing about the book was that it seemed to have no beginning. As far back as I turned the pages, there was just another chapter, and then, after enough chapters, another writer. I could tell those changes by the penmanship. The angles of the letters, or even the language itself. I had started reading words in English, but I had seen other chroniclers of other nationalities. There were reports scribed in other languages, I was sure I recognized the French, the Spanish, and possibly Italian. Definitely the Latin.

I flipped past writings that looked like Chinese symbols. A stretch of hieroglyphics. And now, after hours of going back further and further, I was reading what I believed was Norse. Old Norse. Or I was trying to read it, there was no way I could really understand the language. I knew some of the symbols, especially the things I had been shown, like the doors to Fenrir's lair. Like other symbols, like the ones etched onto the side of my pen, an ink-filled thing of gold with Norse symbols naming the instrument Gungnir, which I thought an odd bit of poetic license, and likened it to mean that the pen would always strike true, always find its mark in its words.

At least, that was my thought.

I noticed other runes. Symbols that meant Asgard. Or Niflheim. Or the great rune for the tree on the front of the book, Yggdrasil. In the beginning there were chapters and chapters written in old Norse, and I saw the symbol of the tree a lot, but hell if I could make sense of it. Asgard, Niflheim, Midgard, plenty of runes. Plenty of worlds. Plenty of talk about gods.

I saw the rune for Freya. A number of times. Frey as well. Thor came up, and Loki, of course. The great watcher, Heimdall. Mimir, of course.

Plenty of runes. Plenty of worlds. Plenty of talk about gods. And, also, gods conspicuous for their absence. At least, absent from the pages I flipped through, from the runes I had very little knowledge of. Fenrir's mother, of course, Angrboda… and Kvasir, Bragi, Sif, Tyr—the beautiful and kind gods, the gods of wisdom and poetry—and of course Odin. The All-Father's rune, the stark vertical line with two arm-like lines angling down diagonally from its top, like a god placating supplicants, I saw nowhere.

And nowhere did I see mention of Fenrir's daughter. Not in the beginning of the book, and of course, I wouldn't know it if I did. I couldn't guess what her name was in Norse. Hell, I couldn't guess what it was now. I wouldn't know her, probably, if she had walked up and said hello.

So I came back to where I started. To my chapters, my reports on the world. My running commentary of humans and their slide into darkness. To my words, always tinged with sadness and regret and a foreshadowing I could not keep from them, as much as I might try.

I have tried not to read other's writings. I felt like they might bias my own thoughts and feelings, of what I observed today. It was what great writers did, they wrote to such a degree that their story impacted the reader, left the reader changed. So I didn't want to be changed by what I read, not in this case. Not with this book. Not with the Ragnarok-like feeling I already held, the cleansing waiting over the horizon. I wanted to observe, and to hope, and it was to these two things I had clung in my years serving Fenrir.

Having tried the far past for mention of the god, or his daughter, I decided to start closer and work my way back. From the Chronicler right before me. I had been nervous, always nervous, about reading his words. After all, the reason I was now the Chronicler was because this guy no longer was.

Which meant he had met his end. And that, as much as anything else, wasn't something I wanted to know. I had come too close on my own, to read—perhaps—another way I might meet my own death.

I took a breath and blew it out. Went to the chapter right before I had started. The very last thing the Chronicler before me had written about.

He had a clean script, and his writing had some note to it that had me thinking the author had been born outside of the United States. Their hand was elegant, precise, their letters remained straight up and down where mine slanted from right to left and from top to bottom, as if I tried to pull each letter backwards across the page from where I started to write it, as if I wanted every sentence to go back in time, to the moment before I had written it.

I read.

Today Fenrir sends me to New Orleans. He seems particularly edgy today, Fenrir. Full of brim and fire. I ask him why New Orleans and he chuffed at me and asked me who was the leader, and who was the pack?

So New Orleans it is. It has been decades since I have been called to visit America, I could use the respite there. They hold a festival there, I'm told. It is called Mardi Gras, and it is a religious observation, although the stories say that a person must—during the celebration—drink in plenty, reveal a lot of flesh, and toss beads over the heads of other practitioners.

Odd, to me, to be sent there. A city, a tradition... so like the story of Salem, and Lot. The world today, so much like that particular tale, and I wonder how true it might be. How close we are, here as humans on Earth, for all of us turn into our own pillar of salt...

See what I mean, about bias?

Still, I will enjoy the respite. You would think Berlin would have been kinder. That the experience would have filled me with more hope, and yet, it was opposite. There were crowds there, surely happy crowds, celebrating as the wall came down. But there was a darkness there too, a darkness only I seemed to notice, something that clung to the bricks as one was pulled down after the other, a blackness in the alleys and the streets, in the crowds across the way. A deeply unhappy expression, one of quiet, long intent and hidden rage, of plotting and planning and a future as yet undetermined…

I believed I will start at The Black Penny. It was the first name I had seen; such an odd turn of phrase, and one that appeals to me now. It has me wondering how long it has been in New Orleans, and if it is cheap and yet somehow always in circulating, if the bar has appeared in one form or another through its lifetime in the city.

Black Penny, bad penny… the thought makes me smile, just a bit. Smile, even after leaving Berlin, after my months there. I can't help but shake my head, writing this now, even after my report to Fenrir, remembering all the people there celebrating. The coincidence is not lost to me, the partying without end there, the yearly party I head towards.

Where, I wonder, will those people tearing down the wall be on the morrow? What do they think now, days after the first brick had been pulled? Will they plan ahead, stand guard against those forces of darkness, will they plan for a better future just like those who plan against? Will they hold fast to their ideas of freedom and bettering their fellow man, or did they wake up the next day, after all the celebrations, with a hangover and go back to their countries, their governments, their gods, and not realize that taking down the wall has stopped nothing? That taking down the wall didn't remove their illusion of working towards a better world, but only hid those who worked to destroy it in open sight?

I stopped there for a moment, feeling the pages between his entry and my first one, and knowing there would not be much left there. Trying to rub them in the way people did, trying to pull apart pages stuck together. It was only after a moment of effort I realized there were no more pages. Nothing more to report. There was this page, what was left of the man's writing on the back of it, and then the very next page was my own hand.

My spine tingled with that thought. This man had gone to New Orleans, and had plans to visit The Black Penny, and that had been his last thoughts. I didn't even know, not really, if he had made it there. To the city or the bar.

Something did strike me though, strike me aside from the spine-tingling thoughts of death, and I went back to look at it. There was an interesting line in the beginning of his tale… *it has been decades since I have been called to visit America.*

It made me wonder when the wolf had come here. It must have been recent. Perhaps it would be better to wonder when he had been moved here, and how, and from where. I flipped backwards through the book, taking quick peeks into each of the Chronicler's tales—these stories were not long, each of these scribes had not survived long in their role—and I found little mention of the god, and nothing about when he had moved, or why, or from where.

Hmmm.

I shook my head. Flipped past the short-lived Chronicler entries, the chapters and reports short, maybe covering a few years each. The early twentieth century seemed a brutal time for a scribe, with the World Wars and everything else happening at that time.

I gave another, thoughtful hmmm. Continuing to flip back, Chronicler by Chronicler. The style of prose and writing changed from one to the next, all with three or four entries before their writing disappeared into the next style.

It had me wondering. Had they died during a World War or from a car accident? A sinking ship, or a plane crash? Perhaps they had been killed in a violent mugging, or if—as the wolf had always warned me—they each had met up with another god. A Thor or Loki, or a giant like Surtr in some fiery angry spat.

It had been a time of wars. A time of lies. A time of fiery machines rushing across battlefields.

They all had had bad runs. I surfed through each, never seeing anything I was looking for, always going backwards in my search for something that might hint at Fenrir's daughter, without looking too closely. I didn't want to know what had sent them to their end. Where they had been. What they had been doing. It spoke too closely to the here and now of my life. To the cleansing, to where humankind was, and where they were going.

So nothing in the few short chapters of the short-lived Chroniclers. Nothing about Fenrir's daughter. They headed to foreign lands all, Russia, South America, Egypt. I held myself back from reading the last page of each, thinking maybe one day. Thinking it might be better to be prepared than not. Thinking the whole time how curiosity had killed the cat.

I flipped back further. Finally found a looser hand, scrawling chapter after chapter, for a long period of the book. Another long-lived Chronicler. At least, comparatively.

Their script was one of large loops around curving letters, even the T's had a tiny embellished swirl on either side of its top. The writing was elegant and perhaps a little feminine. At least, that was my idea of it, reading their words. It could very likely have just been the prose at the time, where the writer had learned, who they had learned it from, but something about the words and the way they were written pulled me in…

I saw Wyatt Earp again today. It had been a long time, a long time since he had been a child, I his schoolmistress, and he had told me his dream of being a lawman. He looked tired now, riding his horse with his posse, tired of hunting those who had killed his brother. Tired and worn, the way an iron spike looks years after it had been pounded into the railroad tie, years of weathering and of trains rolling across it, years of doing its service with nothing to keep holding it there, holding it in, other than a tool fulfilling its job.

He never recognized me. I knew he wouldn't, and yet part of me still expected it. Both of us had changed since then, and perhaps where his older eyes had thinned with the years, and perhaps grew more unfocused with use, mine had remained sharp, but still…

No matter.

It made me sad, being here. Sad, and yet comforting. China had been something I had never seen before, and couldn't imagine to want to see again. I don't know what the final death toll had been, ten million, twenty, thirty? It was hard to tell. I think it will always be hard to tell. Rebellions—I was certain—must always be a bloody business, yet I had never seen a rebellion like this one; I would likely never see one like it again.

Although the wolf tells me different. He tells me of times when that many people would die in a blink of an eye. In blink after blink, when they would disappear from the face of the Earth and never be missed. Of ending after ending… when the gods might laugh and drink and carry on without a thought or care or wonder.

China had been horrifying. I don't know that I could have dreamed of human depravity that way. Of the sheer amount of evils men could do to other men. Of not just the murders, the rapings, the violence, but the sheer uncaring of it all. The lack of simple human kindness that I thought should exist somewhere inside all that horror… I don't know that I can dream of a time of gods doing the same.

There's a darkness in the world. A shadow that only grows darker, something I only seem to see and feel. Perhaps because I am just human, even if I have lived a lifetime. Perhaps because I am human, with a human's thoughts and feelings, in a universe of gods who have lived much longer than I.

Now here I am, observing a ride. Oddly comforted, watching a ride of vengeance, of an older man's quest for justice. A small thing, perhaps compared to China, although the wolf never sends me to small things. Everything is a lesson to the wolf, and I should remember that.

Everything.

Perhaps I need to learn my own lessons now, too.

I paused here, feeling I had something. Feeling that I had found something in this Chronicler. Not just because of how she had spoken of Fenrir, but how she had spoken of the god in the way I thought of him. As *the wolf.*

It made me feel like I was connected with the writer. That I shared something with them. And now, reading just this, about Wyatt Earp and the Chronicler's observations, it all had pulled me in. I was there, looking into the sad eyes of Wyatt Earp. I could feel the exhaustion in the man, in his thin frame, his hollow cheeks. I could feel the fire in him, a fire that had once blazed, and perhaps now was banked, but still there. Hot. Holding on.

I felt like here, with this Chronicler, there would be something I could learn. There would be something here. I would find this daughter through them. I knew it, because it started with Fenrir. Their observations of the wolf. Done in almost a familiar way. As if they had spoke many times.

I was certain here, with this Chronicler, I would find where I needed to go. I measured the thickness of their entries, it went back a ways, it went forward a ways. They had travelled quite extensively. It would be a lot of reading.

A horn beeped, loudly, insistently, from right outside of my window. I jumped a bit at the desk. Lights flashed, headlights, illuminating a square behind the closed blue curtains in quick flashes. I glanced at the time, it was well into dark now, past midnight. I had read for a long time.

I decided to check it out. I wasn't worried, although I should have been, perhaps. I slowly got up from the desk and stretched, feeling my back ache and the muscles there pull in a way that told me, when I woke, they would hurt even more and need even more stretches.

I moved to the window, turning a bit sideways again between the foot of the bed and the dark oak dresser. I leaned a little to the side and pulled the curtain aside, just a bit.

A truck was there. A black F-150, with a chrome grill. It idled there, motor chugging, some guy behind the wheel I couldn't make out, with the glare of the motel lights against the windshield.

He flashed the headlights again. He had his high beams on, and the flashes were bright. I winced and let the curtain fall shut. Blinking a few times before—being curious (I was a Chronicler, after all)—I pulled a tiny corner of the curtain aside and peeked past it, once more.

The truck was still there. Idling. The lights glaring back at me.

And there was a clicking sound, the kind made by cheap high-heels, against the sidewalk outside my door. A young girl, perhaps too young, walked to the side of the F-150. She wore a tight halter top and a very short skirt with the heels, revealing a lithe, thin body. A body that might need growing into, and walked almost crookedly. As if she wasn't used to the heels.

She opened the door. The man inside reached down and yanked her inside, more than helped her. Her face was moving behind the windshield, her mouth was moving, his was too, in the fast rapid way that usually meant an argument, one that had happened many times. Then the man raised his hand, the girl ducked, the truck flashed its high beams at me again and then it was backing out of the spot and then they were gone. Leaving an empty space between broken white lines of teeth on the pavement.

I had already let the curtain fall back.

I hadn't been worried at the first beep of the horn. I hadn't been worried, even in this little run-down motel in the middle of nowhere. But maybe I should have been.

Not worried for my safety. But worried about what I thought. Worried about what I might observe. What I might *see*.

I was glad I had already written today. I didn't want to write more. I didn't want to find a way to add a touch of hope to something like this. Something I didn't want to put into the book's pages.

Still, I made sure I just observed the young hooker and her pimp. Light could never truly exist unless darkness surrounded it, and I guess I felt the same way about hope. That people should see a little of the bad of the world, in order for the hope to mean anything.

But I did promise myself to just observe. To never write of the lost face of the girl. The twisted face of the young man. I promised myself to just observe this, remember it, carry it, and never write about it. Never report it to the wolf.

There was no need to hasten along what didn't need hastening.

CHAPTER SIX

E ven with the late night, I got up early the next morning.

As I predicted, my lower back ached from hours of reading on that shitty chair. From getting lost in the words of the other chroniclers. From reading the words of the last.

I stretched in the bed, feeling the muscles in my back stretch some too. Feeling the ache there. The bed was soft, too soft, and other parts of me ached. Parts of me more used to sleeping on something firm, of being supported.

It had felt like a much longer night than it had been. Maybe it was the feeling of Ragnarok hovering in the background, looming over me. Maybe it had been the mournful howl of the wolf, the memory I had seen, the sunlit field and a pup rolling in flowers. Maybe it had been the pimp and the girl who was too young to be a hooker, too young to peddle her body for money.

There had been too many instances of that lately. Too many things I should have written down, that I hadn't. Things that I thought tipped the scales too much towards the world-destruction way. My dreams had been full of things, things I had seen while observing for the wolf, things I had seen and not put into the book, dreams—nightmares—where a slow pen wrote down what I had seen, the words changing as I moved the pen across the page, the ink shifting and morphing into all the things I had seen and not written down.

It had been bad. I remembered a small place in Africa. Ethiopia. One of those villages occupied one day by the liberation front, the next by federal forces. A place with starving families and those kids you see on the commercials with the too-swollen bellies, stomachs distended from hunger.

My dream had pulled an old memory out. Maybe the girl last night had brought the memory to my subconscious, and it had played it over again in my sleep. It was one where a young girl had been sleeping with soldiers for food. I remembered a time where she had come out of an alley with a ration bar in her hand, taking it over to her brother.

She had sat next to him in the dirt. Hugged him close, with one arm. Made sure he took small bites of the bar, swallowed it down with old water.

The next day the federal forces rolled in. There had been a small fight, a little gunfire. Most of the rebels had escaped. And then, like what always happens, the forces took it out on the villagers.

The dream had turned bad. In real life I had written of that girl in the book. The magic of the moment, of what she would do for her brother. For food. For family.

I wanted more of the world to be like her. To understand sacrifice. I wanted Fenrir to see that, too. The good in humans.

So I had written of that moment in the book. In the dream, reality took its place. New words ran like blood down the page. The federal forces shooting those who conspired with the rebels. Shooting a little girl who was just trying to get food for her brother. Shooting her and leaving her in front of her younger brother, the boy crying in the street, squatting on bent ankles, the half-eaten bar carefully tight in his fist.

That had been one, one of many. Many dreams, many nightmares. I had tossed and turned on the soft bed and woken to a world that was, and wishing that I had woke to the world it wasn't.

My room was quiet. The rest of the rooms around me weren't. The motel had the thin construction of all cheap motels, with thin walls and thinner floors, so that I could hear the heavy guy above me pound his way to the bathroom and back just as easily as I could hear The Today Show in the room next door.

I left my television off. I used to watch a lot of shows, but now just couldn't. Thanks to the wolf. I left it off for the same reason Fenrir had given me, back when I asked him why he didn't get his information by watching the news.

The wolf had laughed. Not loudly, the chuckling, chuffing sound that I understood wasn't meant to be derisive, was just something a parent might do in front of a child that doesn't understand how things worked yet. He questioned me about the news, and wondered if, when I looked through the glass of the television, if I was looking at things with my eyes or through the eyes of another. And if, looking through the eyes of another, if I could filter the tint of their bias from the image, like a person might filter the color from a picture.

I remember his final words that day: *Can you truly look into the surface of a pond and see yourself, without imagining what might lie underneath? Without wondering if a serpent doesn't wait there, below what you believe you see, waiting for that moment you lean into it, and it can strike?*

Odd, the wolf.

Odd, my turn of phrase. I had usually called him Fenrir. One night of reading the Chronicler from the night before, and I was already calling him the wolf.

Anyway, I listened to the muted, unintelligible words of The Today Show and the heavy-footed thumping of my upstairs neighbor. I left the television off, like I always did now. I hadn't at first, after the wolf had cautioned me, but then I began to understand it. I started to see things common between all the channels, a message, a bias, and I was unhappy that I did so.

I struggled up and took a shower. The water was thankfully hot and had good pressure to it. I peeled the wrapper from the small square bar of soap and lathered it up, breathing in a scent that was described as cucumber aloe. I let the hot water rinse that off of me, let the pressure beat on my back a bit, at least until my skin felt red and hot, thinking of how I had stopped watching all the different news stations to see what was going on. That I had, back then, just left the sports channel on.

Even sports had its own particular bias. Seemed to have something guiding it. When I was a kid there used to be a football team, every time one of their players scored they would get in the endzone and celebrate, jumping up all together in a bunch. I think they called it the Fun Bunch.

One time, a player from the other team had gotten in the way. Pushing in on the group celebrating. He had caused enough of a ruckus that the league had banned group celebrations.

That had been a few decades ago now. Fast forward to today, when celebrations were again allowed. It had started with individual players celebrating, after making a tackle ten or twenty yards down the field. Where a player celebrated a first down by doing that little chop thing with their arm, even if their team was down twenty or thirty points.

It was odd, to me, looking at it from the outside. It had taken some time, after turning off the television, for me to see what the wolf had been trying to tell me. And it was something I could never make other people understand, not if I tried to explain it.

There was something wrong about banning the celebration of a group of people who had worked hard together, who had worked *together* to become victorious. There was something more wrong about promoting these individual, meaningless celebrations. There was something insidious tying these things together, the banning of people working together, the celebration of meaningless individual stats, that I could see everywhere now. Not just in sports, but in all news.

It was something I couldn't explain though, what I felt and saw. A darkness, maybe. A shadow I could never get someone else to see or believe. It was like there was something behind it all. Some malignant force guiding us to Ragnarok. Maybe I didn't understand it in the beginning, maybe I first thought the wolf's chuckling chuff silly, but I thought I got it now.

No wonder Fenrir felt the way he did.

I was gloomy this morning. And while I wasn't always the cheerful, hopeful writer I had been as a youth, I wasn't always like this. I thought the Chronicler I had read, The Black Penny, bad penny one, had gotten to me. Especially with where I was headed.

Sometimes these thoughts struck me, though. Struck me with wonder. I never saw the gods, not that I knew. I had it on pretty good authority that Odin hadn't shown himself in a long time, other than his silhouette on the cover of the book. The wolf just growls if I mention his name. I figured Loki was still alive, being not only Fenrir's father, but you know, Loki. I hadn't seen Thor, even in the middle of some of the worse thunderstorms, and I knew Baldur was still dead, and I knew that while Freya was alive and walking catwalks, Frey hadn't been seen in a while.

Some of the Norse gods were dead. I knew that, even if I wasn't sure who. Some were still alive, like Fenrir, although I also didn't know who. Gods were secretive, at the best of times, and now didn't appear to be the best of times.

Was it any wonder that I thought these thoughts? Here I was, living in a world of gods, and yet I followed and wrote humanity instead. Here I was, feeling like Ragnarok was on the horizon, as if I could feel the storm there, hovering over the edge of the Earth, and yet instead of finding Odin or Thor, I was heading to a bar in New Orleans, following the path of the guy who had been writing words in the book before me.

I took a breath and let everything go. Swung the shower off, the inside of the small room was muggy, the tiny mirror by the sink fogged. I wiped it off and saw my hair, thick and dark again, and smiled a bit at the vanity. Sometimes it's a little thing that gets us through the day.

Then I got dressed. I had packed light, I always did while travelling, and grabbed another pair of jeans and another white T-shirt out of the bag before shrugging the same blue-and-white checkered flannel I had worn yesterday overtop that shirt. I tucked my wallet into one back pocket, a dark blue kerchief in another, and checked out of the hotel and went back to the sedan, not quite shivering in the dim morning sun, the early morning chill.

An eighteen-wheeler had been parked in the back of the motel, where the broken teeth of the parking spaces ended, where a little gravel lot swung around behind the building. The cab of the truck faced my way, angling almost at a right angle from the back; it fit in the parking lot like a dragon, head bent and sleeping. The rig hadn't been there the night before, and I hadn't heard it come in, and I wondered how much sleep the driver could have had.

A large man walked the outside of the truck, pausing beside each tire as if checking the pressure. He wore one of those big, thick jean jackets with some kind of white fur lining the inside and poking out a bit outside the collar overtop his own dark jeans. He had dark hair, cut short and tight to the sides, and a beard manicured to look the same, sharp along the sides and filling out as it grew to a square on his chin. A cigarette burned, hanging from his lips, a tiny wisp of smoke following the man around. His belt was tight at the waist, cinched so that for a moment I could believe he was Thor, the giant of a god, with his belt of strength, Megingjörd, around him.

I waved at him. Imagining waving to one of the Norse gods that might walk around us, each and every day. The man frowned, and I imagined he grunted, though he was far enough away I couldn't hear him back. Then he turned back to his tires and his pressure checks.

People today.

I got in the sedan, thinking about going back to the diner. Part of me wanted to be a part of the smiling waitress, the bashful cook, even the somewhat brooding dark-haired man. And a part of me wanted to see if Emma-mae was there. Which wasn't a thought I had about a woman, not in my new life.

Instead I moved on. Maybe it was the power of threes. If I did see Emma again, I'd think it was a sign, and then I would always want to look for her. Best to let that kind of thing go, to let the fancying go before it dug too deep.

I headed to the car rental place. It had just opened. It was one I had used before, there were only so many around in the little towns around the Adirondacks, though the clerk didn't remember me from the prior times, even if the waitress of the diner had. It was nice to be remembered, I felt, even though I had been warned by both Fenrir and Berley that there would be people, and powers both, wanting to find the cavern.

I shrugged, thinking about it. Handing the keys of the sedan to the clerk. He looked at me a little funny. I wasn't going to tell him I was taking the best precautions I could.

It was time to move along. And it occurred to me, that in the first time since before my service to the wolf had begun, I was more free than I thought. I was going to a place of Fenrir's choosing, but not to observe and report. I was going to where he had asked me, but for a different reason. I wasn't there to observe and chronicle, though maybe the wolf expected that. I was going there seeking and finding.

It was oddly freeing. It felt like an unshackling, of sorts. As if the purpose I had been chained to no longer was there, or the chain broken. I felt thoughtful, but also different; reflective, but also—in some way—new.

Maybe it was the words of the schoolmistress. She had read the other reports before her, and now I found myself wanting to do the same. Of the others, and of her accounts. I felt like she knew more about Fenrir than I did. And something in me told me that was important.

Silly of me, right? Here I was talking about writing something that mattered. About words that mattered, because books carry their meaning with them. Here I was holding the very book that might have the most meaning, and up until now it had been one I had refused to read.

I would fix that. I would fix it while I searched for Fenrir's daughter. I would fix it while I searched for a way to prevent Ragnarok, while I searched for a way to stop my back from tingling with fear, each time my mind brought up the image of the wolf there at the end, in his cavern, with his rattling, rough voice. Telling me it was *time*.

New Orleans was a place where all great parties began, I was told.

Might as well start this one there, as well.

CHAPTER SEVEN

Having been in this particular town, I took a left out of the car rental place and walked down the sidewalk. Away from the main road and up into the hills behind the town. Past old red-brick stores, a closed barber shop, a closed garage, an open Dollar General. A dentist office with no cars in the parking lot. A tiny bank on the corner, also closed, and then a cannabis store. Open.

Just observing, that's all.

I walked past all of that and out of town. It was a small town and the walk was short. Past all those places, then past small blocks of old wooden homes with faded yellow and blue paints, with sagging porches and even more saggy roofs, with tiny threads of gray smoke twirling up from stained chimneys and the scent of burning oak. I walked past all of that, waving to an old lady struggling out in a heavy yellow and red robe and black galoshes, grabbing a paper. I walked past all of that and into the trees beyond the town, up into the hills of the Adirondacks, heading a small clearing surrounded by woods that I knew was there, and secluded.

There's a part of you that might wonder, reading this account, reading the others, how a person could travel the world so quickly to observe something in China and then be in the wild west of the United States. Especially in the late nineteenth century.

You might even wonder how people had done it centuries before that. After all, Fenrir wanted to know what was happening in the world, in Germany and Britain, in Africa and Greece, in Australia and Brazil. How could a Chronicler travel so far, so fast?

The magic of the gods.

Literally.

I pulled the kerchief out of my pocket. It was a dark blue silky thing, thin, but from experience I knew that thinness did not mean fragile. The kerchief was folded into a small square, and I carefully unfolded it to a certain size. Knowing in this, as in most things, size did matter.

The kerchief unfolded to the size of a scarf. The translucent-silk like material rippling a bit in the still morning air. Translucent, and thin, but still supple and strong.

The scarf changed color as it did. From the blue I usually favored to something darker. A black, streaked with silver. I kept unfolding the scarf larger, until it was larger than a person. Then larger, like a couch.

One of my hands remained on the corner of the scarf as I unfolded. When it got to couch-size, and darkened fully to the black and silver color, I flicked that hand. Flicked it and smoothed out the scarf in the air with my other hand.

That's the best way I can describe it.

The corner I held grew harder under my finger and thumb. It *twisted* in shape there. The rest of the scarf fluttered in the air, taking a firm shape underneath my hand as I ran it along the material. Everything became firm, solid, black and silver under my hand, the scarf disappeared in that instant and instead of holding the corner of a scarf I instead was holding the handle of a motorcycle.

A Harley-Davidson. A V-Rod. With a black tank and a silvery figure, a chrome-like emblem almost etched into either side of the gas tank: the long glimmery form of a wolf in mid-run, its paws stretching forward, its hair ruffled by a gale of a wind, its eyes holding some inner spark, the jaw open as if the beast were ready to howl...

The rest of the bike looked lupine too. The foot pegs and the long chromed-out pipes spoke of ready paws and long legs, ready to run. The black seat was leather but somehow spoke of fur, and its haunch was curved and rounded along the back, as if the bike was ready to spring. The handles of the bike, the front tire angled underneath it, the short curve of the cowling that broke through the wind, all of it spoke of a long, wolven jaw ready to eat up the road.

I'm a writer at heart. Sometimes my imagination gets the best of me. And while I hadn't really ridden a motorcycle when I was younger, something in me loved it now. The solitary aloneness of being on the road. The hunt of riding, of digging into a corner of some back-country and powering out of it. Of the roar of the engine as I rolled down the highway.

It might sound like I wasn't happy in my service to the wolf. If not happy, frustrated. That wasn't quite the case. Maybe I argued, and maybe I questioned, but there wasn't a place I'd rather be. There wasn't a place I really couldn't be. I had been on my deathbed, before the wolf had found me.

And now, there was this. I mean, I had written some fantasy in the past. I had written science fiction. I had written about alien worlds and gods and swinging magic swords among a host of enemies, swinging for everything I was worth. I had written about spaceships and magical beasts and all kinds of ways of teleportation.

Now I lived it. Now I had this.
Skidblandir.
Ship of the gods.
And now, motorcycle of a Chronicler.

CHAPTER EIGHT

Travelling in Skidblandir—or on it—was something to experience. Hard to capture in words, but I'll try. Imagine travelling along a road where the cars around you, you start passing them one by one. Where every car seems like it's moving slower and slower, until each one seems almost frozen in time. Where the trees on the side of the road start racing past, one after the next, until they become a blur. Where even the great mountains roll by faster than you can count.

Still, even at that great speed, you are in full control. The bike sinks into every curve. You lean into the round section of road, you feel your gravity sink with the bike, and then you roll the throttle back and roar out of it. Down the next straightaway, with the wind rushing by you so that it felt like you were flying.

It's a weird juxtaposition. You are almost completely out of control, and yet you manage every move of the bike. You travel too fast to see the sides of the road, the trees and homes and gas stations turn into some kind of whitish blur, and yet you see every pothole, you miss every deer, you easily navigate around every slow vehicle in front of you.

And then, you go even faster. Faster until the world is a blur. Until everything has faded white, like you see the world rushing by you through a thin film of cloud, rushing by at a speed nothing human can track, and yet you know exactly where you are at.

Yeah. There's a reason I chose a bike for that. I rushed ahead on the road, rolling my right hand back, squeezing a bit occasionally on my left and feeling Skidblandir leap ahead on the road. Feeling it leap with every squeeze, and relishing the moment. Knowing it wasn't too long ago that I couldn't use that hand anymore. That I couldn't even see. That if I had tried riding a motorcycle, back when the cancer was eating me up and leaving my hand unresponsive, my eye blank, I would have ended up in a jumble on the side of the road.

Now I laughed. Now I roared; the twin engines roared underneath me. It howled and I howled with it, rolling my right hand back even more, feeling the wind rush by me. It was always clean on Skidblandir. Always clean and fresh and bringing the faintest hint of snow. It was never cold, the racing wind was never chill, I was part of the ship and it was part of me. I was part of the motorcycle and it was part of me. We were beast and machine and man, and I loved it.

Other chroniclers may have chosen a ship. They might have chosen a horse, or a carriage, or a blazing red Ferrari. I didn't know, I couldn't know with my avoidance of the knowledge of them. Whatever they had chosen though, a bike beat them all.

Google Maps tells me it's about fifteen hundred miles between the Adirondacks and New Orleans. It would take a fast driver around a day to drive it, even without the normal traffic jams, the packed interstates, the long stretches of roads under construction, with the orange cone after orange cone and no worker in sight. Maybe twenty-two hours, at their fastest.

It took me thirty minutes.

At least, thirty minutes before I began to slow down. Before I eased off the throttle. Letting the thin white film of cloud dissipate, and see the long flat stretches of marshland on either side of I-10. Seeing the swamps, and the low-lying trees that—wherever I saw them—gave me a *Gone with the Wind* kind of feel. The unique southern blend of trees, of Spanish moss, of lush and green landscapes mixed with shimmering bodies of water. I could see and feel the trees, the moss, the scent of thick branches and tall grass decomposing in the muddy-watered marsh.

Then I was cruising along, west, at a comfortable eighty miles an hour. The bike humming underneath me. Content. Homes and houses poked out from the landscape, to the north and south. The urban sprawl grew tighter, the home and houses packed closer together, even though the swamps and the lush grass and the low-lying trees remained.

Part of me wondered if Frey had ever taken Skidblandir out like this. If the god had gotten onto his magical ship and flew at such a speed that the world rushed by. If he had slowed down, observing the blurred images coalescing into recognizable features, of trees and homes, if the god had left his home of mountains and fled to a land of trees hanging with moss, from frozen ice to this expanding —small waves crossing its simmering surface—lake.

Which told me I was on the Lake Pontchartrain Causeway. Crossing over the lake itself. The huge body of water glinting under the early morning sun, as if it were one big mirror reflecting the open blue sky above it. The shimmering seemed to move with me, the light reflecting on the tiny waves as we rode the causeway, as if the sun itself shone a spotlight on the bike as we rolled along. Highlighting the world around me, the glinting of the water, the bright blue sky, the pure white clouds, the glossy black surface of the bike, the sharply reflective chrome, the flashy, silvery emblem of the wolf.

And the hidden expanse of the lake. Its waters seemed too high to me, as if the lake swelled underneath me as I rode into New Orleans. As if the shimmering brightness masked the true intentions underneath the water, distracting us with the sun highlighting those who rode in.

Then I was over the lake. All thoughts of the hidden waters gone, the causeway was past, in a flash of small piers and tied-up boats, to either side. There were still the marshy lands here, but more homes. Clusters of trees dotted landscapes. Streets trailing to either side, as individual homes turned into suburban neighborhoods.

It was odd to me, seeing this now. Thinking about the Hurricane, not so long ago. Not the one in lower-letters, but *The Hurricane*. Katrina.

Reports from back then had been devastating. A city under water. So many homes torn away. Lives lost. Businesses gone, restaurants and shops that had been in families for generations. People bussed and shipped to other places, most never to return again.

It would have been a good place and time to chronicle. I would have hoped to see the best of people. I wouldn't see the isolated groups, those with masks pointing to those without, those without pointing to those with. I wouldn't see the rage and anger those groups held, the how dare they of it.

I imagined Katrina would have brought out the best in people. At least, I hoped it had. It had happened in my youth, at a time the cancer had been eating at me, so I didn't quite remember what had happened that well. I hadn't been watching a lot of news then.

I slowed down on the motorcycle, taking in the outskirts of the city. There wasn't a sign of a hurricane had passed through here, at least not coming in this way, along I-10 East. There were just the homes, those homes became blocks, those blocks had buildings that swelled up, adding floor after floor, growing taller and larger as I rode in. Homes became offices in places, or banks. There were the Creole cottages you come to expect when you think of New Orleans, grouped with shotgun houses. Palm trees, oddly enough, lined the occasional street.

I realized, not seeing anything from the hurricane, how much time had passed between the Chronicler before me, and my own time. It must have been a fifteen or twenty-year gap. I wondered if that was normal, and if I shouldn't perhaps time-line the book out some. Maybe I'd find something.

And then the thought passed. Just like I passed the Creole cottages, the ones that make you feel like you're a part of history. The old homes full of a soul you've never been a part of, just something you see on television, or maybe get a glimpse of from an Anne Rice book. You see it and feel it, just like I felt it riding in, the hidden spirit and vibrancy of a city that never stopped partying. That never stopped loving life, in its own mystic way. There were local shops along the streets, cafes, bars, restaurants. At some point you leave the peaceful feel of the long lake you had crossed and you enter a different world. A vibrant world. A world built of the living and the dead.

That's when you know you're there. When you're really in New Orleans. You can feel the French Quarter, long before you arrive.

I swung off of I-10 and headed deeper into the real part of New Orleans. The old part, full of mysticism and ghosts and spirits. Into the French Quarter. Looking for The Black Penny, the first place the Chronicler before me was visiting. I knew it was off of N Rampart Street, and I navigated in that direction, looking for the right spot as I rode.

I found it. A tiny alley between a café and a restaurant. A tiny thing of old brick just wide enough for a pair of motorcycles to enter with a guy lying back by the side of it, a homeless guy with an army jacket on and a blue bandana.

I pulled Skidblandir in. Throttled it down, as the shadows of the brick fell over me. Looking back and making sure no one was paying particular close attention to me. Which no one was, not this early in the morning, in a city known for its nightlife.

The darkest of the shadows fell over me. No one was looking. I stopped the bike, and in the same motion as getting off, pinched the corner of the handlebars with one hand, and reached along the side of the bike with the other, leaving the small backpack of toiletries sitting there on the back of the bike, knowing that Skidblandir was not just a bike, and not just the ship of the gods, but a ship with cabins and beds and closets, a magical place of storage.

I ran my hand down the side of the bike, thinking all those things. Holding the handlebars with one hand. For a moment, if anyone had been watching, they would have seen a biker patting the side of his bike. Maybe running a hand lovingly alongside the seat.

And then the bike was gone. Between the fingers of my left hand, the hand holding the handlebars of the bike, was the scarf. Again just a dark blue square, silky and smooth. Something that snapped quickly in the air as it folded back up into a square. A square I stuck back in my pocket.

And then I was walking back out of the alley. In my jeans and T-shirt and a flannel shirt that now seemed perhaps too hot for this far south. It was a cool seventy degrees now, even this deep into fall, down here.

The homeless guy looked up at me. He looked middle aged, with the kind of tanned white skin that came from sitting outside all day, and had a scratchy beard kind of face. His eyes glanced at me, a little blurrily, and the cardboard sign lay flat on his lap. The cardboard sign looked too new for a man who had been homeless long, and scrawled across the fresh cardboard in the blackest of magic marker were the words I've got nothing, but this street's got soul.

He looked at me, not really asking, just the kind of look that said it was early in the morning and what was the effort really worth anyway, but if you could spare a buck or two, well here I am.

I wasn't sure if he was really homeless, or just one of those panhandlers that worked being homeless like a job, but I felt caught in the stare of the ask. I couldn't really call it, and felt like I'd be wrong whichever side of the coin I landed. I guess in the end I defaulted to something my mother always had done.

We hadn't had a lot of money to speak of. I'm not sure if people use these today, but food stamps were sacred words in our home. We counted those things like cash, locked the booklets up, in all their fancy red and yellow and purple colors, with the little Liberty Bell off to the side surrounded with empty stars, with the value listed on the piece of paper. The value that wasn't real value, was something most people hid in the register line and pull out at the last second, with me watching my mother do it with grace and patience, with her head held high in dignity.

We hadn't had a lot of money, yet every time we passed a store with a bucket in front of it, and someone ringing a bell. Whenever we passed a table with a kid holding a sign in it, my mother always pulled out money and gave it to them. It might be just a dollar, but it was a real dollar, a real thing, and not some colored booklet of coupons.

She had always given at least a dollar. I had asked her once about it. I had grown into a teenager, with perhaps some of the selfish thoughts teenagers have. There had been this big reveal on one of the news stations, how some of the bigger charities had chief executive officers with bigger salaries, where the money people weren't getting the donations they might have in the decades before.

I had watched that, and Christmas was coming round, and whatever dollar my mother was giving out, well, it could have been something put to a new book, a new movie. A real turkey, maybe, for dinner for the holiday.

She had looked at me, with a tiny smile. Something maybe sad, not for me sad, but for something else. Her voice, like it always had been, was small and soft and held just a tiny bit of wishing deep within it.

"You have to hope, son," she had told me, "You have to hope, when you give something, that something of it does some good."

Then she would tuck the dollar into a bucket, with her head high. Say Merry Christmas to whomever. Or pat the kid with the sign, with the basketball team needing new uniforms, on the head. Wish him, and the team, good luck.

Those thoughts always popped into my head, when I saw the people ringing bells in front of stores. Or a homeless guy. And while money didn't mean much to me anymore, I did have a certain amount provided by the wolf. A livelihood of sorts. So, even if it didn't mean much to me, I pulled a ten-dollar bill out of my wallet and gave it to the guy with the funny sign.

It was the least I could do, the very least I could do. After seeing the world, and the way it was going, I understood what my mother had inside of her. What she had tried to pass on to me. Very possibly it was the very thing that drove me now, to save part of the world. To try, in the times and places I didn't know the truth or couldn't call, to err on the side of being human. Of what I'd want humanity to be. To err on what my mother would do.

I tried to believe in things like goodness, in the gift of giving. I tried to believe there weren't people on this Earth that would take advantage of that gift. I tried to believe that and walked away, hoping that I hadn't just given money to a guy who had a new car parked a block away and a home out in the suburbs.

Then I walked on, shrugging the flannel off. Tying the arms of it around my waist. It was cool here, but not cold, and the flannel felt like too much. I kept walking, a hand running along the strap of the satchel, making sure it held the book tight against my hip.

I was sure I looked like a bit of a tourist, and maybe a bit of a rube, with the flannel shirt and the backpack and satchel. But I had looked worse, and much different, in other places I'd been. I found I didn't care so much now, knowing the place I was at today could be a wildly different place the next week, the next day, the next hour.

So, dressed somewhat in a mix, like some country singer, like some college student nine years into a writing degree, like some tourist rube, I walked to The Black Penny.

CHAPTER NINE

It seemed like a beautiful day. The sun was out, arcing along a blue sky with just a white, puffy cloud or two drifting through the air. Its rays were warm on my face, warm on my bare arms, I was glad I had tied the flannel shirt off around my waist, even if the air was cool enough that the tiny gusts of it brought a slight chill.

I walked the sidewalks of the French Quarter. The stones, the concrete, the mixed pavings of the streets, all of it was old, and a good amount of it was uneven. Flat rocks slanted into the next, so that I had to watch my step. The square blocks of concrete mostly held spider-webbed cracks, the centers of the spiderweb splotched with dirt, the concrete dark with age.

The streets of New Orleans were mostly empty around me, still. Even though it was heading towards noon, it seemed as if most people were still sleeping in, or they had gotten up early and were already at work. There was little traffic on the streets, which varied from flat blacktop to cobblestone in no discernable pattern.

Just like the streets themselves. I walked by historic shops, bars, restaurants. I passed shops with voodoo dolls hanging from windows, with beads hanging in strands. I walked past vintage lamps along the sidewalks, unlit in the late morning. I walked underneath many a second-story porch, with old iron railings showing signs of rust, or painted a flat black, depending on the porch.

Everything was old and new. Some of the sidewalk was broken, some of it was the bright new white blocks of replacement sidewalk. Some of the cobblestones rose and fell, in patterns, as if a wave rolled by underneath the streets. Some of the roads were flat. The iron was rusty, the iron was painted.

Just like the sky. It was empty and not. There was the warmth of the sun, and the chill blue of a fall morning. The air was both clean and fresh, and yet it also held other scents. The wake-you-up scent of hot, bitter coffee. The spicy Creole scent of gumbo, even this early in the morning. The sweet, sugary smell of beignets. And an older, earthy scent. Something that had been around perhaps even before New Orleans. The wet scent of old mud, of a watery grave that had pulled in the land around it, that had pulled in the grass and the graves and even the trees, that had sucked it all in, so that the grass and the bones and the trees had lain there for hundreds, if not thousands of years, had lain there decaying so that the smell of the grave was always, always an undercurrent here.

I shivered. Part of me felt, then, a storm coming. Something riding that background scent of decay. Something that had built in the depths of New Orleans, had built like the pressure of gas contained, something that had built and was ready to explode.

Even on this beautiful, sunny, fall morning.

Part of me observed this. Part of me acknowledged the feel of it. The writer part of me, the part prone to these types of sobering descriptions. But another part of me—the primal, hindbrain part— realized that what I was witnessing was the state of the thing. That

New Orleans was undergoing a process, a change, that the city was taking a step in a different direction.

Like me walking the sidewalk, I felt the city should watch its step. There were cracks a plenty where it tread. The old, slanted rocks could trip a person, when they least expected it.

The feeling of the storm, the pregnancy of the empty sky and the underlying smell of the grave in New Orleans had me wonder about Fenrir's question to me. About the difference between gods and men. About there being no difference.

I had yet to meet a god, other than Fenrir. But the wolf had cautioned me, had always cautioned me that the gods were there. That they worked and planned. That some of them wanted Ragnarok, they wanted the destruction of everything. They wanted to watch the world burn.

Others wanted it as a test. They wanted to face it to see if they could survive the cleansing. They wanted to pitch themselves against the final battle to see if they would survive.

The last group wanted it for vengeance. There would be an accounting, at Ragnarok. A tally-board. There would be gods settling old scores, and that, to me, felt like the vengeance group outnumbered the previous two groups. That felt more human to me, the pettiness of something like a god-like vengeance. The need to not only right a wrong, but—in the righting of it—to cause a thousand more wrongs that would need righting, as well.

The breeze blew again. A stiff morning gust that rushed by me and then died off. I shivered again, perhaps with the feel of it, perhaps with my thoughts. There was a feel here, a feel to the city, a reckoning I felt was coming.

And reckonings usually meant gods. They came in plagues, on battlefields, in great storms and floods. They came without warning, out of the bluest of skies.

I walked and wondered about all of that. I walked and wondered why The Black Penny. The bad penny. Why the Chronicler had chosen to come here. And what he had found.

I had only his final page, his few words written on the back. A few jots of a paragraph, as if the man had wanted to write more, before he had left the Earth.

New Orleans is what I thought it would be. Especially now, especially during Mardi Gras. I had thought it would be better than Berlin, with the celebration, with the dark feel there of something watching from the other side of the wall, as the bricks came tumbling down.

But there's a different darkness here. Something threaded in the undercurrent of celebration. A more permanent darkness, something that always exists. Something that puts on its costume of celebration, its mask of revelers and bead-throwers, and hides in plain sight. Something that perhaps had been here long before the city had come into being, and planned on being here long after the partying ends.

Man, I didn't like reading this guy. I got it, I understood where he was coming from with the world today, but he dwelled deeply in the dark currents. I felt like at least I was still treading the water, I kept doggy-paddling in the mirk where he was sinking and I kept my head above the darkness, no matter how hard his currents pulled at me.

Which brought me to his last few words.

It's late. Too late tonight to go to The Black Penny. Even if it is a place for locals, a place that tourists might forgo in the name of something more dark, in the name of something with a bit more name to it, a bit more story, still The Black Penny would be packed.

It was Mardi Gras. And it was like all the stories. In a way better than Berlin, and in a way worse. Better, because most of the people here party with a will that I have rarely experienced. A zeal of sorts.

But worse, because of that undercurrent of darkness. A current that would steer a ship onto shoals the captain would never see. A guiding of a hand I can sense, but only lightly. Like the feathery touch of the lightest gaze upon the back of my neck.

I will take my repast tonight. I will sleep, as much as I can. And tomorrow I'll get up and make my way to The Black Penny, and see what I can find.

I'm sure Fenrir already waits for word.

So that's what I had. I wondered if the man before me knew those would be the last words he would ever write. I wonder, as he put pen to paper, or kugelschreiber to the book, if he had been aware that he had finished writing everything he would write in that sentence.

Would he have written more? Less? Should I, even now, write more in the book myself?

I shivered, thinking of his words. Of the undercurrent of darkness. Of the unseen, guiding hand. It was too near what I felt now, with the undercurrent of decaying scent of the streets. The musty, moldy smell of carcass too long in the grave.

There was no record of the Chronicler's death in the book. There never was, with us. I had asked Berley once, about what had happened to those who had gone before me, and he had told me all people die. Even ones granted longer lives by the wolf. Him, me, the rest of the scribes, all of us couldn't live forever.

More true now than ever, I suppose, if Ragnarok was more near, than far.

There was a time I had planned on asking Fenrir himself about the fates of those who went before me. It was early on in my service, and I had been huddled there in the cavern. I had formed my question and had my mouth half-open, and something in his yellow eyes told me the wolf was waiting. Waiting for that question.

Maybe Fenrir had seen it in the way I sat. In the lean of my body. In the titled angle of my head. Maybe the wolf had seen it hundreds of times before, in all the other men and women who had journeyed the Earth for him.

And, trusting my gut, I closed my mouth and sat back. For some reason, not wanting to give the wolf what he waited for. It occurred to me, in that moment, that I might not want to know what had happened to those who had written in the book before me. That, if I knew how they had ended their service, I might somehow glimpse what might come of mine. And my future—so recently almost ended—I wanted to leave wide open. I didn't really want to know. I didn't want curiosity to kill this particular cat.

The wolf chuckled his chuffing laugh then. His eyes caught mine between the tiny chuffs. And I saw there, he knew everything I was thinking. Knew it, and let me have it.

So I didn't know. And didn't want to know. The Chronicler before me could have died for a million different reasons, heading to The Black Penny. Our long lives wouldn't save us from a drunk driver, from an olive pit stuck in our throat from a too-dry martini, from walking up on a god or some mugging in a side street. Anything was possible, and I liked to keep it that way.

Those were my thoughts, I guessed, walking in New Orleans. Maybe I should have been more focused, but in my defense, I was observing. I was in the state I normally was in, when sent to a city. I took everything in, I took it in with my own particular thoughts, coloring those thoughts with my own bias, and knew that I would write these thoughts in the book later. Write them down and let the wolf hear them.

Vain, maybe, to want my words to still matter. Vain for a man who might never again write a story another human would read. Whose words may never again leave a reader smiling, or crying, or hugging a loved one.

Vain, but one can still hope, I guess.

CHAPTER TEN

I walked through the early morning crowd, sparse as ghosts on the sidewalks. There was no Mardi Gras happening, not now in the late fall, but there was still a feel to the people of a late-night crowd. Of people whose lives were spent in the darkness of the evening, of sleeping in past the sunrise, of stiff, thick brunch coffees mixed with deep-fried beignets sprinkled liberally with confectioner's sugar. There was a slow move to most of the people, the people not working, a stumbling that reminded me of zombies in some of the older movies.

I got to N. Rampart Street. The Black Penny was just ahead, a brick building framed with iron accents, the face holding large windows and a set of rustic doors. The sign was small and understated, a round black circle with the Black above the Penny, and it all together seemed to contrast the vibrancy of New Orleans, and yet I found it oddly comforting.

Across the street from The Black Penny was a large, open grassy area. A park, with the faded green grass of late fall. Of a lawn that had been pumped full of enough fertilizer and chemicals to hang on as the oak trees began their late-season slumber, as the leaves on the branches gave up their colored ghosts and drifted down to the earth.

Very few people were in the park this late in the morning. A couple of birds fluttered around the park. Black birds pecking at the grass, late in the day to be looking for worms. There were some benches in front of the park, benches down the street and along the sidewalk, though just a black-haired young man sat on one now. Sat with a white cup in one hand, staring straight ahead in that focused way that told me his mind was elsewhere.

It was early enough I wasn't sure the bar would be open. Mid-morning, heading towards afternoon. I was hoping there wasn't a time when people officially started to drink here, since there didn't seem to be an official stop time. I shouldn't have worried, it was New Orleans after all. So, happily enough, I found the door unlocked when I tried it.

Inside the bar seemed much like the outside. There was an industrial feel to the place. One of the walls seemed like it was built of an old stone, surfaced with some plaster that had fallen off over the centuries. Other walls were made of a newer red brick, and I use the word new only in the way that the brick wasn't two hundred years old. Archways divided an interior wall, also made of red brick, although some of the brick had been painted a lighter, pale color.

Cream-covered booths that could seat ten or fifteen people surrounded small tables that might not be able to hold fifteen drinks. Vintage photographs dotted the walls, along with the occasional black-and-white piece of art and in one place a round copper tray or plate. There was a splash of color here and there, red unlit candles on the tabletops, some in old sconces on the wall. The counter of the bar was a dark wood, with dark-covered wooden stools before it, and zig-zagged through the bar in a Z shape. There were plenty of taps, and even a larger selection of craft beers behind the bar.

And there were a few people. A bartender behind the bar, a younger man. A man with the light tan skin of someone who spent fall in the south, with dark hair and sharp eyes. He wore a clean white shirt and a pair of black pants. A small cord hung around his neck, a golden cross lay tucked there underneath the V of his shirt, something with what looked to be Latin inscribed above and below the figure lying, arms spread and feet hanging, across the bars.

There were a few couples in as well, an older couple at the far side of the zig-zagged bar, sitting by themselves and sipping from two glasses with umbrellas poking out of their tops. Each of them had long gray hair, and older clothes. Perhaps something from the sixties, that kind of vibe, loose bleached shirts and vests that spoke of Woodstock.

There was another man, older, if not of the age of the gray-haired Woodstock couple. A musician in the corner of the bar, with the sightless gaze of the blind, sitting on a small stool and fingering a guitar. It was a light brown, faded, acoustic guitar, and the blind man held it loosely in his lap, cradled a bit against his body, one of his hands gently strumming a string or two, the other turning a key at the top of the bridge.

I felt a little sympathy for the musician. It hadn't been so long ago that I had been losing sight in my own eye. I could imagine what two might have cost me, even without the tumor behind my sight loss. Not being able to read, or write just what I wrote now, I wasn't sure I could live that life. Even knowing what living mine now was.

I sat and watched and listened. The notes were oddly melodic. And haunting. Even briefly strummed. Even as he turned it. Each single note fell quietly into the bar, fitting perfectly between the murmured words of the old man and woman. Each note almost hummed after the setting down of a drink, as if in counterpoint to the sharp clink of glass on wood. Quiet notes that seemed to both echo the atmosphere of the bar, and yet oddly contrast it.

"Get you something?" the bartender asked. The young man moved around the bar efficiently, wiping down the counter, checking stock, making sure all the bottles were ready, that the liquors ready to pour were clean and they all had their spouts tucked into their tops. That all the beers, bottle after bottle of different craft beers, all faced outward, out into the bar, like soldiers at attention.

"Maybe," I said. "Been here long?"

He flashed me a look. As if measuring me. The kind of glance someone might give to someone out of town, or perhaps one of those looks a snitch might give when deciding what information to parcel out to their cop.

He came down squarely in the middle of whatever he had been thinking. In a way that said he was still reserving judgement. "Sometimes it feels like forever, my man."

"But not decades?" I asked. Already knowing the answer. He looked perhaps thirty. At most.

The man rose his eyebrows.

Yeah, I hadn't thought this out well. Even if this guy had been tending the bar back then, it wasn't like he was going to remember the Chronicler before me. Even if it hadn't been over decades, it wasn't like I could even give the bartender a description.

A feeling like a wild goose chase came over me. It wasn't something I could shake, even if Fenrir had sent me to New Orleans. Part of me wondered why I thought coming to The Black Penny had been a good idea.

"I'll take a beer," I said.

"Glass?"

"Nah," I said. I never got the pouring a beer into a glass thing. Straight from the source is kind of what I preferred.

"Got a flavor?"

"Surprise me."

The bartender didn't quite grunt. It was more of a humph, just kept to himself. But he swung around quickly, pulled a bottle out. Popped the top with a practiced motion and, in the same muscle-memory type of movement, set the beer in front of me while sliding a coaster underneath it.

The beer foamed the slightest bit out of the top. There was a picture of a skeleton on the front, a skull with kind of an iron hat on its top. One of the triangle-pointed caps you see on the heads of some of the old templars, or Crusaders.

Dead Guy Ale.

I grinned. The bartender had a sense of humor. I tipped it to him and took a sip. It was hoppy and cool and refreshing, and if for some reason I thought I could smell the undercurrent scent of New Orleans when I was drinking the beer, that scent of a muddy grave, I ignored it.

The bartender watched me. The corner of his lip may have turned up a bit when I had tipped the bottle towards him. His eyes always seemed alert, as if they were ready to flash, as if he were ready to rush to wipe down a spill or grab a drink at a moment's notice.

"X," he said, after a moment. As if whatever he had decided a little more in my favor.

"X?" I said. Finally getting that he was giving me his name. "Like ex-husband?"

"More like axe," he said. "Without the 'A'."

I grinned and tipped my beer back again. It was the potato-potahto thing. It was everywhere. The beer was fresh, it was crisp in my mouth, with a mellow hoppy taste that stayed on the back of my tongue.

Then I set the bottle down. It thunked a bit on the wood, the sound muffled a bit by the coaster. A high, ringing note followed the sound, something that hung in the air long after the blind musician had plucked it.

"If you're looking for something, or someone," X said, nodding to the guitar player, "Old Hode's been around here forever."

I followed his glance. The blind musician sat in his corner, tuning and strumming his guitar. Occasionally I caught a faint humming, a crooning, as if the man quietly sang to his instrument. He wore light blue jeans and, much like me, a white T-shirt, if his T-shirt sagged a bit around his frame, and was more the pale, yellowed stain that colored a shirt after its hundredth or two-hundredth wash.

Maybe he was older than Mister and Misses Woodstock. He didn't appear to be, not at first glance. Some age spots dotted his forehead, and cheeks, and though his skin appeared dark and weathered it was mostly unlined.

Maybe he just aged well. His hair was mostly gray, gray with slight streaks of black threading through it. The hair hung loose around his face and lay back high from his forehead as if a hand had recently been run through it.

His eyes were the youngest part of him. They were blue and unfocused. They were open as if taking everything in, so open they were striking. It was a gaze that stopped me, even though I knew the musician couldn't see me, it was like I could feel the eyes rest on me.

That was silly, though. Surely the man wasn't looking at me.

"He drink anything?" I asked X. Or Ex, or Xe.

"Just out of his mug," the man said. "I can fill it, if you'd like."

I nodded, laying some cash on the counter. I hadn't seen the mug, or maybe I had and thought it was a tip jar. It lay on a small table next to the blind man, a large earthen thing of brown clay. Large enough a man might have to grab it with two hands.

"That enough?" I asked, measuring the mug, looking at the cash.

X just took the money. I wandered over to the blind musician. I knew he couldn't see me, his gaze straight ahead, as if he looked out and over the bar, but it was odd that every strumming of every note seemed to follow my steps towards him.

The notes slowed down as I did. They slowed down as I neared him, and took slower steps. They slowed down until I was standing before the blind man, until his fingers lay on the string, neither one of us moving.

"Hey there, old man," I said. To say something. Hoping my words sounded more respectful than they might have.

He smiled. "Hode."

"Hode," I said. "Finn."

The man grunted. He had a rough voice, long used. His face shifted, turned, as if he looked past me. I looked back to see someone else entering the bar. A younger man, thick in the shoulders, but quiet on his feet. The man looked around and headed to the bar.

Good hearing by Hode. I guess you get to practice that kind of stuff.

"A bit of the Irish in you?" Hode asked, his raw voice taking on a light brogue accent. "You a young Finn MacCool? A warrior, leading his merry band of heroes?"

I smiled. I got the reference. "Not really a warrior, no."

"That's a shame," Hode said. "The world what it is today, it could use a warrior or two."

There was a feel to Hode's words, something in the undercurrent of them, something I felt in the plucking of his guitar as he had tuned the strings. I looked at him then, and though Hode couldn't see me do it, his face paused under the scrutiny. His voice was gruff. It had the deep bass that a singer might have, that sound that comes from deep in the chest, but it was scratchy, too. Raw. It broke between words. It wasn't a singing voice at all, and maybe that's why the man crooned, softly.

His smile widened a hair. "Never was the singer of the family."

Maybe Hode could read thoughts as well.

X came by then, with a large glass pitcher of something dark. The liquid poured almost like honey until the mug, and X filled it, and the whole time Hode waited as if this was something that happened enough times between the two that both understood their place in the moment. X finished his pour with a slight twist of the lip of the pitcher, and then patted Hode's shoulder one time before he left. Back to the bar, the old couple, and the young man, who was tapping his foot a little impatiently.

The moment might have gone on too long. I get that way sometimes. The observation of a thing, instead of the doing of it.

"What can ol' Hode do for you?" he asked. "Young Finn MacCool?"

I paused, my mind searching a bit. It took a bit, to remember the Irish Skald. A leader of a band of sorts, a bright, light-hued poet and fighter. A leader of a band back in the day, someone perhaps like the Robin Hood of later years.

I might have a light complexion, but my hair was more of a dark, sandy color. I definitely wasn't fair-haired. It was questionable how bright I was, that was for sure. And while I might be a writer, of sorts, I definitely wasn't a fighter.

The bottle of Dead Guy Ale was still cool in my hand. I took a quick sip while thinking about it. Asking around about a guy that had come here years ago seemed foolish, but I would get nowhere by not asking the question. "You know what, I guess I do, and I guess I don't."

"Why don't you start with the guessing that you do," Hode said.

"And if'n I can help you, maybe we can move to all the guessing that you don't."

"You've been here a while?" I asked. "The Black Penny."

"As long as I can remember. Played here a lot through the years."

"You remember Katrina?" I asked.

Hode's gaze went long. I don't know how to describe how I knew that, the focus on them didn't shift, he didn't open or close his eyes at all, but I had the sense he was looking back into a memory. One hand lightly ran along his strings. Left a little chord behind. Not haunting or melodic, but discordant. His words, raw and rough, were simply spoke. "I remember the storm."

"Was it as bad as they said?"

His head nodded a bit. As if he were agreeing alongside thoughts running in his own head. I imagined a blind man back then, with a hurricane hovering over New Orleans, with a hundred and fifty mile-an-hour winds and the water rising up over the graves of New Orleans, rising up to claim more.

Probably as scary a thing a person could go through. Blind or not blind.

"It was bad," Hode said, finally. And then, as if that wasn't enough. "It was a real world-ender."

I got that feeling that I was on to something. That feeling in our hindbrains that says this may not make sense, but go with it.

"Tell me about it?"

Hode let out a snort. "Told that story enough, young Finn MacCool. You want stories of the seas rising and swallowing a town, of the vengeance of the gods, of the battling winds and waters and the swirling knowledge of what may or may not be here on the morrow, you come back sometime when I've had a little more to drink."

He took a sip then of his own mug. Reaching out as if he knew exactly where it was, bringing the large brown clay mug to his lips, drawing from it deep. Wiping his mouth with the back of his arm when he finished. "Besides, that in't what you're here to ask about."

"It isn't?"

He pointed to his ear. "I can hear it, you know," Hode said. "The truth of a thing."

I smiled. He had me there anyway. "I'm looking for a man," I said. "A guy who was here before Katrina. I don't think you'd remember him, if you were here." If the blind musician was even playing The Black Penny then.

Hode though, shook his head. Not with the memory of the man I was looking for, or the lack of a memory, but with Hode saying, "That ain't it either."

I cocked my head. Hode did the same, mirroring the motion. As if he could see me, even though I knew he couldn't and didn't.

That was some good hearing.

"I'm here to find a girl," I said. "A daughter of a—"

Hode's head cocked further.

"—friend," I finished.

He measured my words, his blank eyes somehow both looking at me and through me. He chewed on his bottom lip while he measured, and thought, until Hode finally said. "Guess it's good enough."

"Good enough?"

"Close enough," he said. "To the truth, for ol' Hode."

I hadn't mentioned more than that, but Hode leaned back. He plucked a string, that string vibrated, and a low sound vibrated with it. The sound went through the room and died there, died around the bar, where the young man drank from a tall bottle and stared at me, or the musician, or the both of us.

When Hode spoke, it was with a bit of the storyteller voice all musicians have. The carefully pronounced words to the crowd they faced, be it large or small. In a varied rhythm, in a tone both loud and intimate. "A lot of people come here looking, young Finn MacCool. You probably think you understand what you're looking at, where you're at in this city, but you don't. You can't, unless you live in this place. Live here, live with all this." Hode waved a hand around the bar, a small, slow gesture. "For a long, long time."

The spell had come over the place quickly. Everyone else seemed to be glancing this way. The angry young man with his bottle of beer. The other couples in the booths. Mr. and Mrs. Woodstock.

Not wanting to break it, I didn't say anything. If not understanding what Hode was saying, or what he was hinting at, understanding my place in his story. Understanding my role in the here and now. The listener.

Hode plucked at his strings, letting the notes fall between the pauses in his speech. "You got to know, this city is a place of things," he said. "It's got a magic all its own. It's seen a lot of death, and a lot of life. That kind of dichotomy, that yin and yang of a thing, life against death, death against life, it has a power. A power that pulls at the world around it. Pulls at the magic of the world. A power that pulls at other powers."

He snorted, with a hard twang of a note. "Even pulls at gods."

Then he paused. There was another pluck of a string, as his blank face looked around The Black Penny. As if he could see everyone watching, before Hode turned back to me. Lowering his voice to almost a whisper, a raw whisper that still carried through the bar. "So you come looking, just like others have. And I'll warn you, just like I've warned those before, what you seek ain't gonna be what you find. There's more here to the eye. There's more happening than what might fill a book, and what you're gonna stumble into, well, that kind of thing isn't for a musician to say, or face.

"It's something for a warrior, that's what Hode always says to those that come, not a story to tell, not a song to play, not a canvas to paint or some words to write in some book somewhere."

His raw, rough voice stopped then. His last words stopped me. There was a resonance in them, something that gave me the feeling Hode knew more about me than I knew about myself and this world I found myself in. That there was magic here in New Orleans, magic and powers and perhaps even gods. That even blind, Hode saw me sitting in front of a desk, scrawling away in my book. "You know I write?"

Hode smiled. It was as rough-looking as his voice sounded. It was an old smile of crooked teeth, and older things. His free hand tapped a finger against his temple, right by his ear. "Ol' Hode knows an artist when he hears 'em."

I tried to play that connection up. One artist talking to another. Putting an urgency in my words, a knowledge of the Ragnarok I feared was coming. "If you know I write, then you know the story always ends, right?"

Hode shook his head. Plucked a low, vibrating string. Something that ran a bit through the air. "You want to keep writing, young Finn MacCool. Keep writing and hope there's never an end to your story. That the story itself is the life you live, right?"

Another note. This one higher in pitch, and wavered long in the air. Wavered back and forth, back and forth, like the trembling of the guitar string itself.

Finally, long after I had taken a last sip of beer from an empty Dead Guy Ale bottle, long after that sound had died away and been replaced by scattered murmurs at the bar, of the low talk between Mr. and Mrs. Woodstock, or X asking the young man if he wanted a refill, Hode spoke again.

"I'll give you some final words of my own though," he said, leaning a little forward over his guitar. "Artist to artist. You ain't going to find what you need here. Not at The Black Penny. You ain't going to find what you need in New Orleans, no sir. What you're looking for, you have a better chance of finding at the Blacksmith."

He tapped his guitar. As if he wanted to strum his guitar but had run out of notes, and instead patted the body of his instrument. Leaving a hollow echo between the two of us, something that died quickly, unfinished.

Hode nodded at the sound. "I'll tell you another thing, young Finn. Mayhap because you asked about Katrina. There's another storm coming, and it's not one you want to write about. It's not a storm words'll survive, not written or sung, not painted or spoke. It's only something that is, it's something that can only be weathered, and it can only be weathered by those with a bit of fight."

That was the last thing Hode would say, then.

Even if I did buy him another round.

Even if I hung out and watched him tune his guitar, endlessly. Playing an occasional note that would carry through The Black Penny at just the right time, at just the right inflection, no matter what was going on. No matter if I hung there and thought about what he had told me, his last words, about the pen to paper and the weathering. About the final battle, about the fight.

I never saw him play a song. Not while I was there. Not after nursing a second beer and wondering what Hode might know that he wasn't telling me. Not after the angry young man left the spot next to me, not after some back and forth with X about what the Blacksmith was, and then getting that was Lafitte's Blacksmith Shop Bar. I got a little more there from X, the history of the bar, where I could find it.

I never saw Hode play a song, just the notes, and it seemed as if he knew that I was watching. Occasionally his face, sightless, would gaze my way. His hands would pause, as if he was ready to play something with real meaning, ready to fill the bar with chord after chord of a real song. Of real music.

It was then I thought the hardest. About a young Finn MacCool. About a writer, putting pen to paper.

And it was then his hands paused. Hode paused. The blind musician would nod a bit to himself and go back to his finger plucking. Never glancing my way. And he did that, all the way until I left the bar.

CHAPTER ELEVEN

It had seemed like I was in The Black Penny forever. That the talk between me and Hode had taken years. That I had mused upon his last words for hours, nursing that final beer. Wondering about the storm he referenced. Knowing he meant Ragnarok. And yet hoping he was just some crackpot musician who had drank too much, for too long, in a city known for both.

So it had felt like forever. The moment, the music, the talk between us and the musings. Stepping outside, I wasn't sure it had even been an hour.

It was still nice out, the streets were still filled with the sounds of the occasional car and the mixed scents of simmering gumbo, steeping hot coffee, and sweet sugary beignets. There were the sounds of people waking. More people walked by, along the crooked faces of sidewalk. There were more shouts from shopkeepers, from all the little stores selling the beads and voodoo dolls and bags of New Orleans Creole spices.

The mid-morning was still bright. The sky perhaps a paler blue above, with a puff of a white cloud trailing across it, the rich blue of the morning fading as the day neared afternoon. There was a whisper of a wind on the street. A whisper that brought a chill, even if it was already cold out. A whisper that brought the feel of a storm. Something hiding on the edge of the horizon, the tip of something much greater coming, a storm unlike anything the world had ever felt.

I took a breath and felt it. Nervous. Felt it like I had coming into New Orleans, just more of it now. Felt like the pale sky, the sun overhead, the little whisper of a wind down the street. The wind chillier now, the currents of air had an icier edge to them, colder now than when I had rode in. A whisper of wind speaking of faster winds behind it, of greater turbulences, of something circling round out there over the water, faster and faster, winds that whispered of *more*.

I shuddered. Turned to head down the street to Lafitte's Blacksmith Shop Bar. X wasn't sure it was open yet, but he thought it might be, and he had given me directions. It was south of here, less than half a mile, on Bourbon Street.

Ten minutes maybe, walking. And though my feet felt a little sluggish, as if I had to force my legs a bit, I turned south and headed that way. The faster I got there, the faster I could figure this out.

That was when the fist hit the side of my face.

I hadn't seen him. I should have. I was pretty observant most of the time. Hell, I was observant all of the time.

Or so I thought.

I had been standing there. Then I found myself sitting. I hadn't felt the blow so much as the strength behind it. A powerful blow, a fist cracking against my cheek and all of a sudden there I was, my ass on the sidewalk. The side of my face thumping with blood. Shaking my head a bit. Blinking and holding my jaw with one hand.

The angry young man squatted on the backs of his legs before me. He was young, younger than me, I thought. His hair flat and black and brushed around his head almost in a Caesar cut, with flat bangs perfect on the front of his face. His eyes were dark and angry and focused. They looked like they would be focused all the time, but right now they were focused on me.

"Stay away," the man said. His voice angry. Firm.

"What?" I asked, blinking. A small part of me worried, and another small part, a small, growing part, angry. Angry and growing angrier.

"Stay away," the man repeated. "Stay away from Hode."

"Who the hell are you?" I said.

His face never moved from his angry expression. His lips didn't twitch. His eyes didn't narrow. His frown, his expression, seemed carved into his face. "It doesn't matter who I am. It matters what I'm telling you."

"And you're telling me to stay away?"

He nodded. "Hode isn't right in the head, anymore," the man said. "Best if you just forget what he told you."

I pulled back a bit from the moment, because as a writer, I know how things work. I could follow the thread of a story. I knew this guy warning me was warning me off from what Hode had told me, and that made Hode's words a little more important to me than they had been just a moment ago.

I started putting two and two together from that. I was quick enough when I needed to be, even if my observational skills weren't what I thought they were.

"You tell everyone that who speaks with him?"

His eyes did narrow then. So his face wasn't stuck that way. That was confirmation enough, to me.

I took a deeper look at him. Like I said, I was a writer. I could infer things. I could take the threads of a story and follow them to a conclusion.

The angry man was young. He *appeared* young. The strands of his flat black hair lay perfectly straight along his forehead, like soldiers.

His anger was something he carried with him. Something he had carried for a long time. Longer than a year or two. Longer than ten or twenty.

It was then another emotion wedged its way past the worry and the anger inside of me. Something that shuddered a bit. Fear. I was looking for what had happened to the Chronicler before me. The one who had come to New Orleans and then disappeared.

Chances were, I had found it.

Chances were, I had found my first god. The first one outside of Fenrir. The first one I realized I had met.

And he was warning me away.

Which meant—in my mind—he didn't know who I was. Not really. I was something who had taken an interest in a blind musician, who Hode had taken an interest in return, and the two of us had a talk.

That kind of talk might happen ten or twenty times in a year. I could hope. Other artists surely had stumbled upon the blind man. Other writers, even. People who might be looking for things, as well. People who might have a similar conversation.

The worry was fading a bit. That always did, once I understood a thing. Once I could see a way around it. The fear remained, which, if I was honest, would always remain too, once I understood a thing, a fear of something I couldn't work around.

But the anger, the anger grew a bit more. That anger I had held deep within myself. The anger of a young man raging in a hospital bed, raging against his death, against the unfairness of it all.

Maybe it was in those moments, we get to truly know ourselves.

The moments right before death. The moments of the darkest pain. And the moments when we faced something we might not be able to overcome.

I looked at the young man in the Caesar cut. "What's it to you?"

The man—the god—scoffed. I was pretty sure that was the term. He picked me up easily with both hands, standing as if he was carrying a loaf of bread, and swung me around to put me—with a heavy thump of flesh to stone—against the outside wall of The Black Penny.

Then he pressed his face against mine. So that the tip of his nose, warm and hard and pointed, pushed into mine. So that his forehead with its straight-lined strands of soldiers mashed against mine. So that his breath, a bite stale and smelling a little like the sweetness of a dark honey, washed over my face.

"The question is, what's it to you?" the god said. "Your life?"

I felt like the god was still stuck in his human mode. As if he believed that I thought he was a human. And he was acting, loosely, in those terms.

Because he didn't know who I was.

I guessed, like in the stories, sometimes the gods weren't as appreciative of human intelligence as the rest of us.

I certainly appreciated where I was at. That this god could kill me. And I was even more aware of my book, the Chronicles, hanging in the satchel by my side. The satchel was closed, but it wouldn't take much for the flap covering it to open, and if this god saw that...

I pushed the tiny bit of anger down. I let the fear show. Enough to widen my eyes a bit and raise my hands, as if saying no harm, no foul. "Hey man," I said. "It's fine, it's fine. I've just had a couple, is all."

The god's face remained carved. Like from rock. A stone-like anger forever in place. I couldn't tell what he was thinking. I just had the feel of his thoughts, something my intuition spoke to, but I also wasn't a hundred percent sure of.

Gods thought themselves better than humans. I got that. In the stories though did they just kill those who got in their way? That bothered them? Were humans inconsequential as gnats?

My memory ran back through all the stories of all the Norse tales I had read. Both the tales I had read as a kid, and the ones I had learned after taking service to the wolf. I didn't recall murderous killing sprees by the gods, but then, maybe they had made sure those tales hadn't survived.

The stone face remained unmoving. Finally, the angry young man's hands opened. He dropped me. And stood there, watching me.

I didn't look at him. Being appreciative of the delicateness of the moment. Afraid too much would show on my face.

I was being given a chance, and so I took it.

We writers find other ways to get our point across, sometimes. If it's not one sentence, it's another. If it's not one plot, it's something right next to it. We meander when maybe we should cut to the point, and we cut to the point when meandering was expected.

Part of me smiled at that. I was speaking to myself like I was Stephen King. Like I was a best-selling author. Here I was, some guy who had one short story published in his entire life. Who only chronicled things now, instead of any real writing.

Still, I brushed myself off, making sure the satchel holding the book was tight to my side, wincing a bit at the pain in my jaw. And I chose to go another way. To not head south on N. Rampart Street. To not walk my way down to Bourbon Street to the Blacksmith Shop Bar.

I headed north instead. Feeling the wind push slightly against my back. As if hurrying me along.

I kept heading north, keeping all thoughts from my head, and—right after turning into a side street—glanced back.

The young man wasn't still standing there. He had made his way across the street. Directly across from The Black Penny there was a park, with a few benches. I thought I remembered seeing him at one, when I had walked in. With a cup of coffee in one hand.

A lookout.

The god walked past those benches now. He continued south. Towards the French Quarter.

I know, I'd be stupid to follow a god back to wherever it was he was going. A god that likely would and could kill me the next time he saw me. A god too full of himself and his warning to even worry about someone like me.

But, I'd also be stupid not to follow him.

I had read plenty of detective stories. Plenty of mysteries. And here was one before me, now.

A storm was coming, I could feel it. Ragnarok?

Maybe, certainly the wolf thought so.

I was here looking for Fenrir's daughter. Somehow that had led me to following the Chronicler's steps before me. And I had found his ending, I thought, in the god I had met.

Fenrir had told me to find his daughter. Certainly he thought the moment was right, whatever that moment was, for me to find her. Whoever she was.

But that moment had led to this. And this had led me to here. And here, I had found gods. Angry gods. And a storm coming.

I had to see what all that was about. This guy had been a lookout. A lookout meant there were more gods, a group of them. A lookout meant there was a plan for something going on, and I felt like the most important thing I could do, here and now, was see what that was.

After all, a Chronicler had died for it.

I'd be stupid to follow the god. But I'd also be stupid not to follow him. There were threads upon threads, and plots upon plots, which meant there were sides, and there were other sides.

I needed to know more, to separate one from another.

I flipped a mental coin. You probably know where it landed. I waited a moment longer, the way McGee might, the way Spenser might, and then followed the god down the street.

CHAPTER TWELVE

The sky was just as pale as it had been moments ago. The sun still that yellow orb making its way across the blue. Passing a white puffy cloud, perhaps trying to race the orb to the horizon.

The wind was different though. The blowing of it still felt like a storm. It still cut with a chilly edge. It just pushed against me now, instead of ushering me away.

I started putting things together as I followed him. I had read a lot of the Norse stories. When I was young I had loved all the old mythologies. I had read some of them again after taking service with the wolf, for obvious reasons. I thought I could figure out who he was.

He was a young man, and angry. He held an anger that spoke of vengeance. A rage that had formed his very identity. He was quiet too, he spoke little, which was another clue.

Vidar, I thought. A son of Odin, and born almost with vengeance. Born with the need to avenge his father's death. Death at the hands of Fenrir.

My steps slowed a bit under that realization.

And that one was followed by another.

If I was following Vidar, then it was likely Ol' Hode was Hodr. The blind god. The one that had killed Baldur with a sprig of mistletoe, fashioned by Loki.

My steps remained slow. If there was one thing Shakespeare had taught everyone, it was never get in the middle of a family feud.

These were heavyweights. I wasn't dealing with dwarves fashioning trinkets, or chopped-off heads spouting wisdoms. I wasn't dealing with a fair maiden, with the golden hair of Sif, or with sneaking into a beautiful woman's bedchamber.

Vidar, Hodr, Loki, Baldur, Odin. Gods at the very center of Ragnarok. Gods who—if they hadn't began it—threaded their way through it. From Odin, binding Fenrir with Gleipnir, thinking to prevent the very thing he would cause. From the vengeance of Fenrir, after that one act, the vengeance on the All-Father. From those promises to others, from the sons of Odin promising their own vengeance, from gods challenging giants, from giants facing gods, from the battle lines being drawn and the sides being chosen, all from that day, all starting with Odin and his sons.

I looked up, wondering if even then a lightning bolt might strike down from the white puffy clouds of the sky. If the white clouds would turn tumorous and black and gray and swell out over the horizon. If Thor would appear in the middle of that storm I felt, and swing his hammer, leveling all.

Vidar kept walking ahead of me. I had wondered when I might meet a god. Now I tread carefully. Now I thought that wondering more a foolish wish of a young man who really didn't understand what Ragnarok would be.

I had wondered why Fenrir sent me out into the world. He wanted real acts. Real captures of what was happening around the world. I thought it had been so he might know when to finally release Ragnarok.

But now, perhaps, it might be this. It might be for a Chronicler to stumble onto something like this. Into stumbling into a pocket of gods who were plotting to kill the wolf.

Hodr, Odin, Vidar, Vali, Thor, any of them.

Perhaps that was the reason behind the recent runs of Chronicler deaths. Maybe the longer-lived Chroniclers had just been lucky. Or less observant than someone like me.

Vidar was farther down the block now. I was losing him. I forced myself to walk faster, and hide myself the best I could along the open shops we walked past. The few people who walked around me, stopping to look into one of the shops with beads. Stopping to gaze across at the park. Stopping to look into a café.

I could only hide for so long in this sparse crowd. Just trying to blend in wasn't going to be good enough. Not if gods were involved. Not even if Vidar was human. All he had to do was glance back.

I pulled Skidblandir out of my pocket. Reached inside the soft folds of silk and pulled out a ballcap. Just red and white something with a Bitches Be Serious slogan across the front. I rolled my eyes, tucked that hat back into Skidblandir, and pulled it out again. Though this time I thought a little harder, and something else came out. A black hat with a golden fleur-de-lis on it.

It looked like just a ballcap, but it was a Hulinhjàlmr. A magic hat that wouldn't make me invisible so much as make me part of the crowd. For whatever reason the Hulinhjàlmr I had been given had a sense of humor to it. I wasn't sure if it was the magic in the hat or whoever had created it, long ago. I just always knew that I had to usually think pretty hard about what I needed before getting something that would work.

There was a reason I usually packed light. That I didn't have to pack much for whatever city I was going to, whatever country, whatever weather. I could throw on a pair of jeans and a T-shirt and Hulinhjàlmr and fit in anywhere.

I put on the New Orleans Saints hat. There was no feel to it, no magic sense I felt from the ballcap as I slipped it on. I felt the hat fit itself to my head, like any good fitted cap. I tugged the bill down once or twice, and I knew as I did so I looked just like a million other Saints fans here in the city.

Still, I saw Vidar pause as I tugged the bill down. The angry god stood there, and even a block away I could feel his chest swell with a breath. I almost saw his back stretch with it. His head tilted just a bit to the left, as if the god had felt the magic. As small as it was.

I remained very still.

He shook his head and continued.

I let out my own breath, and followed.

Stupid is as stupid does.

He headed down the street. Closer along the way I would have taken following X's directions. Towards Bourbon Street, towards Lafitte's Blacksmith Shop Bar (Try saying that five times fast).

The crowd thickened a bit on the sidewalk. Either more people were up and about, or this area of the French Quarter was a little more busy than back at The Black Penny. I kept following Vidar, more carefully than I might have had he been just a regular person. I noticed, as the god walked, other humans step to his right and left long before they crossed his path. There was a subtle current about the god, something that pushed others aside as he strode.

It'd be nice to have something like that at a bank line. If they had those anymore. I wasn't sure people went to banks anymore.

Maybe the movies. That thought led me to Athens, and the masks, and the groups of people masked and unmasked pointing to each other among the empty streets.

So—I guessed it'd be nice if they even had movies anymore.

Maybe it was just a nice power to have for now. For a god

walking down the street. Because I kept getting jostled. Maybe it was the Hulinhjàlmr. The hat had a sense of humor. Maybe it made me so almost-invisible the people closing the gap behind the crowd didn't really see me.

That seemed pretty likely.

So I followed Vidar as he waded through the crowd. I followed the god as people subconsciously stepped to his right and left. I followed him as those same people closed in and bumped against me with a pahdon mah sir, or watch where yah going, or a hey there, pahdner, for the most point always said in that New Orleans twang, the little drawl with the softness on the harder consonants and the drawing out of almost any vowel to sound like an *ah*.

I followed Vidar through all that. Down Bourbon Street and past Lafitte's Blacksmith Shop Bar. To a little café there, a thing with tables on the sidewalk and a couple of people sitting there. One of those iconic two-story New Orleans buildings with a porch on the second floor and black iron rails around the porch.

I slowed, down the block. I watched Vidar walk up and take a seat at a table, a seat where there was a young woman sitting, a tiny white cup of expresso on a white china plate before her. A second plate next to the expresso, with a few half-eaten beignets. I watched him take a seat without saying a thing, I imagined his carved face staring at her much like he had looked at mine. I imagined him staring at her, but I wasn't really seeing him, because I knew the woman, and all my attention was on her.

CHAPTER THIRTEEN

There's real power in threes, Emma-mae had told me.

Yet this was only the second time I had seen her.

For some reason, the thought calmed me. Because otherwise my heart was racing. My chest pounded with the beats inside of it. My lungs worked, quickly, as if suddenly wanting or needing more air.

Emma-mae looked a little the same as in the diner yesterday. Her long legs stretched out across the sidewalk, one crossed over the other at the ankle. She still had on tight jeans, though her wool coat had been abandoned for a dark blue denim jacket with a little white fur fluffing out around the back of her neck. Her dark red hair still back in the ponytail, simply there, and her eyes glanced over at Vidar, and then past him down the street.

It was a casual glance, casual and yet not. It was the practiced gaze of someone who was alert. Of someone who was always on alert. It was a gaze from emerald eyes flashing with a joke she wasn't telling anyone. A gaze with an inner knowledge she wasn't going to share.

A gaze that had me freeze there on the sidewalk. Even though I hadn't been moving. My body stiffened as the gaze moved through each of the persons around me: the older lady with a walker at the corner; a pair of young men with sleepy, blood-shot eyes, one of those men wearing the same hat I was wearing, thank heavens it wasn't the Bitches Be Serious; and an older couple standing right beside me, the older man wanting to get coffee and a beignet, his wife telling him—apparently for the millionth time—why he couldn't have either.

I froze there, watching the old lady pause on the corner with the walker, as if deciding when to chance her trip across the street. I froze and let the two young men slowly walk by me, as if not yet ready to face the afternoon. I froze and let the old man and woman argue about the possible health benefits of caffeine and the definite not-healthily risks of a beignet.

I froze and let the flashing emerald eyes move down the street, past me, then let them draw their way back to her table. I stood there and watched her glance at Vidar and say something, something I couldn't hear down the block. I saw him barely shake his head, and then she said something else and reached out and grabbed her coffee.

There was a part of me that was confused. Our meeting back in the Adirondacks couldn't have been chance. It had been planned, I had to be sure of that. Her talking with me now, looking back, seemed almost as if she had been measuring me. Testing me out.

Maybe.

She had read my story. That should have clued me in. It wasn't like *Reagen's Journey* had been widely known. In the short time we had been together, we had talked a lot. About everything and nothing. There had been a connection there, I felt, something that had scared me, and something I thought had surprised her too.

It was tough for me to figure out. I observed, but I'm a writer. Sometimes I inferred things that weren't there, and I was inferring a lot here. It's what I do. It's what I try to keep out of my reports to the wolf, but I'm sure some of that gets in there too.

Still, let's say this meeting wasn't chance. That Emma-mae had searched me out. And now I discovered her in New Orleans, in the here and now.

Had she known I was coming here?

Or was this a place she was planning to be at, already?

And—here I was thinking of the Chronicler before me—did she have a role in his death? In why I was here now, instead of him?

I didn't know enough. So I had to get closer. As close as I dared.

Which was going to be pretty freaking close.

I took a very large breath. As I did goosebumps rippled up and down along my skin. Not just my skin, but the cold tingle of them ran down my back, along my shoulders, down both arms. They ran in waves.

I wondered if the Berlin guy had done the same thing, had seen the same thing, before taking this step I was taking now.

I said it before, and will probably say it again. Stupid is as stupid does.

Still, I stepped along bravely. I walked with a firm step. Walking like I had always taken this walk, to this café. I walked past their table, tugging on the bill of my Saints hat with the hand closest to Emma-mae and Vidar, and took a second seat at a table behind her. Trying to place my chair so that the stone-like gaze of the angry god was blocked by her form.

The table was small and round and white, with white chairs, a blend of painted white metal iron legs and back with a painted wood seat and back. The table had that thing in its center all tables at restaurants do, the metal thing with packets of sugar and a salt and pepper shakers, with a menu tucked into the middle of it.

My heart still thudded in my chest. If not as hard as when I had first seen Emma-mae, hard enough that I worried she could hear it. I worked to settle it down, I forced myself to lean back, to take long, even breaths, to slowly reach out and slide the menu from the two metal prongs it hung in.

The wind blew. It carried her scent, the sweet smell of jasmine blooming under a full moon, and I almost caught myself leaning closer. Instead, I flagged the waitress and—not trusting the hat to quite cover how my voice sounded—pointed to a few things on the menu. An expresso and a pair of beignets.

She came over, bringing a tall glass of water, cold enough even in the fall to have condensation running down the sides. The waitress asked if I'd rather have a café au lait instead of an expresso. Still not trusting my voice, or at least not trusting Emma-mae to not know it was me, even with the Hulinhjàlmr—the magic hat did have the oddest sense of humor—I nodded.

The waitress was young, and gave me a small smile. An understanding kind of smile. Maybe she thought I was a late-night reveler still struggling to wake up. In some ways, I felt like that was true.

The waitress left. I took a sip of water. It wasn't the pure water of the Adirondacks, it was more like the tap water found in any other of the hundreds of restaurants I had been in. Something dull and lifeless, something ice cubes could only bring a hint of life to. I sipped that and listened to Emma-mae and Vidar. Trying to lean back and see what I could, without being obvious about it.

Of course, the angry man spoke first. "We waste our time."

Her response came slowly, in the same tone and inflection Emma-mae had back at the diner, her voice light with just a hint of a southern drawl (I thought). A light voice with light words, though I sensed a hard iron core at their center.

"You should be there still," Emma-mae said. Almost ordered. "Watching."

Vidar's face remained unchanged. Angry. Brow-furrowed. "I

have been watching for a long time. Watching with no results. Watching with nothing to watch for."

There was a pause. A small clatter of a small china plate being set on another, from back in the café. "He wants to kill him."

I couldn't see Emma-mae's face, but I heard the roll of her eyes. I almost saw it, in the tiny movement of her head. "Who wants to kill who?" she asked, as if wondering, though I got the sense she knew from her next words. "You all are all the same. You have all lined up some god or giant or creature in your sights, and all you want is to kill it."

Vidar's jaw moved. It grew tighter. And that was saying something. "Vali wants to kill Hodr. You know this. And he waits."

"Vali has been wanting to kill Hodr for thousands of years," Emma-mae said. "He can wait a bit longer."

"It is always waiting with you—"

Emma-mae leaned forward, across the table, not like she had with me back in the diner. Not the gentle lean of someone who found themselves interested. But in the quick, decisive lean of someone who meant trouble.

"Waiting is something I'm good at," she said. "It's why you have me here, now. It's why you wanted me here, now. Because you gods, for all your eternal lives, can't seem to wait for the right moment."

She blew out a breath and leaned back. Closer to me. Close enough that—even at the next table—I leaned back just a little.

"Go watch," she said. "Or go kill. Go tell Vali to get his vengeance on Hodr. Go tell him to kill Hodr for whatever reason he wants to, let him believe it's for Baldur, and tell him the real vengeance will just pass him by."

Vidar waited another long moment. More clatters of china. Waited and followed the waitress as she brought back my order. As if his mind was telling him I was here, that the guy next to his table had followed him, as if that thought circled around the god's brain but just didn't quite land.

The waitress was unaware of the stare. Or maybe Vidar was here enough she was used to it. She set before me a plate of beignets (not two, not three, but four of the things; I could smell their sugary fresh-from-the-oven warmth) and a nice-sized mug that smelled of chicory and steamed milk. She set it all down with a wink and a tiny chinking of china on the table, telling me she had them brew the coffee extra strong for me, and walked away.

Vidar's gaze followed the waitress. Went back to me. As if the plane of thought had kept circling. Then back to Emma-mae.

"You press, woman," he said. "I will go to Vali, but I will not tell him, as of yet."

Then the god got back up and left. He headed back up the street, as if walking to The Black Penny. Breaking off to head northwest, before being lost to my sight.

I took a bite of beignet. It was as sweet as it smelled, full of a buttery light-bread-like sweetness, covered with the powdery sugary sweetness of the confectioner's powder. I savored that for a bit and then sipped on the café au lait. The mug was still warm in my hands, the coffee was bitter and a bit spicy, mellowed a touch by the steamed milk, and the combination was perfect with the sugar.

Emma-mae seemed to like things less mellow. At least here on her own. She took another bite of her beignet, and mixed that with a sip of her dark, bitter expresso, and sat there as if thinking. She sat there, sipping and taking smaller and smaller bites of beignet, with more of her expresso. At one point she tore the corner off of one of the treats and tossed it onto the sidewalk.

A black raven landed there. A large black raven. It cawed, loudly, and pecked at the bread. Another raven landed next to the first and they pecked at each other, then the bread, their beaks stabbing at the sidewalk, and Emma-mae laughed a bit. "Relax," she told the birds. "There's plenty for you both."

She tore the last of her beignet into a few last pieces and tossed them to the birds.

Tossed them to the ravens.

Two black birds.

Which I had seen before. I had seen them, and I had seen them three times. In three different places.

It was then I knew that they had seen me too. Each of the times. They had watched and seen me at the diner in the Adirondacks. They had watched and seen at the park outside The Black Penny. And they watched and saw me, even now.

One of them let me know that. Looking directly at me and cawing, loudly.

Huginn. Or Muninn. The two ravens of Odin. Thought and Memory.

The birds knew I was here.

Which meant Emma-mae knew I was here.

Which, nicely enough, she let me know.

"Well, Finn," she asked, her voice an odd mix of resignation tangled with some slight sense of pleasure. "What are you doing here in New Orleans?"

CHAPTER FOURTEEN

Huginn cawed loudly at me. Or Muninn. The bird hopped up on my table and opened its beak, wide. Then it cocked its head and stared at me, glittering black eyes unflinching, as its feet shuffled a bit from side to side.

Right in front of my beignets.

Which I had discovered I kind of liked.

"Shoo," I said, waving a hand at the bird. Odin's ravens or not, Norse ravens or not.

Huginn or Muninn called again. It danced away from my hand, turning its head quickly, as if thinking about stabbing my fingers with its beak. We did a few back-and-forths, me waving my hand saying shoo (why is shoo the word people used to scare away birds?), Huginn or Muninn dancing around the table and cawing, and Emma-mae laughing from beside my table.

She got up from hers and came to mine. Holding her plate and expresso in one hand. Huginn or Muninn looked up at her and danced its way off the table, landing on the sidewalk with a flutter of its black wings. Emma-mae winked at me, much like she had back in the diner, and looked at the empty seat in front of me, giving a little lift of her eyebrow as if asking permission.

I nodded, sitting there. Trying not to breathe the scent of jasmine in too deeply. Wondering what was happening. Curious about Emma-mae, and trying not to infer anything about her. Trying to really understand.

She had known about me, even before I had come to New Orleans. She had checked me out, measured me, for something. Then she had gotten down here—she had beaten me, with Skidblandir—a place she had been at apparently a long time. Long enough to be working with Vidar, and possibly more gods. Vali, at the least.

Waiting in the place the last Chronicler had met his end.

Whatever that had been.

So I watched Emma-mae, carefully. Observing. Seeing her casually take the seat next to me, her long legs stretching before her again, her legs next to mine, her feet again crossed at her ankles. She leaned back, her dark denim jacket tight around her, showing a bit of the curve of her body, a lean, lithe body with just enough rounded chest to make things there interesting.

Like I said, I observe things.

And try not to feel them. Not this much. I tried not to feel the sparkling of her eyes, the humorous glint of her smile. The knowing of a thing, the thing between us.

Maybe it was my imagination, but she took a sip of her expresso, holding the cup there in front of her face a moment, even though I thought it was empty.

The waitress came by then. She looked between the two of us a moment and seemed to sense the same thing I was. Her happy interest, her quick smile seemed more muted now, as she asked if she could bring us anything else.

I looked around. The café was still a little slow. Just a few patrons sitting further inside the restaurant.

Emma-mae nodded to her cup. I held up my fingers for a second. Even though my café au lait still had some coffee and milk left in it.

I thought I might need more bitter.

We sat there in silence, waiting for the expressos. Emma-mae seemed to be doing the same thing I was. Observing. Watching. Maybe even inferring. At some point she reached out and grabbed one of my beignets, smiling a bit at me as she did so, and took a smiling bite of the dessert. Her teeth were white and sparkled with an inner joy as she did so.

A raven cawed below her. Huginn. Or maybe Muninn this time.

Her smile grew wider, though it became a little less real. A little something she put on, as if the mask was a face she put on when she was enduring a great weight. Still, she smiled in a wide fashion; she tore a few pieces of beignet and tossed them as far as she could, so that the two ravens flapped and fluttered their way down the sidewalk.

Her eyebrows—both of them—waggled up and down at me. Knowingly. As if she was inferring everything I was thinking, as if Emma-mae knew everything I was observing about her.

Then the waitress was back. Depositing the expressos quickly in front of the two of us. Smaller cups than the café au lait mug, but almost full to the brim with a dark, viscous liquid. She took Emma-mae's empty cup in the same motion, but left my café a lait, giving me a quick second glance before leaving again.

We sat there. Cups untouched. The wind puffed, and the bitter aroma of hot expresso came to me. Hot. Hard.

I look at it. Wondered why I had ordered it. And grabbed the café au lait and sipped from it. Warm and definitely no longer hot. Bitter and a bit spicy but mellowed with milk. I forced myself to drink it and took another beignet from the plate, and ate the sweet dessert and finished up my drink. Wondering at where I was at, and the why of being there. Wondering at the storm I felt coming, and why it was coming, here and now. Wondering at the woman before me, and her role in all of those things.

"Funny, isn't it?" Emma-mae said. "Knowing so many things, but never all of them."

I sipped more on my café a lait. Nodding. "It's like you've read my mind."

"I notice things."

"Yeah," I said. Knowing she did, and knowing I did, and knowing both of us knew that about the other.

"Why did you come talk to me," I asked. "At the diner?"

She shrugged, a delicate lift of one shoulder. A delicate lift that moved the curve of her chest.

I notice things, too.

"I think I had to know," she finally said.

"Know?"

"You're a writer," she said. "You know these stories. There comes a time when you have to measure the person in front of you. You have to know."

I got it, and I didn't. I knew things like big boarding and character sketches, I had done thousands back when I was a writer. So I knew what she was talking about, having to know a person. Having to measure them. Having to understand their deepest motive, in an effort to understand what they might do, when the time comes they have to do something.

I understood those things, but not here and now. Not why I was being measured. Or the why. Or who Emma-mae was, and where she might have decided she fit into this story.

Was Emma-mae her real name? Had she told me a real story about her parents? I had never read about a Norse god quite like her.

There was Sif, with her golden locks. There was Freya, with light, flowing auburn hair. There was Hel, Fenrir's sister, with her half-dead face. Emma-mae was none of those, that I could tell.

"You understand what's coming, right?" she asked, but it really wasn't a question. She knew and I knew. "You understand, and you know, and so you know you're going to be a part of it."

I didn't know much about my part in things. I knew even less about hers. Or the gods she was with. "Just like Vidar is."

Her eyes widened. "You recognized him then?" Emma-mae nodded, as if checking something off a list. "Good, good."

"What do you mean good?"

I asked because none of this made sense. She was with Vidar. Vidar wanted vengeance on Fenrir, just like Vali wanted vengeance on Hodr. Both likely would want Ragnarok sooner than later, for that very day or reckoning.

I hated thinking that. Because, for the first time in a long time, I had met someone I had felt a connection with. It was almost funny that she turned out to be with the gods wanting Ragnarok. Funny, and a bit sad.

"Good, because there's a part to play here, for all of us," Emma-mae said. "Vidar, Vali, you and me, the other gods." We stared at each other before her face turned down the street, her eyes still on me. Her other hand reaching up as if to touch the side of her head, as if to straighten a stray hair. "You know the story. You know how it ends. You just have to take it back from there."

"Take it back from where?" I asked. I knew the story, but I couldn't tell you how we got to the end. The whole reason for me going out into the world was to write things down so the wolf could determine that little part.

Fenrir had warned me other gods wanted Ragnarok. I never thought I'd stumble into them plotting it. "There's the ending. And there's now. There's you and me sitting on a corner talking about it, and nothing else."

Emma-mae's eyes flashed, briefly. "There is everything else, Finn. There's the breath of fresh air in the mountains, the press of a dog against your leg, the cry of a child wanting their parent." She circled a finger around the empty plate of beignets. "There's sitting at a café eating the sweetest of treats."

"With the bitterest of coffees," I said.

She blew out a breath. "Maybe you have to have one with the other. Maybe that's the only way to tell."

Interesting, I thought. Not having figured Emma-mae for a pessimist. The woman I read now, she was like the woman back then and not. Maybe gods were fickle that way, changing on a whim.

I wasn't an optimist. Not really. Maybe I had been when I was writing, back before the tumor had struck, but any optimism had been burned away from the cancer. And then cauterized in the service of the wolf. No matter I still wanted to save those I could. No matter the empty feel of a torn-off teddy bear paw, each time my fingers touched upon it.

"There are things you are looking for, things you are thinking," she said. "You should take them further."

"Further?" I scoffed. "Here I am, watching gods determine the fate of us mere mortals. About petty things like vengeance, and ending the world to get it. How much further can I take that?"

Her eyes were sad. "Things rarely end cleanly, Finn. Unless it's a true end."

"An end of everything."

The sad eyes remained. "They'll be a part for all of us to play."

Part of me fought getting up. Fought marching away. The part of me that somehow wanted to reach the woman with the sad eyes, and make those eyes flash again like they had back at the diner.

That wanted to bathe in the scent of night jasmine and the sound of her laugh, god or not.

"You speak of it like it's a play," I said. Then thought again. "No, a game."

Her finger still circled the empty plate of beignets. Right beside her cup of bitter expresso. "When you're around it long enough, it starts to feel that way. Ideals you once held dear become memories, those memories become pieces, and all of a sudden those pieces don't fit together like they used to. Not in the way you remember they did." She looked up at the sky, and I was surprised to see a moistness to her green irises. "Thoughts you believed you would never betray, they betray you. They change you, and you change them. No matter how hard your core is, no matter how tightly you hold onto it, it, everything, it all… changes, with time."

Her last words were almost a whisper. "Especially if you have enough time. The things we've seen Finn, the things we endure, for what? Why?"

I couldn't speak to her long life, what she had done and seen. I couldn't speak to the long lives of gods, and what they might endure through the ages. I even couldn't—perhaps—understand the singular focus a god might need to keep their smile up, when the world was the way the world was. When it descended ever deeper into a darkening hole. When things that people couldn't imagine doing fifty, a hundred years ago became commonplace.

I couldn't speak to them, and I couldn't perhaps imagine them. I shook my head, because right now all I could do was be myself. Be the person I wanted to be. No matter how long I lived, right now I knew I would never change. There would be things that mattered to me, that would always matter, no matter how many centuries passed. People would never be things, things would never be acts in a play, pieces or a board, or a game to be won, or lost.

Emma-mae looked at me, as if part of her understood what I

was thinking. Understood, and looked at me much like a parent might look at their child, with the patient understanding of one who had lived much longer than their son or daughter. She drew her long legs in, leaning forward in the same movement. Something lithe and athletic and which brought the scent of night jasmine closer. "Your book, the one from back in the diner?"

I nodded, maybe not trusting my voice in the moment. The deep-welled anger at an end I could do nothing about. The frustration of a man who still remembered who the teddy bear belonged to. And the fascination of a man who couldn't stop his body from responding to the woman across from him. The fastly beating heart. The quicker than normal breaths. The understanding of a connection between us.

I knew she felt that connection too. I saw it in the way she leaned in, with the subtle shifts of her body. With the circling of her finger on the plate, and the looks at me from the sides of her eyes. With the moment when she reached back and touched her hair, slightly, as if wanting to fix it.

She hid it, I felt, no better than I.

"You know the cover of it what's on it?"

I nodded. The Tree of Life. Yggdrasil. I knew the stories of it, the roots of the tree that burrowed through the universe and tied all the worlds together. The roots that would dig into Asgard, into Midgard, into Niflheim and Muspell. Roots that drank deep at the wells in each of the worlds, wells that contain things other than water, wells that contain wisdom, and more.

Emma-mae waited. Watching me. Observing.

"I know about Yggdrasil," I finally said.

Her smile seemed to tell me I didn't. "I think you believe you do."

"I know about the tree," I said again.

She tsked me. Waving her finger. "Be careful, saying a thing a third time."

That had me pause.

"There is always more to the story, Finn," Emma-mae said. "There is always more. More to the story. More to the tree. More to its roots. More even, than all the worlds the tree has burrowed into."

She leaned back again. Like she was about to tell me a story. Like she was a storyteller, I got a sense she would have played a note or two on a guitar, like ol' Hode. "It's the Tree of Life, Finn. Every root is a connection, the roots have dug in everywhere, touched everything, everyone. *Everywhere*. There are more roots than branches, and I know you've seen those, tried to count them maybe, get lost in the cover. The roots are infinite, they embed themselves and flourish, they exist like strings on puppets, they pull and tug and..." Emma-mae let out an exhale then, something long and cut off, quickly. "If it's not directing us, the tree is aware. It *knows*."

This was new to me. A left when I thought we were going straight to the ending. I wonder if Emma-mae viewed it the same way, or if she had lived so long, seen so many things, like so many gods, that she just couldn't see what she was saying as different. As another way.

The way she described the tree fascinated me, in the way a story with good depth sucked me in. I had looked at the cover, I had been lost counting the branches, I had taken to avoiding looking at the tree directly all together. I ignored the branches, the squirrel on the branches, the birds that would appear there from time to time, the pair of ravens, the eagle, the hawk.

I especially ignored the body swinging from the rope.

I was fascinated. And, like all stories you might be fascinated by, a little unbelieving. "It knows, huh?" I chuckled. Not from any sense of disbelief, but just at what Emma-mae's words hinted at. "Whether I'm bad or good? Naughty or nice?"

The corner of her mouth moved, as if she understood. "It knows, Finn," Emma-mae said. "And you need to, as well."

Maybe bitter was the thing. This conversation had been a wild ride, and I needed something steeped heavily in grounds. I needed grounding. I picked up the expresso, if the white cup had once been hot it wasn't any longer, and I sipped the lukewarm coffee.

Ugh. Not cold, not hot, just bitter. Perhaps just right. "What do I need to know?" I finally asked, setting the expresso back down. "Why Fenrir sent me here? Why I'm trying to follow the Chronicler before me? Why Vidar and Vali want their vengeance this bad?"

I knew I sounded exasperated, but I couldn't help it. All I could do was continue. "Did Hodr send that Chronicler to die? Does his send all of them to die? Does Vidar kill them, or do you, after these conversations of endings and roots and things I *need to know*?"

The exasperation reached a peak. I was here for a different reason, not to find an ending of the world. Not to find gods plotting to kill Fenrir, or those who might be helping him. I threw up my hands. "I mean, why in the world does the wolf even want me to find his daughter?"

None of it made sense.

To me, and maybe, now that I looked at her, to Emma-mae.

She had frozen. Not frozen, I guess, not really. But she had paused at my last question. Paused, briefly, and covered it up. Covered up her surprise.

"His what?" she asked. Her voice maybe lightly surprised, maybe more-than-lightly curious.

"His daughter," I said, a second time.

"The wolf," she paused, as if testing the words out, "asked you to find his daughter?"

"Yes," I said. Knowing, if Emma-mae knew the wolf, she would understand Fenrir never really asked a person to do anything. Especially someone like me. He had told me, and now here I was.

Her gaze looked lost. I wondered during that time about gods, about, for all their long lives, what they knew and didn't know. What they had learned, and what might have escaped them. What sides they had stood on before, and what they stood on now. What the stories remembered, and what they had forgotten. Like a daughter of a certain god.

It seemed I wasn't the only one surprised by it.

"He has no daughter," she said. As if she had searched her whole memory, maybe her life, and had come to the firm knowledge.

I shrugged. "It's what he told me."

And, like it or not, I had pledged to do the things he had asked. I had pledged his service, I had pledged to it in order to save my life, and I was going to follow through with that pledge.

Not just because I liked to think I was a man of my word. But because Fenrir had asked. And because of something I had felt from the wolf, of the image I still had in my brain, of a little pup with a shaggy tail prancing about a field of flowers under a warm, yellow sun.

We all have last requests. And if anyone deserved theirs to be fulfilled, I felt like that little pup did. Someone who had grown into a wolf, a beast responsible for the cleansing, a monster responsible for releasing the end of the world…

And still a puppy at heart. Somehow, in some way, the wolf had kept that part of him, through all the centuries of being bound with Gleipnir. Through all the pain he had endured there. Through all the wars with all the other gods, gods that wanted and did not want the end.

It was my time to lean forward. "If you know Fenrir, you know he's not well."

Emma-mae still looked, if not surprised, if not shocked, then befuddled. Which is an odd term, but I thought it fit. Her eyes had looked past me, looked back at some memory, who knows how far back.

I tried again. "He's near the end, Emma-mae, and he's asked me to find her. I think he just wants to say goodbye."

Her eyes returned quickly then. As if she was calling me on that. As if she knew, like I knew, the wolf wasn't like other men or women. That the last thing the wolf would want, on his deathbed, was to have his child see him in that state.

Emma-mae's mood changed. It firmed up from the sad, regretful game-playing goddess she had been and became someone who had made a decision. Who had decided to move a piece on the board. A piece she might move sadly, but also perhaps with fingers crossed. There was a quiet hope to her now, I felt. Something that had steeled her resolve in some way.

Was it hope for the ending of the world? Or hope the world would survive? That I didn't know. Perhaps couldn't know, not having lived Emma-mae's life before, nor the length of it.

I could only hope, myself.

It was an odd feeling for me. I had understood, from the very beginning, that I was a piece on Fenrir's board. That I was something he would move to another place, at a time of his choosing. And I had come here with that understanding.

Now, sitting at this table, in this café, I stared at Emma-mae across from me. Seeing a board between us now. Seeing her have that same realization, in that same moment.

I had no idea of the game I played with her. I didn't know if we played for fun, or if we played with Ragnarok at stake. I only knew she was across from me, in the here and now, and it had been her hand moving the pieces across from me.

Her smile told me, she understood the same thing. The same

moment. She saw the same board. Her eyes glimmered a bit. Perhaps they sparkled. Perhaps it was the very beginning of the glistening of tears.

She made her move.

"Go back to the Penny, Finn," she finally said.

I just nodded. Like I did with Fenrir.

"Go back to the Penny, and figure it out," she said, a second time. "See what game is really being played."

I wanted to tilt my head, but kept her gaze. Her glimmering eyes locked with the steel-gray of mine. Slowly, very slowly, I allowed my lips to curl just a bit, into a smile. Knowing what was next.

Emma-mae saw it, recognized it, and understood it. She had warned me, after all.

"Figure it all out," she said, for the third time. Invoking the power of three. "The game, the tree, the world and all our parts in it, Finn."

CHAPTER FIFTEEN

I left Emma-mae with more questions than I had coming in.

The feeling of the storm swirled around me. Maybe there had been a slight break from the feel, maybe I had sat in the café, in the eye of the hurricane, while the winds built up around me. But built they had.

The feeling of the storm coming intensified. The winds whispered with it, tossing bits of paper past me on the streets. The warm sun seemed to lose to the chilly air, late fall was winning its battle. There were even more clouds now in the sky, larger, puffier things, mostly white but with tiny streaks along their bottoms, lines that spoke of stretchmarks, of holding in something that was growing too large to hold much longer.

Coming to New Orleans, I was on the search for Fenrir's daughter. I was sure the wolf was dying. In some way he wanted, needed his daughter, for some reason I did not know, and I was here to find her. The wolf always knew more than I did, he always had a reason, and maybe he was playing a game too. Maybe he had sent me here more than just to find his daughter.

I could never be sure. Fenrir would never say, just like he had never told me if he understood what might happen to me, back in Sendai. No matter his look, when the wolf caught me fingering my bookmark, the teddy bear paw.

The words of the other Chronicler came to mind. Not the man I had come to find, but the schoolteacher.

A small thing, perhaps compared to China, although the wolf never sends me to small things. Everything is a lesson to the wolf, and I should remember that.

Everything.

I had connected with those words. I had connected with her writing. And I understood, more than most, maybe, that what she spoke of was true. Everything the wolf did had a lesson attached to it, be it large or small.

I needed to remember that. Especially now. Especially with the feeling of a storm coming, with gods walking around wanting nothing more than vengeance, with Emma-mae and her rules of three.

I hadn't found Fenrir's daughter. Not yet. I had only found more questions, following in the footsteps of the Chronicler. A man who maybe had been sent on the same quest, though he hadn't mentioned it in his writings, or perhaps hadn't had time to write those intentions down.

Still, following the man had led me here. It had led me to a small gathering of gods wanting Ragnarok, and the reason I felt like the storm gathered in the distance. It had led me to Emma-mae, who apparently was the queen plotter of those gods. A woman I had connected with, for some reason, because it wasn't often a man like myself, a man who had seen a lot of the bad in this world, felt something that deeply, that quickly, for someone else.

Her and I were playing the same game, it seemed. We were at the same board. I was playing for the side of the wolf, she was playing for the side of the gods wanting Ragnarok. Wanting revenge.

It seemed like a small game, now, thinking about it. A small, petty game for what I felt from Emma-mae. However we want to think of it, vengeance is both large and small. It feels large to those who want it, it feels personal, it envelops everything around them. And yet, in the grand scheme of things, it does very little. It is just another death after thousands, millions of them.

A small thing to end the world on, right? No matter how long any of us live, would we really throw everything away for something as small as a god's vengeance? Would we end the world, just to kill someone else?

Vidar would. I certainly could feel it from the angry god. I don't think his feelings had changed at all, in the thousands and thousands and thousands of years he had lived. He seemed to have taken every waking step with that purpose. To kill Fenrir.

But Emma-mae? I had felt something different from her, back in the diner. She had lived life, I could sense it. Feel it. She had lived real happiness and real sorry. And those qualities, in anyone, would make it hard for them to just end it all. End it all, and the world with it.

There was more to her. I was betting on that. And—the part of me who still was taking deep breaths of the night jasmine scent of her—I was hoping I had convinced her there was more to my side as well. More to the wolf.

Maybe even more to me.

Those were my thoughts. At least, the largest ones. Many others ran around those, like the green shoots of a sapling digging deep into the earth, winding around older, thicker roots there. New truths, circling older ones.

Yeah, my mind was on that as well. What had Emma-mae meant about Yggdrasil? About the roots being everywhere? About us perhaps all being puppets on strings that the tree pulled?

There was a justice there, maybe. Marionettes, after all, were made of wood. Wood came from trees. Maybe Yggdrasil was just taking its own vengeance. Maybe it was a murderous tree bent on ending the world of puppet-makers it lived in.

I grinned at that. The writer in me liked to take a little license, sometimes. Take a left when I was going right.

If I was being honest though, her words had struck me somewhere. I certainly felt like a puppet sometimes. A puppet on Fenrir's strings. Could it be that something pulled the wolf's? Was there something that could bend us all to its nature, human and god alike?

That question, though small, seemed large in import. It hung in the air in front of me, felt like the king piece on a chessboard. A piece seldom looked at, moved only when it was safe to do so, moved if no other piece could be moved, or moved at the moment when danger was greatest. A piece that almost hid behind all the other pieces, and yet was always the last remaining, towards the end of the game.

I had always moved my gaze from the book's cover. Now, maybe, I understood why. Who of us could ever look someone, or something, in the face, if that someone or something had mastered them? I felt the question dance around. I wonder if other chroniclers had gotten lost, like I had, in the book's cover. I wondered about the birds on the cover, the squirrel, the roots that dug deep into other worlds, about the man swinging on its cover.

I knew who the man was. Who he should be. I knew Odin, the All-Father, had hung himself from the Tree of Life's branches in his search for wisdom. For sight. For knowledge.

Was he still hanging there now, in real life? Was the dust jacket just a cover with an image that seemed to move, or did it depict reality in some kind of dimensional way? I had never seen Odin, nor Thor, nor Loki. Nor any of the other gods, until now.

Funny, now that I think of it, that I wasn't seeing some of the major players of the upcoming apocalypse. It made me wonder when they would show up.

Or if they would.

I mean, Huginn and Muninn were Odin's ravens. They were Thought, and Memory. Odin had drunk from the well. Why wasn't the All-Father here, if they were? If he was only supposed to hang from Yggdrasil for nine nights, then why did I often see Odin on the cover of the book? Where was he, truly?

A nervousness ran up and down my spine. The nervousness that came with that knowledge that something you knew, something you thought you knew, was coming back to bite you. That spine-tingling you had when watching a scary movie, and you see that girl walk past the closet hiding the guy with the knife.

I didn't like those movies.

I didn't like that feeling. Not having it. Not knowing what it might mean.

It was odd to not have some of the most important gods of Ragnarok around. They should be at the heart of this story. Odin and Thor should be readying for the battle, their great battles against the giants, against the serpent, Jormungandr. Loki should be stirring the pot, stirring the apocalypse on. Fenrir, the wolf, should be straining at Gleipnir, aching to kill the All-Father.

Odd, the things we see and understand, late into the game. As if moves that had long been played were finally, in a slow glimmering awareness, seen. Seen by the empty squares they had left behind on the board, the gathering of the pieces left.

Where were they?

I had no answer. Having just met my first opposing god today, I wasn't sure I could answer. That, to me, might be what Emma-mae had been hinting at. What she had invoked upon me, telling me three times.

Figure it out.

I kept walking. The park appeared on my left, the Louis Armstrong Park with its oaks of dying leaves and its faded green lawn. More people were at the park now, people sitting on blankets and eating something they likely called brunch. There was a young couple, likely still in college, a young man who leaned close over a young girl, their faces close together, and I knew for both of them there was no storm coming. No world ending. There was just the here and now of that moment.

I looked this time for a pair of ravens, a pair of black birds dancing along the lawn, but neither Huginn nor Muninn were there. There were other birds, but not the two black ones. No thought or memory of what was, what is, and what might be.

Perhaps Emma-mae had other work for them.

I guess she had work for me too. The sign of The Black Penny appeared, the little black round thing with its two simple words on it. For some reason the sign grounded me, brought me back to Earth, reduced all the wild musing my brain was playing with.

I laughed a bit aloud at my earlier thought, of her and I playing at some game, opposite each other. I laughed at the thought that I could even play such a game against someone who had lived as long as she had. Who tangles with the gods and lives, right? I laughed at the thought, then chuckled, then sighed, and wandered my way out of the storm of New Orleans and back into The Black Penny.

CHAPTER SIXTEEN

The bar felt much the same as before. It hadn't been long, so I hadn't expected it to change, but some part of me had changed, so maybe something deep in my mind had expected The Black Penny to change with it.

It felt the same, though. The same industrial feel. The walls of old stone, the arches of red brick, the arches painted a paler color. The half-plastered walls with the vintage photographs around the place, the long cream-covered booths with the tiny tables, the tiny copper tray hanging by that one arch. The zig-zagged bar with plenty of taps and rows of craft beers behind it.

Most of the people had been changed out. I had been gone long enough for that. The Woodstock couple perhaps had retired for this part of the day, it being somewhere around noon, and older couples needing their naps. A younger couple had taken their place, the woman a little heavy, the guy perhaps too thin. She was dressed in a huge white blouse that seemed to hang over her curves and tuck in around her boots, leaving her looking much like a peeled potato. He was dressed in jeans and a wife-beater T-shirt, and had a cigarette tucked—unlit—over one ear.

A large crowd had gathered in one of the booths to the side. Close to Hodr. He was still there, playing a little more earnestly now. Not with the occasional strumming of some cowpunk backroads early morning twang, but something with real chords in it. He didn't sing, not much, but his humming to the chords had its own kind of magic to it. A resonance felt in the bar, and which could be seen in the heads bobbing over their drinks, the slight sway left and right of bodies to a music felt, more than heard.

The blind musician couldn't see me, but it seemed as if Hodr sensed my entrance. His hands never stopped moving, he never stopped playing or crooning in his low hum, but his face turned my way a moment. Nodding, in a brief, music-kind of playing. And then he returned to the song.

The young man tending the bar was still there. His shirt still clean and white, the cross still tucked into the V there. He was still efficient in his movements. Always cleaning, or turning a bottle just so, or checking on customers. Checking stock, checking the taps, checking the levels in the liquor bottles that were plugged and primed for a pour. Always ready for a quick order.

He saw me, and smiled. A quick flash of a grin. As if he was still reserving judgement on me, and had a bet with himself whether or not he'd see me again.

Emma-mae had told me to figure things out.

I guess I'd start with X.

The feeling of the storm outside seemed to come in with me. It was a weight, a pressure, that I always felt. It pushed down on me, reminding me that the end was coming. That Ragnarok was coming. And everything I did here, every moment I spent trying to *figure things out,* was delaying a moment where I could be trying to save those who might need saving.

I went back to the same place at the bar I had been earlier. The same stool. I held up a finger in that universal signal that said, beer please.

X smiled and went to grab another Dead Guy Ale from the long fridge behind him. There, his hand paused and moved to another shelf. Picked up a can and put it in front of me. A light-colored greenish can with a mountain on top, a beer made by a company called Odyssey, called Here Today.

I liked the name. Or I thought I liked it. I was still here today. New Orleans was still here, too. Maybe the world would be, by the end of it all.

X popped the top, gave me a look as if to ask if I wanted a glass. I shook my head and took a sip, it was hoppy and fruity with a bit of citrus finish. Something clean, after the sweet beignets and bitter expresso. A fresh start.

I looked at X curiously. With a decided tilt to my head.

He stared back, unflinchingly. Ready for anything.

Seems like forever, my man.

My guess is, that he had been.

X was a god, too.

I had asked him if he had been here decades. And he hadn't answered. Maybe part of his own judgement on me, whether or not I could tell more about the world around me than what it revealed. More about the people than they showed.

I looked over at Hodr. X. Thought about Vidar and Vali. Took a sip of the clean, citrusy beer. Then walked over to the vintage photographs.

Black and white, all of them. From older times, other ages. From a time when most people dressed up a little more than a potato blouse or a wife-beater. From a black suit and evening dress kind, with shimmery satin and sequins, and sharply-tailed jackets that cut in to a narrow waist from wide shoulders.

There, if I looked closely enough, was X. The same young man, with hair greased up with some kind of wet oil and ran back along his head. With a white shirt and a well-tailored vest, the cord around his neck tucked deep into his shirt. The picture might not hold up in court; he was a small figure in the background of a group shot, a group of people in front of the bar, but I thought it was him.

I looked at all the women closely. Trying to see if one would be Fenrir's daughter. Trying to identify her by a shaggy mane of hair, by a nose that might be longer than it should be, by eyes wide enough to see you with, or shiny bright teeth big enough to eat you with. I wasn't surprised, but none of the woman I saw fit any image I could conceive that might be a wolf's daughter.

I did see another picture had another side of the bar. Where Hodr played. The musician wasn't in the shot, but I saw the same guitar there. At least, it looked like the one he held now, if it was more of a lighter color in the black-and-white photo, and not the old, pale brown of the body Hodr held now.

My eyes picked out other people. I looked for Emma-mae and was disappointed not to find her. I did see Vidar once, the god—not surprisingly—not smiling for the picture. There were older pictures there too, older black and white photos of older times. Some with what looked to be sailors, not the sailors of today but the rougher kind, with homespun cloth, with gold hoops in their ears, perhaps from the very beginning of New Orleans.

That picture wasn't of this bar, but another. There was no zig-zag bar, no stone arches, and there appeared to be candlelight every-where. Candles even hanging in little round chandelier things from the ceiling.

That picture couldn't be real. That place had to be a backdrop of some stage. Photography just didn't exist back then. So whatever this picture was, and whoever it was in it, it was staged.

Had to be.

I mean, I thought I saw one of those sailors, someone in the back of the group, sitting on a stool and facing whatever bar that was, with a satchel much like mine. The dark brown strap over the corner of their shoulder. The lighter color leather pouch, square and the size of the book, over their hip. In the middle of all the old sailors, or pirates, whatever and whoever they were.

I sat there sipping on the Here Today. Thinking of those people in the picture back then. And, with that in mind, headed back to the bar.

X was coming back from serving the table in the corner, the table of young guys and girls listening to Hodr. His tray held quite a few empty bottles and shot glasses, and one tall empty martini glass. In a quick motion, he had cleared it all, and returned to me.

I searched my mind for every story I had read. Every Norse tale. Every story of every giant, of every beast, of every Vanir and Aesir I had ever read. And trust me, that had been a lot. It had been a lot growing up, and it had been more after I had first met Fenrir, and found out the Norse gods were real.

X didn't fit any of them, that I could see. He wouldn't be the warrior Frey, or Thor (I could see Thor drinking at a bar, sure, but bartending?), he wouldn't be Odin, or Bragi, the god of poetry, or Tyr, the god who had given his hand to Fenrir to trap the wolf, or Hoenir, the god of reason, even if X felt a little reasonable. He wouldn't be any of the fire giants, or Kvasir, the wise kindhearted man made of the spittle of the Vanir and Aesir.

Would he? I mean, in the stories that man had been killed. He had had mead made from his body. Mead that made others sing, and play music, and recite poetry the likes of which had never been heard.

I looked over at Hodr playing. I arched an eyebrow looking at his mug there. Then I turned back to X and tried the name out. "Kvasir?"

X smiled. "Reading up on some mythology?"

I set my Here and Now down. "I thought that might be your name."

"I told you my name," he touched the can, frowned, and grabbed me another. Popping the top and swapping the full can for the empty in a long-practiced motion.

"X isn't really a name," I said. The full beer between us, the snow-topped mountains under a pale sky, the slight sizzling sound of bubbled carbon dioxide leaking from the can hinted at something. Perhaps the slight shift of ice, before an avalanche crashed down from those wintering peaks.

"It's definitely short for something," he agreed.

I thought again. The god waited patiently there. Tending his bar. Swiping a white cloth over a pristine countertop, the wood there polished to the point it shined. There, behind him, was row after row of liquor bottles, each label pointed carefully ahead. The beer bottles in the fridge, the cans, each one of them aligned like soldiers in parade formation.

I thought back to his picture. The one with his hair greased back and the white shirt and—in that picture—a black vest. He had been here decades. In this bar, The Black Penny.

Who was he?

I ran through the Norse gods I knew, and came up with the same names I had moments ago. I thought about Thor's sons, the angry Modi (who would be a pair with Vidar) or Magni, who might be strong, and a little dense. X didn't fit those bills.

I dove into the dwarves, and I couldn't see X as any of them. They were grumpy in the best of the stories, and not the most patient. Same with the giants, I thought. Large creatures with large appetites, very seldom the image of a young man cleaning a bar. Not drinking himself. So he wouldn't be the mead-drinking, Hymir, with his great cauldron of the tastiest mead.

Would he? Could it be a cover? Or was I just reaching the end of my guesses?

"Hymir?"

X shook his head. He had an odd look of expectation and disappointment. "Strike two." He wiped down the bar once with a cloth, then his gaze went over my shoulder. To a corner table behind me, where a young couple sat. The young man's drink was finished, the girl's colored drink was maybe halfway done, and he waved X over, as if the young man was drowning in something and needed a hand.

A hand giving him another drink.

X gave the man a nod and a smile. "One sec," he told me. Leaving our back-and-forth unfinished.

I grabbed the new beer. Sipped it. Saw X talking to the young man and getting into a conversation. The man seemed a little more drunk than he should be, and was trying to explain the drink he wanted. The young girl with him looked on with a sad eye, as if this was something she had seen often, or perhaps something she was expecting, with whatever they were talking about.

A note twanged then. A discordant note. Something not the melodic plucking of earlier, a note from a guitar that had kept playing in a way that I hadn't realized Hodr was still there. Not until he drew my attention with what might have been a too-strong flick of his finger across a string.

I headed that way. Hodr's face followed me. If he couldn't see me, his hearing was good enough that he knew exactly where I was. Knew each step I placed. Knew exactly when I stood before the guitar-playing god, sipping on my Here and Now, thinking to myself the citrus aftertaste might be more sour than sweet.

"Young Finn MacCool," Hodr said. "Back from a battle?"

"No," I said, and maybe I even felt the untruth of that statement. "Maybe."

Hodr grinned. His teeth were old too, if still white, the faded white that came with age. The faded white of bones left long in the sun. "I see."

The words weren't hollow. It wasn't a pun by the blind man. I felt like Hodr did see, sitting here. I wondered how long he had been here playing. I wondered how long he had been here, waiting.

And then, I wondered why.

Why was he here. Why was a god playing here in a bar? Why here, for years, decades, who knew how long?

Surely Hodr knew Vidar had been here earlier. Surely he knew that mean Vali was around too, and that sooner or later Vali would come in and kill him. So why make it easy? Why sit here and wait?

I decided to go at this another way. To lay it out. The truth of everything I was here for. That Ragnarok was coming, that it was here, and that I wanted to do everything I could, if not stop it, delay it. Save who I could.

And see where it goes.

"You know Vidar was here, earlier," I said.

Hodr nodded. His fingers found the strings again. Started playing, as if he was a storyteller of old. As if the two of us were storytellers of old, and needed a little sound in the background for our tale.

"I see you know as well, young Finn," he said.

"If you know that," I asked, "then why are you here? When you know Vali is here, too?"

"Ah," Hodr said, plucking his strings slower, and slower. As if slowing the moment done. "I always forget the youth. The young. The rush to the end of things, the haste to the answer, when the question remains hanging in the air."

He knew. Of course he knew. Knew, and was waiting. I kept my hand from tightening around the can. "But you know that's real," I said. "You know the end is coming. The actual end. You *know*."

Hodr was sitting there and waiting for the end. The actual end, of this world. He knew and sat there, playing his single notes, crooning to a few chords, waiting for the end of the world. Waiting for Vali to come kill him, waiting for Ragnarok.

I knew too, and it was everything I could do to not cry out to the world to stop it. I couldn't, not really. Not with my role, no matter what I wrote or didn't write into my book, the cleansing would come. It would always come. It was fated to come.

"Dammit," I said. Thinking of all the stories I had read. All the hints from the gods, all the tricks, all the things they hid. Thinking of all my time with Fenrir, where the wolf would never tell me exactly what I was looking for, he would just chuff and tell me a place to go. To write. And then mock me, each time I came back. Mock what I wanted. Mock the desire to save what I could. "Why don't you gods just say what you mean? Just this once. Just stop playing your damn songs, strumming your damn hints, and just say something worth the sound?"

Hodr chuckled then, his blind eyes narrowing just a bit. Not in an angry way, or in exasperation of the young man in front of him. But as if in thought. As if carefully composing a song, and deciding on the next line.

"I'll tell you something true, young Finn MacCool," he said, leaning a little forward. The strumming of his guitar soft now, so soft I barely heard the notes. "The end is always coming. Ends always come, they just vary in the telling of them, in who tells it. There is always an end, it is always there, it waits, and one day," he plucked a second discordant note, loud and sharp in the bar, "one day it'll all just be over."

Hodr leaned back from me. Playing his guitar again, smoothly, melodic. Not crooning to the words, but playing in a rhythm that had the group in the corner swaying again. Sucking them in.

His face stayed on me though. His sightless gaze. He played and sightlessly stared and waited.

I sat there and returned his blank stare. Not moving. But thinking, furiously. Taking a sip of the now citrusy-sour beer.

What he said didn't make sense. Not really.

Maybe a little.

Maybe if the end was always there, maybe if Ragnarok was always above us, its executioner axe poised high in the air, ready to come down on the neck of the world, gently resting on its chopping block, maybe that would explain Hodr's patience in waiting for it. Maybe he had felt the sharp edge of that axe for too long, and had decided to sit in a bar and wait for it, wait and drink whatever he drank out of his big clay tankard, and play and torture those of us coming in looking to stop it with his secret knowledge.

That felt more on than off. Just not complete. But a start.

"If you really believed that, you wouldn't call me young Finn MacCool."

"Maybe," Hodr plucked and played. "Maybe it's still interesting, to see the fight in the young. To see the desire, the want, the need. After a while, you see, that starts to fade. Even if it doesn't get bitter, young Finn, the flavor is something you get used to. You never enjoy the sweet anymore, because you've had it too long. Things aren't sour, not anymore, because you've eaten that lemon so many times it's just another piece of fruit."

I felt like I'd heard this before. Something like it, at least, in another way. An explanation, a *reasoning*, that it was okay to sit around and do nothing, and just accept things, just because the world had become something you had gotten too used to. "That's just a chicken's way out," I said.

It was. Saying that the gods had become bored of the world, bored of their roles in it, bored of what they did and what waited for them, I couldn't imagine it.

Much like I couldn't imagine what Emma-mae had told me. Much like I had imagined her, speaking with the wisdom of someone who had lived longer than me. Seen more than me. Experience more, and longer than me.

Wisdom had to be earned, after all.

But what was wisdom, if it always came to this? To the single-string plucking of Hodr, waiting for the end to come. Waiting for an end he always felt, and perhaps just got tired of the waiting?

What was any life, if it ended this way? With sad acceptance? Without any kind of fight?

Hodr nodded, gently. His words soft. "I feel a truth circling around you, young Finn. It's a truth many don't see. A truth many will never get."

"I don't like it," I said, honestly. "I won't be that way."

He smiled again, with the sun-bleached bone color of his teeth. "We'll see how that holds up, in time."

He played then, and played something incredible. Hodr stopped playing the single strings that he had played, the single notes that echoed in the bar, the little chords he had been crooning to. He sat there, leaning back, sightless eyes on me, while his fingers danced along the neck of the guitar. While his pinched finger and thumb swiftly strummed the strings.

Music burst over the bar. The sweetest of songs. Something that ached and cried, long and loud. Chords that banged away at my heart, that pulled out every beat. A melody that went on and on and on, that seemed to draw out my every breath, until I stood there breathless, my mouth open, I stood there on weak knees and then —

Then the music stopped. Immediately. It stopped and went back to a single note, singly struck. A hollow sound now, an echo of something I had heard and would never forget. A pluck at a heart-string that would never forget that one note. That one moment. That brief song where everything had been beautiful and *alive*.

There was a thump of something and a crash. It took a moment to realize it had been me, dropping the beer. I shook my head and went to pick up the can, rolling away from me. Pick it up and curse a bit, the beer fountaining from the can, fountaining and going all over the place.

X was there. Quickly. Somehow he had a mop and a cloth and was already wiping the floor almost before I could apologize for the error. His gaze caught me with a knowing smile, a ready acceptance of what was, and he just slightly edged me away and cleaned up the floor with his rag and then swiped it with his mop, leaving the floor with a gleaming white shine of clean streaks of water.

I stood there, puzzled, as a god cleaned up after me.

Holding a can of beer that still was wet with foam.

X kept up the smile. Plucked the can from my grip. Handed me another towel, a clean fresh one. And then took the mop and the half-empty Here Today back to the bar.

I watched him.

What god did that?

Not any Norse god, or giant, or creature? The gods of the Norse, they were large things. Beings of power, and desires, and wants and needs. They would drink much, fight hard, and lust heavily, but there weren't many tales of any of them that would do the things X was doing.

Not always cleaning. Not always ready. Not just always prepared, but expectant.

"Who is he?" I wondered. And then realized I had whispered those words aloud. Realizing I was about to have another understanding, I was about to gain more wisdom, and perhaps take another step to a place where Hodr now sat, and played.

The blind musician's smile widened. A parent, or grandparent, or great-great-great-grandparent, watching their boy group up. Gain a little knowledge of the world they had lived in for so long.

"You come upon a different world than you once knew," Hodr said, with a pluck of a string. "Best go find out, yea?"

CHAPTER SEVENTEEN

That was a second person, telling me to go figure it out.

After Emma-mae had told me, three times.

I felt like a third person telling me would be too much. It would be three times a rule of threes.

I walked away from Hodr slowly. As if I didn't trust my feet. As if I didn't trust the world to be yanked away from underneath me, with each step.

My eyes went around the bar. The people there were all in a similar state. They all had heard the brief, momentary burst of song from Hodr. Its magic had paused them all, in everything they were doing. They all sat there, blinking, gathering themselves. The large group in the corner maybe first, jostling each other as if asking themselves if they really had heard what they had heard.

My gaze went around The Black Penny as I took each step, almost in slow motion. I picked out the photograph with X in it, from decades ago. From a lost century of black tuxes and evening gowns. His hair slicked back, but with his white shirt and black vest and cord.

The guy in the wife-beater's face looked a bit lost. His jaw worked a bit, as if he wanted to say something, something to the white-potato-dressed woman. He finally shook his head, picked the cigarette out from behind his ear, and put it—with no ashtray around—into his empty drink.

Which X took, quickly and promptly.

Ready.

I looked at the young man. Really looked at him. His young features, perhaps Mediterranean, along the lines of classical Greek or Roman. Rounded forehead, well-defined brow, a pronounced chin with a square jaw. A strong and prominent nose, almost hawk-like with a bump on its bridge.

So, more Roman then.

Not just Roman, I realized. Not with the cross on his chest. Not just a Christian cross. But a cross of two thick bars of gold, with Christ crucified on them.

A Catholic cross. And not just a Catholic cross, because around the figure of Christ were two words, inscribed there. One above and one below, the letters vertical on the long gold bar.

My mind raced from there. I had been raised Catholic, even if I didn't practice. Raised Catholic in Mississippi, which was tough because that was in the heart of the Bible Belt. Baptist country.

My mother had made me go. I had been to Sunday school. So I could recognize Catholicism when it slapped me on the face, a couple of times. The figure of Christ on the cross.

But there were other signs here too. I had read a lot of mythology as a kid. I had been entranced with other realms and other gods. Norse gods, Greek ones, Roman. How close some of the gods were to the other. Egyptian, Asian, Indian.

Even Christian. Not just their god, but their saints.

And something circled then, there. Some thought. Some hidden piece of knowledge. Some great awareness that had hidden there, ready to leap out in a moment.

Like now.

Red candles were a hint. The candles in the sconces, unlit. The candles on the tabletops.

The platter was another. The one hanging on the wall, as if for a donation.

The cross on the man's chest.

Those threads gathered together, became a larger picture. A small piece of a tapestry I couldn't fully see. They colored the corner of some map, of some place I was going, but had yet to arrive.

I kept walking. Thinking of Emma-mae. Of her telling me to go figure it out. Figure out what I wasn't seeing. What I couldn't know. Or didn't know. Of her telling me, much like Hodr had, that there was something large I was missing.

She had mentioned Yggdrasil. Had told me, almost angrily, about its roots. Much like the threads I was weaving together now, the roots of the great tree circled the world around us. Touched everything. Connected as all. Almost steered each of us.

Steered me, in a way, here to New Orleans. A place of mysticism and magic. The only place, had I really thought about it, where I could come to this realization, here and now.

I paused there, foot hanging in midair. That last phrase sticking in my head, sticking as if those words by themselves should clue me in. As if one of those words in particular. As if whatever was coming was too large to really fathom.

Then it came.

Then I made my final step.

Ending up right there, in the place I had first started. The very stool I had taken, when I first had met X.

The bartender stood there, wiping the counter. Always ready.

Another clue. The young man holding another beer out to me, the slight hissing of gas telling me the can was open and waiting, the label turned towards me.

Here Today.

Here and now.

Here. Today.

My eyes caught the young man's eyes. They waited, expectant. Full of readiness. Ready to keep wiping the bar, if I didn't get it. Ready to help, if I did. His golden cross hanging outside of his chest, on his shirt, with the slim figure crucified on it. With two words in Latin, above and below Christ. Latin words, Hodie and Cras.

Hodie. Today.

Cras. Tomorrow.

The two words of a little-known Catholic saint. Someone whose name, if the stories weren't made up, came from a word scrawled on a box that had been shipped to a place, almost by mistake.

Two words for a saint that would only be around in places of the greatest emergencies. A patron saint of only the most urgent causes. Someone who would be prepared, with quick actions and solutions. Who would help those with immediate need.

Those with the greatest need.

Maybe not a Chronicler looking for another. Maybe not a Chronicler looking for the daughter of Fenrir. But perhaps, a Chronicler trying to stop the oncoming ending of the world.

The realization grew. Threads wound around more threads. The tapestry spread. Hints of things, foreshadowings of others. Mainly, though, a few things flashed through my mind. Glimpses of where my thoughts were going, at a speed so fast I couldn't quite catch up. Quick flashes of true knowledge I might one day piece together.

Endings of the world, flashing by, one after the next. Volcanoes. Floods. Plagues. Wars. Other endings, that perhaps spoke to missing gods, gods I had expected to be here in New Orleans. Lost gods. Angry gods.

Endings always come, Hodr had said. They just vary in the telling.

More images passed me. There, a flash of Emma-mae's eyes, glimmering. Glimmering and lost themselves, lost in the roots of a tree, of Yggdrasil, winding around us all, tapping into worlds greater than just Asgard and Midgard and Jotunheim, then all of those. A tree that wound far into other worlds, and bound all those together. A tree with branches from which a god still swung, gently in an unknown breeze.

A god who may have seen a truth even he could not handle, after drinking from the well.

A truth he had tried to prevent with the binding of a wolf.

A truth that would come, regardless.

A truth that would come as an ending, and when that ending came, this person I faced would be there. A saint for the greatest of emergencies. Perhaps a bit of a god, here locally, in New Orleans.

It was then it really hit me, the Norse gods weren't the only gods around in our world. The knowledge had been circling in my mind, but it hadn't landed. Not fully, not until right now. I didn't live in some mythical world where the Norse gods walked among us. Or, that they weren't the only gods here on this Earth.

There were other endings, after all.

This here, in New Orleans, was just one of them.

I grabbed the beer. Nodded to the man, the saint, the minor god before me. Knowing, finally, what X was short for. "Saint Expedite?"

His smile didn't widen, so much as grow. As if he understood, the same as I, why I understood where I stood, here today. Knowing his own place in these things.

"At your service."

CHAPTER EIGHTEEN

I guess Fenrir had warned me. Well, he hadn't warned me, but had let me know, in the wolf's way. That there would be other gods, both for and against Ragnarok. Other gods that each wanted, or did not want their end.

The wolf hadn't explained that the other gods would be those from other mythos. From other religions. He hadn't explained to me that little detail.

And I hadn't asked. I had taken the job, having met the wolf. Having that world-shattering realization, that the Norse gods walked our Earth, that they were real. Having had that, in the time of my cancerous madness, had it and accepted it, and moved on with my life. Moved on with my job. Had it, without thinking to myself, if the Norse gods were real, might there be others?

Silly now, right? That there could be other beings of power in the world? Here I was in a city of mysticism and voodoo. Of gods and ghosts. Walking through it without a second thought. Secure in my knowledge of the world and the gods who walked it.

It was a large realization. One Saint Expedite let me come to, in my own time. I thought about my foolishness, back in the hospital. When I had been raging in my cancerous madness. Raging and cursing the gods. One god in particular, being raised Catholic. Saying things I had meant with the whole of my being at the time, things I likely couldn't just take back, now that I was aware of a larger world than one I walked.

I wondered how long that god's memory was. I looked, uncomfortably, at X. The Saint gazed back at me, quietly, a small smile on his lips. He looked as if he knew where my thoughts were. What I had been thinking of. He lifted a shoulder, just a little, as if saying, *who was he to say?*

"It's a lot to take in," he said. Waiting patiently. Ready. Polishing the counter with his clean, white cloth.

The knowledge gave new light to things, but brought more questions as well. What if Vidar wasn't here for Ragnarok? What if they weren't here for their end, but for someone else's?

Forces gathered here, that was for certain. I had come here looking for Fenrir's daughter and found a storm. A storm gathering today, and coming tomorrow. Relatively speaking.

Which explained Saint Expedite. A saint who was called upon in times of greatest emergencies. Not to fight battles, but someone who helped prepare those for storms that were coming. It made sense to find him in New Orleans, a city under constant threat of storms, a city of the dead, a city built lower than the seas around it.

He would probably be here a lot. Maybe even own a home, with as many hurricanes as came up from the Gulf. He would help get New Orleans ready. He would prepare those who had called upon him. And, after the storm, he would help those left to bury the dead, to clean up the living, and start anew.

Feels like forever, my man.

I shook my head. Not with any kind of negation, or thoughts of no. But just with the too-heavy thoughts of someone who had too much information pushed into his mind too quickly. I drank more of the Here Today. Hoped there was a beer somewhere called Here Tomorrow. Here Cras?

I smiled at the thought.

Then I got to business.

If Saint Expedite was here, in The Black Penny, then a storm was coming to New Orleans. A storm unlike what I had thought was gathering. Not something built of vengeance, not something where a god was ready to step onto the field of the final battle, but something more cunning. Not an ending of an ending, where Thor faced the serpent, where Vidar faced the wolf, where giant and serpent killed god and god killed giant and serpent.

This ending was perhaps more devious. It was an ending of everything. Not a plan built out of anger, of rage. But something more devious.

A *planned* ending. Something cold and calculated. Something that might tie all the endings together and call upon Satyr's fiery sword to cleave this Earth in two.

The world was certainly different than the one I knew. Different than a world of Norse gods, hidden among us. Living lives. It was greater than Norse, greater than Greek or Roman gods, of Horus and Ra, of any and all of them.

Maybe someone had grown tired of all of them. It could be any god. Any of them, here in New Orleans. They were here, planning, ending, and the wolf had felt them. Fenrir would surely feel something tugging inside him, something begging to be released. He would feel it and know the end was coming, coming soon. He may even feel the direction of the pull, and send a Chronicler there.

Never with direct knowledge. But in the wolf's way. Laying a scent out and allowing the Chronicler to track it on his own. Never pointing to the kill and telling him to eat.

That scent could lead to anywhere in the world. Anywhere in

the worlds, if I could believe what I had been told about Yggdrasil and its roots. It could be here and anywhere, and although I had found Vidar and Hodr and Emma-mae, I had no idea if that was the beginning or the end. I had no idea where to follow the scent from here.

I took another sip of the Here Today. Trying to remember that the beer had been citrusy sweet as well as bitter. Trying to think of a question that may get an answer that I could use. A trail to follow. A scent to track.

And then I finally remembered, the guy before me wasn't the wolf.

So I said the words I might say to anyone. Any human, that is.

"I may need some help."

X nodded. "It's what I'm here for."

CHAPTER NINETEEN

I almost let out a breath of relief. Finally, straight answers.

"Who's behind it?" I asked the Saint. Maybe if I knew, I could go back to Fenrir with that knowledge. Maybe there was something the god could do. Because certainly a writer couldn't do anything in the final battle, as much as Hodr had called me a young Finn MacCool. "The storm? The ending? Ragnarok?"

He laughed. Not anything rude, it was polite, but still a laugh. "I think you're severely misunderstanding my roles in these things." X waved his towel. "I mean, I'm tending bar here."

Well, damn.

I had hoped someone here to help me would be able to actually, you know, help.

X's chuckles went on a bit. It was an odd side to see from the always serious, prepared man he had been. "It's not like I could have ever went up to Adam and Eve, and tell them not to eat the apple."

That made a little sense, in a frustrating way. Saint Expedite was there for emergencies. Not to fight the emergency, and not to avoid it, but to endure it.

Which was a little ominous, for me. In my particular situation. In this town, with the storm that was coming. I felt a little insignificant, like a bug, in the middle of a dark tunnel, with a light rushing towards him, with no understanding or idea of what that light might be. Or who was bringing it.

X seemed to understand that particular part. The storm that was coming. A storm no one could endure. "If it was something I could tell you, I would."

I guess straight answers were off the menu, if X couldn't point to a god like Loki, or some other god, of some other mythos, and say *there's your huckleberry.* Maybe all gods were that way, or maybe X was more like the wolf than I thought. Maybe all gods, all powers were that way, like Emma-mae, like Hodr, with more hints and prods and pushes than answers to real questions.

"I get it," X said, smiling a bit more, watching my face go through the expressions, from understanding to relief, from relief to frustration, and then perhaps to some kind of understanding, again. A different understanding than before. "But gods never know everything, no matter how much they pretend to it. It's much the same for them as it is for the rest of the world; sometimes they think they know things they don't, sometimes gods hide things, sometimes, as much as they might not believe it, things are hidden from them. And me," X shrugged. "I'm a great deal less than a god."

I smiled, a small, bitter thing. "If you're here to help me, it's poor help."

"Maybe," he said. "Maybe not. You know more than before, right? You're aware of more?"

I nodded. Sure. I just wasn't sure if knowing the light towards me was a bullet train, or a locomotive, I wasn't sure knowing that was much help. Not to me. Not to the bug. It was going to get squished either way.

"Awareness is a funny thing, my man," X said. "A small thing, maybe, but without awareness, nothing else can happen. A problem can't be solved if you aren't aware a problem exists in the first place."

"I knew the ending was coming, though," I said. "I know what the storm is. What's bringing it."

"Do you?" he asked.

I thought about it. I had felt this storm coming, but how? When had I first had an inkling?

Perhaps a while, though I had put it down to my job. To what I did. After all, when you go around writing down details of human nature around the world, just to give those details to the god responsible for bringing around the end of said world, you might tend to feel that weight.

I hadn't been observing for the wolf long, but it didn't take long for something like that to soak into your soul. To perhaps color your thoughts. Shift your view.

So I had always written with the idea that the end could happen. But lately I had been arguing with the wolf, more and more. He had remarked upon it. Prodded me. Poked me. Laughed when I said I wanted to save some. Chuffed when I had asked him why we couldn't save some.

All or nothing, Fenrir had said. All or nothing.

So, in a world of absolutes, I had to feel something. And it was either all or nothing. It was either the storm, or not the storm.

So I had started feeling the storm. It had been subtle, in my writings. I had even stopped writing about some events, like back at the motel, even though I felt like the wolf still gathered something, just from the things I didn't put down.

I had started feeling it subtly, but I hadn't really felt it until I was headed here. Here and now. New Orleans. Right after the wolf had howled, and moaned, and told me to come here.

So there was something there. An awareness of when I had first become aware of the storm. Was there more to it?

More to the awareness?

I could say so. I hadn't given it much thought, after seeing Fenrir. The world had become very narrow to me, as much as I had travelled it. As many different things as I had seen, witnessed, scribed, it had become about the end of the world to me. About Ragnarok, a Norse ending to the world I lived in.

But now I knew there was more to the world. More than just Fenrir and Odin, of Hodr and Vidar, of Thor and Loki or Fenrir's daughter, of more than all the other Norse gods and giants and the flaming sword of Surtr, cleaving all the worlds into pieces. There were other gods in play, gods I hadn't even seen yet, other gods with other desires, with their own battles and fights.

Did that awareness help in some way, too?

I didn't think so. It only made it worse. There were too many, too many different religions. Too many gods. Too many wrongs that wanted to be righted.

With one great right-wronging storm on the horizon. Here and Now. Here Today. Coming to New Orleans.

I was back to feeling like a bug. And the light coming was from a million-ton train thundering down the tracks. Tracks that bounced and shook as if an avalanche stirred them.

There was nowhere for me to go. Nowhere to run. Nowhere to hide.

And no place to bring others.

I shook my head. "This one, X, this one that's coming, I don't know that it matters that I'm more aware of it now than before. This one, there's going to be no tomorrow. No next day. No one left, no saint to pick up the pieces."

X nodded. "I know it feels that way."

"You're saying it's not?"

"I don't know, either way," X said, one hand polishing the bar top, almost like the motion was performed subconsciously. "All I can do is prepare for it, and if the town survives, help pick up the pieces."

He looked to the beer can. "We're here today, my man. Here today, and that's where we have to be. Thinking about tomorrow is tomorrow's thing. At least for me. All I can do is prepare today, and if tomorrow comes, then I can prepare tomorrow. If something happens between today and tomorrow, something that almost ends the world, then I can help those that survive, survive."

"And if there is no tomorrow?"

X smiled in a way that reminded me of the wolf. Of Emma-mae. Of even Hodr, over there plucking along on his guitar. "I can tell you this, I've been around for a few of these. Sometimes one comes around that ends *almost* everything. Sometimes, something can be done at the very last moment that derails the storm. Allows the world to keep spinning."

I felt a connection to his words. Something in there spoke true for me. It was what I wanted, most of all. More than writing words that mattered, I wanted to save a few.

It's why I wrote, after all. To write things for people to read and smile a little more. To pick themselves up after a long, hard day and repeat it the next day. To realize, the moment they are hugging someone, that this hug may be the last with this person, and to maybe pull them in a little harder, for a little longer.

Maybe I had to stop thinking about writing words that mattered. As much as I wanted them. Maybe I had to start doing things that mattered, instead.

Or at least, too.

It was then I thought X's words might have helped. But I hadn't given the Saint enough credit. Because his next words gave me hope, and that might be the one thing I hadn't really felt in a long time. Since, maybe, Gaza. Sendai. Among the first times I had gone out for the wolf, with a dream of doing something important.

"This storm that's coming," X said, "you feel like it's going to end the world. And it may, I can't say whether it will or won't."

He stopped wiping the counter. Bent over a bit, like a bartender about to share his world wisdom. Which, in a way, I guess he was.

"But how many stories exist where another person has felt the same way, only to save it at the end? How many humans, saints, gods, how many have you read of?" He smiled, just a bit. "Do you think Noah felt the world was ending, during the Flood? Or was he just aware, and prepared to save what he could?"

CHAPTER TWENTY

I left The Black Penny, not knowing if I'd be back.

Not knowing if there would be a Black Penny to come back to.

Not knowing if the white-potato-dressed woman and her man wearing the wife-beater would still be there. If the Woodstock couple would be, or the young man drinking with the girl sadly watching on.

Or X, or Hodr. I may never know.

After all, I knew all about the past, hell I was writing chronicles. *The* Chronicles. A tracing out of our human history for thousands of years. Stories, with the barest reading of them, of some of the worst things we have done as humans over our past.

I had written some of the most recent.

I had written about the past, feeling the future. I had felt the weight of the oncoming Ragnarok with every scribed word. I had thought about it, almost single-mindedly. About the coming cleansing. About saving who I could.

I thought it was the job. But perhaps I had been too focused on the past. Or the future. Or both. Maybe it was time I started living in the current moment I was walking in.

Living in the present. Living in the here and now. Living Here, Today.

I smiled a bit. Not a happy smile, just one of self-realization. Of how the mind could take a couple of words and change your perspective about a lot of things. About how words could tint the glasses you peered at the world through. About how words resonated, long after they were penned on the page.

I looked around. The sky was still blue, though less a brilliant blue of an empty morning to something hazy and gray. A good amount of time had passed. The sun was lower now, and the sky had that dark afternoon feel of a darker, oncoming night.

Tomorrow would be even darker, I felt. Something threaded through the sky, almost mist-like, hazy gray tendrils stretching across New Orleans from the south. The white puffy clouds of earlier were gone now, disappeared into the west. Instead, there were the hazy gray tendrils, of clouds unseen in the south, from the storm that had appeared there, almost without warning. The gray fingers were long and delicate and stretched far beyond anywhere I could see, as if they led back to the darker, thicker palm of a god waiting far out in the Gulf.

A storm was definitely coming.

A world-ending storm. One from which there may be no future. No tomorrow after tomorrow. A time when everything could possibly end.

Was I Noah? Certainly not. I hadn't the man's faith, even if I had his fears and doubts and questions.

I thought about other things. Other endings. Plagues and locusts. Cities turning to salt. First-born sons dying. Hell, I had been raised Catholic, I knew all about The Apocalypse.

All endings of something. Possible endings of the world. With one great ending of the world.

I had grown up reading a lot of mythologies. Watching a lot of movies. I knew a lot about Apophis's war to end the world. The Mayans certainly believed an end was coming. There were floods everywhere, from Greek mythology to Chinese, and, shaking my head at this, the Hindus forever believed in the cycle of rebirth. Cycles of creation, destruction, and preservation.

That last word had me pause and glance back towards the Penny. Far down the street now. I wondered if there was a Saint Expedite in the Hindu mythos, or if X had dual roles. Or more than dual.

Funny, thinking about it, how closely some of the stories linked up, across all cultures, throughout our history. Looking out over the world, thinking of the things I had witnessed, the things I had scribed, the apparent decline of society, the widening of freedoms at the cost of morals, maybe the Hindus had the idea right.

Maybe X had it right.

Maybe there were always almost endings. Maybe they had to come. Maybe the world had to end, or almost end, to shift the course of humanity a bit. Maybe we *couldn't* shift, until we knew there was no way to keep going as we were. Until we had to finally turn left, because the bridge ahead was out.

Permanently.

It was a lot to think about. More than I had known that morning.

I was hungry. All I had really eaten that day had been beignets, espressos, and beer. And though the beignets had been delicious the espresso had been dark. The beer, oddly enough, had been a bit of both. Sweet and sour, hoppy and bitter.

I needed something more sustaining. And some alone time. Not that I could sleep, at least, I didn't think I could. Not even being up late reading the book.

I good meal would help. And a place to stay, with maybe some liquid fortification (see X, I could prepare as well as the next). Some liquid fortification and the book.

If there was one thing that might have answers, I felt, it would be there.

After all, in a book of endings, there had to be a beginning.

And, I thought, with the god still swinging on the book's cover, there was a beginning I needed to know more about.

CHAPTER TWENTY-ONE

I figured, if the world was going to end soon, if a storm was coming to New Orleans, I might as well have a nice meal and stay in a place that felt like the city. Who knew if that place would exist tomorrow, or the next day?

Who knew if any of us would?

I walked the French Quarter under the hazy gray tendrils above me, the wisps of fingers clawing at the pale blue sky. The clutching hand that would swell and grow and—once it was big enough—crush New Orleans in its gale-like grip.

Others seemed to notice the oncoming storm. I could tell, the way you notice these things. A couple on the corner of a street, an older man and woman, the man holding his hand on his hat as a gust shuddered along the street, the two of them gazing south with narrowed eyes. The younger people, sitting in chairs on the side-walk in front of restaurants and shops, even walking around, phones held in front of their faces, watching the red and yellow and green lines swirling out in the Gulf on some app.

Seeing the same thing on an occasional television, something hanging from the corner of a bar, or through a shop window, the swirling winds of a storm building. The perplexed look of the weatherman, trying to puzzle out the beginnings of this storm. Looking at things like fronts and trade winds and jet streams.

The feel of most was that it was the Gulf. It was the south. It was New Orleans, and sometimes storms just came along. They'd come along, blow in, and blow over.

But the ones that knew, knew different. The older hands, the ones that felt the storm in their bones, they knew this storm wouldn't just blow in and blow over. They felt this one could stay. That this one would come in with bad intentions, with turbulent lungs full of a monsoon-like wind, would come and huff and puff until all the homes were blown in.

It wasn't quite odd to watch. It was something I had seen in other places. There were those that knew, and those who only saw the surface. There were those who prepared, going to the stores to buy water and eggs and candles, who were battening down their hatches, and others that pointed at their app and wondered if they'd still be in New Orleans when that storm hit, others that talked about things like porch nights and hurricane parties, about sitting out somewhere drinking and watching the storm hit.

It took all kinds, I guessed.

I ended up picking Hotel Monteleone. An old hotel, old with a capital O, it had that grand Beaux-arts real New Orleans type of feel. One of those places you imagine you'll visit when you see the city on the television, with a grand entrance of pale stone and motifs, with its name scrawled above the doors, with extravagant chandeliers inside and rich, elegant furnishings.

The place even had a revolving bar, that you kind of have to see to believe. An actual bar that turns in a circle, like a carousel of horses circling around, only with chairs instead of horses on a pole and so, so many lights, lights like a casino.

Before getting a room there, I had a meal at Antoine's. I had asked around, and had been told it was the oldest family-run restaurant in any of the states, which I couldn't really verify but kind of felt like it might be true after stopping by. The inside of Antoine's was a labyrinth of dining rooms, of diners walking sideways down corridors passing waiters and waitresses doing the same, and smelled heavily of butter, pasta, seafood and Creole.

Everything smelled heavenly and tasted the same. I was never an oyster guy, even if Antoine's might have come up with Oysters Rockefeller. Another claim that might be hard to verify but could be as true as not. I can tell you the chicken Rochambeau was delicious. It was moist and tender, the ham was sweet and cooked just right, and the demi was rich and savory and provided a nice backbone to the dish that the bearnaise sauce complemented perfectly, with its hint of citrusy, herbal tang.

I took a breath after eating everything, needing to find a little more room in my stomach, then got a baked Alaska. It had been a long day, it was going to be a long night. Might as well load up on calories.

Besides, I felt like having a sweet treat. Even with the end of the world coming. Let's not judge.

A few more deep breaths later I found myself in the hotel. The front of it was like I described earlier. Grand entrance of pale stone, motifs carved on either side, name of the hotel scrawled across the marquee over the doors. Inside everything was white, or pale cream, the lobby was large with high, high grand ceilings holding grander chandeliers. Extravagant, rich furniture lay beside walls, on top of thick carpet.

The room was the same. Rich and elegant, with a beautifully thick carpet, pale walls, and gold curtains over the windows, with a matching gold skirt around the bed. The bed looked like it would suck me in, large and fluffy, with a coverlet that looked the same.

I ignored the bed for now. Even after eating that much. I found a chair, a thing of wood and velvet, with a warmly red, round cushion to sit on, and a matching red velvet back to the chair that looked almost heart-like. I pulled that chair to a desk, a thick mahogany square thing, and set some beer on a coaster there. A beer from a six-pack I had picked up on the way to the motel, some Holy Roller IPA, and I'm sure you know as well as I do why that particular name jumped out to me.

I wondered about X. I didn't know if I would see the Saint again, but I thought I might. I thought he'd probably appear, if and when I needed him. Especially with who I worked for, and the particular job I performed.

Provided the world went on long enough that I kept performing it.

I popped the top on the beer. Sipped it. It was juicy with a scent of tropical fruit, and its finish was smooth.

The thought of X appearing was a positive and negative. It was positive, because I apparently was in the mood that I would see him again. Which meant another day might roll around.

Negative, because I didn't know if I'd see him for this particular Ragnarok, this ending of the world, or, if I happened to stop it, another one.

I took another sip of the beer. Still tropical. Still a clean finish. And offering no comment on my current thoughts.

Maybe it was all negative.

I set the beer back on the coaster and brought out the book. Took the pen in one hand, and fingered the teddy bear paw of a bookmark. Feeling the soft edge of the paw, and thinking, without thinking, of a different hand, if one just as small. A small, delicate hand of a young girl I had never known. A hand I had held once, had held until it had been torn from me. A hand I had never seen again.

I stopped fingering the paw. I stared at the cover again. Forced myself to stare at Yggdrasil. Stare at the tree in all the ways I had avoided looking at it before, in the way I always avoided thinking about the little girl.

My hand ran over the spine. My fingers splayed over the dust jacket. The cover, like always, was supple. Smooth. Yet I could feel the bark of the tree—just a little rough—under my hand. I could feel the scratch of it against my palm, almost like I was standing in the forest, leaning my hand against the trunk of the largest tree. Breathing in the thick scent of earthy loam, of deep earth, feeling a breeze brush against the side of my face. I could feel the tree there, the bark, smooth in places, rough in others, cool to the touch. Cool, almost cold, like a grave. Cool with the passing of years. Cool, with the vastness of space—

I shook my head, pulling away.

The tree was like that.

Maybe it should have clued me in, from Berley handing it to me in the very beginning. I always knew there was more to the book, more to the tree on the cover, that it was more than just a dust jacket to a book I would never name.

I always knew it, and yet carefully avoided thinking about it. Looking at it. Seeing the eagle near the top of the tree, the hawk sometimes on its beak, sometimes not. Seeing the squirrel, even now, running down the side of the tree, its small shadow winding around and around, flickering at the edges of my sight, before disappearing over the edge of the bottom of the book. Not seeing the ravens, Huginn and Muninn. Wondering if the ravens on the cover were in some way reality, that I would see them at times because they were there, in the tree, for real (yeah, I rolled my eyes at that particular word), and then at times they were out in the world, maybe snapping at pieces of beignet on a sidewalk somewhere. Or watching for me to leave the hotel, and follow me to wherever I was going next.

It was an interesting thought to me.

I sat there, thinking, the pen in one hand, the book under my other. If the tree was real, if this tree was real, and was everywhere, if it touched everything, then I also held it in my hands. I had a piece of it, like it had a piece of me. Like it had a man, swaying in the tree, from a noose.

Not a man, but a god.

Odin.

The Allfather.

The stories said he hung himself for nine nights, in his quest for wisdom. That he had taken his spear and cut his side and hung himself, offering himself as a sacrifice for true understanding.

If that were true, why was he still there? Why did I see him, his silhouette, gently swaying in that cool breeze, the breeze I felt on my cheek, the breeze that brought the scent of deep, earthy loam and the cool feel of smooth, yet rough bark under my palm —

I shook my head again.

Knowing, and fearing, more understanding myself.

There was an order to things. And order to what I was seeing. An order to what was still going on.

And an order spoke of direction.

A direction spoke to an ending.

And endings, always, spoke of Ragnarok.

I sat there, looking at the cover—without really looking at it— for the longest time. Understanding in some way that this was the beginning. The beginning of the book. The first point from which everything else travelled.

My fingers twirled the pen in my hand. My right hand. It was an automatic motion, something I had learned as a kid, the little flick of forefinger over thumb, a snapping motion that twirled the golden pen over my cupped fist before catching it in the same place, so that the point of it rested between finger and thumb, ready to write.

Gungnir.

I had thought the name perhaps ironic. That my words always found their mark. There were mysteries here. Mysteries to my life. Knowledge that had sat before me, knowledge the wolf hadn't shared, because the wolf thought of me as a cub, thought of all chroniclers as cubs, and he would let his cubs find their own way in the world.

Boy, when awareness hits you, it really hits you. Especially when you started becoming aware of all the things you *didn't* know. It was almost too much, all the information that should be there, if I just opened my mind to them. Things I had shied away from knowing, in my brief time with the wolf. Things perhaps I should have taken closer looks at, before the end came.

Things like reading of the chroniclers before me. Of understanding more about them. About our work for the wolf. About understanding each of their steps, in their journey from the beginning. About each step they had taken away from the tree.

Those steps were a direction.

That direction led to now.

And now seemed pretty important.

It was time, then. Time to open the book. Time to figure out what I was missing. What lessons I had to learn. Time to gain more knowledge, more awareness, of what I had to fight. What I had to try to stop.

X had been right about that, after all. Knowledge brought awareness. And awareness brought a readiness. I could be ready for the end, or I could be ready for stopping it.

And I didn't know which it would be, until I looked.

CHAPTER TWENTY-TWO

I opened the book. It opened to the same page it always did, a blank page. A blank page after my last entry. The book of endings sat there, waiting. Sat there, open and ready.

I took a sip of beer and tried something I had never done before. I sat there and wrote of my day. Not what I observed, not the people I watched and the things they had done, not observations of the good and bad of humans, but my day. What I had done, who I had seen, what I had experienced.

The words flowed smoothly. Until I got to Emma-mae. Then the pen stopped. Literally stopped. And would not write more.

I moved on to Vidar. I could write down about that god. About his quest. About Vali and Hodr. Then I got to X, wondering if it would be okay to write words about another god here in this book. Thinking, in a weird way, that maybe a book written by Nordic Chroniclers might not be okay with writing about other gods, about other powers, about saints.

Maybe that's why I couldn't write about Emma-mae, because

this book was for an exclusive club. A members-only set of chronicles. For those of the northern mythos.

The pen wrote smoothly, though. I described the man to a T. I wrote about understanding his true nature, that he was a Saint, that he was Saint Expedite. I wrote about his job and what he did, about him talking about the Flood.

I even wrote about Noah there.

Every word went smoothly.

Hmmm.

I tried to write about Emma-mae again. Again the pen froze in my hand. It wasn't my hand that stopped, it was the pen itself. Gungnir. An instrument that always found its mark, that always struck true.

I wanted to experiment more, but didn't. Because me writing down things about Apophis or Ra, about Zeus or Mars, about Achilles or Hercules or any other god from any other religion would just be fiction. It would be like me writing *Reagen's Journey*. It would be something I made up, because I hadn't met them.

Because I hadn't met any of them.

At least, I was pretty sure I hadn't met any. I had travelled the world, seen a lot in my short time with the wolf. Who was to say that I hadn't sat next to Ryujin in Sendai? That I hadn't watched the god— maybe wearing a nice little dragon-printed shirt—call up the wave that had swallowed the town with a tiny smile on his face. Or a frown.

Maybe I had sat next to Athena in Athens, maybe the god had sat right across from me and watched the same young man I watched struggle to carry his medicine home. Maybe she had been in the group of people mocking the man. Or just stood alone, one of the solitary figures in the masks.

Hell, Moloch himself could have been holding that pistol on me in Gaza, and I wouldn't have been able to say different.

I just didn't think I'd know.

How could I?

So there was nothing for me to compare to, in order to figure out why Gungnir would not find its mark. For why the pen would not scribe down Emma-mae into the book. Nothing I knew of right now, at any rate.

I could write about Huginn and Muninn. About them eating the beignets. About my conversation with her. Just not the words Emma-mae.

Frustrating.

So I stopped. Things like this, I had to give them time. It was a puzzle whose solution wouldn't jump out at me. I couldn't power my way through it, for all I might want to. For all I felt like the two of us were playing a game, that she was on one side of the chessboard, I on the other, both of our hands slowly moving pieces and tapping the clock to the side of the board. Tapping the clock and — with a quick glance — seeing the little time that remained for the rest of our moves.

Like I said, trying to solve this puzzle was frustrating. And I had to move on, because it was frustrating with an urgent side of time running out. There was a storm coming, a storm whose beginning I didn't understand yet, and not understanding where it was coming from, I couldn't quite understand how it would end.

And that was the key, I felt. I needed to know who had called the storm. And why.

Then, and only then, did I think I had a chance to stop it.

No matter what the wolf said.

So I tried another thing I had never done before. Have you ever read a book, and come back to it later? Maybe there was something in it you wanted to show someone else? Or you just liked a certain paragraph, a description, perhaps a sentence made you laugh? Maybe the way a character looked at another, maybe you wanted to read it and feel that again, feel it in a way you felt that emotion in real life, for someone else?

Have you ever had any of those thoughts, and come back to a book, and just opened it right to that spot? The spot you were thinking about? Even though you had no idea of what page that paragraph or sentence or scene was, just a general sense of beginning, middle, or end?

If you have, then you'll understand what I was trying now. It's kind of a magic all its own, right? Pulling a book out you haven't read in years, and flipping it open to the exact page you were thinking of?

I thought about what I needed. Thought about the storm, and wondered where I needed to go next. Where I needed to go to figure out the heart of the storm.

Thought, and opened the book.

And it didn't work. Not the first time. My hand was a little moist from holding the beer can and I thought maybe the pages stuck to my hand. They kind of flopped over all at once, and there the book opened, on the last entry of the Chronicler before me. The page where he had written that he was heading to The Black Penny. The page that was only half-full, because he hadn't written into the book anymore, because wherever he had gone that night, he hadn't come back from, and the next page my chronicles began.

I gave a tiny smile to myself, and sipped my beer. It was still the first can, and more warm now than cold. Less tropical fruit now, less of a clean finish. More of that taste of warm hops that stays in your mouth.

Then I wiped my hand dry on my pants. Closed my eyes for the second time. Closed my eyes a second time, and closed the book again as well. Closed the Chronicles, felt the cover in my hand, felt the tree underneath my hand (without trying to really feel the bark rubbing my palm) and then opened the book again.

This time I tried something different. I didn't think about the storm coming, and where it might have began. I didn't think about Ragnarok and gods and where I might need to go next. I opened it to the page I felt like I needed most. The reason I had been sent to New Orleans in the first place. I thought about Fenrir's daughter, about the wolf's daughter, and thought about finding a clue as to where she might be. Who she might be.

Then I opened the book. Opened my eyes. Read the words, and blinked.

They weren't what I thought they would be. Not some comment about a chronicler talking about the wolf. Not some Nordic runes that might describe some congress between Fenrir and another god. Not some date of birth, place, location, parents, nothing like that.

The words were simple. They were the words of a schoolmistress. The words of a schoolmistress travelling with Wyatt Earp, along his ride of vengeance.

I had flipped it to the very last page I had read, of hers.

Everything is a lesson to the wolf, and I should remember that.
Everything.

Huh. Not what I would have thought. There didn't seem to be much about the wolf in this, or who his daughter might be. Part of me wanted to try again, close the book and see if the third time really was the charm. But something about doing a thing three times had me avoid that.

Instead, I decided to trust this flip. I read back up a ways, re-familiarizing myself with where the schoolmistress's observations began. About her meeting Wyatt Earp again, decades after teaching him as a young boy. As I read, like I had before, I felt connected to her. Her words drew me in, I could see them, feel them. Feel them in my bones.

I felt her admiration, in the man Wyatt had become. I saw him there, standing by his horse, looking west over dry land sparse with brush, with the mountains of the Rockies in the distance. I felt her… it wasn't pride, and not satisfaction, but something close. About having known the boy he had been, and now, having met the man, knowing the direction the boy had headed out in had become the destination the man had wanted to be.

There was admiration there, in her words. The dedication of the lawman in his ride of vengeance. Admiration about how tired Wyatt Earp was, but how a relentlessness drove him. About his desire to push himself to do what was right, what was just, no matter what. To hunt down each of the men who had ambushed one of his brothers, and killed another.

Other emotions colored her words. There was sadness, and yet also comfort. She felt sad for Wyatt Earp, sad in the man he had forced onto himself, sad in the dressings of a man who might have chosen different, in a different time or world. But she also felt comforted, comforted that a man could put on those clothes. That he could become such a thing. That a person could hone his edge to such a fine point, that he could become the instrument of vengeance he desired to be.

That he could right this particular wrong, in this world.

There was something there, in her words. I felt it. I knew it. Perhaps not about Fenrir's daughter, but about the oncoming Ragnarok.

I knew it like I knew she knew Fenrir, much like I did. Knew the wolf better, perhaps. There was a level of comfort there as well, of debates, almost as if they were equals. As if they had bantered many times.

There was an image there, something coming to life in my

mind, the way a good story will bring something to life. An image of a girl lying back against a wolf, lying there in the warmth of the crook of his great neck, lying between his jaw and the length of his great paw. Lying there in the cave and reading aloud, the wolf's eyes partially closed, as if in a sleepy slumber.

I paused there, flipped back through her pages. All the pages she had written. I was surprised to see them go on a long way. A long time. Hundreds of years, perhaps.

Way more than the other chroniclers after her.

Just like with Wyatt Earp, I could sense a certain feel from her with the wolf. I could see him in the cavern, much like one I had sat in. Although her wolf's cave seemed different. Older. Darker.

The two bantered. Debated. Argued. I flipped through the pages, they got longer through her service. There was a level of comfort, as if they had had these discussions many times. As if they had sat and talked philosophy and religion and politics, as if they had debated human nature, greed and justice.

But there was also a divide. Small at first, growing over time. It was just a feel, maybe the odd placement of something she had written down. A word, a particular choice of description. A certain chosen adverb over another.

But I could feel it.

The schoolmistress wrote on. About the wolf telling her of other endings. About other gods, laughing and carrying on without care or wonder. About floods and plagues and volcanic eruptions…

And that, that was where I felt the edge inserted. The sharp edge of misunderstanding. The slow draw of a knife that had divided her from the wolf. Reading her words one more time.

I ask the wolf about the darkness. About how it feels different to me. The darkness of this world, the shadow that only grows darker. I feel it, I feel it and see it… it's as if the world perches on the end of a great chasm, as if in' the great cycle of death and rebirth this world is stuck in the dying.

There is no light to the shadow. Nothing to guide us. No small glow of sunrise over the horizon. No firefly blinking in a dark field, letting us know we are not alone.

There is just the darkness.

Although the wolf tells me different. He tells me of times when that many people would die in a blink of an eye. In blink after blink, when they would disappear from the face of the Earth and never be missed. Of ending after ending… when the gods might laugh and drink and carry on without a thought or care or wonder.

No matter that the wolf looks aside as he tells me these things. That he chuffs and turns the topic to other things. No matter that he knows something I do not, that the wolf hides something about the shadows gathering around this world, that the wolf knows why no light brightens the horizon.

I felt the divide then. The beginning of something. Of something that might have led to now.

I moved back and forth in her pages. I felt certain truths strike next to me, like lightning dancing ever closer along the horizon. I could feel every word I read strike closer and closer to some truth I needed to understand.

I stopped, during her observations in China.

She had mentioned them, at the end with Wyatt Earp.

Now I read them, understanding she was writing about the Taiping Rebellion. A brief period of time, maybe ten years, maybe twenty, where unspeakable acts were done. Where thirty million people had been killed.

Unspeakable, but written.

She had been there. She had been there to observe, from the very beginning. The wolf had sent her there, and the schoolmistress knew, knew like I knew, what she was observing. And why.

It was dark. Bleak. She lost herself, there, I felt. Lost herself in the rebellion.

How could a person not?

There had been things like back in the middle ages. People's heads were cut off and placed in villages as warnings. Other body parts had been chopped off and left scattered down streets, for nothing but reminders, reminders of what happened to those who didn't take part in the rebellion.

Reminders, in other villages, of what happened to those who did.

It was odd, to me, with what I did. With who I had just met. Understanding the revolt had been started by a man who had claimed to be the younger brother of Christ.

More gods among gods.

The revolution had caused people to flock to Nanjing. Millions to join the cause. And millions more followed, the Ever Victorious Army, to quash the rebellion.

The schoolmistress wrote on. I got the feeling she had tried to push herself away, distance herself from the words she put on the page, but she hadn't been successful. Maybe couldn't have been.

She had written of entire regions destroyed. Of village massacre after village massacre. Of seeing people lie against homes, lie in the dirt and the mud, lie there with a hand or foot missing, with a leg missing below the knee. With pus-covered stumps and the black streaks of infections and sickness. With people wasting away before her, over and over. Wasting away and dying.

It got to be where the quick kills were at least merciful. Where the starvations and the forced marches and the live burials, these things she had witness with a shaky hand, the rapes and the flaying alive and what she called slow slicing, executions of rebellion leaders by slowly disemboweling them. Pulling out their intestines and stringing them in the dirt.

I felt the cries in her words. The cries of the people there, the villagers, the townsfolk. Those who just wanted a simple life, maybe wake up and farm, go home to those they loved. I felt the cries of all of them.

And I felt the cries of the schoolmistress. Felt them as she lay against the side of a home herself. Lay there holding a little girl to her chest. Lay there crying, crying over and over, holding the girl to her chest. Feeling the lifelessness in the child, the way her arms and legs dangled there in the air. The blood trickling over the schoolmistress, from a tourniquet on one of the young girl's arms.

The tourniquet there because the girl's hand wasn't. Because she had been caught trying to steal food. Having no parents, no family, from one of the villages that had been mowed through by both armies, leaving nothing but devastation, loss, and hunger in their wake.

The girl had been so thin. I could feel her thinness, in the words I read. I saw her, I saw and felt the girl as the schoolmistress hugged her to her chest, felt the thin body of the little child, the fragile bones, the cold press of the girl's cheek to the schoolmistress's own. I felt all that like I felt the schoolmistress's fingers holding the girl's arm, squeezing the wrist tightly, as if she could stop the blood pouring out of the stump there…

I felt that scene intensely. It pulled me out of the book. I did not look at the teddy bear paw, off to the side. I did not look, and could not think, of that little girl in Sendai. I could not put the two together, because I knew if I did, I would follow the schoolmistress into her world of hurt and pain and suffering.

And I knew, if I did that, I would never return.

I already felt the darkness she felt. I could see the

schoolmistress look out over a great chasm, I could feel her stare into the dark pit. I could feel her biting her tongue, wanting to scream out *why*. I could feel her searching for a bit of good, something to fight the atrocities of the rebellion, of the horrors of other places she had been. I felt the darkness circle her even as she searched for a light. I felt her wonder where the good was, in a universe of bad.

I sat there, taking large breaths. Looking at nothing. Seeing nothing. Hearing and feeling nothing except for the breath. Feeling nothing except the ticking of a clock inside me, of the counting of the moments before the storm struck.

Slowly, I came back to myself.

Slowly, my feelings and emotions became my own again.

I took a sip of the beer. Warm now, too warm. Warm and flat and bitter, in the way most warm beers are.

I flipped those pages of the rebellion away. Feeling the storm mired in those words. I flipped forward until I got to Wyatt Earp again. Realizing, that I did so, that this observation was the schoolmistress's last that she would write. That she travelled with the lawman, wrote down her observations, and—as I flipped to the end—came to her end.

The lightning danced ever closer. It danced over the horizon, the bolts nearing with every strike. Nearing and bringing with it a subsonic rumbling, something I felt in my very bones, as I sat there, looking at the very first page of hers I had ever read. The same words I had started with the night before.

I swallowed, knowing that here was where the storm had began.

Knowing that what I read now would lead to what was happening in New Orleans, here and now.

Knowing that I was reading about the beginning of the Ragnarok of now.

And, knowing that, I settled myself in. Forgot about the beer.

About the sun dying in the west outside, about the late afternoon becoming evening. Forgot about the storm.

I forgot about all of that, and just focused on the chronicles, as they were written by the schoolmistress. I read about the ride.

Wyatt Earp's last ride, his ride of vengeance.

CHAPTER TWENTY-THREE

Wyatt Earp stood there, framed against the Rockies. The lawman stood there, his duster swaying a bit around his legs as the breeze picked up. He stood there, facing west, looking out over the scrub-filled plain, watching the sun fall.

She watched him. The lawman stood this way every night. The wind brought the smell of the plain, the earthy scent of dust, over the camp. It had been a hot day, but the breeze seemed to promise a coolness this night. A chilliness, not as a comfort for the heat of the sun, but as a contrast. A cold that would be a yin to the sun's yang.

His horse snickered next to him. A black thing, for perhaps a black purpose. The tall animal stood there next to Earp, its mane fluttering in the same breeze that moved the lawman's duster, the two of them watching the sun die. Watching the orange and yellows and reds spreading over the edge of the horizon. Like a dream, dying.

Or, perhaps, a waking awareness.

"I can't help but feel like I've known you somewhere before, Miss Easley," Wyatt Earp said. Like he had said before. Like he would say, glancing at her, his eyes narrowed just a bit, as he searched through his memory.

He said those words, and if something inside of the man could read her. Read her even though she knew she looked nothing like the schoolmistress she had been, first meeting Wyatt Earp, as a kid.

She stood a little bit behind Wyatt Earp. She—who never felt uncomfortable around many—always gave Wyatt Earp his space. Her arms were hugged around herself in the chill, so that the wind tugged the ends of her own coat, laying overtop her pants. She was dressed much like Earp and his gang, to the great delight of Doc Holliday. A man who always had a ready grin, a quick joke, and a general delight in the people around him.

She huddled into her warmth, gathering herself in her arms. Even knowing Wyatt Earp would never recognize her. Could never recognizer her, with the beret in her hair. The Hulinhjàlmr that would keep her disguised.

Still, the wind was cold. And the man was sharp. There was something inside of him that other men lacked, that other humans lacked. That other gods… lacked.

"You've met a lot of women out here, on your ride?" she asked.

He blew out a breath. She imagined, though she couldn't see his face, the hairs of his mustache blowing out with the breath. Then he chuckled, once, and the chuffing motion of it reminded her so much of the wolf. "Not at all, Miss Easley, not at all." A pause. "Where did you say you were headed, when we found you?"

Funny, she thought, how he kept trying to figure that out. As if it was something he needed to put together. As if a puzzle sat there in his mind, one he was perhaps unaware of, yet the puzzle sat there, deep inside the man, driving him to figure it out.

Just like something drove him now.

"I didn't tell you," she said, once more. Her standard reply to his question. "I don't think I know, myself."

"Strange," he mused, like he always did. "Strange for a woman to be out here alone."

"I've heard that before," she said. Once or twice, or a million times. She wondered, again, why the wolf had picked her out of all the men and women he could have chosen. Why he had granted her life. About the whims of fate, and the direction of destiny, and if one could survive alongside the other.

Or, despite the other.

"Mighty strange," Wyatt Earp said, again. Softly. Watching the sun die, next to his horse.

Tomorrow they would catch up to the last of the gang. The last of the Cowboys. They had killed Stilwell and Cruz and Curly Bill Brocius. She had heard about that last fight, the one at Iron Springs, where Curly Bill and a group of cowboys had ambushed Earp and his gang. She had met up with Wyatt Earp and his group of shooters shortly after.

Doc Holliday had grinned, telling her the story. Standing about the flames of a campfire, motioning widely with his arms, his eyes lit with gleams of dreams and fantasies. He had regaled them all about the god-touched Wyatt Earp, how, with bullets raining down all around them, how Wyatt Earp had pulled his shotgun out and charged Brocius and his crew. How bullets had torn through his duster, had taken off his hat, but not one had found the man or his horse.

How Earp had charged the group, bullets tearing holes through his coat. How Wyatt had charged up the hill and laid the shotgun in front of Curly Bill himself. How he had pulled the trigger and torn Brocius in half.

The very angel of vengeance, Holliday had said. His hands out in front of him, like he was holding the shotgun and pulling the trigger. Eyes grinning, and the man waggling his eyebrows.

It was a hell of a story. One that would likely go down in histories other than her stories. Than her book. A legend maybe that would carry on, of a man so committed to who he was, in his core, that nothing else could touch him.

"The world is strange," she said. Trying to explain, or perhaps hint, at where she had been. What she had done. What was required of her. "I don't know that I understand it at the best of times. I travel, Wyatt, I travel and go where I'm supposed to."

There was something in the man that fascinated her. She knew about angels and devils, both. About the gods and who they blessed, and who they didn't. What they allowed, and wouldn't.

She knew and, after China, wanted to know that no longer.

"I figured, Miss Easley," he said, his tone still one of memory. As if he recognized something in her voice, as if he searched back for the lessons of the young kid she had taught. "I see you writing in your book. If it's not too much to ask, I hope you color me kindly."

She liked Earp. Admired a man who took on odds greater than himself. Who had set a limit, had decided that he knew what was just, and what wasn't. Who had decided that he would take it on himself, if no one else would, the protection of those who couldn't protect themselves.

A man who did *something*.

Because he was capable of it. Because he felt, in his heart, people needed protection. And because he had built himself into a person capable of delivering that.

The wind stirred again. Wyatt Earp's duster flapped around him. Occasionally the dying sunlight poked through the holes in his coat, as it lay open in a particularly long exhale of the wind. There was something comforting in that image, she thought. She felt. Something comforting in a man who faced impossible odds. Who had given himself a quest for justice, even if he called it vengeance. Even if those around him called it vengeance.

It was still justice. Still a reckoning. A holding accountable of those who should be.

Those feelings resonated in her now. Resonated in a way that she recognized. She felt them, as she wrote them down. A growing divide, between her and the wolf. Something she had thought had been a misunderstanding, something that she could debate, but now it had become more. A divide. A gulf. Something she feared could no longer be crossed.

"Why do you do this?" she asked him, like she had asked him many times. It was the crux of her problem. She knew it. And it bothered her, because she knew the wolf had sent her here for this very thing. Some lesson she was supposed to learn.

She feared that she was learning the wrong thing. She didn't know what the right thing was. There was a divide now, a divide between her and the wolf, there were two sides to her life now, where before there had been one. What she was learning, it was the flip of a five-cent piece. She could flip it and it could be heads. It could be tails. And, flipping the nickel, she didn't know what she wanted to call. What the wolf *had* called.

Wyatt Earp stood there for a long time. Hearing her words, but standing there. Watching the sun. His head lowered, lowered for a moment, then picked back up. As if he didn't understand her question so much, as if he understood her need to ask it, and had given his reply deep and measured thought.

"I don't rightly know," Wyatt said. His words simple, but also solid. Firm. "I can just tell you what I've told you before, Miss Easley. There are just things I feel, I feel in my bones, and there's no half-measure when it comes to these things. In the end, I think it comes down to either a man does what's necessary, or he stands by and lets the wrong go unanswered."

Another blow out of his breath. Another snicker of his horse. A stamping of the horse's hoof, on the ground. As if it was already ready for tomorrow.

Then Wyatt Earp continued. From a spot he never had before, when talking to her.

"I just knew," he said. "I knew from a very young age, that I wouldn't be able to let wrongs go unanswered. That I wasn't a man who would live with that, and if I'm being honest with you, Miss Easley, if there are other people who can, well, I don't think that much of them."

Maybe it had been China. Maybe it had been the wolf. Maybe it had been the little girl she had hugged, the little girl who had died almost the moment she had found her. Maybe it was all of them, or nothing, but with his words a coin finally landed in her mind. It landed, and whether it was heads or tails, whatever the wolf had called, none of that mattered.

Because she felt, in her bones, the truth of what Wyatt Earp said. And his truth, his words, they didn't strike her as much as become her. Alter her. Transform her in some way. She felt them, twisting her insides.

Knowing then she couldn't do things as she could before. She couldn't sit and write and observe, and let wrongs go unanswered. She didn't think much of the person who could. She didn't think much of herself, not anymore, and she could no longer live life the way she was living.

Her pledge be damned.

The edge of the horizon flared then, briefly. A flash of red and burning orange, of simmering gold and the longest reach of yellow, north and south over the hills. It flared and died away.

Though Wyatt Earp couldn't see her, it was like the man had felt her transform. As if he understood the core of her had changed, to something he said. As if he had found a kindred soul, recognized her, and in recognizing her wanted to share.

Something very human.

He kept speaking. Still facing forward, still facing the west. His words measured and thoughtful, as if speaking directly to her.

"A man doesn't choose this life lightly," he said, one hand patting the neck of his horse, almost absentmindedly. As if telling his stallion that tomorrow would come, soon enough. "And once you're on it, you're on it. You have to see it through, no matter what it costs."

She knew that, now. She perhaps had grown in that understanding, in the lives she had lived, but now that understanding connected with her, in her bones. She understood that if she committed herself in the way Wyatt Earp did, to stop, to alter course, to do anything other than see it through would make her choice worthless.

There could be no half-measures. No stopping. No saying, this, here and now, is enough. There was doing the right thing, and there was commitment, and one could not survive without the other.

She saw it, in the weariness Earp stood with now. Saw it with the man staring at the sunset, and she knew he stared at the burning flames over the horizon and wondered if it was the last one he'd ever see. She knew that, because she had watched him do the same thing, night after night, as she had travelled with him and his gang.

Knew it, even though he never mentioned it. Knew it in the way kindred souls knew more about each other, than any spoken words. So she gathered herself and watched Wyatt Earp face west watch the sun die away. Watched it on his own, taking these questions from her, questions she knew he wondered about, but was perhaps too much of a gentleman to directly ask.

She watched the man, and found herself doing the same. Staring at the dying sun. At the tiny flickers of flame, the subtle embery glow of orange, after the red had burned away. Stared at the sun and wondered, herself, how many sunsets she might see again. Having made the choice she had made.

Was it the lesson the wolf wanted her to learn?

Her eyes were wet. Her chest felt both tight and loose. Tight with worry, and loose with the decision made. Her breaths came uneven, until she stared at the sun and let them out, one by shuddering one.

The two of them had talked in this fashion, for the past week or so. Around each other's meanings. Circling their own truths. It was now, though, that it had come to this. Now that she had learned something, a lesson, and she would take it and go. She would take what she had learned, about a single man driven to do the right thing, no matter what he faced. Driven for a concept he called justice, but to her, was just not standing by as ends come.

Her end, Wyatt Earp's end, or the end of a little girl, it didn't matter. All that mattered was setting your course, setting your course by what you feel, deep in your bones, and seeing it through.

There was comfort there.

The sun slipped over the edge of the mountains. The embers of orange, the simmering gold, the tiny flares of red slowly slipped away with it, as if the colors themselves were being pulled in after the sun, as if quicksand sucked both the sun and its fingers of color in. Just a few minutes, all told, between the dying embers of day, and the darkness of the oncoming night.

Wyatt Earp still stood there. The lawman's eyes still west. He chuckled and patted his horse again, one more time.

"Mighty strange," he said again, as if musing. He turned back, and like always, his eyes lit into her.

His cheeks were thin and covered in dirt, his skin was tanned and dark and leathery from a lifetime of chasing down those who had thought to impose their will on the world, to do unjust things, and to bring them into the light. He was thin and tired. Old and battle-worn, and even if his shoulders slumped in weariness, his back remained ramrod straight under the duster.

His back was straight, and his eyes always flashed. With an intensity of purpose. With an internal fire of a sense of who Wyatt Earp was in this world. The confidence of a man who believed in what he did and was willing to see it through.

There was the flash of his eyes, and a quick turn up of his lips. As if he understood the dance they danced. As if he knew the puzzle of her existed, somewhere in his memory, and that he might never figure it out, but didn't mind always trying. "I ever tell you, Miss Easley, I can't help but feel like I've known you somewhere before."

She wrote all of those words down that night. In the darkness, her back against a low stone, cold against her back. She wrote them in darkness, her eyes able to pick out the page and the lines and the ink. She wrote them, knowing Wyatt Earp stared at her from where he lay, wrapped in a blanket, on the cold earth, with the small fire cracking and popping in the middle of the gunman's posse.

She wrote those words and thought about them. About how, even if Wyatt Earp couldn't remember her, he still remembered something inside her. Something he recognized, as kin did with kin. Something he might have recognized in her, even as far back as when he was a kid. Something that had existed in her, long before she had become aware of it.

She sat there, writing what she knew would be the last words she wrote in this particular book. Knowing the lesson had taken, the coin had been flipped, and it no longer mattered if it was heads or tails.

She neared the end of the page, and wrote towards her own ending.

. . .

And now here I am, observing a ride. Oddly comforted, watching a ride of vengeance, of an older man's quest for justice. A small thing, perhaps compared to China, although the wolf never sends me to small things.

Everything is a lesson to the wolf, and I should remember that.
Everything.
Perhaps I need to learn my own lessons now, too.

She flipped the page, to finish her thoughts. To finish out her chronicle. To end her story, in this particular book.

I flipped the page with her. And then immediately yanked back. Yanked back from the book. Yanked back from the story of the schoolmistress and Wyatt Earp. About the lady the lawman had called Miss Easley.

I pulled back because I had read her next words. I had flipped the page as Miss Easley had back then, as she was writing, following her thoughts and feelings. As I flipped the page it was *then* that the lightning bolt fully struck, as I followed the words of the schoolmistress from one sentence to the next.

The final sentence. The final page of her chronicles, the words I would have read, had a pimp not blared his truck horn in front of my motel room.

Tomorrow I leave this life. I will set this book aside, and go think. Perhaps I will go to the place Doc Holliday keeps telling me about, a place full of evening parties and balls, of people laughing in the streets. He called it New Orleans, and describes a yearly festival called Mardi Gras, a place of magic and merriment. I could use that kind of place, at least I could use it on the outside. A place that I hope can soak into me a bit, before my insides become too dark, too bitter.

The wolf is wrong. I know it. I believe he knows it, too.

I can no longer stand aside and let these wrongs go unanswered. To allow gods to walk around unpunished. To walk a cruel world where the weak suffer, and the strong ignore. To see a world of sorrow descend into despair, while those with real power stride over those who hurt in apathy.

Justice, thy name is Emma-mae Easley.

CHAPTER TWENTY-FOUR

It felt like I sat there for long moments, as the lightning struck. As it danced over the horizon and pulled the curtain back. As each bolt revealed more and more of the mysteries I had been mired in. As each strike of revelation made me more aware of the world I lived in, now.

The largest strike was Emma-mae. I had been sent to find the wolf's daughter. I believe I had found her. There was a reason Fenrir's daughter wasn't in any of the stories about the wolf, it's because he never had one. Not a real daughter, of flesh and bone. Or fur and claw.

A daughter in spirit, perhaps. Someone the wolf had grown close to, over time. Someone he hoped to reclaim, before it was too late. A lost cub he wanted to bring back to the pack.

I sat there for a long moments, in the hotel room. Tiny sounds happened around me, sounds I noticed without noticing. The click of the heating unit turning on, the rushing of air from the vents. The thumps of someone moving around in the room above me, the loud sound of the dropping of a heavy suitcase. The muted garble of a television next door, something turned up way too loud. The same muffled sounds from outside, not a television though, but shouts of people in the streets.

Winds swirled around me. There was a storm coming, today, tomorrow, this week. There was a world-ending storm coming. I felt it, the wolf felt it, the beginnings of that particular cleansing was happening here, in New Orleans. Here and now.

And, like the tornados and waterspouts that briefly appeared at the edges of hurricanes, there were other storms. Whirling winds that swirled around me, of Emma-mae and the wolf. The tangle of the thing between them. Those threads whipped around me and brought in other gods, Saint Expedite, Vidar, Hodr, Huginn and Muninn, Hodr, and who knew what other powers were here. The winds and threads spun around me, they pitched and tossed me around until I could find neither headwind nor tailwind. They were winds I couldn't unravel, from storms I couldn't count, there seemed so many.

What did I feel? So much. The tiny fingers of a little girl, slipping away in the hardest of waves. The stump of a wrist of a dead child, in the slim, fragile fingers of an older woman. The well of sadness from all of that.

So much awareness. So many bolts striking. From just a few pages. What did the bolts reveal about me?

I had began this life with a dream. A dream of writing words that mattered. Of writing something that remained long after I was gone.

That dream had died, and yet a part of it remained. A part of me fought, wanted to save what could be saved. That part of me fought with the wolf, stubbornly argued, with Fenrir. No matter how many times he chuffed and decried, all or none. No matter how many times he howled in pain, his muzzle on his great pillow, no matter the saliva dripping from his slack mouth as the morphine was pumped into him.

Storms upon storms. Winds upon winds. Threads upon threads.

I sat there and stared at the open book. Sat and thought and felt. I had felt a connection to the words of the schoolmistress, from the very first time I had read them. I had felt a similar connection to Emma-mae, from the first time she had sat in front of me, in the diner. No wonder those people had been one and the same.

No wonder, but also a bit of a surprise. Maybe not to the back of my mind, maybe the writer in me had always known, had always felt that connection, but to my front brain, it had been a revelation.

I thought about it. About the flashing of her eyes, as she sat in the booth. The real smile. The real interest she had shown in me. Genuine interest, that I had mistaken for a young girl seeing a young man and being confident enough to come up and say hello. I still remembered that first smile, the first breath of night jasmine, the feel of her across from me. Something both exciting and sweet and wild.

There had been a measuring, back then. I remembered feeling that now, from her. A measuring with a bit of wonder. At the time I had felt it was one of those things you get when your eyes lock with someone else's, and they are sitting there thinking about a future with you, while you're imagining one with them. The few, brief moments of gazes locked that feel like a lifetime.

I understood now, what I had felt wasn't a measuring. It had been a testing. She had come over, testing the waters. She had known who I was, she had given me her name, her real name, wondering if I would know her. If I had read the chronicles of those before me and would recognize her name.

She hadn't been just testing the waters.

In some way, she had been testing me.

I must have passed that test. Passed it, because I was alive now. Alive and still talking with her.

What had Emma-mae been looking for? What had she sensed in me? What had it been, in that brief meeting, that had kept me alive.

Not only kept me alive, but had Emma-mae telling me to dig further. Deeper. To figure out more. Because the meeting at the café had been along the same lines. Almost a second interview, of sorts. A feeling out. A test. As if she was curious about me, about what I'd do, where I'd go. She had told me to go figure it out, told me three times, and here I was, at the bottom of the hole I'd been digging.

I called it the bottom. But there was more there, there would likely always be more to dig up in this particular hole. More I needed to know. I got the same feeling in the air, in my bones, that Emma-mae had described in the book: that of a coin flipping in the air, flashing heads and tails in the light, over and over, wondering how it would land. Wondering if it would be heads or tails. Wondering which was which, wondering what I wanted it to be, what perhaps the landing of the coin *needed* to be.

Was I even figuring this out for Emma-mae? Or was I still digging for the wolf? Could this be a weird three-sided coin, could there be a version where I was digging just for me?

With Ragnarok coming, did any of this really matter?

I shut the book, with the same muffled whump it always shut with. A book too heavy for its size. Too large to be closed easily. I sat there a moment, my finger playing with the teddy bear paw I had stuck between its pages, thinking of two little girls. Emma-mae's, and my own.

The little girl I had lost, back in Sendai. The lesson I believed I had learned there. A lesson Fenrir had sent me there to learn. I played with the paw and let the tears come. Let the sadness come. It always did, thinking of the last moments. Of me holding onto the girl, running, feet pounding the street. The tsunami crashing into the town. The weight of the water slamming into me, the wave picking me up and flinging me forward. The little girl's last screams, as the water swallowed the two of us and tore us apart.

I had written of this once. And shied away from the words, the thoughts since. Because there were forces too great to fight. There was a strength greater than my own. I had learned that, I had learned the little girl would always be torn from my grasp, no matter how hard I tried to hold onto her.

No matter how hard I always wanted to hold onto her.

I had wrote more, then. About all the things I had seen after. The devastation. The old lady, walking around, calling out in Japanese for someone, before she finally collapsed on the wet street, face down, and sobbed there. The young man who had gone over finally and pulled her up, who had hugged her to him and let her cry, for what seemed like forever.

The broken buildings. The dead bodies, stacked along the streets. The hopeful eyes of the men and women digging out those trapped, timber by timber, stone by stone, brick by brick. The sadness the rescuers all turned away with, over and over, as they found more bodies. The continued hope that warred with the repeated sadness.

And, occasionally, a shout of exclamation. Not one of joy, but one of life. Of finding someone who lived.

I had wrote about all of that.

I still cried about it now.

And I would never forget it. Never forget wishing for my own death, moments before the wave crashed into me. Never forget the tiny body I held clutched in my arms, the soft warmth of a child, pressed tightly to my chest. The silken hair brushing my cheek one last moment and then—with enormous, overwhelming force—just gone.

I took a large, hiccupping breath, and followed that with a large sniff. There was wetness inside my nostrils, and I sniffed harder through my nostrils again. Took the palm of my hand and pressed it into the corner of each eye. Once. Twice. The finger of my other hand still playing with the teddy bear paw.

Storms upon storms. Threads upon threads. The book sat there, mocking me with its silhouette of Yggdrasil. Huginn and Muninn had returned, they sat there, perched above Odin, swinging slightly in an invisible breeze, and I felt like I could hear the ravens cawing.

Thought and memory, mocking me too.

I realized, then, that my first flip of the book hadn't been an accident. The one earlier, before reading about Wyatt Earp. I hadn't opened it to the last page of the Chronicler before me because my fingers had been a little damp from holding the beer. I had asked the book where I needed to go, and it had told me, as much as the book could.

It had told me to go to The Black Penny.

Then I had tried something different. I had thought about the reason I had come here in the first place. To find the wolf's daughter.

I had been to The Black Penny. The book was telling me to go there again, but I felt like it was just reminding me that's where I had gone. That's where I had gone, following the Chronicler before me.

He had left there, I felt. He had likely been given the same information I had, to go to Jean Lafitte's Blacksmith Shop Bar. A place Vidar had strongly discouraged me from going.

Had that Chronicler failed Emma-mae's test, then? Had he failed Hodr's test, had he been less of a Finn MacCool than I? Or had Vidar just decided to kill that Chronicler, decades ago?

Threads upon threads.

Like the one tied around Odin's neck. The shadow of Huginn's beak opened and closed on the cover. Once, twice. Muninn stayed quiet, to the side. Odin hung there, drifting. In the stories he had hung there for nine nights. He had been on the cover of this book far longer than that. There was more information there. More thought was needed, perhaps there was more memory to be read, more the birds mocked me with. Mocked me, or tried to tell me.

Likely whatever they wanted me to know was old. Maybe written in the Nordic runes I had seen, in the beginning. Awareness of an event that had happened tens of thousands of years ago.

I had enough of awareness for now. Enough of sad feelings and wonderings. Enough of the feeling of the oncoming storm, the worry and fear and the wondering if it was something I need to stop. If it was something I could stop.

I was just a writer, after all. I wasn't Thor, or Odin, or Tyr or Frey. I wasn't a god of war like Mars, or an Achilles reborn, someone who could fight as naturally as I drew breath. I had a good size to me, but I wasn't strong like Hercules. I wasn't any of the warlike gods.

Hell, I wasn't even any of the unwarlike gods.

I was just a guy with a pen. As much as they say the pen is mightier than a sword, I have yet to see someone take a pen into battle. Especially a battle with gods.

If Ragnarok was coming, how the hell could I stop it? How could I stand up to that tsunami of a wave, waving my pen, and hold onto anything here in this world? How could I stand among gods who warred with each other, warred over the ending of the world, and save anything, much less myself?

The curl of my lips was... bitter. Frustrated. I was aware of more, that was for sure, aware of everything but how to stop what was coming. How to save those who might need saving. How to prepare, so that a few remained, after the crashing of the wave.

I shook my head and got up. Slipped the book into its usual place in the satchel. Slid Gungnir in its spot next to the book.

I wanted a gun. Or a knife. I had neither. I had gotten into the same fights as a kid all kids did, but I wasn't a brawler. I hadn't served in the army or the marines. I wasn't a fighter. Or a killer.

I was just a writer.

A writer who felt like he was going into battle.

A writer who felt like he was standing there, looking out the window of his room, into the dying sunset, of orange and reds that slipped into the dark night hanging above New Orleans. Wondering if that was the last sunset I'd ever see. Wonder if it was the last sunset New Orleans would see.

Would it be tonight that the storm hit? Tomorrow night? The day after? I had no sense of Ragnarok, other than its nearness. The swelling strength of the winds. The wild push of a front. The rising tide of the sea.

I let out a breath. There was no sense putting it off. Whatever I was going to have to face next, I needed to face it. Now, tomorrow, the day after.

Face it without a gun or magic sword. Without a mirror-like shield or golden knife. Without anything but what I had, even if I felt like I needed more.

All I had was what I carried with me. The book, the pen, Skidblandir and Hulinhjàlmr. Those things, my wallet, some I.D., and a little cash. And whatever I felt like I needed, all I really had to have were the last two things for a night out on the town.

I took a final breath and headed out. To Lafitte's Blacksmith Shop Bar. Something I had trouble writing without misspelling, much less saying five times fast. I headed out with a book and a pen, a wallet and some cash, to see what more I could figure out.

No sense in putting off tomorrow's troubles, today, right?

CHAPTER TWENTY-FIVE

Lafitte's Blacksmith Shop Bar looked exactly how it sounded.

It certainly looked old, with dark brick and wood on the outside, with a rustic feel that felt like I stood outside a shop a hundred years in the past, and could have easily been a hundred years older than that. It was low, squat, with a pitched roof and shuttered windows. It felt a bit like a French Creole cottage, and the shuttered lanterns and flickering candles around the outside of the bar made me feel like any moment Paul Revere would ride past me screaming the British were coming.

I shivered. It was colder now, cold and I hadn't worn a coat. I wasn't wearing Hulinhjàlmr, either. I had left the magic hat off, wanting to step into this place as myself, for whatever reason.

I had felt the time for disguises were past. If I was going to face my end, I was going to face it as me. I might rage and scream, I couldn't say I wouldn't, but I'd do it as myself, and not some New Orleans Saints fan.

A man has to have some dignity.

I walked up to the door. A sign hung above it, a light wooden thing with the words Lafitte's Blacksmith Shop Bar burned into it, long scrawls and etches and streaks of black. There was a little plaque to the side of the door, talking about the bar, how long it had been there on Bourbon Street, its use as a smuggling base back in the days of Jean Lafitte and his probable or non-probable piracy. There were a few dates, some words about how it was the oldest known bar in the states, and that was it.

I got the feeling, reading it a bit, that it was probably missing the important stuff.

Like what I might find inside.

There I paused, on the outside of the bar, for a long moment. Wondering what I was doing. I finally shrugged to myself and opened the door.

The inside felt much like the outside. It was dark, intimate, with shadows everywhere that could hide anything. The walls inside were of the same old, rough brick as those on the outside of the bar. The only light came from candles, candles hanging from the ceiling, candles in sconces on the walls, candles on tables, all the flames flickering and dancing on their own, out of tune with each other and the rest of the world.

There were no televisions playing sports, there wasn't a jukebox playing something jazzy or bluesy. There was a good-sized crowd. There was a brick fireplace in the center of the place, with a small fire burning in it. A few chairs before it, the chairs taken with people tipping back beers.

Wooden stools and benches were everywhere, as well as an odd, authentic blacksmith tool or two. Tongs here, an anvil there. A hammer in the corner, on a small table, handle high in the air. The bar area was compact, with bottles lined up on wooden shelves behind it, a few shelves with the same liquors I'd expect in any bar, as if the bartender was serving the same things he had been serving for centuries.

The bartender wasn't X. He was a heavy-set man with a broad chest, wearing a white shirt with the collar open. His hair was long and unruly, hanging around his face and head, and shifted to move around his face as he looked around and took, then made, orders. His hands seemed too large for the bottles and glasses he shook and poured into, and poured from.

Some music played from a piano off to the side. The woman playing it was dressed almost like a pirate, white shirt and black vest, red bandana holding dark hair back from her forehead, gold rings in her ears and nose, gold bracelets up and down her wrists. She played something that wasn't fast, wasn't slow, something that seemed to just keep things going as they were. Keep drinks pouring. Keep people talking. Keep some of them swaying in their seats. Like water flowing.

There were a lot of people there. I looked for Hodr and Vidar, saw neither. But there were a lot of others in the crowd. Of all sizes and colors and genders. Of humans and gods and saints alike, if who I thought gathered here were drinking, tonight.

Jean Lafitte had used this bar as a base of operations. For his probably pirating, sure. For his definite smuggling. He used it as a place to take out the British, too, in an oddly placed sense of nationalism. It was an old place, the stage of a play where plenty had happened, and plenty would happen, through life. A place where plenty of happenings had happened, through history.

And quite possibly one more.

The bar was packed, with men and women standing, holding out their hands with fingers out, signaling one, two, or many drinks. As big as the bartender was, he seemed to keep up with the constant orders, making a mixed drink as fast as pouring a round of shots.

Still, the crowd was thick. There wasn't a place for me to order a beer. Or a person to ask. Until my eyes got to the end of the bar.

There was a stool there, at the corner. An empty stool at the edge of the bar, next to a woman.

A woman with long legs, long red hair bound up loosely behind her head, a woman sitting and facing the door of the bar. Holding a little shot glass of something dark in her fingers. Holding the glass and sipping from it, just a bit, before tipping it to me in a little salute.

Emma-mae.

Something shifted inside me. I felt like a kid, like I was eight years old and about to ask a girl for the first time onto the gymnasium floor for a dance. Wondering if I even knew how to dance. If I was about to muck all this up.

I almost shook my head. Silly is as silly does. I put on a brave face and pushed my way through the crowd. I didn't push too hard, not knowing who was a god and who wasn't, if any of them were, so I figured on being careful all the same.

Still, a crowd was a crowd. A drinking crowd more so. And the place seemed to have more patrons than seats. It was a bit of work getting through them.

The piano played in that flowing way some pianists have. Where the keys are struck so hard as rolled over, so the music isn't banging out so much as drift from one note to the next, where one chord glided into the next, so that the song never really just began or ended, it just continued. It sunk through the crowd in a way none of them seemed to notice, even if the occasional eyes glanced over to the pianist, or a person caught themselves starting to sing words to a song they may never have heard before.

When I got to the empty stool Emma-mae had finished her shot, and had held up two fingers. The big bartender had just slid them down in front of her when I sat down. I winked at her and picked up mine, sniffing the liquor before tasting it.

It was cold. Dark. And licorice-scented.

Jaeger, to those of us who know her.

Jägermeister to those who have missed that particular introduction.

I tried not to frown. Much. Jaeger and I had a history, but then I think you could say that about a lot of college kids.

The bar was packed. Packed with people, shoulder-to-shoulder, but for some reason everyone left enough room around Emma-mae, and by extension me. There was a pocket of space around us, that the loud-talking of those around us didn't seem to penetrate. It was like we had a little world just for the two of us.

Emma-mae winked at me, a quick thing. We tinked our shot glasses together. And sipped, carefully. Her words maybe just as careful. Her eyes locked with mine.

"You figure it out?"

It was an odd feeling, I had then. For a long time I had been the only person doing what I was doing. The only Chronicler in the world. I had been on the outside of life for a decade, writing, observing, journaling.

And now there were two of us.

Two of us who had served the wolf. Two of us who had travelled the world and observed humanity for him. Two of us who had been sent out to observe, and quite possibly bait, other gods.

Two of us together at one time, when in the history of the book, there had always been one. Two Chroniclers together in one time, and one place. Two of us, who had shared some of the same sorrows, even if we had lived different lives.

I'm not sure I'll describe this well. It was like being the only man in the world, and then walking up on the first woman. Like being alone all your life and never knowing that your life was something you could share, until you met another human and realized that possibility. Maybe, perhaps, something like Adam might have felt, walking up and first seeing Eve.

A flood of emotions ran through me. All quick and sudden, and nothing I could really identify in the moment, but understood more after they had left. There was a curiosity, and a need. There was want and warmth. There were dreams and wishes, all of them unknown, or unrecognized, until this moment. There was all of that with the thrilling feel of rushing down a rollercoaster, of being on something that was too late to stop.

There was all of that, and more. More because all of a sudden there was someone here who would understand. Understand me. Who I was, what I did. Understand, and who I could share understandings with.

There was someone with which to share sorrow. To share that particular burden. To talk about children neither one of us had known, and yet each of us still carried around that particular loss.

I nodded. "Wyatt Earp, huh," I said. I had never been next to someone like that, not a legend, not in my time chronicling. Other than Fenrir, and now the gods here in New Orleans. "Seemed like an intense kind of guy."

Her eyes went back a moment, in memory. Just a tiny fade before coming back to the here and now. "You read it," she said, as if checking another thing off that list I felt she had. "Good."

She took another sip. Didn't grimace, but allowed the bite of the black licorice taste to show itself in her face, before nodding. "He was, Finn." Nodding some more. "He certainly was."

The taste dissolved, and Emma-mae sat there, thinking. Her eyes on me and not. Seeing me, and seeing something else. Maybe something in her past.

"Is that what you're doing, now?" I asked. "You on Emma-mae's last ride?"

A laugh burst from her. "Come on, Finn. You're a writer. Does the ending come first? Or do you have to work your way to it."

I shrugged. "Thought I'd try."

The laugh disappeared from her face. We both sat there, on the edge of something. The crowd drank and murmured around us the way crowds in bars did. The chords of the piano came and went, soft and hard, through the murmurs and laughs and clinks of drinks.

She leaned closer. Her Jaeger loose in her hand. Her face both here and lost to me, both here staring at me intensely and somewhere else.

"Let me ask you a favor," she said, and all of a sudden the scent of night jasmine was the only thing I could smell, even in the bar, even surrounded by all the people here. All of a sudden I felt her there, felt her, and felt all that nervousness that came with that feeling. The sad memories, the quiet hopes, the slight chance of shared dreams. From me, and from her.

I had come here expecting a battle. I had come here expecting to find gods, and some thick plot about destroying a world. About vengeance, long in the planning. I hadn't come here expecting this.

Even if I felt like I wanted it. Wanted her. In that way you meet someone and know that your souls are close enough to be shared. Know that two people can all of a sudden become one.

I was pretty sure my voice didn't squeak. "Sure."

Her eyes had been on me, that whole moment. That whole moment that felt like years. They glistened a bit, happy, sad, I couldn't tell and couldn't know. She brought her hand to her mouth, the hand holding the Jaeger loosely between her thumb and forefinger, and tipped a bit into her mouth like pouring a bit of fresh milk from a pail.

She swallowed. Long and slow, the muscles of her throat contracting with the motion, something I couldn't, for some reason, pull my eyes away from. The skin there, long and pale, delicate and yet firm. Strong.

"It's been a long time," she said. "Hundreds of years, of being Emma-mae. Of being around other gods, and powers. It's been a long time, just to be around someone like me. Someone who might understand, someone…"

She was just saying the same words she knew I felt. The connection. The things that tied us both together, that we both were. The things we both had seen and endured. I sensed all of that in her, just like she saw and felt it in me.

Those things, and more. There was something like weariness in her face, the flickering of a candle burned to the very last bit of wick. Shadows, haunting the corners of her eyes. Weariness and a haunting that spoke of a long ride, a long ride that had begun with something like purpose, and was closing in on desperation.

Emma-mae knocked back the rest of her shot, quickly, looking away. Or not looking away so much as tucking her forehead onto her forearm. A motion again hinting at exhaustion, of a will rode long past weariness. She sat there a moment, head tucked against the crook of her elbow, the fingers of her other hand slowly raising, calling for more shots.

Four fingers.

I didn't quite gulp.

Her head moved, just a bit. Emma-mae looked at me from over her forearm. Her eyes glistening in something that could be happy, could be sad, could be both. Her words soft and close, spoken with a timbre that resonated deep inside of me, words that brought a shiver-like feeling to my spine.

"Can I just be Emma, tonight? Can we be Emma and Huck, just for this night? Just for now?"

Her eyes stayed on me. Knowing what she was asking me. Knowing what she was asking, with what I was doing here, and with what was coming. She knew it, and still asked, in that soft, close timbre. Her mouth curving into something small and delicious and just between her and I.

"Just the two of us, with a devil-may-care to the rest of the world?"

Her eyes were locked with mine. The rollercoaster I was on sped down the longest of hills. It brought a rushing with it that blurred the rest of the world. That blurred everything around by the descent, the pounding clickety-clacks of metal on track, the pounding of my heart, the rush and pounding and the blurred world around me, around us, just me and Emma-mae.

"Emma—" I said, slowly, and stopped.

I hadn't known what I was going to say, and I don't know that I would ever know. I don't know, even now, if I was going to say no. If I was going to ask her about Ragnarok and her role in it. If I was going to ask her to stop whatever was happening so that the world could go on revolving, like it had for millions of years.

I'll never know.

Because when I had said Emma, at the first mention of the first of her names, her face took on some glow. Something that came from deep inside her chest. Something screaming of relief, some intense mix of desire and want and need, of letting go, of burdens carried and burdens demanding to be shared, all of that threaded with the thinnest of hopes, it was all of that and more with her looking at me and *my god*, if you've never been around a woman who looked at you with all of that, I'll tell you, it's irresistible.

It's a power all its own.

So forgive me, if I ended up putting the world aside for a few hours. For a night, even. For at least, here with Emma, here and now.

After all, there might not be too many moments left. And when you find one that might be special, that might be incredible, no matter what you're doing, no matter where you are or what's happening in the world around you, no matter how short or long that moment might be you have to take it, no matter the cost, if you're staring into the eyes of a person who feels the same.

CHAPTER TWENTY-SIX

I have to say, that first group of four shots of Jaeger weren't the last soldiers we stood upside down on that bar top.

I don't know what kind of regiment we finally set up. Or battalion. Or army. Armies. I lost count after the first four, and I'm sure Emma did too. We drank and sat and laughed in the beginning, we talked the way people new to each other do, with our stools slowly sliding closer and closer together, until I was right next to her, until she was leaning into me. Until I was sipping from the shot of Jaeger she was holding against my lips, and her from mine. Until we felt alone in that bar, until I felt her hair against the side of my face, lying with a silken feel against my throat, as she tucked herself a bit against me. Until the world passed by in that drunken blur we've all seen at some point in our lives.

We sat that way, Emma against me, and talked. Not about the important things. Well, not about the things that other people might think were important. Not about gods or endings, not about wolves and Ragnarok, but little moments we could share about our own lives. Little laughs, little cries, moments we were proud of. Moments we were ashamed of.

Emma was that kind of person.

Me too.

I told her about the cancer, about the raging in the hospital bed. About the steaming burns of the expresso machine, and the tripping on a piece of sidewalk I could see, about the pain behind my eye, about losing the ability to write, and she gave me the oddest look then, a look full of that wondering that lots of alcohol brings, about that brilliant insight you almost have in the drunken middle of swirling shot after swirling shot.

She told me about her own time. About being born with something wrong with her heart. About not knowing what that might be, back in the days she had been born. With medical care, with science then not being what it was today. The doctor just told her parents she had a weak constitution, there was a faint murmur over the chest, a congenital defect of the heart.

She had air-quoted the words. Rolling her eyes. I got it.

She told me about her shortness of breath, just moving around. That she had gotten tired easily, and even as a kid fighting that tiredness with a sheer force of will. That she worked herself into long fatigues, then after long weeks of rest would get up and work herself into another.

I felt like she was restless, then. A restless spirit, something primal. Something searching for meaning, even as a kid.

She had told me about *Reagen's Journey*. About how much she had connected with the story, of a girl who thought she had been walking a world alien to her, before realizing the world was her own, just seen in a different light, from another angle, from a shifted perspective. She had loved to read, from back as a kid, during her sickness. Her parents had made sure of it, buying whatever books and stories they could, letting her read in bed until Emma could get back outside.

That had been her life. Emma fighting her body until she collapsed back into bed. Reading there until she could get back up. And that cycle continuing until her heart had finally decided it was giving up and she was on her deathbed. At the young age of twenty-two.

There was no Doctor Berley then. But the wolf had found Emma still. Had hooked her, with his promise of life. Of a life where she could be restless forever. Where she could read and write and discover everything she had been missing.

And that was just perhaps the surface of what we talked about. The surface of what I remember, at least. The drinks kept coming, and there were other moments of other things in the middle of the night. Interruptions.

Looking back, I'm sure they were gods. There was a dark-skinned young man, tall, impossibly tall, with a thin gold circlet holding back a short length of dark hair, hair so short it almost didn't need the band. There was an older man with white hair and a long white beard, walking around with a long stick that might loosely be called a cane. Another woman, small, lightly browned, with a bald head under a colorful robe. There was a young group of women, women who almost felt like warriors, and plenty other men and women, even a shorter fellow who might have been a dwarf, though I wasn't sure I could use that name in today's world, even if that was what he might actually be.

All of that was lost in the blur. Those brief interruptions would pull Emma-mae off of me, would pull the both of us in the deep lake of being together, and the two of us would surface and speak to whomever had done the interrupting. She would introduce us, though the names escaped me now. There would be some loose talk among us, a measuring frown, and then they would be gone and we would be flinging up four fingers and diving back into the deep lake of us. Finn to Huck, and Emma-mae to Emma.

She mentioned *Reagen's Journey* once or twice to some of them. To my surprise, they nodded. With us drinking, sometimes even the two of us talked about it. Emma, smiling, just a bit, her lips wet with Jaeger, talking about how it was a story about hope. About no matter what kind of world we think ourselves in, that just the smallest shift of perspective could change everything.

Had I written it about hope? I hadn't thought so at the time. I had just wanted to write something that mattered, and so I disagreed. With a smile and a shot of my own. Emma smiled, and much like pancakes and hash, we both talked and dreamed and looked towards a future that may never exist past this night.

The night rolled on. Forever in my mind, and yet a blink of an eye. There was a very drunk time where we had sat with the woman playing the piano. The pirate-looking woman, with the gold bangles and jewelry and the red bandana. I think her name was Gaia. Though I can't swear to it now. And, likely enough, couldn't then. She could have been a god just as much as she could have been a woman who liked dressing like a pirate; I just remembered sitting next to her and singing (I have no idea what song) and laughing and drinking together, with the occasional banging of accidental keys by yours truly.

There were laughs, then, with Emma and me. Emma and Huck. We laughed and drank and sang. We laughed and drank and danced, the dance of people far younger than us, dancing with energy and zest for life, with being alive. Then the piano changed its tune and we ended up in something much slower. Something where I felt the curve of her body against mine, where she fit in all the right places, where she breathed and I felt her lungs swell up, where her heart beat and I could feel the pounding of it in her chest, where I felt the shuddering, aching exhale of her breath, warm and soft, against my throat.

It wasn't long after that we both were gone. Gone from Lafitte's Blacksmith Shop Bar. Gone to her place.

I couldn't tell you where that was. Because when the moment had happened, it had happened fast. That rollercoaster was rocketing down the hill, it was racing and pulling the two of us with it, and there was no getting off. All of a sudden I went from slowly dancing, little side-to-side steps, feeling Emma's warm body against mine, my arms around her back, holding her in a way that I knew I never wanted to let go from. My palms open and on the very small of her back, my fingers there at the top of her waist, feeling the slight curve there rounding out her backside.

There was the shuddering exhale. The warm breath against my neck. A small sound, something that might have been oooooooohhh, that lowercase o-sound that was soft and could have been me, it could have been Emma, and which could have gone on forever.

And then we were gone.

Back to her place.

To a night I'll never, ever, want to forget. As much of a blur as the evening had been. As much time rushed by me, as much as blurred by us. There was her, and there was me, and for this moment, for this time, that's all I think I had ever wanted out of life.

CHAPTER TWENTY-SEVEN

I woke to a pounding headache.

In an unfamiliar bed.

In an unfamiliar room.

Bundled in a thick blanket. An old blanket, cream-colored with streaks of red, threadbare in places. Old and heavy and thick and warm, the mattress lumpy and soft and too small for me, much less the two of us.

The headache was to be expected. The bed and room too. The bed frame was old black iron, with a curved iron headboard, flaky in places. Something smaller than a queen bed, larger than a full, built of another time and for other-sized people. I remember now the two of us, Emma and me, figuring out how to both be on it at the same time. Figuring it out and laughing, and then… figuring it out and not.

I remembered the feel of Emma against me as we slept. Waking up at times throughout the night, feeling her warm skin against mine. The rise and fall of her chest against mine. The beat of her heart, beating soft and slow, with mine.

The warm exhales, stirring the hair on my chest.

Warm exhales, missing now. Her warmth missing. Her body missing.

I looked around the room, a place I hadn't seen much of the night before. There was an old light above me, a lightbulb in a socket with a string. The room was dark, the dark of early morning, the light revealing a small bedroom, with the not-a-queen-and-not-a-full bed in it.

I groaned, softly. Moved, just a bit. Looking around and blinking, rubbing my eyes, my face, feeling thirsty, my throat dry. The wallpaper of the room was old and peeling, wallpaper of cream and flowers, flowers hanging in strips here and there.

The wall was dark, shadowed, even if there was some light in the room. Among the strips of wallpaper were objects, hanging on hooks, set on the wall like someone might put a hunting rifle on a cradle. Only there was no rifle. There was an old sceptre hanging upside down from a hook, with a yellowed bone-like rod thick as a wrist ending in a round, bronze ball. There was a pair of sharp bronze wings on either side of the ball, the wings covered with an intricate, lotus-like motif. The end of the sceptre was bronze or gold, aged, and words were inscribed along the shaft and ball of it. Words from a language I didn't understand and couldn't see fully in the shadows, but which could be Hindu.

There were other objects there. A collection. There was a long, silver, two-handed sword, the tip of the blade with a tiny chip. There was a long spear, white like it was made of bone. A katana, slightly curved, in its dark wooden saya case. A claw made of stone. A rounded circlet with a stick figure through the twist of the circle. A single arrow on a tiny shelf.

And more. All on the shadowed wall. A collection, from someone who might have spent decades or more collecting them. A lifetime, or more.

My body ached a bit. I stretched and kept holding back a groan. Somehow I was still wearing pants, but not my shirt. Sometime during the night I must have put those back on. Or Emma had.

The hangover was massive. It pounded in my skull, even if the wolf's powers had already reduced it some. They would even heal it completely, in time, though I may never have tested his powers to this degree before, with that much Jaeger. It had been a hell of a night. Huck and Emma and really poured one on.

There was a bookshelf to the side of the bed, with a number of books on it. Old classics, like *The Count of Monte Cristo*, like *The Woman in White* by Wilkie Collins, *Paradise Lost* by John Milton. There were newer books mixed among the classics, a few Jack Reachers, another book called *The Red Shirts*, even some romance, like *Angels Fall* by Nora Roberts.

Plenty of variety, on the tiny shelf. None of the books new, all trade paperbacks with torn covers and yellowed pages (on the older books, at least). Well-worn books, read many times, classics and science fiction and romance and fantasy and a stack of Asimov's magazines—which I knew, embarrassingly enough—if I'd looked through them I'd find the issue with my only published work.

My eyes followed the wall around the bookshelf. Seeing the strips of flowers, hanging and peeling from yellow, faded wallpapered walls. Feeling thirst, my throat rough, wanting some water to quench the dryness in my throat. Feeling the quilt of the bed move around me as I moved, rustling a bit, the mattress moving, the wire springs holding the bed above the frame squeaking just the tiniest bit.

My head hurt. It pounded. It had been a lot of Jaeger. I stretched with another groan, my head pounding with those beating thumps that I knew would get worse throughout the day. My hand reached out of its own accord, searching that warm spot Emma had lain in next to me, feeling just a coldness there now.

There was a little light in the room. It came from a window, in the wall across from the foot of the bed. An old, thick curtain had been pulled the slightest bit aside, letting in a sliver of sunlight. The small yellow beam poured through the slim gap between the curtain and the edge of the window, it fell at a slant across the room, dividing the room in two, as well as the small oak desk in front of the window.

The desk was an old thing, like the room, an old thing with wax fading in patches and peeling away in others. The beam of sunlight cut from that back corner of the desk, across the wood to a chair in front of it, to Emma sitting in the chair, sitting with my T-shirt hanging around her, a glass of water on the desk and the book open before her, the sunlight burrowed in the book's open spine.

Not just any book.

The book.

The one I wouldn't name.

It was open, but Emma wasn't reading it. She was looking back at me, her fingers playing with the teddy bear paw left in the fold of the book, the fingers moving almost absentmindedly. As if she had read something and had looked back at me, lost in some kind of thought or wonder, lost watching me sleep.

Her eyes caught mine.

I felt the same thing I had felt last night. The whole thing, from the whole night. Everything I had felt from her, from the beginning until the end. I felt the will in the woman, the drive, the restlessness. I felt the shadows and the haunting and the weariness. The desire that consumed her.

I felt all of that, and I felt the dead girl in her arms, Emma's tight hug around her. The hug that seemed to go on forever. I felt all of that along with an unrelenting force in Emma, a force that would be almost unrecognized if you passed her by in the street, until she looked at you like she was looking at me.

Then you would feel it. You'd recognize it. The sheer strength of it in her gaze would stop you in your tracks.

I felt all of that. I felt the anger and the pain and the quiet rage. The haunting loneliness, the weariness of the ride. I felt all of that just like I felt the thin thread of hope running through everything else, as if the barest hope could hold Emma together.

I felt all of that, even as Emma looked at me and offered the shiest of smiles.

Wow.

It takes a moment to recover from a gaze like that. From an offering like that. From that kind of intensity colored with a mix of wishing and fear.

"Hope you don't mind," she said, her fingers leaving the teddy bear paw, her hand smoothing the page of the book in a zig-zag motion before closing it with that soft, muffled whump. "It's been some time."

She had been reading it. And it was hard to tell, with the book being the way it was, half-open, what she had been reading there. I thought it likely she had been reading my stories, my chronicles, and I guess I might have done the same in her place.

Funny, how it had taken me forever to read the stories of those who had come before me. To read Emma's story. And how quickly she had gone to read mine.

I think I understood myself a little better now. Maybe it was something human in all of us, to avoid reading what's happened, but to keep reading ahead. Maybe there was always something in us that hoped for a better future, and some part that still refused to study the past, no matter what we might learn from it.

I wondered what it might be like, to read the direction of the world long after I had finished writing. To know where I had began, to see the world years after I had written in a different place, a different destination than perhaps one I had written of, and wonder at what point had the direction of everything changed. And if it had changed for the better, or the worse.

I thought about my wondering. About what it might mean in the scope of what I faced. And thought, for the better or the worse, at least there was someone else writing. At least there was a world to write about.

Natural, right? To hope we still have time to make things better. To hope that things do get better, no matter what we've left in our past.

Emma's hand lay on the cover of the shut book. Her fingers traced the tree now, as if they had to do something. First the teddy bear paw, then zig-zagging down the spine of the book, now tracing the branches of Yggdrasil. As if, even now, Emma was restless.

"It's funny," she said. "You call this the book."

I rose my eyebrows. Feeling like if I spoke, at best it would be a croak. Eying that glass of water on the desk next to Emma.

"It's always been Sogur Endalok to me."

I tried an answer. "Yeah."

My voice definitely croaked a bit. I understood that, as much as we were the same, in this Emma and I were different. In how we thought about the book. After the night before, everything we shared, as close as we felt to each other with all our understandings of who we were, what we did, and why… this one thing we thought about differently.

A small thing, perhaps.

"You know the story?" she asked. Her fingers tracing the branches, her hand placed in the center of the cover, where I knew Odin usually swung.

"Of Odin?" I croaked again.

She smiled at me and got up, bringing me her glass of water. It was an old glass, an old country glass, a little yellowed with age, with tiny pits in the surface. As if she had found it in an alley somewhere, or a trash dump, or some country farmhouse a hundred years ago. I tested it, and then sipped heavily. The water was cool, refreshing, and I tried to not finish it all before handing it back.

Emma took the glass, sitting on the bed next to me, in the place she had lain in for the night. The tiny spot on the edge of the lumpy mattress. She sat there holding the water in both hands, her T-shirt hanging loose from her shoulders, her red hair unbound and free around her head.

She moved a little, settling in, and the bed leaned a little under her weight, the iron springs squeaked again, which brought back memories of the night before, even as all I felt was the warmth of the side of her leg pressed hard into mine.

There she sat. Sipping the water in tiny sips. Waiting.

"I know he hung himself on the tree," I said. "He stabbed himself with Gungnir, right? And hung there for nine nights."

He had stabbed himself with the spear Gungnir, of course. Not the pen. He had offered himself as a sacrifice, for greater knowledge. At least, that was the story.

She nodded. "But do you know why?"

I felt like she was testing me. I felt like she already knew me in this, knew what I knew, and this was her way of telling me things she felt like I needed to know. After all, I only knew what the stories said. The same stories she had heard and read, as a child.

"He wanted wisdom," I said. Slowly. "Wisdom for the runes."

She cocked her head, and let me think that through.

I had said *for the runes*. The words had just come out, following the word I had said before, wisdom. It had been a natural sentence, maybe even something I had thought about before, so it was something I had read or known. And yet, thinking now, it was something I had known and never really wondered about.

What runes could Odin need? What might he sacrifice himself for? He was a god. He was a god of gods. He helped create the world we lived in today. That was power, a universe-creating type of power, all its own.

What rune, or runes, could Odin possibly need after that?

I frowned. Wincing a bit as I thought. Feeling the heavy hammering of a headache in my head.

Emma kept watching me. Carefully. Following the train of my thoughts, not saying anything for fear of derailing them.

Odin, along with his brothers, had created this world from the remains of the giant Ymir. The primordial giant. Ymir's flesh became the earth, his blood turned into the oceans, lakes, rivers. His bones formed the mountains, teeth rocks and pebbles, his skull created the sky, his brain the clouds. Odin and his brothers had formed Midgard, this world, and bound it to all the other worlds by Yggdrasil. Bound it to worlds of fire and ice, of dwarves and Vanir and Aesir, of all the worlds, by the eternal tree.

If I thought about that, really, the power needed for that type of creation was something I just couldn't fathom. Gods themselves and their powers were hard enough. Understanding they existed, and then understanding their powers were vastly different things. Understanding how much power was needed, well, it was like trying to think about infinity. And whatever number you think of, no matter how large, no matter how many digits, there was always a number larger.

If you think of ten, there's an eleven. If you think of a billion, there's always a billion and one. A billion and two. And so on. Trillions. Zillions. No matter how big the number, no matter how large the power, I couldn't get it. I couldn't understand it.

I just knew a god's power was large. Larger than I could truly understand. So understanding the power of creation of creating humans and the world we lived in, of the cosmos, of all other worlds, of Muspelheim and Niflheim and Asgard and Vanaheim and the rest, it was just too immense for me to *get*.

So why would Odin need more power? Why would he look for more wisdom? Why, in particular, would he look for the wisdom *of the runes*? He had already created the world and everything in it, what more would Odin want? What more could the god of gods need?

Then it struck me. Creators had a certain ego. If you asked any of them, a painter, a rock band, a god, they all would want the thing they created to survive. To last forever. To last long after they themselves had left the Earth.

I grew cold at that realization, but the understanding went deeper. Further. It tied together with something else.

Before Odin had hung himself from Yggdrasil, before he had went to seek the wisdom of runes from the Tree of Life, the tree that had its roots *everywhere*, he had gone to a well. And not just any well, to Mimir's well. To the Well of Wisdom at one of the oldest roots of the great tree, in Jotunheim.

Odin had gone to the well seeking wisdom—again—wisdom for knowledge of the universe, to be given a greater understanding. To see beyond time and space, to see out in the cosmos and understand *it all*.

He had done that before seeking knowledge of runes, so something in the well had scared the god. Something in the knowledge he had gained, knowledge given to him from the Tree of Life, had driven a fear deep in the god. Something so deep he had offered himself as a sacrifice, for the runes to stop it.

My eyes connected with Emma's. Her brow was narrowed just a bit over her emerald irises, shadowed now in the early morning of the room. I could feel her, right behind me on the train of thought, urging me to keep going. I could feel the connection between us, urging me to take another step.

Like she had told me to figure it out, back at the café. Like she had told me, *three times*, to figure it out. Telling me to go back to The Black Penny.

To meet X. To understand there were other gods in our world. Other powers, other saints.

The coldness inside me widened. A shiver ran along the chasm of ice, a shiver that threatened to run across my spine. I understood, then, what Odin had seen at the well. What he had given up his eye to see. What had the god shaking him to his core, and had Odin offer his life up for knowledge of the runes.

A creator might have power over their creation. But not of all creations. Yggdrasil had shown Odin other worlds, other creations, other gods. It was the Tree of Life, and as Emma had told me, the Tree of Life was bound to everything, it was the *Tree of Life,* its roots dug everywhere, touched everything, and it had shown Odin all of it.

And as much power as Odin might have, over his world, his creation, he didn't have power over them all. He had seen many universes, many gods, many other creations.

And, Odin had seen many endings. All the other endings, of all the other creations. All the other endings of all the other worlds. Ending to their world, their universe, that would also end all worlds, because an ending wasn't really an ending unless it ended it all.

That knowledge must have shaken Odin to his core. He had seen all of that with his single eye, and had known he would need something infinitely more powerful than any force Odin could bring on his own. He had needed a power that would hold, not just against an ending of Norse giants and other Norse gods, but a power that would stop the endings of other gods, of other mythos. Of all the endings of all the gods throughout all the universes.

He had needed wisdom of the runes.

Odin had gone to that well and had been shown all the other

worlds Yggdrasil was connected to. He had seen past all its branches, deeper than all its roots, beyond time and space, past *all* the beyonds of all the times and spaces.

He had seen Ragnarok wasn't the only ending to his creation. That there were other endings, and those endings would end his world just like Ragnarok. How could he stop those endings? He would have to sacrifice something great for that knowledge, Odin would have to sacrifice himself for that wisdom. For knowledge that would not only prevent the Norse Ragnarok from happening, that would prevent from *any* Ragnarok from happening.

For his sacrifice, Odin had gotten runes. Runes—once inscribed on Gleipnir—that would forever bind a wolf in his place. That would bind the ending of the wolf not just to the ending of Midgard, to the ending of the Norse worlds and gods, but to all the endings of all the worlds and all the gods.

And a third chill hit me. This one colder than the previous two, an icy knowledge that would never warm. A depth of coldness, like a cavern buried deep under the mountains. A chilly cavern with a wolf, a wolf bound with a silken thread, a silken thread illuminated with the smallest of lights and the dancing of figures upon it, small things that could be drawings, or runes.

It is all or nothing, human, the wolf had told me. *It is always all or nothing.*

My eyes widened. The word escaped me. Slow, long, like air escaping a leaking tire. "Noooo."

Emma waited still, sitting there, the glass with just a bit of water in it in her hands, her eyes hidden, the beam of sunlight falling across her back. She waited, patient, the glass forgotten. She waited, pushing me that final step, allowing the enormous realization to finally sink in.

The tree had known. Odin had known. The wolf had known.

"Odin saw..."

"Everything," Emma finished. "He saw everything. He saw all the other gods, all the other religions. He saw the birth of humanity in a million different ways. He saw all the births, and…" Emma leaned closer, not consciously, but as if the words she spoke were too fragile to be spoke loudly. "…all the deaths."

I blinked. Then blinked again. Then wanted something more stout than water.

When I had first taken service with Fenrir, I had thought the wolf was looking for the right time and place to release Ragnarok. That he held on to his life, through his powers, through medical science, using Dr. Berley, so that he could release Ragnarok at the time it was supposed to happen.

The wolf had allowed me that understanding. Maybe because the larger one wasn't something I would have believed. That the universe was greater than just the Norse gods. That it was greater than this Earth. That it was the ending of all the universes, of all the earths, and that all of them were tied to the slim thread around the wolf's ankle.

Not just Ragnarok. The Apocalypse. The other endings, the Kataklysmos of Zeus, the Dissolution of the Hindus, the Pralaya. Gleipnir bound all of them and more. The Celtic battle of Moytura, the destruction of mankind by Sekhmet, and more.

As many destructions as I could think of, there was always more. Always another. God, religion, ending.

I got it, then, why Odin hung from the tree still. Why his silhouette swayed on the cover. He had left himself as a warning. A warning, not to other gods, but to humans. Letting us know that a price had been paid, a price for our future, for all the futures, and that the ending would not come so long as we stood watch.

And then I found out that the slim thing that was different between Emma and me wasn't so slim at all.

"Some things, Finn," she said. Slowly. Carefully. Measuring.

Her hands around the almost-empty glass, the sunlight still dividing the room, the beam lying across her back, her eyes deep in the darkness of the room, "aren't meant to live forever."

CHAPTER TWENTY-EIGHT

I didn't get it at first.

Like before, Emma understood. Watched and waited.

I had been sent to find the wolf's daughter. In the beginning I had thought the wolf was dying, that Ragnarok was close, and Fenrir had sent me to bring his daughter back. To say goodbye. I hadn't understood, really, that everything is a lesson to the wolf.

Everything.

He had sent me here, knowing what I would find. Knowing what I would discover. Knowing that I would either discover it, or die. It was what had happened to the Chronicler before me, and maybe others before him.

It was the way of the wolf. He would never send me somewhere with foreknowledge, it wasn't in the wolf to impart knowledge in that way. He spoke to me, to all of us, like we were cubs. Wolves didn't explain, so much show. They didn't tell a cub where to hunt, so much as allow them to follow the barest scent of a trail.

After all, a cub who could not hunt on their own was of no use to the pack.

Still, had Fenrir spoke of this at all, to anyone? Had a cub made their way through the world, learned how to hunt, become its own master, and had come back to the wolf so that Fenrir could speak to the cub almost as an equal. Speak to the cub in a way he would not speak of it with me? Had the wolf lain there, with Emma leaning back against the nape of his huge neck and spoke about other gods and other endings?

An odd flare of jealousy rose up at the thought. I had to fight it a moment, fight it and fight the feelings inside of me. The man who was so tied up in all of the woman before me, in everything she was and did and felt, and who also was a Chronicler trying to save the world.

How did Emma learn this? Everything about other gods and other universes and other endings? How had she learned about what Odin had seen, how could she have known what the god had refused to tell anyone?

Could she have learned it another way, if not from the wolf?

She watched me, carefully, still. As if Emma could follow every connection my brain made. As if she followed each, and knew when I got to that very question in my mind.

"Huginn," she said, with a slight shrug. "And Muninn."

Thought.

And Memory.

Odin's thought and memory.

Oh.

A fluttering came then, the beating of wings against the window, along with cawing. Lots of cawing, from loud, large birds. As if they wanted to interrupt whatever this was between Emma and me. As if they feared the knowledge she had shared with me.

I pulled myself up to a sitting position. The bed squeaked as I did, the springs stretching underneath the old mattress. I settled there, already missing the warmth of Emma's leg, the cold iron bars of the headboard pressing against my back.

I had come here to find the wolf's daughter. I had come here fearing Ragnarok was close. I had found her, and I had found Ragnarok, but I understood now the storm I felt wasn't like the other endings. It wasn't like the flood X had hinted at before. It wasn't like plagues or locusts, it wasn't like tidal waves swallowing a coast or volcanos erupting.

This was something much greater. Much darker.

What the gods planned here, what *Emma* planned here, was the ending of everything. Of all the universes. Of all the gods.

Of all the humans.

Why?

"Why?" I whispered. Knowing what she would say. Knowing she had said it, when she had said some things weren't meant to live forever. Knowing that I understood her, because I had read her story. I understood the feelings of loss and rage and despair she held deep inside her, held like she had been holding that little girl, holding her long after the body had cooled in her arms.

I understood the feeling she had, following Wyatt Earp, understanding the amount of will someone had to have in their pursuit of justice. I understood some things lasted much longer than they should. Especially things evil in nature.

We always say the good die young. And perhaps that was true. Perhaps that was the way of our world, of our universe. Certainly the things that lasted longer seemed to have a twisted center. There seemed much more evil in the world than good. That those with the longest lives had accumulated the most power, and seemed to use that power for their own ends. That lives existed long after they should be a corpse, buried deep under the earth.

Emma saw my thoughts run across my face. The awareness, the assimilation, the comprehension. She let out a small breath, understanding the same things I did. Understanding that as much as the two of us were alike, we were also different. Different in one of the smallest ways, in the slightest shift of perspective, small and tiny and yet possibly large, like a bottomless chasm.

Still, she tried to explain it. "Do you know why I live here?"

Here? New Orleans? This house? This room, with its hanging strips of old wallpaper, its smell of dust and mold, its water-stained walls?

The caws kept up outside the window. The fluttering and flapping of wings. Emma rolled her eyes, just a little motion in the dark shadows, giving a tiny smile before going back to the window and pulling the curtain aside.

The slim beam of sunlight widened, illuminating the room. It looked older now than before, when shadows had hidden the tears in the wallpaper. Now the flowers hanging on the wall looked faded, and the tiny peeling strips looked like bandages unwinding from an old wound.

The birds almost froze there, outside the window. They paused, with their black eyes glistening on me. They hung there in the air for a long moment, the bird in front, Huginn or Muninn, that bird cawing loudly, its beak opening wide, before they both flew off in a flutter of wings.

Past the ravens was another building. An older building, a two-story apartment or home, looking much like the age of the room Emma and I currently were in. The spine of its roof, once arched high in the air, now broken, the tiles missing in places, sliding down the roof in others. The walls of the home were stained black with grime, stained as if water had run down the sides of it, leaving dark waves spreading from the broken roof to the ground.

I got up and went to the window. Feeling sore as I did so, my head still pounding, my throat still dry. When I got there, I understood the room I was in. Why it looked the way it did. Why the glass Emma still held was old and pitted.

Row after row of homes lie there after that first home. Most of them with the same look. With broken spines of a roof, with water-stained walls, where walls stood at all. With shattered windows and missing doors and trash and rubble piled up on lawns, lawns overgrown with weeds and grass.

The ninth ward? Maybe. Maybe part of Saint Bernard's Parish. A place that had been flooded and torn apart in the hurricane. Whatever this area was, it was a part of New Orleans. A part that had never been healed after Katrina. Homes, neighborhoods, that may never be rebuilt.

"It's to remind me," Emma said.

Remind her. I wasn't sure she needed the reminder. I could feel the strength of it in her. The iron will. The hard grip around a dead child. The ride of vengeance.

The damage of Katrina had been immense, but no less immense than the Taiping Revolution. No less of a horror. Just a gentle reminder, like we got when we saw ourselves in a mirror. Just something saying this is you, this is you, this is you, so many times that you will never mistake yourself for anyone else.

I understood her then, in the way I understood the rest about Emma. Through that connection we both had, from the people we both were. Were, or had been.

Not just Chroniclers of the book. Not just servants of the wolf. But people we had been before then. Readers, writers, we were both one and the same. People who had loved the story of a thing, the dream, the promise of a good ending. People who had faced death, real death, and had fought it to the end. Fought it until the wolf had found us.

I got why Emma had started on her own ride of vengeance.

Even if I didn't fully know why. Even if I didn't understand where she wanted her ride to really end.

Her voice was soft. She, too, understood where I was at. And maybe, like the wolf, was trying to allow me to find my own way. With maybe a gentle nudge of the muzzle, here and there. "All these gods Finn, all these gods, everywhere, and look at this."

I looked. I saw. I imagined.

The strength of the hurricane. The people being swallowed by the storm. I felt it like I felt a tsunami, like a giant wave of water rushed over me and buried me under thousands of tons of ocean, like a hand of cold, wet force held me there. Held me under the ocean, until I was forced to let the hand of a little girl go, until that hand was ripped from me, until I was pounded and shattered among the homes in Sendai.

I will never let that go. I understood that about myself. I thought Emma understood that too, if she had read what I had written about it. If she had read that part of my chronicles and looked back at me, her fingers playing with the paw of a teddy bear.

I knew why I needed to always remember it. I knew why I needed the reminder.

Her voice was a whisper. A gentle nudge. "They let all this happen, Finn. They let all this happen, they've let it happen, throughout all of time. They've let it happen, and they've done nothing."

Did they? Perhaps. The stories—the myths—were full of uncaring gods. Of gods that took human form just to walk the world, but also gods who left that world, like a child tired of building sandcastles finally left the sandbox.

There were great injustices in this world. Emma had seen them. Had lived them. The Taiping Rebellion. The World Wars... the Holocaust. She had been alive through all of them, and more. Had seen the atrocities people would do to others, and had lived through all the evils a person would do hidden, behind people's backs.

She had lived it all, and she was tired of it.

"Someone needs to stop them, Finn," she finally said.

In all the myths gods fought other gods. They rarely took sides, or were invested in the outcome of a fight. They rarely stepped in to make a difference, unless there was an Achilles or Heracles or Horus, around, unless a Gilgamesh or Krishna or Cu Chulainn needed a hand.

Funny, how all the tales seemed to get that right. Seemed to show that gods existed, but never really helped. Not when the lowest of humans needed it, not when they were starving, or when armies were marching across their land, cutting off hands and heads.

I could see Emma's side. I felt it deeply within me. The angry cry of *why?* It resonated in me, just like her.

Why wouldn't a god want to help? Why wouldn't a god want to answer the world's cry for help? Why wouldn't they reach out and just do the tiniest thing, to ease a little suffering?

I didn't know, as much as I could see it. As much as I felt it. As much as I felt it from *her*. I could see and feel all of those things, but part of me knew there was more. There was more to this, more to life. More that I didn't know, couldn't know, just hope that it was there and it was worth all this pain and suffering.

The world wasn't a paradise. I knew Emma wasn't looking for one. Like me, she had lived in a world of grays. But her grays had grown darker through her life, as if she had sank in a pit. A pit she knew she was in and could see no way out of. A place where it was all or nothing, now, because if a paradise didn't and couldn't exist, then a hell shouldn't either.

It was a tough thing, all or nothing. I had fought it with the wolf. Life should have meaning, and for me, I knew that meaning meant there would be pain. There would be suffering. I hated it, I held that teddy bear paw and *hated* it, but I still understood it.

Maybe I wouldn't, if I had lived Emma's life. If I had lived as long as her. Maybe life would lose its meaning, maybe it wouldn't have the highs and lows and all kinds of middles. Maybe I would stop seeing it the way I did now, and stop discovering the little moments, the shocking awareness of finding someone who thought as you did, and yet perhaps loved pancakes when you preferred hash. It should have things that make you cry, because then when you laughed, when you really laughed from deep in the belly, you could feel that joy, recognize it, and hold it all the more dear.

Emma knew what I was thinking, all those thoughts, even as I thought them. I saw it in her face, I saw what was going to happen and what she was going to say even as I knew my own part in the story. Even as I knew that Huck was gone now, gone after last night. That he had been put away, and Emma too.

"Emma—"

"Don't," she said. Her voice hard. Firm. "Don't, Finn. You weren't there. You'll never be there, you'll never have seen what I've seen."

She was talking about China, but she was also talking about more. We both knew that. We both could see the words between us, the *I hadn't been there* and the *you don't know*, the *I've been to bad places* and her reply of *not like that place, you haven't.*

All her words were true. They would be true if I said them, if Emma said them, but neither of us needed. The real truth was, I hadn't ever been to Taiping. I could never be there. I could only read her story and live it in her words. In her chronicles.

I had never been to Taiping. By all accounts the things done during that time had been as horrible as humans could do to each other. I might have seen and witness something close, in other places. And, as they say, close only counts in horseshoes and hand grenades.

I had never lived Emma's life, as much as I had read her words and felt them. I would never really know the depths of the things she witnessed and lived. I would never, really, understand—not fully—the depth of her sorrow, her pain and rage.

I looked at her then, and I found myself crying. Not loudly, not sobbing, but tears fell from my eyes. Because I stood next to a person I wanted to spend the rest of my life with. Someone who got me and understood me more than anyone I had known or would ever know.

And yet, it was someone who I had to stop.

Because she wanted to end not just this world, but all of them.

And I wanted to save, if not everyone, at least a few.

The slimmest of differences, and yet the greatest of gaps.

Emma's eyes were wet, too. Tears ran down her cheeks much like mine. I understood then, what she felt from me. About me. I understood she had known it before I had, and that she had asked for last night because she had known this moment was coming. She had felt something different, something special, and had needed it, much like I felt something different, something special, and had wanted it.

"I can't let you," I said. My words a whisper.

She nodded, not trusting her voice. Her hands found the book, her fingers played across the cover one last time, and then she was tucking the book back into the satchel and wrapping that satchel around my neck.

The weight in the strap on my shoulder had never felt heavier.

Emma wrapped her arms around me, and pulled me close. It was the longest of hugs, like she never wanted to let me go, and I wrapped my arms around her and felt the same. I never wanted to let her go, or this moment go, because I knew where the next moment would take me.

"I just," she started, her words in the same whisper mine had been, her breath along the back of my neck, warm and soft and reminding me too much of the night before… "I wanted someone to understand. I wanted you to understand." Her head seemed to softly shake, left and right, as if she still was trying to figure that out, as if she knew she could make me get it, get *her*, if she just could find the right words.

I sat there for the longest time. Emma warm and soft, vulnerable and torn in my arms. I felt her there, with that slim thread of hope there, holding her together. Hope for what, I didn't know. Just hope.

Maybe that's where we all ended, in our last few moments. Of our last few days. Hope for a longer beat of the heart, a longer strike of the clock, a longer day or a longer night. Maybe all we wished for was another day before the end. Maybe we hoped at the last second for someone, for some god, to swoop in and save us. To stop whatever it was.

I felt and got it and understood that moment, like I understood her and I holding onto each other now. I knew what would happen, when I unwrapped my arms and left this place. I knew what would happen next, and where that moment would lead, and what would happen from there.

Emma had said things weren't meant to live forever. I could see what she felt when she saw the darkness. I could feel her *know* the cycle of death and rebirth was a natural thing. That without death, none of us could really feel life.

Something that lived forever felt like a tumor. Something that would live and grow until it could not grow anymore. From there it would divide and divide, over and over. It would turn malignant, it would eat other lives like cancer, it would eat until the host was dead.

No matter if the host was a human, a god, or a world.

Emma knew that about our world. She knew it, and it was nothing I could gainsay. No fault I could find in her logic. Things that waited to die only rotted, I knew that as well as she did. And if all I had to say was that I wanted to save a few, in a world that had turned this black, well, I could feel the balance on those scales.

This world had gone on a long time since the schoolmistress had begun her service to the world. It had gone on and gotten darker, waiting for a death that never had come. It was a world that had lasted far longer than it should have; it was a life long over, and there was going to be a reckoning to it. For it. An end to the ride.

Emma's ride. Her vengeance. An all-or-nothing throw of the dice to stop the rot, to halt the darkness, to end everything before it all became completely black.

It was all, or nothing.

And for me that meant that I would have to choose. I could choose her, Emma, and be with her for the short time left to us. Or I could choose against her, and allow life to continue in the way it has. For the bad things to continue in this world with little relief, like Gaza or Ethiopia, like Taiping or Sendai. For life to continue with the slow clacking steps of a girl too young to be a hooker walking to the truck her pimp waited in.

I understood now the hope Emma had inside her. The thin thing holding her together. The slim thread of wanting to be enough, for someone, to choose her over how she viewed the world. The tiny chance that someone might believe in what she did, might believe in *her*, to follow her onto this path.

It broke my heart, to not make that choice.

A part of me always wanted to save some. To save a few. That whatever might end this world, I could save the best of those remaining.

I slowly unwrapped my arms from her. She felt the motion, and held me tighter, her arms squeezing me. I moved my hands to the sides of her temples, feeling her hair under my fingers, as I moved her head lightly away from me, so that I could kiss her forehead.

There my lips lingered, a long, long time.

Then I broke the kiss off. I pulled away. And, after the longest of moments, Emma let me go.

She was crying harder now. I could no longer look at her, look at the tears streaming down her eyes, feeling the understanding from her, the awareness from Emma of knowing that I was always going to make this choice. There was a hard lump in the back of my throat, something I couldn't swallow down, and I felt her awareness of my choice that just like I felt the hurt inside of her, the betrayal, the knowledge that she, alone, wasn't enough for me to choose anything else than standing against her. The knowledge that she, as a person, wasn't enough.

As much as she had hoped she was.

I almost said I was sorry before I left. The words almost escaped me. I think because of the moment, because of seeing her there, her head tucked down, her arms wrapped around herself, as if Emma held herself together, now that hope no longer could.

But I didn't want to cheapen her with those two words. I didn't want that between us. What I felt for her, and what she felt for me, was much deeper than that. We both knew the world we lived in was much deeper than that. Emma knew I was sorry, just as she had known I would make this choice. Just as she had known what choice she had made when she first cast aside the book.

CHAPTER TWENTY-NINE

I stumbled out of the house, almost zombie-like. Finding my shoes, my coat, leaving my shirt with Emma-mae. My thoughts were racing with emotions, racing with wanting to rush back to her. To convince her to come with me. To give up her ride. To not be on the other side of the coin I found myself on.

I knew those thoughts were foolish. Just like Emma-mae had felt, from her side of things. Just like she knew she could never convince me.

The smallest of differences, the greatest of gaps.

My feet shuffled along the floor of the old house. I didn't notice the warped floorboards, the water-stained walls, the longer strips of wallpaper. The faded paint. I didn't notice the squeaks of the floor as I walked along it, or the dead, cold feel of a two-by-four as I steadied myself with a light press of my fingers against the stud.

I didn't notice the door to the home missing. I didn't notice the gap I walked through, leaving Emma-mae's home. I didn't notice the morning's light, dull and gray, nor the harder gray fingers of clouds stretching overhead. I didn't notice the thundering feel of the air, the weight of the storm. I didn't notice the cold breeze, brushing against me, nor the smell of mildew and rot the breeze brought with it.

I felt all of that, stepping out of Emma-mae's house, but I didn't feel it, either. I noticed but didn't notice any of that. I didn't notice it at all, because my mind was on Emma-mae. On her, standing there by herself, up in her flood-damaged home. Of a life, however short, of Huck and Emma, and what it could have been. Of the choice I had made, knowing that I couldn't have made another, and yet desperately still wanting to.

So my thoughts were there. On Emma. On my choice. Not on the sun or the feeling of the oncoming storm. Not on the cold chill of the breeze or the darkening hand of clouds. And definitely not on the fist connecting with the side of my head, knocking me into the side of the home and then onto the darkly-stained front walk.

Two strong hands gripped me.

Two very strong, very *angry* hands.

Vidar.

The god picked me up, his hands curled around the outside of my shoulders, his grip tight and painful. His Caesar-cut hair framing an angry face. His eyes burning with it. And yet his lips, his lips were curled in a smile.

It was a very chilling expression. A very real one.

"I believe I told you to stay away," Vidar said.

I wanted to struggle, but didn't. I knew it was useless. I was just a human, a human with a little longer lifespan, and Vidar was a god. A very angry god.

Who wanted a very specific end.

The funny thing of it was, I was ready to go away. I had run into something too deep for me to figure out. I knew the storm was coming, I knew the Ragnarok of all Ragnaroks was coming. I had found the wolf's daughter, I knew what she planned, and I had no idea to stop it.

The only thing I figured I could do was go back to the cave. Go back and talk to Fenrir. Tell him everything, this whole story, the chronicles of New Orleans.

And hope the wolf had an answer. A direction.

I tried to shrug. It was hard with my head pounding, with the remnants of the hangover, with the recent applied force of a god-like fist. It was harder with Vidar's tight grip on my shoulders.

"I'm guessing it's too late to say I'm ready to go, now?"

"Give a piece of candy to the winner." The god swung me over his shoulder like I was a sack of potatoes. Or a sack of laundry, because potatoes seemed too heavy for him to have swung me that easily. I saw then his shoes were a little different, they looked like tennis shoes, but they were thick straps of what might be leather. Leather wrapped tightly to give the appearance of shoes.

Vidar headed down the walkway with me over his shoulder. As if I weighed nothing. Towards a car I had glimpsed, briefly, when he had swung me up. What appeared to be a nice Lexus sedan, dark blue in color, windows tinted.

"Where are you taking me?"

Vidar grunted. "Where she wants you."

I looked back. Emma-mae was in the frame of the missing door. Her eyes, even from here, still sad and wet.

There was nothing left, I thought, of the young girl from the diner. The joy I had felt from her. The mischievousness. There was just sadness. Sadness and weariness and a fierce determination.

She stood there, one arm on the door frame, leaning a little against it.

Watching me.

She had known, I thought. She had known even before last night what would happen. What I would say. What last night would lead to. She had known and had Vidar waiting outside the next morning, waiting for me.

She had known, and still taken that night.

I couldn't fault her. And I didn't regret it either. Some things you have to live, good or bad. Some things you always wanted to remember. Last night, Emma, that was one. I knew, if I ever had a chance, if I lived, if the world lived, I would do my best to put that night in the book. Put it there with everything I had felt about her, and everything I felt she had felt about me.

It had been that kind of night. Magical. Haunting. A night that I would never forget, just like I would never forget Emma.

Even if Emma-mae had.

The ravens sat above her. On a sagging, if not broken, roofline. Shingles lay all over the roof, as if they had all been paused as they slid down it, leaving open gaps of tar paper. One bird nibbled at something under its wing, Huginn or Muninn, whichever, tucking its great beak under its flapping of feathers. The other one, the one on the right, seemed focused on me. Its beady eyes locked onto me.

Vidar got to his car. He swung open the passenger door and dumped me into the seat. There was a heavy smell of new leather, and something minty from Vidar as he leaned in to strap the seatbelt over me. There he paused, his face right in front of mine, his eyes still burning with anger and intensity.

"If you run, I will pull your arms off, and feed them to the ravens."

I got his point. And believed it.

"No running from me, chief."

He nodded and slammed the door shut.

I looked back at the house. At Emma-mae. She stood there in the door, still wearing my T-shirt, her face sad, but composed. Resolute. There was a tiny lift of her fingers, as Vidar got into the driver's side of the Lexus. The car shifted with his weight, and then fired up underneath the push of a button.

Funny, today, watching a god thousands upon thousands of years old, start up a car with a push of a button. It was a thought that hit me heavy enough that it pushed most of all the other thoughts from my mind.

A decade ago I would never have believed gods existed. Now look at me. I was being kidnapped by one. Kidnapped and being taken to somewhere else. I guess, ostensibly, to watch the ending of our world. Maybe even to write it down in the book.

Perhaps that's why Emma-mae wanted me alive.

Though I could have hoped for another reason.

The car pulled away. Surprisingly Vidar did not drive with an angry foot. We drifted away from the curve like a ship gently leaving a pier. Leaving a crowd of people behind watching the ship, some waving at loved ones, some already turning away. Leaving Emma-mae standing there, in the open door of her house wearing my T-shirt, her head following us until she disappeared. Until the ship itself sailed away on currents unknown, with a fickle wind behind its back.

CHAPTER THIRTY

Vidar was a good driver, I'll give the angry god that.

His hands stayed at ten and two on the wheel. He was always glancing, at either side mirror, the rearview. He stopped carefully and fully at every stop sign and stoplight. He used his turn signal, not only to turn, but every time he changed lanes. He accelerated smoothly from every stop until he got to the exact speed limit, and there he let the car roll along.

Strange, somehow to me, a god driving like that who wanted to end the world.

The radio was off. No music played. There was just the hum of the engine, soft and smooth, and the rolling of the tires along the road. The bumping of potholes, the slight jogging of weight of the new car over speed bumps. There was a tiny sound of the ventilation fan running, the whooshing of air, recycling the heavy scent of new leather in the car.

We headed west, in a fashion. Sometimes northwest, sometimes south. Sometimes circling a bit before going west again. I didn't see very many people, and I thought maybe they were finally getting it, that the storm coming wasn't just a storm, wasn't just a hurricane forming somehow right outside New Orleans in the Gulf, but something much darker. Much worse. Something that you could never run from, even though they might try.

The world went by us. Broken homes, old homes, every now and then signs of rebuilding. Of frameworks of two-by-fours and drywall. Of a crane overtop an apartment's roof. Of people in jeans and rough coats, some with orange hard hats, moving around the buildings. I thought maybe Emma-mae's house had been in the parish of St. Bernard, sometimes we passed long stretches of wet marsh, always in a fashion heading west according to the little blue compass W lit up on the driver-side dash.

I sat there, taking it all in. Feeling the cold leather against my back. The feel of the door pushing the satchel against my side. The hammering of my head from the hangover, receding. The hammering of my face from Vidar's fist, still strong and present.

The angry god. Powerful. But also silent and thoughtful. In the stories he wanted revenge for the death of his father, the death of Odin, at the hands of a wolf.

I understood, then, why he worked with Emma. Or why the two were a pair. Vidar desired revenge... No. He didn't desire revenge as much as believe in vengeance. He was one of the most powerful of the Norse gods, perhaps second only to Thor, and in the stories he was often thoughtful. He used vengeance as a restorative force. As a balance.

Emma-mae and he would get along just fine, there. He would admire her ride of vengeance. He would help her, especially if it helped him achieve his own.

"I know your story," I said.

The crook of his lips twitched. "You think you know it."

Maybe I did. Maybe I was getting part of it wrong. Vidar was supposed to kill Fenrir, because the wolf had killed Odin. But I hadn't seen Odin, I had only ever seen his silhouette, left as a warning on the book.

Was the god really dead? Was he really hanging there? Were Huginn and Muninn all that was left of the greatest of the Norse gods?

"Where do I have it wrong?" I asked.

"I'll tell you where you don't have it wrong," he said, turning the wheel slowly. Making a left and heading towards the French Quarter. "The stories describe me as the silent god."

With that he shut up. I wanted to ask him more, but when I did Vidar gave me one of his angry looks. The one that reminded me about the whole pulling-my-arms-off comment. So I kept quiet.

We left the broken buildings and wet marshes behind. Entered the French Quarter, with its shops opening and its balustrade-lined buildings, its cobblestone streets and old stone sidewalks. It was early morning, just like the day before, and again just a few people were around. Fewer now in number. Perhaps just the early risers, the locals after a night of revelry. The people who loved getting a coffee and a beignet at a café, reading a paper, or walking quiet streets.

Less in number now today. Less of them walking, looking south. Looking at the gray clouds stretching up from the Gulf. Shuddering, glancing at their phones, probably trying to figure out what was happening down there. Catching the news, the weather reports, the weather apps or even some guy on the television telling them to maybe stock up on water and canned goods and toilet paper.

We stopped at an intersection close to where I had first parted Skidblandir. We rolled by there, past a few alleys and a few public parking spaces. There was a new BMW in one, a BMW 3 Series, long and lean and sporty looking. It was gray with chromed wheels and fenders and grill, with heavily-tinted windows.

As I watched the homeless guy from the day before got out of the BMW. He grimaced in the cold air, pulled his old coat out of the backseat and tucked his arms through it. Then he wound a blue bandana around his head, and reached in and pulled out his sign: *I've got nothing, but this street's got soul.*

I couldn't help myself. I shook my head, my jaw tight, my fist clenched. "Come on, man."

Here I was, trying to save the world. Trying to save the human race. Here I was, sent to New Orleans to find Fenrir's daughter, and discovering that I didn't only have to fight her, but that I had to find a way to stop her. No matter how much I liked her.

Here I was, in the seat of a car, kidnapped by another god trying to end the world, trying to figure out a way to stop it, and now even humans seemed to be standing in the way. This panhandler. The young girl and her pimp from a few nights ago. The next thing I'd see would be Santa Claus pickpocketing someone.

All I had against that was what I felt. How I felt. What I thought the world should be like. What Sendai had shown me, in both the best and the worst of what the world had to offer. How sad was it that the thing that had me wanting to save the world had been a tsunami crashing over a town, killing tens of thousands and ripping a little girl from my clutching grasp?

Emma-mae had said some things weren't meant to live forever. The hardest part about the choice that I had made was the truth resounding in her words. The truth echoed back at me by the panhandler.

Rebirth was a common enough theme. In mythos. In stories. In other books and movies. It made sense to destroy something old, so that something new could be born in its place.

So why was I fighting it? Why was I fighting Emma-mae? Why was I standing across from a woman I found incredible, in every way?

I thought the answer for me lay in Sendai. In the tender arm of a man pulling an old lady up off the street, with her crying and sobbing and calling out the name of someone she would never find again. Of giving her a cup of something warm and sitting there on the wet stone of the sidewalk and holding the old lady against him. Of the people there, pulling timber after timber from shattered homes, digging through brick and rocks, of working without food and water to find someone else still alive, even as corpses were stacked like cordwood behind them.

It is at those times, the most bitter, the hardest, that the brightest lights are shown. It is at those times the best of our spirits rise up through the gloom and shine over the world around us. It is always during the darkest of times that the smallest of candles, the slightest flickering of a flame, would reveal the most about us.

About who we are. Who we could be. Who we should be, in the moments when the world needed us the most. I guess that was my only answer. I had seen the worst of the world, but I had also seen the best. And, even if the best of us were too few in number, even if we only revealed ourselves in the darkest of nights, the world deserved to keep on spinning, if only for them.

It is always darkest before the dawn, after all.

And yet, still, all I could think about was Emma-mae this morning. Of her ride of vengeance, of her feelings standing there behind Wyatt Earp, admiring his strength of will, his desire to do something *just*. All I could think about was the delicious curve of her smile from the night before, the haunting weariness of her soul, the determination to see her ride through.

How might it feel, should I get on the horse with her? It would be easy for me, right now. Especially after choosing not to write about pimps hustling customers with girls too young for the life. Or this guy with his 3 Series BMW and his funny, fresh-cardboard sign.

The streets here might have a soul, but that guy didn't. None of them did.

Gods. I pressed my eyes tight for a moment, then opened them. Taking a deep breath. Trying to relax my jaw, my fist. Looking away as the car started forward.

Vidar was looking past me, to where I was looking. The god offered a grunt. I couldn't tell if it was a mocking comment or a sympathetic one.

"I get it," I told him. Feeling like I could understand why he was on Emma-mae's ride. Why he was on his own ride of vengeance. I could understand why Vidar felt it was time to burn it all down. I could certainly see why.

He looked over again. At me this time. Quickly, still keeping an eye on the road.

Such a careful driver for a god.

His voice held a little less anger. It was more introspective. "You think so?"

I thought so. That was the scary part. I could understand the other side, I could understand it and it tempted me, it tempted me in the way looking over the side of a tall cliff might, in that pull of the depth of it, in that weird desire that made us all want to look over a bit further, and a bit further, and then possibly jump. "I get it," I said again. "I get what Emma-mae thinks."

Another grunt. "I can admire that one," he said, and I heard the admiration in his tone. Very different from his anger earlier, not just the anger at me, but the quiet anger when he was speaking to Emma-mae at the café. "Very few humans can follow a path of vengeance that long. You all lack the will. The conviction. It's something reserved only for the strongest of us."

"I get it," I said, a third time. A shiver running down my spine even as I uttered them. Something had come over me, some need to convince this god, trying in some way to stop the Ragnarok that was coming.

"This world is full of crap. It's full of people who do wrong things at the wrong times. It's full of people who want nothing but power, and who want to hurt others, who want to control everything, but there's still good in it. There's still a few people who want to do good things, who want to help, and *who knows* what those people are capable of? Who knows what they might do, if the world's allowed to continue?"

Maybe someone would come along who would make it all worth it. Maybe there would be a thought, a saying, a stand someone would make to balance out all the evil in the world. All the injustice done to so many. Maybe they would do something that mattered, mattered to such a degree that the world would not only keep spinning, but would brighten the shadows flung around it as it spun?

Vidar's face softened. It surprised me, because it had always been stone-like. Made of granite and angles and anger. Even his hair shifted, as his brows lifted a little, as the ventilation fans blew, a few strands stirred.

"You say you get it. You understand *her*. You understand me," he said. "Let us say you like apples, and you have an apple tree in your yard. A large tree, and every year it blossoms with flowers. Those flowers become apples, big and red and streaked with tiny rainbows of orange and yellow. Sweet apples that hang from the limb, ripe to pick."

His words caught me. I said nothing, observed, felt. Saw his glance to the sideview mirrors, the quick flick of his eyes to the rearview. The gentle nudge of the turn signal, and the accompanying *click-click* as Vidar turned the car. The slightest shift of my weight in the seat, the push of my hip against the book, and the book against the door.

The god continued. "Every year you go out there. You pluck the ripe apples. You eat them and they are sweet, delicious. You do this year after year. You perhaps take up canning, and can what you can. You have jars of apples lined up in a pantry, and still every year you eat more."

The hum of the engine grew a little more intense. The car accelerated. The tires began to whir. The god drove, in a fashion that wasn't quite a straight line, at least to my way of thinking. We were headed west, towards the riverfront of the Mississippi if I understood how New Orleans sat on a map, and the buildings grew more industrial and more warehouse-like. Bigger buildings, older buildings, with tall walls of old wood and newer buildings made of concrete and metal, with signs in big letters telling everyone what company owned what building.

The god seemed to be waiting. One of his glances to the side-view on my side paused a moment on me. "Well?"

I felt like his story, as much as it was about an apple tree, wasn't quite apples-to-apples. "Well what?"

His brown lowered again, just a bit. "What about all the apples that lie on the ground, year after year?" The god asked. "What about the ones too high in the tree, that only fall after you leave? You've canned what you could, you've eaten the sweetest apples, and still there are hundreds of them rotting on the soil. There are hundreds more in the branches that never drop, at least, that drop while you're gone, or after you've eaten, or after you've done your canning."

Click-Click. Turn. Shift of weight. A slowing of the car, as we passed larger and larger warehouses. One that might have been a cotton mill, at one time. Another that looked like it had been a warehouse once, but was now a brewery.

"Have you saved every apple? Is there a sweet one still left somewhere in the branches? Is there one on the ground, lying on the ground among all the other rotting apples, lying there with bees buzzing around, is there an apple there worth eating? Is there one worth canning? Worth saving?"

Maybe I got it then. Humans were apples to the god. Apples he had eaten for thousands upon thousands of years. Maybe millions.

"After a while, perhaps you lose the taste," the god mused, pulling up in front of a large, concrete structure. "Perhaps apples aren't as sweet anymore. Perhaps you're tired of the work of canning. Perhaps you're tired of walking among the rotten apples, looking for that one that is still ripe and juicy. Perhaps you're tired of getting stung by bees."

He stopped the car there and shut it off. Like everything else, the Lexus's engine turned off smoothly. Without a shudder or an extra half-rotation of pistons. He sat there, his face starting to harden again. As if the anger could only be put away for so long.

He motioned for me to get out, nodding to the warehouse.

I did get it then. I got what Vidar was telling me. I understood him now, perhaps better than I ever had. I had a brief thought, as I unbuckled myself and got out of the car, to run, but the god had told me what would happen, and I didn't fancy getting my arms ripped off.

CHAPTER THIRTY-ONE

Vidar led me into a large square building of concrete and a solid roof. It was a new building of new construction, perhaps three stories tall. Something raised after Katrina, built thickly with dark gray concrete blocks that reminded me of a castle, or a fortress. Something that might last against the next hundred hurricanes.

If none of them were Ragnarok.

There was a large set of doors, something you might open if you were going to drive tractor-trailers into the building. The god led me past those to a small, thicker door. Something metal with a small, square windowpane of glass in it. What might be an emergency exit, once upon a time.

He opened the door and motioned me through. From the outside, from the storm, and what could possibly be causing it inside.

I took a breath and crossed the border.

The inside of the warehouse was the size of a football field. It was brightly lit, from bright white fluorescent tubes stretching in row after row along the high ceiling. There were large windows on my side of the warehouse right underneath the ceiling, large windows facing south. The floor of the building was a large concrete slab, stretching from where I stood to the end of every wall. There was a balcony around the inside of the wall along what I would call the second floor, metal stairs ran up to it in places, and doors there and glass windows lining the wall spoke of offices and bathrooms and supply closets.

People stood in the center of the building. There was a large structure there in the center of the floor. Large in width, if not quite height. The structure was colored in blues and greens and whites and blacks, it glistened in places, like mirrors or glass. It shone and shimmered, and perhaps the tallest part of the structure was shoulder height. Curiously, a grayness hovered above the structure, almost like wisps of smoke of a cigarette, or more like a cloud of cigarette smoke.

Tables sat around the structure and the cloud. The flat, long metal tables you have to unfold the legs from. Cheap things, with cheap folding metal chairs around it. On the tables were papers, Styrofoam cups, and on one table were platters of croissants and donuts and beignets, and a tall silver canister that looked like it held coffee.

Men and women sat at the tables. They stood around the structure. They moved around it, glancing, sipping coffee. Some held their hands over it. Others watched. A few stood by the coffee canister, pushing the little lever down and filling the small white Styrofoam cups.

Vidar directed me that way. Towards the center of the building. It felt very *Ocean's Eleven* to me. Maybe *Fast Five*. Those movies with mockups of a vault in some warehouse and everyone there was planning how to pull off a heist.

Only this wasn't a heist. Or a movie.

Even if this was a mockup. Not of a vault. But of something… greater.

The two of us neared the center of the warehouse, Vidar heading over to the table with all the pastries and the coffee. I realized what was being mocked up as we drew closer. I realized it as I felt the lifelike-edness of the model. The vibrant colors of the grass of the parks, the dark green marshes surrounding the outskirts of the model, the shimmering surface of the lake to the north, the rivers and smaller ponds. The shiny glass reflections of millions of windows, the yellows and blues and greens and everything else of the French Quarter.

It was a complete reconstruction of New Orleans. Every tall building, the tallest skyscraper shoulder-height. Every broken-down home, even from Saint Bernard's Parish. Every piece of water, every street, every bar and restaurant and shop, even down to the people walking on the street.

I blinked.

There were people walking on the streets.

Real people.

It wasn't a mockup.

I was looking at the real thing. I was looking at the real New Orleans. Just in miniature.

I slowed down under that realization. I slowed down when I realized what the gray cloud was above the city, the finger-like tendrils of smog, with the grasping hand reaching out from the south, from the Gulf. I slowed down until Vidar tugged me forward, his face slowly drawing back into granite.

I took a look at those standing around mini New Orleans. They weren't people, and I knew they wouldn't be. All of them were gods.

I recognized some of them, from the night before. There was the pirate woman who had played the piano. She had her hip sitting on the corner of one of the tables, overlooking everything. When she saw me she smiled, tipping her coffee cup towards me, the other hand holding a chocolate donut with all kinds of sprinkles, one large bite taken out of it.

Off to the side was the old man with the white hair and the white beard and the cane. By the pastry table was someone who looked enough like Vidar to be Vali, the god's brother. There was the shorter man who would be a dwarf. There were those, and there were more.

There was a striking-looking woman from out of classical Greece. Her long robe flowing with blues and whites. Her dark hair bound by a simple circlet, her face stern, her hands held out over the mini New Orleans. There was a tall, light-brown skin man, carrying himself like a warrior, a sword on his back. I blinked, because he had four arms, one holding a drink and the other a croissant, and two arms laid back against his side.

That kind of definitely clued me in to the whole these people are gods thing. It's not every day you see someone with four arms. With four arms and a large sword on his back, eating a pastry.

There was a shifty man in a pinstripe suit, with a smile that felt snaky. A shorter, darker woman holding an ankh. A Japanese man, his hand on the katana on his belt. Other gods, a man wearing a feathered headdress that looked South American, a shorter Chinese man with a scroll in his grip, a raven-like woman with dark hair, the hair barely showing from her cloak, holding a spear. There was a very large man, very stout in thick, black leather armor, his beard flowing over his chest. He could be Russian, I thought, though that might just be the feel I got from him with his balding head, his great gray beard, his tattoos along the side of his temple and intense gray eyes.

All those gods, and more. Maybe twenty of them, twenty-five.

Such a large collection of gods and powers, from all different myths and religions. With different outfits and looks from all across our history. All here, at the end of the world. All here, *causing* the end of the world.

They all stood around New Orleans. The model, the mock-up, the mini city, whatever you wanted to call it. Some of them spoke softly to each other, others spoke in tongues I recognized, some I didn't. All appeared, as I watched, to briefly call on a power, like the classical Greek woman.

I felt that power in the room. Felt it stir, even if no fans spun in the ceiling, even if there wasn't ventilation to speak of. The power shifted, the air stirred, it brushed across my cheek with a chilling tingle, bringing with it, oddly enough, the smell of dusty concrete, dark coffee, and that sweet scent of sugar and warm pastries.

We finally got to the table. The scent of coffee and donut was strong. The god grabbed one off the plate, something white and round and powdery, and the man I thought was his brother Vali handed Vidar a cup of coffee.

"Today, brother," that man said. His words quiet, if not with the anger of his brother.

Vidar nodded, taking a careful bite of the donut, leaving no sugary powder on his lips. Sipping the coffee.

Vali looked at me. "The Skald?"

"We're to hold him here," Vidar said, taking another bite of donut. It looked like it was cream-filled. One of my favorites.

"We should kill him."

The angry god shrugged. "She wants him alive."

"We should kill him."

Vidar looked at me. I had the feeling my life could have ended right there, with perhaps the tiniest of gestures. A lift of the shoulder. A brief nod of the head. Perhaps even a motion that could be mistaken for permission, as he took another bite of the donut, another sip of the coffee.

"She's been right so far," the god said, finally. "What's it matter to hold him a few hours more?"

He looked at me, as if Vidar knew what I had been thinking. "Coffee, Chronicler? Something to eat?"

I shook my head, slowly. Even though powdered, cream-filled donuts happen to be a favorite. Getting close to the table meant getting closer to Vali, and now I wanted to stay a bit further away from that than what might be considered polite.

Vidar nodded his head to the mini New Orleans. To a desk behind it, hidden by the structure from where we had first walked in. The desk was a nice thing made of what looked to be mahogany. Waxed and polished and clean, with an office chair tucked into the cubbyhole of the desk. Sitting there, empty, like a throne.

"Best get to it, then," the god said.

"Get to it?"

"Writing," Vidar said. With the slightest roll of eyes in his hard face. "Isn't that what you do?"

I realized then, what Emma-mae had Vidar capture me for. Not to kill me, because that didn't really make sense. Not if the world was about to end anymore.

She wanted me to sit and write. To capture everything about this moment. Everything that had led to it, all the way up to the very moment the world ended. To capture her part in it, and the gods that were here. The who and the why.

I wondered if that mattered. If the book would exist after the universe was wiped away. I would never know, and maybe that was the point. Maybe that's why Emma had me here. Hedging a bet, in case everything was wiped away. Planning ahead, in case there would be a new world, another seed sprouting from the corpse of the old universe, leaving something behind as a lesson, so that the next group of gods, the next people would perhaps do better.

"Perhaps you'd like to stay here," Vali said, with the slightest of smiles. Not anything happy. More sinister instead. Like that winding smile of a copperhead, its head high in the air, before it struck. "Next to the two of us."

I definitely didn't. I walked over to the desk, wishing I had grabbed a donut and some coffee. I was hungry, I hadn't eaten anything but Jaeger since the night before, and Jaeger just didn't have the nutritional value one might need.

Still, I thought, glancing back to Vali, watching the god watch me, better safe than sorry.

I sat in the chair. It was comfortable, soft. It had been placed at the perfect height for me, so that I could lay the book in front of me, place my elbows just so on the desk, and write. As if the two pieces of furniture had been placed here just for me.

Which, maybe, they had.

I sat in the chair. Feeling, and not feeling, the eyes of all the other gods on me. Feeling and not feeling their warring desire, to kill the Chronicler of the Wolf, and to allow me this last task. Feeling the intensity of their power, as they stood around mini New Orleans and called their own powers. As they stirred up the storm.

As they prepared to end the world, as I knew it.

CHAPTER THIRTY-TWO

I sat there, ignoring all of the stares. The feels. The glances. I sat in the comfortable chair and pulled out the book, feeling those glances intensify in that moment.

The book came out of the satchel easily, as if ready. It slid out and I laid it on the mahogany desk with the familiar muffled whump. I grabbed Gungnir from its place in the satchel, and laid an elbow next to the book. The mahogany was hard there, under the bone of my elbow. Hard and cool.

My fingers traced the cover of the book. Much like Emma's had, earlier. I felt and saw the thick trunk of Yggdrasil along the spine of the book, the tiny circle at the top of the spine, the serpent eating itself. I saw the thousands upon thousands of shadowed branches spread out over the front and back of the dust jacket. I saw the eagle there, at the top of the tree, though the hawk was missing from its beak.

The ravens too, were missing. No surprise there, although Odin missing from his noose might have been. Maybe the silhouette was nervous, around all these other gods. Maybe the warning the god had left behind had given up and gone, now that it had been ignored and the world was ending.

There was the squirrel though, running up along the trunk. The smallest of shadows, the smallest of silhouettes, a tiny flicker of black moving along black. Disappearing for a moment, and then reappearing to run down along the tree until it vanished at the bottom of the book.

Hmmm.

How does one write the end of the world? I didn't know, but I guess it had to start with a first sentence. Then I'd take it from there.

My fingers moved to the paw of the teddy bear, one last time. I felt it there, the soft cotton, worn from years of me touching it, from years of being my placeholder in the book. The softness of the paw, the flatness of it, the collapse after all the stuffing had been pulled out.

Then I opened the book and wrote.

I understand this, I started.

I understand this, the why of it, even if I don't like it.

I understand this, what Emma is doing, even if those who read this after me don't. I understand the pain, I felt it in her story, in China. With the rebellion there.

Perhaps today others might not understand the same. Maybe it's too easy, with social media being what it is, to see something that horrible and let it go as the next thing goes viral. Maybe it's too easy to put a thumbs up on a post, to send a dollar to someone's fundraiser for some charity and cause, and feel like you've done some good.

But I understand it. I come from a time when people went places. Where they endured what was thrown at them. I understand being in a place where something so terrible comes at you, something you can do nothing about, and watching that terribleness crash down around you. Rip those you love from your arms. Kill and maim and destroy and end lives.

So I understand Emma's decision. I hadn't been there, but I could imagine it well enough. The months of wandering from village to village. Of standing outside unspeakable horrors. Of wearing Hulinhjàlmr and having some protection, but just the protection offered by a disguise. A protection she couldn't share, as she watched the rapes, the murders, the starvings. The rebels moving through a city and killing those who opposed them, placing heads on spikes. The emperor's forces following and doing the same.

I could understand what Emma saw, as she wandered and wrote down things for the wolf. At some point she must have broken. She must have seen all this and wondered when it was going to end. When she was going to stop seeing a man kill a child for a handful of rice. Or a woman kill a man for the same.

I could understand and take it forward. Emma wasn't wrong, when she had started her ride. That rebellion had been horrible, but then there had been World War I. World War II. The Holocaust had followed the rebellion fifty years later, and had killed millions and millions of Jews. Not just killed, but done so in ways still hard for me to write about, even if I hadn't been there.

Emma had seen it coming, I thought. She had seen the great furnaces burning people alive. She had seen greater weapons, of a race of humans who found new and greater ways to kill. She had seen, without knowing, nuclear bombs being dropped on Japan. Of the hundreds of thousands of people who had died, and the hundreds of thousands left behind to wither as radiation ate them up from the inside.

She had seen all that, without knowing, and more. Of weapons of war, like napalm. Of weapons made of food, where nutrients were replaced with chemicals so that things we eat are made of things like red dye number forty, compounds with tripotassium phosphate, with glyphosate and aspartame, with all the chemical preservatives like hydroxytoluene and hydroquinone.

She had seen all of that, and more. With drugs that might cure one thing but cause a dozen more. She had seen what humans would be willing to do to another, for power, for control, for a buck. What humans wouldn't be willing to do, to help. And she had seen all the gods standing by, watching all of it happen, day after day, year after year, century after century.

She had felt the darkness coming. She had seen it, endured it. She had survived longer than most humans thought of living, and saw where the shadows grew blacker, and darker, with no relief.

It was no wonder she wanted to end it.

I don't know if anyone will read this. And I don't know if anyone will read this and understand. Will know. After all, the person reading this will never be where she was. Will never truly be where I am now.

I stopped there, for a moment. I wasn't sure it captured what I wanted, but I didn't know if I could do better. For all the pain I had felt in Emma, I couldn't put that on the page. There was only so much words can convey.

So I left that, there. Left my words on Emma and understanding where they were. Knowing that in my heart I understood. Knowing that in my heart I even wanted to join her. Maybe the largest part of me wanted to be with her, because I had seen a number of things that were wrong in this world, and very little right.

Maybe just a thing or two.

And—for some reason—it was that thing or two that kept me on this side. For all the pimps and young girls, for all the wars and all the people making money off of foods that slowly killed those eating it, for all the panhandlers without souls, there was something that kept me here writing. Maybe it was the dollar my mother didn't have, getting placed in a charity bucket. Maybe it was the grip of a little girl, torn from my grasp. Maybe it was the arm of a young man around an older woman, comforting her.

I couldn't tell you for sure.

A thundering boom shook the warehouse, a boom of thunder that resonated long after the strike. The windows facing south had grown dark, even though the day was young. There was a rustling, whistling of wind one hears when a storm is brewing, when it is about to grow violent. The air whipped outside and battered the warehouse, I could hear it. See it, in the occasional flickers of the lights.

Some of the gods smiled. More stood around the mini city now, their arms out, eyes closed. Tiny spits of lightning circled the Greek woman's fists. Strikes of the bolts hit the city, stabbing it here and there. Other gods had fire around their hands, and I saw tiny flames dance down streets. Others might have something that looked like wind, rushing around their fingers, winds that took the flames in the mini city and fanned them larger.

Just the beginning now. The booms of the thunder outside like the gong of a bell striking midnight. I tried to figure out who was who, from what I knew of mythologies. Some of them were hard. I could not figure the Greek woman, nor the raven-like girl with the hood and the spear. I thought the man with the four arms might be Kalki, the god of Hindu who embodied justice.

Strange, to me. Here at the end of the world I would expect to see gods who wanted to drive that about. Gods like Kali, or Shiva the destroyer. Like Sekhmet or even Anubis. Or even Sutr, the great Norse giant with his flaming sword.

None of these gods were about destruction. I made sure to write that down. These gods, they were about vengeance in some way. If not vengeance, then justice, which might be the opposite side of the same coin.

That seemed important to me. Something to write down for the next world, if there might be one. Something about the lesson, that if a world was going to be destroyed, if a universe was to end, it wouldn't be from some god or evil whose job it was to destroy it. It would more likely come from something done to another, something small or large, something creating the feel, the want, the need for vengeance.

And the vengeance taking it from there.

The ride.

A plate was dropped next to me. A plate of donuts and pastries, things covered in white icing or syrup. Quite a few of them, an abundance of croissants and donuts. Even a powdered, round one.

I looked up. The pirate lady was there, with a bandana holding back her thick hair. With her content, small smile, and a cup of coffee in one hand.

She set the coffee down too. A full cup of dark, black roast.

My stomach rumbled. Funny, how the body needs to keep going, even at the end of the world. I *was* starving. I ate the powdered donut fast, almost not tasting the sweet cream inside, the confectioner's sugar dusting the outside. The coffee was hot and dark and black and washed away any sweet quickly, and with a bite of bitter, and fit my mood perfectly.

The god sat there, waiting. Her eyes with the smallest of twinkles. Tangles of her hair moved a bit, slightly, as if the blows of the wind outside stirred them.

"Thank you," I said, between mouthfuls of some sticky pastry full of nuts and honey.

"You're welcome," the god said. Her voice was nice and pleasant, and I remembered part of the night before, when she had played the piano and sang parts of songs that I didn't remember with Emma and me. "How goes the writing?"

I looked at the pages. I had written more than I thought. I

wondered how much more I could write. I wondered where the book might go, when this world, when all these worlds and universes ended?

Would the book even exist? Would the silhouette of Odin return as a warning to the next race? Or would there be the image of the last Chronicler swaying there instead?

Would the tree remain? Would something grow from the roots of Yggdrasil, after the tree was burned? Or would it all just be gone?

I didn't know. And what's worse, after writing what I had written, I kind of wanted the latter. Wanted the latter, and hoped for anything other.

I answered the god truthfully. A plate of donuts earned her that. "Not great."

Her smile widened a bit. I got the feel of her more from it, the wind stirring her hair, the quick wince of her eyes as a bolt of lightning struck both the mini-city and the real New Orleans in the same moment. Her name popped into my head. "Gaia."

The smile stayed there. "You remember."

I did. Gaia. A Greek god born from Chaos. Born from the primordial void. Born into existence, and bringing with her creation all the gods and planets, the skies and the seas and the mountains.

She was here.

And—I realized—she was dying. I saw it in the tightness of her face, behind the smile. The tiny winces at the outside edges of her eyes. The occasional glance back to the miniature city, or the storm past the windows.

These gods were killing her, and if she wasn't happy about it, she also wasn't... stopping it.

She saw I understood. Not just who she was, but what was happening.

"Why?" I finally asked.

She seemed to think about it a bit, although I felt like Gaia already knew her answer. Had likely known it the moment she had been birthed. It had been a question long in the making, long in development, with an answer just as long in its own maturation.

Wind battered the windows. The thunder rolled on long and low outside. It came with bright flashes outside and sizzling, electric spats, each spat causing the Earth mother's eyes to wince.

"It's not really my place," she finally said. Her tone thoughtful. As if she had this answer, had had it forever, and still studied it. Turned it around in her mind, over and over. "I was created from the void; surely one day I must return to it." Her head tilted, just a bit. "Who am I to say when and where that time might be?"

"But..." I paused, looking at the gods around the model. The gods ignoring Gaia, even if they had listened to her songs the night before, if they had listened to her play the piano and sing and even had joined in. "They're killing you."

My head tilted, in the opposite direction of hers. Both of us turning something around in our minds. Something we might not fully understand.

Gaia smiled, though. As if she had been turning that thing for far longer than I had. As if she had seen all the different facets and sides of the object, and understood far more about it. Even if it wasn't everything.

"There is always death," she said, her eyes past me, in the distance. "Life springs from it, and if there is no death, Chronicler, there can be no rebirth."

She wasn't talking about the other gods, or at least, I didn't think she was, and their lack of interest in humans. She wasn't talking about suffering, or things like Sendai. She was talking about something perhaps larger, a lesson of the seasons maybe, from the mother of all the Earth. Gaia had lived and seen and endured far more than I ever would, and having done all that, what turned around in her head would be something greater than maybe I could understand. Something only she could fully know. Something she had lived and experienced and learned over a lifetime far longer than my own.

I guessed, having just written about something like that, about the difference between being there and reading about it, the difference about being there and being told about it, maybe I understood. Maybe Gaia's feelings and thoughts were enough for her, even if they weren't for me. Maybe I would never get it, why she was happy to sit here at the end and watch these other gods kill her. Maybe I could never understand what Gaia was telling me, because as much as I heard the words, I would never truly be in her place. I would never live her life.

I could only listen, and pretend to understand.

Gaia watched me, as all that ran through my mind. She watched me swallow the last bite of honey and nuts and pastry, and pause. She nudged the plate of pastries closer, turning the plate until I saw a chocolate-covered donut there facing me, something covered with a lot of sprinkles.

I knew then who had brought all the food. The coffee. The donuts and beignets and pastries, to celebrate the ending of the Earth. It was a slowly overwhelming realization, to know I sat in front of someone who was dying, and who was celebrating that death with song, with food, with drink.

Gaia leaned a little closer. Ignoring the pounding of the storm outside. The heavy blasts of winds battering the thick walls of the warehouse. The flashes of lightning past the windows. The long thundering rumbles.

Her voice, now, resonated. It no longer mused, or was thoughtful. It held a power, and when she spoke now, it was something I could get. Something I could understand, even if the knowledge wasn't pleasant to know. "When you create something, Chronicler, you have to see that creation through to its end. Good or bad. You have to watch your creation grow and learn and stumble and rise up again. You can't help it, because by helping it, you diminish those who might want to help, themselves."

A pause there. A deep breath. And a few more words, words reverberating with the full power of Mother Earth, a sound from the deepest of oceans, from the highest of mountainous peaks. It was low and loud at the same time, soft and yet full of that primal feeling one gets when standing at the foot of the Rocky Mountains and staring up at the jagged, snow-covered peaks surrounding them.

"You diminish those who want to hand a cup of warm tea to an older lady. You diminish the person who might be sick on their own, but goes out and gets medicine for their parents despite what the world might think about them. You diminish everything your creation might do, all the things, large and small. You even diminish the last dollar someone might place in a bucket somewhere, in the hopes that dollar finds a way to someone who might need it."

Her gaze held me for a long moment. With the wind battering outside. The slow rumbling of thunder. With the sweet taste of pastry and the bitter aftertaste of coffee still in my mouth.

My eyes widened.

And a heavy piece of lightning struck hard outside. Hard enough that the lights went out, and stayed out. Hard and fast, but not fast enough that I couldn't see Gaia's eyes close tightly against it, before the entire warehouse became shadows.

Her voice came out of those shadows. And carried not a hint of the pain she bore. "You create something, and you have to watch darkness eat at it. You have to watch the darkness eat away at the thing you love so that you can find the brightness. You have to hope, as the shadows swallow everything, when that day comes, that light you find is bright enough."

CHAPTER THIRTY-THREE

N o.

Gaia couldn't mean what I thought she meant.

Could she?

The lights flickered back on. They fluttered there in the ceiling, all the tubes flickering in the same few moments, so that everything in the warehouse appeared to be under some strobe effect, like I was at a rave. The lights fluttered, revealing all the gods around me in their stop-motion glory.

Vidar, his arm around Vali, the two of them paused there, as if talking. The god's eyes past his brother, on me.

The Japanese samurai, standing by himself. Ramrod straight. One hand on the hilt of his sword.

The white-bearded man with the cane standing, but not straight. Standing bent a little to the side of his cane. One hand clutching the curved piece of wood.

There was Kalki, one fist to his chin, as if thinking. His other hand holding a donut. His other, other hand holding a donut, whole and uneaten. The other hand appearing clenched, at his side, before unclenching at the next blink of the rave-like lights.

The lights flickered faster. The raven-haired girl laughed, her hood thrown back, her spear in the air. The snaky-smile man in a suit next to her, laughing with the raven. The Greek woman's smile widening, the lightning around her fists spitting and crackling faster. Another god stood next to her, with flames around his fists doing the same.

More gods, all paused in that moment of celebration. Gods I knew and didn't. Gods and powers together in the final moments of this Earth. Of all the earths.

And one god who wasn't there anymore.

Gaia, gone.

The primordial god, the Earth mother, had disappeared in the shadowed moments of the lights flickering out. Leaving me the plate with one last donut on it, the chocolate donut with sprinkles, the half-drunk coffee, leaving me with the book and her final words.

Her message.

That there needs to be darkness, for light. That the darkness grows, but in growing deeper and blacker, it's then that the light begins to show. Maybe faint lights at first, but lights that might brighten, given enough time.

It might take a long time, for eyes to adjust to that kind of darkness. To stand out there on a black mountain somewhere, and stare up at the night, until stars began to show. Until the thin strip of the Milky Way appeared.

How long had Gaia been staring, until she could find a light. A light that might be brightest before the dawn. How long had she been staring, until she might have found one. Until she had locked gazes with him and talked about things like watching your creation and diminishing and hinting at things like hope.

No.

I shook my head.

Perhaps not believing. Maybe not understanding. Only feeling that here I was, in a room full of gods, vengeful gods, gods who desired justice and thought they had found it. Here I was in this room, and I was the only one who wanted to save this world. Save just a piece of it.

Here I was, believing there were a few that needed to be saved.

Vidar was watching me, his eyes angry, always angry, but also curious. I was still shaking my head. Slowly. Still not fully understanding.

Was Gaia telling me I could stop this?

If so, how? My hands ran over the book, the pages, the words that I wrote. It was all I had. The book, and the pen. And while the pen might be mightier than the sword, I had no doubt about its ability to kill a room full of gods.

I pegged my chances there at a good zero percent.

The flickering stopped. The lights brightened and then fully lit everything beneath them. The gods in the final state of celebration, of throwing the power into New Orleans. Into breaking the city now, pulling the first thread from the ball of the world, and watching it all unravel. Watching the universe, all the universes, unravel with it.

With the lights came all the sounds of the gods, the muttered talk, the calls to power, the slap of a hand on a back. The laughs and —in the case of the raven-haired girl—an exclamation, a shout. With all those sounds came the pounding weather outside, the sounds of the storm, the battering winds, the spastic strikes of lightning, the rumbling thunders.

I closed the book. Muffled whump. The cover was the same as before. Most of the time that was the case, the silhouettes the same, if a few changed from time to time.

Then I looked closer. A blurry blackness appeared at the bottom of the dust jacket. There was the squirrel again, poking its small shadowy head out of the bottom of the book. Then diving back under the cover.

I frowned.

The squirrel poked its head up again. Then back under. The tiniest tickle ran along my brain. I opened the book back to where I had been writing.

No squirrel there.

Hmmm.

I closed the book again. Muffled whump, of course.

And the squirrel was poking its head out again even before it shut. Ducking back into the bottom of the book. Into the pages again.

Once.

Twice.

This was a first, for me. It was like the squirrel had a message for me, and was trying to communicate it. Trying to tell me something important.

I tried the thing I had the other night. I put my hand on the cover and closed my eyes. Thought about where I needed to open the book to. To the message I needed to hear. Then I opened the book, hopefully to the page the squirrel wanted me to see.

I opened my eyes. And blinked. I had opened it to what appeared to be its very first page. Where a dedication might rest, in other books. It was an empty page though, with the entire thickness of the book behind it, with all the other pages behind that first empty page.

Blank, void, empty.

At least, blank until the squirrel began running across the barren surface. From left to right. Running in a way that words followed it, letters appeared under its paws, so that as the squirrel ran its path it created one letter, then another, as the silhouette jumped from one to the next, until letters formed words, and words formed a sentence.

The wolf calls you home.

Huh.

The words were scrawled, they were thin lines written quickly. As if whoever was sending the message wanted me there, *now*. As if the message was urgent.

My head shaking sped up. Sped up with anger, and came with a laugh. A sound both dark and bitter.

Of course Fenrir would be calling me now. Now, when Ragnarok was coming. Now, when the ending of all endings was coming. Now, when I was in a place where I might be the one person who could do something about it.

Vidar was laughing. I thought he was laughing at me. It wasn't a loud laugh, not a celebration, but one of quiet amusement. He patted his brother another time on his shoulder and watched me, even as I watched his chest shake with tiny chuckles.

Maybe it was Vidar then, that had me think of Hode. Maybe it was seeing him and his brother, of Vali wanting to kill Hode, and that thought leading me to the blind musician in his corner of The Black Penny.

Of Hode's words. Asking me if I was a young Finn MacCool. Asking me if I was a fighter, and then shaking his blind head after my reply. Saying only that the world could use a warrior or two.

And me thinking, I had never been a fighter. That I wasn't a warrior. I was barely even a writer.

Even as I thought that, I questioned it. I hadn't been a fighter, that was true. I hadn't ever fought in armies, in wars, I hadn't cleaned a rifle and called that rifle my own. I hadn't taken that rifle and charged over a battleground.

But I had fought. I had fought for my life. I had fought for life, for that small group of those who I thought deserved better than this world.

I had also fought to save a girl.

So I wasn't a warrior.

But I was a fighter.

Vidar still watched me. Carefully. His chuckles paused. The god was watching me as if he knew I was planning something, but he, like me, had trouble figuring that plan out.

I had nothing but the book, after all.

I had nothing but the book, and the pen.

I had nothing but the book, the pen, and Skidblandir.

An idea hit me then. Hit me with force. Hit me with all the power of the Millennium Falcon arriving, the blazing brightness of the star behind it, taking out Vader so Luke could take the final shot at the Death Star.

I had Skidblandir. The gods, Vidar, none of them had ever searched me. Maybe because they were gods. Maybe they thought there was nothing I could do to stop them. Nothing I could do, as a human. They had never searched me, they had never found Skidblandir, they had never taken the small silken square from my back pocket.

Maybe they didn't know it was there. Maybe they did. Maybe they just didn't care.

And honestly, I had forgotten completely about it, too. I wasn't sure why I thought of it now. The best I could think was The Black Penny. Hode. Thoughts of them, and X. The Saint always polishing the bar. Wiping down bottles. Flicking his white rag in a quick motion, much like I had when I had called the bike, and telling me about being prepared. Being ready.

A second thought hit me then. Building on the first one. Something crazy and out of this world. Something from the movies. Something worthy of a gift of the gods and the ending of worlds.

I stood, staring at Vidar. "Mind if I use the bathroom?"

Maybe he saw it in my gaze. Saw the idea in me, in the way I stood. In the straightness of my back. In the firm, resolute tone of my words.

Still, if Vidar had seen any of those things, he couldn't figure it out. And how could he? The thought was a little crazy, even for a writer. Even for a little girl in a lost alien world.

He yanked his thumb to the side and nodded.

I slid the book into the satchel. Carefully, but quickly. The pen too. Then I rushed to the bathroom like I really had to go.

And I did, but not for the bathroom itself.

Just for the privacy of the room.

There were doors for men and women. I took the men. The bathroom was large, factory large, with a line of four urinals to one side and another row of toilet stalls next to those. A row of white sinks under a large mirror on the other side.

I didn't care about that. I just cared that it was empty. That I had a few moments to myself. Which is all I needed.

Maybe it was just blind chance. Even if luck might favor the prepared. Still, I unfolded Skidblandir. The silken cloth unfolded, like it had many times before, like it was ready now. Larger and larger until it was the size of a motorcycle. There it paused, as if ready, but I had something else in mind.

I tucked the satchel into the kerchief, the satchel with the book. Hiding it in the magic silk's many hiding places. Thinking the upcoming battle wasn't the place for the book. Then I unfolded it even bigger. Held the image of what I wanted in mind. Gave the cloth a snapping motion of my wrist, smoothing out the silk with my other hand, forming the large shape of the silk I needed.

The silk unfurled before me, like a great canvas sail. As if wind took it and held it in the air before me. I ran my hand along it, feeling Skidblandir harden underneath my palm Envisioning thick rods and thick plates. Envisioning motor... *motors*. Envisioning the curve of a joint there, of thick rods connecting with other thick rods.

I thought hard. Not just any metal. Not the silver chrome I had wished when I had created the wolf emblem on the gas tank of the motorcycle. Not even titanium, which was maybe the hardest metal I knew of. I thought about a metal built from the universe, built out of the void, built of something that had created the gods, with god-like strength and powers.

I thought all that and smoothed more. Carefully. Feeling the hardness of the metal underneath my palm. Feeling the firm, thick rods form. Feeling joints take shape and connect those rods together. Feeling large pieces of armored plate form and take shape and lock into their places.

Feeling everything where I wanted it to be. Feeling the motors form, the engine, a place of power from the universe. Feeling a large pod in its center, with all the switches and displays of a starfighter, feeling all of that take place under the smoothing of my palm, the sliding of silk over an object being created from the universe itself.

Maybe it was *Ocean's Eleven* that had given me the thought. Or *Fast Five*. Something about a movie might have edged my mind in this direction, with watching the gods around the center of a warehouse watching the mini-city of New Orleans.

Because I wasn't creating a ship, or a motorcycle, or anything like a train or carriage or horse that previous chroniclers might have created. I was creating something out of this world, because I had only seen it in the movies.

Sure, it wasn't real. At least real, in our human world of today. But it was real enough in my mind, and—with the power of the gods, the powers of Skidblandir—I could make it real enough for today. For now.

For what I needed.

The scarf changed colors, like before. Lightening in shade and becoming brighter. The brightness of a shimmering pool of silver. I gave the silken silver square a final snapping motion. It was large now, unfolding to the size of a bedroom, the silk twisting and sliding in the air before snapping away in a motion David Copperfield would be envious of. Snapping away and leaving my creation there, monstrous in the bathroom.

An exoskeleton, made of metal of the shiniest silver, ten or eleven feet tall. The metal was bright and shiny and lit the bright bathroom with a radiance of the material it was made of. Something from deep inside the void of creation.

It was large, as big as the machine Ripley had stood in, fighting off the alien. It was large, but more heavily armored. Looking like the suits worn in the *Edge of Tomorrow*. A heavily plated jacket of burnished metal, powered by the core of the universe, perhaps even formed from the primordial soup of creation.

I quickly got in the front, standing so that my legs went inside each of the exoskeleton's legs. I pushed a few buttons I had imagined on the panel there, then slid my arms into each of the arms of the machine. Locking my arms in place even as I watched those bright armored metal plates slide over the front of me. Feeling belts wrap around my chest in a crisscross motion, even as a helmet lowered over my head and a heads-up display powered on.

There I flicked through everything I had imagined. The machine guns on each arm. The large square bay of rockets over one shoulder. All of those things loaded with bullets and rockets made of the same void the machine had been made of.

I even checked a last thing. Maybe thinking of the movie I had watched, with all the monsters coming out of portals deep under the sea, and the giant robots that fought them. The large swords and chains and spinning discs those robots had.

There it was. A giant spear resting over the back of my shoulder. Not made of the burnished silver the exoskeleton, though, its blade and handle were the most polished gold. A gold that hurt my eyes, it was so bright. Gold, and perhaps not gold, because this thing had a sharp edge. An edge so sharp it shimmered—almost blurred—in the bright white florescent bathroom light.

A part of me grinned.

I might not be a warrior, but I was a fighter.

I might not be a writer, but I did have a hell of an imagination.

Young Finn MacCool, reporting for duty.

CHAPTER THIRTY-FOUR

It took a moment to get used to the controls.

After all, I had ridden a bike before. I knew how to drive a car. But I had never sat in an exoskeleton made for war before. I had never worked a space dock with a power loader, I had never worn a power suit, I hadn't been trained to fight the mimics. I had never sat in a towering robot-like machine and fought Kaiju.

I was going to have to learn fast. It wasn't like the gods were going to wait for me. It wasn't like I could just magically download the manual to my brain and roll with it.

I had tried to imagine a natural motion when making the jacket, so when I moved, the suit would. And it worked, for the most part. The hard part was feeling the machine move. Feeling the huge weight of the armored plates, the arms, the legs. Feeling the motors spin and whine in the joints, hearing the powering-up sound of the power core on my back. Feeling the crushing of the floor under each step. The heaviness of each arm as it swung. The lurching motion of the exoskeleton as I headed towards the bathroom door.

Lurch. Stomp. Crunch.

Lurch. Tapdance a bit (if a machine could tapdance). Whirl my arms to catch my balance. Stomp stomp crunch.

Deep breath.

Lurch stomp crunch. Lurch stomp crunch.

As I moved, and grew natural in the movements, I watched my heads-up display show things like range to the door. Like the number of rockets in the launch bay over my shoulder. (three rows of five, for fifteen). Like the amount of ammo in each gun (I liked the sideways eight symbol there). I watched things like a vertical, glowing white power bar to the side. Another bar next to it, a darker silver color, for my armor.

Too late, I thought I could have added shields, too. Not like the one the raven-haired hooded woman carried. But the kind you see in the movies, the glowing thing that surrounds a person or a ship and kept them safe.

And that was the thought that carried me through the bathroom door.

Not through it, like opening the door and walking through.

But through it, like breaking through the door. Blowing outward the cheap, easily-tacked-up drywall. Shattering the too-thin two-by-fours. The door, the drywall, the two-by-fours, all of that blew outward as I lurch-stomp-crunched my way through from the bathroom and into the warehouse.

There, the miniature city of New Orleans caught my attention. It was at least half aflame, a large bonfire whipping along the riverfront. The lightning strikes had grown louder, larger, they were thick wrist-like things stabbing into the earth there. The winds whipped the flames around in a circle, spiraling them up into the ceiling, and the gusts were strong enough they even seemed to push the lightning, bend it during each strike.

The gods were still laughing there, around it. Mostly. The samurai wasn't. Kalki wasn't. And Vidar, Vidar wasn't.

Vidar was looking at me.

His eyes opened wide, as he realized what was about to happen in the same moment I did. In the same moment I angled both arms towards the city. In the few seconds I aimed both of my machine guns in the general direction of the party celebrating the end of the worlds.

The angry god's eyes finished opening. They went as wide as eyes could go. They were full of anger: anger at me, anger that he was surprised, anger at being just far enough away to not stop what was about to happen. His mouth started to open, to give a warning shout.

It was then I squeezed the forefinger of each hand. Feeling the fist of the exoskeleton squeeze with it, feeling the mechanical whirs along each metal knuckle, the heavy thick feeling of alloyed fist as the machine squeezed with me. Feeling the power core in the back whine under a new demand, as the barrels on the top of each forearm started to spin.

Feeling a trickling sensation, like shivering cold water running from the power core on my back, running up and around my shoulders, the running power rolling over the back of the exoskeleton like magic from the deepest void of the universe, rolling over my shoulders, down my arms, and into the ammo feeds of both guns.

Feeling all of that, as I opened fire.

CHAPTER THIRTY-FIVE

You might think a machine built of the primordial void, powered by magic, and built somewhat of science, would mow through the gods.

You might think the gods, being gods, would laugh and tear through that very machine.

The truth rested, like always and in everything, somewhere in the middle.

The first volley of bullets did mow through the party of gods. Some of them were fast. Some were slow. The samurai went down quick, while—surprisingly enough—the old man in the cane leapt aside.

Some of the gods went down under the first pass of spinning primordial power. Others took the punches of bullets and rolled with it. Some screamed and turned. Some started immediately, as gods might, fighting back.

Vidar was a fast one. He ducked and danced off to the side. The raven-haired woman did the same, in a different direction, her shield held in front of her. The striking, lightning-fisted Greek goddess took both barrels in the chest and splattered kind of outward from there.

The bullets traced through the air in a kaleidoscope of colors. I wasn't sure if it was because the exoskeleton jacket was magic, or because the bullets were made from the stuff of the universe. Maybe it didn't matter, but the effect sure was pretty.

Vali seemed to be one of the slower ones. Maybe he was too wrapped up in his thoughts of killing Hode. Or taking out his thoughts of killing Hode on me. Either way, he was caught mid-turn, and—I'll say this with a bit of smug reckoning—went down under beautiful trails of primordial power.

Each of the bullets traced through the air, leaving a wafting, smoking, colored trail behind them. White trails. Blue. Red. More. Each of the hundreds of bullets pumped out leaving just the slightest difference in their colors, as if all the bullets came from a black hole, and the colors were all the lights at the edge of the accretion disc.

There were the bright white trails. The light blue ones arcing across the warehouse floor. There were the heavier reds and yellows and oranges. All of the trails, all of the colors shifting in midair, red-shifting as the bullets blurred away from me and punched into their targets.

The bright white trails looked more pink as the bullets tore into the gods. The blue trails deepened into purple as they raced across the floor. The yellow trails more orange or brown. Each bullet with some void-like power, the colored, smoke-like trails shifting across the floor, as if everything I fired fought desperately to escape a black hole, even as that same black hole fought to pull those same bullets back in.

Odd.

But I went with it.

It seemed to be working, after all.

The bullets thundered and thumped out of each gun. I stood there, each lurch-stomp-crunch foot planted firmly on the floor, planted firmly on the ground underneath me. Steady on the concrete, locked in. The force of the guns firing seemed to push the suit back, as if the black hole was pulling me back from the center of the warehouse floor, and the whine of the motors in my legs and back grew louder under the force of the guns firing, fighting to hold the suit steady.

It was wild. And powerful. Gods, the power.

I laughed, tracing my arms left to right before circling back to pan right to left. The bullets chewed through the model of New Orleans. The force of their passage blew some of the fires out. The bullets themselves chewed through the winds rushing down the streets and drew the wind out in that kaleidoscope of colors, along the opposite side of the model, in large sweeping gusts, in rainbow-like swirling clouds of white and purple, of red and yellow, of smoky gray.

I kept my fingers compressed. Infinity was a lot of ammo, I planned on using all of it. More gods went down. More ran, or hid. It had only been a few seconds, moments, really, but some were already calling their own powers. Turning to me with magic-filled hands, with great axes or slim canes, with shouts and words screamed in other languages.

The air grew wild with colors. With smoke from the model of New Orleans. With all the colored trails of my bullets. Their warehouse was clouded with it. I was glad for my heads-up display, which seemed to subdue all that color and fog, and bring all the figures of the gods up to my sight. Putting a tiny bracket of green around each.

There was Kalki, his sword braced vertically in front of him, all four hands holding the blade. Two on the hilt, and two other forearms placed along the flat of the blade, as if supporting it. The sword was on fire and the bullets seemed to curve around both the fiery blade and Kalki himself.

The large man with armor and the beard, the god who might be Ukrainian or Russian, with tattoos along the side of his face, he huddled down in front of me on one knee, with his arms tightly wrapped around his chest, and my bullets wildly ricocheted away from him, springing wild colors in all directions. There was the man with the cane, the old man, standing there *singing* for god's sake. Singing, and somehow, for some reason, the bullets just dropped in front of him. They plinked to the ground, their colors dying away as they fell.

I had been laughing. Those laughs died off a bit. I had known it wasn't going to be easy, and might have been carried away in the first few moments. After all, it wasn't every day a person fought a group of gods. It wasn't every day a man faced powers like this, got the jump on them, and perhaps stood there for a long bit of time, holding his own.

It was time to try the other thing.

I squeezed my middle fingers. Both of them, in each hand. At the time I had been making the suit, waving my palm over the silk, the thought of the motion, the finger I picked, felt appropriate.

Like before, I felt the whirring of the knuckles squeeze. The whine of the power core behind me. The cold rushing feeling of primordial power running up my back, to the rocket bay perched on my suit's shoulder.

Rockets launched out of the bay. Not all at once, but one at a time. One after the next for the first row of five. Then the second row. Then the third. Unguided rockets, heading out to where I was facing, with large payloads.

Each of those launches was staggering in power. Each of those launches felt like someone had punched the suit in the front, trying to knock me backwards. The whine of the power core grew behind me, the whirring of the motors in my knees and feet and lower back spun louder, holding me still.

I kept firing the machine guns. After all... infinity. My arms went a little left-and-right under the launches, though, so that the bullet traces kind of windmilled away from me as primordial power fired from the nozzle of each rocket, as each rocket propelled itself out of the bay, one after the next.

The rockets wound their way through the air. Like the bullets, their trails were colored, but much, much larger. Sparks of the colors dripped behind each of the nozzles, leaving fiery scatterings of shiny colors, falling to the concrete. The sparks spit and spattered, a burning trail of breadcrumbs following each rocket until each delivered its payload.

Those payloads were large.

I had maybe imagined too much.

The world blew up around me. Kalki disappeared under one explosion of the brightest, deepest purples—whether the god had been incinerated or had just left the fight, I didn't know. I couldn't know, because he was there in my HUD, holding his sword against everything I was throwing at him, and then in a blink he was just gone.

The singing old man found he couldn't out-sing the rockets, too. I saw his face, there at the end, his mouth open and loud under the barrage of bullets, then widening further as the red rocket made its way to him, his voice growing louder and louder, until there was a boom and bits and pieces of skin and bone and white beard went everywhere.

A rocket found Vali. The god might have been moving, lying there in front of the model of New Orleans. He might have been getting a hand underneath him. It was hard to say, and it would always be hard to say, because a rocket found him and exploded against his back, and there was nothing left of that god but a Vali-shaped smear on the concrete.

The raven-haired woman took a rocket on her shield. She was still laughing, which I found odd, and then discarded the thought. I mean, what was odd in a battle to save the world, where I was taking on all the different gods of all the different mythos, in an exoskeleton battle-jacket made of the primordial power of creation?

So, let her laugh. I laughed back as the rocket exploded and the god was thrown back through the warehouse wall. Not the drywall, not what I had burst through coming out of the bathroom, but the thick concrete wall of the outside.

She took half of that wall with her. The concrete blocks burst out, some of the roof fell down as the support left it, and the force of the explosion took a lot of the blue and red and orange and yellow and gray with it. As if the warehouse was a balloon, and someone had pricked it, all of the colors and smokes escaped from the building in one large whooshing pop.

Something punched into me. I had been caught watching the colors escape, the rush of them follow the raven-haired god. I had been caught watching, and something burst back into me with incredible force.

The Russian god. Or who I thought of as the Russian god. The large Slavic man with the leather cuirass and the large axe on his back. The large bearded man with the tattoos running down the side of his bald head, from his temple.

His eyes were ferocious. His face grim. He grunted and swung his axe and the blow hit the side of the exoskeleton with all the might of a lightning bolt, with the hardest hammers of the largest of storm clouds.

I went flying, much like the raven-haired girl.

Warning sounds trilled from the suit as I travelled through the air, though there was nothing I could really do about it. There were loud blaring alarms, beeps and boops and the sound ambulances made as they sped down the highway. All I could do was think Danger, Will Robinson, as the suit travelled through the air and crunched into a concrete wall all its own.

Things screamed. Motors whirred and sparked. Armor plates buckled and bent, some of them were torn off as I slid along the wall and then part of the floor. Pieces of Skidblandir fell off, were ripped away as I tumbled along the concrete. The pieces of plate covering my pod. The rocket launcher bay. One of the machine guns on one arm.

More bouncing and sliding. The heads-up display cracked as it snapped against the concrete. The power core itself whined to new heights.

Then I stopped. The exoskeleton stopped. Finally. The beeps and trilling alarms muted. Muted, or my hearing was going. The smoke of the building, the smoke and all the colors from all the bullets and all the exploding rockets, still leaked from the side of the warehouse, leaving just a hazy gray fog inside with thin threads of blues and reds and yellows.

My mouth tasted salty. Blood. I had bit my tongue during my trip through the air. There was a heavy smell of ozone in the building. Ozone, or something like it. I blinked and tried to get my bearings, I tried to learn how to get the exoskeleton up.

Luckily, there was someone there to help me with that.

Vidar.

If I thought he had been angry before, I hadn't really understood the god. He stood there, in front of me, and his face really radiated anger. I mean, literally. His face was red, the darkest of reds, the glow the heaviest of vengeances, the hardest of angers. The red almost glistened along the sharp edges of his granite-like cheeks.

True to his nature, he said nothing.

I didn't think I needed to hear anything, anyway.

I knew I was going to either live, or die, in a moment or two.

I swung the arm with the machine gun still attached to it forward. Squeezing my index finger. Feeling the power core choke a bit under the demand. Feeling the damage there. The gun though, started to spin. The bullets started to leave it, as I swung my arm forward.

Then Vidar stomped on it. Stomped my gun attachment with his foot. His feet, wearing the thick leather straps wrapped around them. The straps formed into the shapes of a shoe.

The machine gun snapped off.

The power core screamed.

Vidar grinned then, and it wasn't a happy grin. It wasn't welcoming. It was the angriest grin from the angriest man in the world. The god reached down and picked me up, easily, thousand-pound exoskeleton or not, his grin turning into a snarl. The side of his nose crunching up with it.

Then he threw me. Backwards. Back to where I came from.

The Slavic god.

This time the flight went worse. If it had been a crash-landing before, this time it was the hard impact of a spaceship accelerating into the Earth. The suit crashed into the concrete and tumbled; I fell out of it, Skidblandir tossed and turned around me and—*thankfully*—didn't crush me underneath it as we rolled together across the concrete, a large ball of both machine and human.

The floor tore into me. Pieces of Skidblandir ripped into me. A sharp piece of something: metal of the universe, edge of concrete, or weapon left by a dead god, shredded the back of my leg. Something in my arm, my right wrist, snapped.

I screamed under the pain. I almost blacked out at the snap of my wrist. The machine and I tumbled together, this snowball of metal and man, until we stopped. Somewhere in the middle of the warehouse. We stopped, part of Skidblandir on top of me, pinning me there. We stopped, and everything was black.

I thought I was dead.

It took a long moment for me to realize that just my eyes were shut. Pressed shut. Against the burning pain from the back of my leg. The sharp shattering pain of my wrist. The thick coppery taste of blood in my mouth, blood that might not just be coming from a bite in the tongue, anymore.

I opened them. Skidblandir was lying on top of me, just pieces of it. The largest part of the torso of the exoskeleton. As if, at the end, it had thrown itself over me to protect me.

Still, the machine was pinning me down. The weight of what was left. The parts of the suit.

It was pinning me down, and there was the Slavic god. Standing there, his huge chest swelling with a deep breath. A breath, a breath that was going to turn into the largest of laughs. The largest of realizations that the battle had been won, that the god had survived and won, that the gods had won.

Only, they hadn't.

Because I was still alive. Because I still had a hand on Skidblandir. And because I still had a weapon left.

The nerves might not be firing correctly, the muscles might not be responding, and oh god did it hurt, but I had worked through pain before. Worked through the numb feeling of losing my right hand. Worked through all of that, as the tumor had grown in my head, as it had pressed on my brain and stole all of that from me, so that I couldn't pour expressos, or type, or write.

So it was easy enough to force my fingers there to close. Just enough on one of the rods of the exoskeleton suit. Easy enough to pinch the metal of Skidblandir with my thumb and forefinger and call it back into the scarf it always was.

The exoskeleton suit disappeared in a blink. Became that deep blue square of a scarf.

In that moment I grabbed the golden spear. The spear that still somehow lay tucked onto the back of Skidblandir. The golden spear with the edge so sharp it blurred in the air.

And in that moment the Slavic god died.

The scarf disappeared. The spear was in my hand. And I struck it, true, into the center of the chest of the god.

His mouth, ready to laugh, opened with a big Ohhhh sound. His breath left his body. His axe fell to the ground.

And the god followed.

His body limp. Dead.

With me standing over him. Standing, somehow, on my shredded leg. The scarf loose in my right hand. The spear tight in the grasp of my left.

I slipped the spear from the chest of the god. Looked at its shaft. Saw the same symbols etched into the pole of the spear. The same symbols as the golden pen I wrote with.

Gungnir.

I guessed that the toys of the gods weren't just toys. The things I had been given as a Chronicler were more than just things. That the pen might always strike true. That it might be mightier than the sword. Or axe.

And thinking that, I looked over at Vidar.

The anger was still there. It radiated. But there was a look of something on the god's face underneath all that. It might not be fear. It might not be panic. It might not be desperation or cowardice.

But part of it *was* recognition.

And with that recognition, the angry god left. One moment there, one moment gone. Leaving me in an empty warehouse. A warehouse empty of anything but the dead bodies of vengeful gods, of the miniature model of New Orleans. Empty of anything but the slowly thinning air around me. The fading trails and clouds of color. The gauziness of the smoke.

Empty of everything but me.

Me and New Orleans.

Finn MacCool – 1. Gods who want to end the world – 0.

CHAPTER THIRTY-SIX

As much as I had saved New Orleans, I didn't celebrate it. I didn't sit there and soak in the win. I didn't light a cigar and like it when a half-ass plan comes together. I didn't take a deep breath and survey what I had done, maybe pump a fist.

Instead, I sank down to the concrete. Feeling the coldness of it on the backs of my legs. Feeling the hardness there. I sat there and tried to figure out my next step, lying Gungnir next to me, the spear clattering a bit against the floor.

The first thing wasn't hard.

I was in a lot of pain. My leg burned and bled where it lay. My wrist was a silent scream of agony. I carefully held the scarf in my right hand and reached my good left hand into it, pulling out a first-aid kit. Reached into the little closet there, where I stored things like my bag of toiletries, a favorite shirt or a pair of pants, and pulled out a first aid kit, a white box with a red cross on top of it.

I set the box on my lap and flipped the top up. What inside wasn't much, but enough. I had packed it to cover a variety of things, having learned over the years that while the wolf's power could heal a lot, there was a benefit to helping that power along a bit.

The biggest thing I had learned was that as fast as I might heal, there was still pain. So the first thing I had asked Berley for, and put in the case, were some syringes and a tiny bottle of morphine. I took a few moments, my right wrist being snapped, to get all that together, and then shot myself with a small amount.

I'll tell you that felt good, the rush of coolness from the injection spot, there on the meat of my thigh. The coolness spread up and over me in a rushing wave, and for a moment I sat there, soaking it all in. The coolness that came when you were under so much pain you couldn't feel it all; and then that pain being gone.

That came with a few deep breaths. A little relaxing of my body. The muscles loosening, a slow bending of my spine. I breathed in, still smelling the ozone in the room, and the slightest scent of smoke that comes from burning old wood.

A breath or ten later, I pulled a roll of athletic tape out of the box. I wouldn't need the wrap for long, Berley would fix me up once I got back, and the wolf's power would fix me more. I just needed to tape my wrist hard enough I could get back to the cavern.

So I wrapped my wrist, heavily, hard. With a lot of tape. Each wrap of the white tape around my wrist grew more painful, painful enough that I winced under each wrapping of it, as the wraps grew thicker. It was painful, but I kept moving my fingers, squeezing them. Making sure that as red as they turned, that they lightened up again. That blood was moving in and out of my hand.

I got to a point where I felt like it was good enough. That the wrist would hold. Even if there might be hell to pay for it later.

As I was tending to myself, the bodies of the dead gods around me started to fade. To disappear from the warehouse, and maybe from this world. Maybe that's what happened to gods when they died.

Near me had been the remnants of Vali, the spattering of the young man who had wanted me dead, for no real reason. He disappeared like a thin puddle of water evaporating under the hottest of suns. Shrinking before my eyes, before just being gone.

Others did the same trick. The bits of flesh left of the striking Greek woman, too. The large body of the Slavic god, fading like from a movie. The rest of the gods lying around, the ones I did and didn't know. The ones that hadn't fled.

Then the miniature city of New Orleans.

It began to flicker in front of me. Flicker like the lights had, when the storm had been raging. Then it too, faded out. Faded like whatever had created it was gone.

That had me feel like it was finally over. Like the battle had been won. That I had stopped Ragnarok.

X would be proud. Maybe not proud, but happy. Happy that his services would still be needed. Maybe even Hode would smile, even if he was tired of the world. Maybe he'd play one for old Finn MacCool.

I smiled a bit, to keep from wincing as I smeared a whole tube of antibiotic around the back of my leg. Trying not to feel the raw, shredded skin there, trying to not see the blood on my fingers when I put more of the ointment on them. I cleaned my fingers up the best I could with a little sterile antiseptic pad, then wrapped some non-stick pads around the back of that leg and wrapped gauze tightly around my leg. Much like with the wrist.

I did all of this, what felt like, slowly. Maybe I was just taking it all in. Maybe it was all the adrenaline leaving me after the fight. Maybe it was morphine.

Next to me, Gungnir had become a pen again. I hadn't noticed the switch. It had been a golden spear, lying there, and now it was just the pen. I saw it there next to me on the floor, small and golden, if still maybe sharp. At least in what it might write.

I needed to put it in the book. At that thought, a breath escaped me. Because the book was a weight, and I didn't want to pull it out and put it back around my neck.

I didn't want to, but I needed to.

So I reached into the scarf of Skidblandir and pulled out the satchel.

And, in that moment, realized I hadn't won anything at all.

I hadn't won a thing.

Because the satchel was vibrating there in the air. Vibrating, hanging from my hand. Vibrating like the largest of cell phones. The feeling of it shook in my hand.

I shook, holding it. Realizing I had missed something. And maybe, maybe it was the morphine. Maybe it was denial. But I had trouble thinking it.

The satchel's flap was hard to open. I had to work it with my right hand, with the tape wrapped heavily around the broken wrist, wincing as I did. I tried once, twice, and then gave up and set the satchel in my lap.

It vibrated even there. I yanked the flap open with my left hand. Pulled the book out and when I did saw the squirrel.

It was running laps around the dust jacket.

Running laps so fast the book trembled under the creature.

Running laps so fast I wondered why the book wasn't on fire.

I opened it quickly. Right to the first page. The squirrel's page.

There I saw the same words as before. This time, though, repeated over and over. The squirrel ran laps around the page, left to right, hopping down a line and starting again.

The wolf calls you home.

The wolf calls you home.
The wolf calls —

The book's vibration felt like an alarm. Like the old alarm on the side of a firehouse. The one they always called the five-alarm fire, when it rang. When that bell rang, with all the other firehouse bells.

The realization hit me then.

What all this had been about.

Why Emma-mae had told Vidar to take me here. To this warehouse. In New Orleans, to fight the storm there.

It had been a distraction.

Maybe she had never had it in her to kill me. Maybe after last night something had been built between us that she had trouble ending, just like me. Maybe she had memories of the first time we met, just like I had. Maybe she still had dreams of two people sitting in a diner arguing about pancakes or hash.

Maybe she hoped she wouldn't have to deal with me. After all, Vidar was taking me to a warehouse full of gods. And the world would end here, or it would end where Emma-mae was going.

Either way, she wouldn't have to face me. She just had to face her task. The whole reason she had set this up, had pulled all the powers to New Orleans.

Not the powers and gods that wanted to destroy the world. Not just them. But those who wanted justice, fairness. Some of these gods hadn't been about the destruction, so much as seeing the right thing done.

This storm here in New Orleans had never been about the end of the world. It had been about pulling everyone's attention, even the wolf's, here. To this city.

While she snuck in somewhere else. To end not just this world, but all of them.

Because the real fight for the world wasn't here. The real fight for the universe wasn't here. It could never be about the storm in New Orleans.

The real fight was—it had always been—about the wolf.

About the Ragnarok to end all Ragnaroks.

And I was missing it.

CHAPTER THIRTY-SEVEN

I rushed as fast as I could. As fast as my morphined body would let me. As fast as my tired, exhausted muscles would work. As fast as my morphined body would go.

My brain even felt like it went too slow. Like it thought the screaming cry for more adrenaline too much. As if it had given what it could, and that was all it could do.

So the first few seconds felt like forever. Picking up Gungnir and stuffing it and the book into the satchel. Wrapping the satchel's strap around my neck. Stumbling up from where I sat, standing there on my legs, almost losing my balance.

It all took too long.

I held the scarf in a shaky left hand. Snapped it in the air, a little less of a snap than an unfurling, calling the Harley-Davidson. The V-Rod.

Even if I didn't snap it, if David Copperfield wouldn't be proud of me, Skidblandir formed under the scarf. Like it always did. Like the magic machine hadn't just undergone a battle and been torn apart.

One moment it was the scarf, and like always in the next it was the motorcycle. With its black tank and silvery figure running alongside it, the long glimmery form of a wolf in mid-run, its paws stretching forward, its hair ruffled by a gale of wind, its eyes holding some inner spark, its jaw open in mid-howl.

Part of me let out a breath. A deep breath. I was worried it would be broken. Or that some pieces of the motorcycle might be missing after the battle. The exoskeleton had taken a real beating. A beating it had taken for me.

But the bike looked fine. Even new. I had no idea how, but I was just going to call it magic. I was just going to thank that thing that powered it, the primordial center of the universe from which all things had been created.

I was going to thank it and go. I finished calling Skidblandir, flicking, unfurling the scarf. Smoothing it out with my heavily taped right hand, in a motion that was both numbing and painful. I did all that until the motorcycle was in front of me.

And still felt like I was going to be too late.

I roared out of there. Through the side of the building that had the large hole in it. Rolling over the rubble with tires that seemed to ignore the broken and burnt concrete blocks. I ignored that and raced for the cavern in the Adirondacks, already knowing I would arrive too late.

Skidblandir was fast. But it couldn't travel in the blink of an eye. And, with the book vibrating even now against my side, vibrating even over the roar of the V-Rod, I felt like blink of an eye was what I needed.

Still, all I could do was try.

I got to the highway in seconds. The interstate. The buildings and homes, the trees in the marsh, the water, the lakes, all beginning to blur around me. I got there and rolled my right wrist back further, opening the bike up, really up, feeling the roar of the engine grow into a world-ending howl, and sped until I saw nothing but a blur.

And still I knew it wasn't going to be fast enough. Each moment was critical. Every second mattered. And I was already too late. Too late, even as cars appeared stopped on the road. Even as the motorcycle sank into the curves and roared out of them. Too late even as the marshlands and the lakes began to swell into the blurred, low-lying foothills of the Appalachians.

The motorcycle howled and roared. The book clanged against my side. Time was critical. I didn't have enough.

It was then fate yanked me off the road.

Literally.

One moment I was there, speeding back north along the highway. With all the cars around me blurring by. Frozen in place. Those cars in slow motion, and me, definitely not. The land speeding by in the fastest of blurs, the swamps and trees and lakes smearing into the low, old hills of old mountains.

The next moment I was spinning out of control. I had no idea what to do, and then it came to me there was nothing I really *could* do. I was on a magic motorcycle going the greatest of speeds, and then I was tumbling over and around in a world that was nothing but smudges and smears. Everything flashed by me. The flat lakes. The grasping branches of trees. The rounded hill shapes of browning grass.

Everything flashed by me, faster and faster. The smears and smudges became their own blur. Became the greatest of blurs. Until even the world was one great blur itself.

Until then even the blur... was *not*.

Until I was standing there, on the side of the road. Standing and not spinning in circle after circle. Standing, having stopped spinning just short of the speed of light, and finding the transition too great for my brain to make.

My brain was still spinning out of control. Still spinning on Skidblandir. And yet, at the same time, here I was, standing not on a road, but a trail. A path of dirt, if not well worn, then occasionally travelled. Walked.

Standing straight by my motorcycle.

Even if my mind was still spinning round and round.

The difference was too great.

I bent over and threw up. My stomach roiling with nausea. My head still spinning in a body that was not.

I emptied my stomach. There wasn't much in it to empty, just coffee and donuts, but I didn't check. I stood there, huddled over my knees, bile raw in the back of my throat, spittle hanging from my lips. I stood there over my knees, the satchel hanging from my neck, taking deep breaths until my brain stopped spinning, until my legs stopped shaking and my feet were steady. And then, only then, did I try looking back up again.

Looking along the path that led up from me.

A path through the woods. Hardwoods, old. Tall and thick. Oak trees with hard bark, smoother barks of birch and maple. Perhaps a redwood in the back of them, a large tree much larger than the others, so large it couldn't possibly be as far back as it looked. It couldn't possibly loom over the rest of the forest, the trees there, the path wandering from my feet, and the cottage at the end of that path.

The cottage. A small thing built of round stones cobbled together, sitting next to a small well made of large stones, with a bucket hanging from a piece of wood overtop the well. Everything looked peaceful, the woods, the well, the cottage with its roof of thatch and its stone chimney along the side of the building, from which leaked a small trail of smoke.

A small cottage, with its door open. Inviting.

A small cottage with a woman in it. Neither old, nor young. And just like all the stories I had read about her.

The woman who would always welcome you to the home of the Fates. The woman of the present, the mother, the allotter, the woman who carried a hint of preservation to her, of the present moment. Of living, and *being*.

Verdandi.

One of the Fates.

I knew her as soon as I saw her. Perhaps appearing a little older than me, with brown hair that might have once been auburn, but now carried the slightest hint of gray. By the slight thickening of a waist that once might have carried an hourglass figure. By the small lines in her cheeks, the smile lines from the sides of her eyes, the earthy green irises. By the knowing smile of someone who welcomes a son or daughter home.

Verdandi. One of the three Fates. Which meant Urd and Skald were inside. Which meant that the well next to the cottage was not a well of water, but the Well of Urd. The Well of Wisdom.

Which meant that the tree in the back of the forest wasn't a redwood, but Yggdrasil itself.

The woods seemed timeless. There was no beginning or end to them. Still, there was a feel to them, a feel of fall turning into winter, a feel of chill air whispering through brittle leaves. A smell of thick wet earth, the smallest scent of old brush, of wet branches and mushroomed logs, the slight hint of a dark loam in which a seed could be planted, with the hope that spring would come.

I held there a moment. Ran my hand along Skidblandir and, after a moment, pulled the silken scarf into a square and placed that square into my pocket. Not because I felt like the magic might help me, but because it was a part of me now, and I didn't want to lose it.

My wrist still ached something fierce. My leg still burned underneath the gauze and ointment. I wasn't in some magic place where everything was healed and everything was okay, but in some place outside of the world. Some place where I was the foreign entity, where I didn't belong, where there were powers beyond the like of anything I had seen or known.

I took a slow step forward. Afraid, like I hadn't been in my life. Afraid not in life or death but the knowledge I may, or may not get. Afraid of knowing a future I didn't want to know.

Still, I took that step. Maybe because the book was no longer clanging its five-alarm fire alarm. Maybe because it wasn't shaking or vibrating or calling me any more, which meant to me either I was in a time or place that had no time or place, or that the world had already ended.

I was hoping, as I took my next step, that it was the former.

CHAPTER THIRTY-EIGHT

I walked the path up to the cottage. There was a slight chill to the air, not uncomfortable, the kind of chill you might find in the mountains in the fall. The woods, at least the trees close by, felt familiar. Familiar in both place and time, even if I was somewhere I had never been.

There were thick oaks with spreading boughs, with wavy, lobed leaves dangling along its branches, the leaves fiery in the dying colors of fall. There were a few birch trees, branches stark, thin piles of crispy leaves along the ground underneath them. There were groups of maples, clumped together, hand-like leaves browning this late in the year, the brown hands swaying in some breeze, as if the leaves clutched at invisible spirits winding through the forest.

It felt normal, and otherworldly, both. There was the scent of the woods, the earthy loam. The slightest scent of pine, from trees I couldn't see, but must be there. There was the clean smell of mountain air. There was even the rushing of a stream somewhere, the pouring-water sound of a stream running along a slope, perhaps whisking around pools of stones.

I swallowed back the sour aftertaste of bile. Some water would be good now. Some cool, crisp water to flush down what I had so recently tossed up.

Normal, this place. And otherworldly. The tree in the background, Yggdrasil, remained both in the background and yet loomed over everything. It was so large it was everything, I felt. The trunk monstrous, that far in the distance.

It had me wonder about the roots. How many there must be, to support a trunk that large. How far the roots must seek for sustenance. How thick they must grow, to fuel something that immense.

My steps pulled me closer to the cottage in front of me. To Verdandi, waving me forward, the gentle smile on her face. The ground soft, like earth would be, underneath my feet. Giving just the slightest amount under each foot, before firming up to support me.

"Finn," Verdandi said, the smile still there. The motherly smile I would expect to see on this Fate. The measurer, the allotter. The preserver, the blissful, bountiful body of the present.

I stopped right before her. The cottage could have come from any story of the Middle Ages. The walls were thick round stones puzzled together in such a way that there were no cracks between them, as if each rock had been selected to fit a precise purpose. The thatch was full overhead, and smelled of the reaped hay of the fall. The smoke trailing from the chimney, like the slow exhaling fires of a dragon, bringing the faintest hint of ash to mind.

I can't tell you how much fear I had then. Or why, precisely, I had that fear. I only knew that it overwhelmed me, so that I stood there a long moment. A long moment of my satchel not vibrating its five-alarm ring. A long moment of which time had frozen, of which time had no meaning.

Of which, possibly, I would find about myself. A person with no meaning. With nothing that mattered.

The smile of Verdandi was always there. It didn't move, her lips didn't widen. Her eyes didn't twinkle any more or any less. But there was something there, something I felt in her, something anyone might feel from their mother. A recognition of the understanding her child was experiencing. An... *enjoyment* of a mother watching the process. Of seeing growth, small or large. Steps forward.

Verdandi stepped aside. "Please, come in."

I want to tell you I stepped right in. But it took a minute. There was something I had to work through, some power or energy or will I had to call up. Something to unlock the fear, unlock my limbs, and work me through the threshold.

Inside was much like I might expect. It was neither larger nor smaller than the cottage it appeared to be. It was a single room of many functions, much like the cottages had been built, back in the times these had been built.

The first thing I noticed was the tapestry. It was everything you would think it might be. It stretched along the back wall, and was large and complex. It held everything you could think of, scenes from all places and times if you looked at it. If you peered closely enough at a corner, you might see a man and woman eating an apple. A heavily tanned man standing by a river, with a golden circle over his brow, a circlet with the tiniest hint of serpent to it. In another place, if you squinted, you could see a warrior with a dome-shaped helmet, pointed at the top, flared out to either side, as the man charged the tallest of stone walls, walls as tall as skyscrapers.

When you pulled back though, it was just a tapestry of colored threads. All blending together in some pattern that was beautiful but also tough to describe. Some of the threads twinkled, others were dark, all contained a range of colors greater than a rainbow, greater than any painting, any picture of the universe with its beautifully deep greens, its vibrant blues, its glowing reds and yellows and oranges.

Odd, there was no picture to be seen there. No picture of the world or universe. Nothing to connect all the dots of all the worlds together, no image to bind the universe into one *thing*. Just a tapestry of threads all tied together, the weaving unfinished even, as I looked at the right side of the colorful mural and it unfinished on that side, the edge of the tapestry unfinished—not bound together but frayed—threads unfinished there, the strands hanging loose, at various lengths.

I looked over the piece for what felt like a long time. Seeing the colorful image that wasn't an image of the tapestry. Zooming in occasionally, to pick out pieces of it. Perhaps pieces closer to my life, to where I lived. A mother taking her boy to a library. A young woman teaching a class of kids, in an old wooden schoolhouse. And there, far to the left, the image of a young cub, a small dark furry thing, rolling in a field of flowers under the bluest of skies.

That had me yank back from the images. From all the stories of all the worlds and universes. It seemed the tapestry, like the Fates, had expected me. Not only expected me, but was familiar with my story. As far back as it had begun.

I took in the rest of the cottage, everything but the tapestry that —like Yggdrasil—both remained in the background of the home of the Fates, and yet loomed over everything. The fireplace was there to my left. Roaring with a fire that seemed too large for the thin trail of smoke coming from the chimney outside.

There were black tools hanging around the rock of the chimney, ladles and larger spoons and forks and things that might stir. There was a fireplace poker off to the side, a long black iron rod, curved at the end, curved almost like a fleur-de-lis, with sharp points at the edges of the curves. There was a pot there, in the middle of the fire, bubbling with something that smelled like a good venison stew, something chock full of carrots and celery and onions, the holy trinity of French Mirepoix, but also the best stock for any good soup.

An old woman sat next to the stew. The Crone. Urd. She was, much like Verdandi, exactly what I expected. Old, wearing a dark robe as if it were cold in the cottage, the hood pulled up over her face to hide as much of it as the hood could.

She sat in an old wooden chair, a thing made of different-sized woods, of split logs, a thick back, a sturdy seat, roughly tacked together. A tiny three-legged table sat next to her, made much the same way, the top a carved wooden disc.

On a little jar and a quill. The quill was made of a large, black feather, and it wasn't standing point-down in the jar, or on a stand, but resting flat on a piece of paper. As if Urd had just finished writing something and had laid the quill down.

That page looked familiar. At least the paper. It looked thin enough to appear like paper of any spiral notebook, but also thick. Heavy. As if it could last forever.

Her face was the leathery face of the old. Well-worn. Well-sunned. With wispy white hairs straying out from under her hood. She had the darkest of eyes, black, irises glinting there even out of the shadows under her face.

There was Urd, to my left. And Verdandi in front of me. Standing in a small room, that might be the welcoming area of a cottage. There were a few chairs along the back wall, right underneath the tapestry. The chairs were nicely put together wooden constructions with soft cushion tops. A loom there, an older type loom with a wheel that would spin as fast as a person could pump the pedals. A pair of shears next to the loom, a pair of shears resting half-open on a book.

Where a table sat, a table with four chairs, as if the Norns always had a place for a guest. The table and chairs were made of wood as well, but they weren't the rough construction of Urd, but something well-worn. Not polished, not waxed, but used for so long that all the surfaces had been smoothed with time. So that every joint seemed to fit where it needed to be. So that heartwood along the table's surface, so that every piece of maple or oak or birch making up the table, every grain of pale white, of rich mahogany, of dark oak melded together into one flat piece of wood.

That would make Skuld to my right. The unturning, the eternal. Youthful in appearance, of course. Young—younger than me in her looks. Perhaps the slightest relation to Verdandi, in the flowing auburn air, thick around her head, moving in a way that her hair always seemed to cover part of her face. A beautiful face, of white skin, pure and unblemished. Of the twinkling green eyes of the earth, of the young, of a spring forever in bloom.

She smiled at me. Or part of her mouth curved, the part I could see. She stood there, stood at a desk that looked more modern to me than the other pieces. Something that might be ordered off of Amazon, or bought from IKEA, something of modern angles and polished looks.

It looked that way, but I knew it was made of the same wood as the other furniture. Even if the desk almost didn't quite fit here, with a small thing that might be a motor underneath the flat of its dark, polished top. A motor to wind the desk up and down, depending on whether or not Skuld wanted to stand, or sit.

No surprise then, that there wasn't a book there on the desk. Nothing flat to write on, no pen or paper, but a computer instead. A computer, and yet not. It was something like an iPad, I thought, perhaps something made by Skuld for Skuld. It was a flat screen, dark and mirrored, angled slightly over a tiny mount that would fold down with the screen so that the screen and the mount would lay flat against the keyboard resting right below the mount.

As I watched Skuld swiped one finger across the dark surface of the screen. A quick right-to-left flick of her forefinger. I didn't know what that signified, maybe she was closing some application out, maybe she was shutting down her computer, maybe she was ending a life. I couldn't see, and I didn't know.

I say all this like it took forever for me to see, and look at. The truth was, like the rest of the place, while it felt like it took forever it was actually timeless. The whole place was timeless. It was in a place outside of space and time, so while I looked around and saw what I saw, the Norns were also moving.

Skuld had been smiling at me, closing out whatever she was closing out. Urd was cackling a bit to herself, ladling her stew into a giant bowl. Verdandi was setting places at the table, putting together polished wooden bowls at each chair, lying down small pieces of cloth under each plate. Setting together sharp, silver knives and forks and spoons just so around each bowl.

Right when I finished looking at everything, at seeing and understanding—some—the tapestry. Of looking at Urd, at Verdandi, at the loom and the quill and the sheers. Right when Skuld smiled at me and swiped, the table was set.

The table was set, and each of the Norns had taken a seat. Verdandi in one corner, Skuld across from her, and Urd, Urd to Verdandi's right.

That left one chair. Right next to Skuld. Right across from Urd. A chair with an empty setting before it, and a big pot of stew. Something that smelled deliciously of game and carrots and onions and carrots, heated for so long together that all their flavors blended together into some heavenly, hearty, thick soup.

My stomach grumbled.

As much as I was scared too, I was hungry.

So I took my seat, adjusting the strap of the satchel, as the three Fates sat there watching me.

CHAPTER THIRTY-NINE

Each of the Fates smiled. Skuld's mysterious, with the slightest hint of flirtation. Verdandi's the smile of a mother, welcoming, comforting. Urd's the smile of someone who had seen far too much, and saw that the person in front of her knew far too little.

"This," I said, finding my voice. "Seems familiar. Familiar, and yet... not."

It did. And it also didn't. The images were like every story about the Fates. Like every tale of the Norns. In any book or mythos. The Crone. The Mother. The child. The forest and the cottage.

Urd nodded. Her voice was a little creaky. Weathered. Dry. "You should expect this."

That didn't explain it. Not fully. Not in my brain.

Verdandi picked it up, with her soothing, comforting tone of a mother teaching a child. "We exist in a place no world does. We are of all worlds Finn, all worlds, and everything." She busied herself with the ladle, pouring stew into each of our bowls. First Urd. Then

Skuld, then me. The steam lifted off the soup with each pour, the heavenly trinity smell thick in the air over the table.

She finished as she spoke, ladling stew into her own bowl last. "What you see here is what you expect, and also not, because it is how your mind frames us."

Those words had me understand.

And, as comforting as they were, they also sent new fears tingling down my back. Because, if what Verdandi had just said was true, I wasn't sitting with three women in a table at a cottage. I was sitting with three cosmic forces, with no discernable shape of their own, no sound that I could understand, no smell I could remember, and my brain was translating everything around me into a cottage, with a tapestry, with the tables and books and pages and iPads, it was trying to show me things I might relate to, even the large, universe-spanning tree over us all outside.

Fear does sharpen the mind, though.

I gathered I wasn't the first person to come here. The first person to look at the three Fates in their cottage. The first person to come visit for wisdom.

I mean, I was here because Odin had come here. But, in my new understanding, I understood other gods and heroes had sat in this very seat. Larger than life heroes. Heracles and Achilles. Cu Chulainn. The cursed Karna. Alexander the Great.

Powerful gods, like Zeus. Osiris. Gilgamesh. Amaterasu.

Gods, kings, heroes, all who wanted consultation. Knowledge. Wisdom. People trying to tempt fate. To fight their destiny. To perhaps change it.

The curtain of my mind shimmered, the curtain that had clothed these cosmic figures with the figures of Urd, Verdandi, Skuld. Reminding me of my new understanding. Reminding me the world wasn't just this one I lived in, but all of them. All of the worlds and all of the universes, everything the Tree of Life had sunk its roots deeply within. That even more forces had tempted fate, had tried to change their destinies, more gods and peoples and heroes than I could imagine had sat in this very chair, perhaps eating this stew.

Though I was, perhaps, the first person yanked here.

"I gather a lot of people come here to visit you," I said, slowly.

Skuld smiled a bit more curvily. Verdandi's eyebrows rose, slightly. Urd just continued to stare at me, in the way old people had. Giving nothing.

"But you all brought me here," I said, my words still slow. Not trying to think of that yank of fate. The force that had pulled me, twisting and twirling, out of my world and into this cosmic place.

I left the word why out there, unasked. Because hanging there, it grew in strength. It grew and swelled throughout the room until I wanted to burst from the non-asking of it.

Urd laughed then. The sharp cackling laughter of an old woman. "Oh, he's a sharp one, in't he?"

I didn't feel sharp. Even if fear had sharpened my brain, I didn't feel that way. I was muddling along here, muddling with cosmic forces greater than perhaps any I had known, and I was careful to tread carefully.

"Eat," Verdandi said. Smiling like a mother with a still-growing teenager.

In the same manner as I had spoken, I ate. Picking up the spoon, stirring the stew. Scooping out a healthy amount, a pile of meat and orange carrots, of pale onions and almost translucent celery.

It tasted heavenly. It didn't heal anything, not physically at least. But it did nourish the soul. It just felt good to eat. Right.

I let out a deep breath. Felt better inside. Stronger. Less full of fear, and more full of something like contemplation.

"You are right," Verdandi said. "We have been visited by many. Many of those who wish to fight their destiny. Change their fate.

Who have the strongest of desires, matched with the most powerful of wills."

She blew a bit on her spoon. Just a bit. Then ate it, slowly.

Skuld took over. "Those, Chronicler, those are usually the ones that visit us. Those with the desire and strength to effect change. Those who want change so badly they are willing to do anything for it. Walk any path. Take any risk."

None of those sounded like me. I wasn't strong like Heracles. I wasn't powerful like Odin. I didn't even think I wanted change so much, as just to save. I didn't want to change so much as to make a difference. To matter.

"None of that sounds like me," I said. Perhaps a bit more bold, after a few bites of the stew. "I'm just a regular guy. There's nothing special about me."

Urd cackled here. Loud and hard. "So you say," she said. Pinning me to my seat with her dark, fathomless, piercing eyes. "What if I tell you that everyone could be special? That the darker the soil a seed is planted in, the brighter it can grow?"

I went to answer. Then stopped. Was she talking about me? Emma-mae? Were the Fates letting me know there was some hope there? Some hope of saving. Some hope, if I could save the world, I could also save the girl?

I went to ask the question, and stopped as well. Knowing I would get no straight answer from the Fates. That was one thing all the stories said, and something I felt was dead-on true, sitting here in front of them.

I found my head cocked, staring back at the old crone. She took a bite of stew, a bite off her spoon, and I saw she was missing as many teeth as she had.

I wondered if her missing teeth was just more of the curtain my brain had pulled in front of the cosmic forces before me. Some detail my mind had put on Urd. Or was it some real difference, or representation, of the powers before me?

Urd's words still hung there. Hung in the air of the cottage with all the things left unsaid. Hung there, and something about it reminded me of the wolf. Reminded me of talks of trees sprouting, of all the whys I had left unasked, with the one I left unasked, even now. They hung there with the talk about seeds and dark soils and brightness, with the thick scent of stew, of carrots and onions and celery. All of the words and thoughts and questions and smells hung in the air there in the cottage, and all of it and everything circled each other.

We should never really know things like fate and destiny. We should never know the shape of the tree we plant, I thought. We should plant the seed, nourish what we could, and hope for the best. Hope for something strong and tall and many-branched, something able to withstand any storm.

Maybe that's what they had brought me here for.

"Something to drink?" Skuld said. Pouring water from the jug into a tiny wooden cup, and setting that jug in front of me.

All of a sudden everything coalesced. It wasn't water in the cup. Well, not just water.

They were here offering me nourishment.

Wisdom.

Wisdom from the Well of Urd.

Wisdom Odin had had to give an eye for. Wisdom that had been turned away from other kings and gods and heroes. Wisdom for me, for just a regular guy, because they saw the end coming, much like I had.

Because they thought I would have need of it. They had pulled me from space and time to give me a moment. They had pulled me to give me a moment and perhaps this, a cold glass of ultimate knowledge, knowledge of anything and everything, of things happening now or in the future.

The cup loomed large in front of me. For some reason it had me think of Odin, hanging there from the branches of Yggdrasil. Not outside, not out in the forest here and now, but on the dust jacket of my book.

As a warning.

I was thirsty. I had lost a good amount of blood during the fight with the gods. I had lost even more throwing up outside. And the stew was hearty, but thick. It needed moisture.

The cup loomed ever larger. The water shifted along the surface, as if a ripple ran lightly across it. The liquid shimmered there, shimmered with knowledge. With perhaps even power.

It was hard. Tremendously hard. Hard enough I couldn't trust myself to say the word. That if I opened my mouth I would be opening it to pour that cup into it.

I shook my head. Slowly. Keeping my hands locked together under the table.

"Are you sure?" Skuld asked, leaning just a bit in. Her auburn hair shifting to reveal just a little more of her face. Her smile even more inviting.

I kept my mouth shut. I kept my hands clasped under the table. I shook my head. Again, like everything else here, slowly.

"Do you even know why you are here?" Verdandi, this time. Her eyes slightly narrowed, not tightly, but open in the way a parent asks a child a very important question. In the way a professor might pause in front of a classroom, standing in front of a student, asking and waiting to see the answer. "Shouldn't you figure it out?"

Did I know? Only in the vaguest sense. Sure, I was here because I was the Chronicler of the Wolf. I was here because I happened to be the guy writing things into a book when the ending was going to happen. I was here because I was the last of the Chroniclers, because there was no one else to be here.

That was what I knew. The vagueness was everything else. Thoughts. Feelings. I was here because of things like hope. Because of all the stories I had read as a kid, of my mother taking me to the library when we had nothing else, of me coming back with story after story of the worst happening to the hero, of a character getting beat down into nothing and yet still finding a way to keep going. Still finding a way to climb out of the pit the story had put them in and win. Still finding a way to protect those they love and care about. Find a way to beat the monster they face, and *win*.

Winning might be relative, in today's world. There were a lot of wrongs in it. More wrongs than rights. But that didn't mean we erased it all and hoped there was a way to start over. That we shook the etch-a-sketch and just started to draw again. The world was a mess, and the only way to make it better was each of us doing just a little better. Doing just a little better, and reaching out to those right next to us. Helping them out of their own dark pits. Each of us climbing slowly to the light.

It would be messy. It would take a long time. Years. Decades. Millennia.

But that would be the only way. Hard work, to climb that mountain. There would be a lot of backslides, a lot of two steps forward, ten steps back. A lot of dollars in a bucket. A lot of people helping someone off the street, offering them an arm and a hot cup of tea. A lot of people willing to withstand the mocking and the accusation, the fear, the hate, to help those they love. And maybe a person willing to withstand that ever-present blame, that thing people rage out with, when the world is unfair and they no longer can see a way out of their own dark pits.

I understood then, winning wasn't the top of the mountain. Victory wouldn't be at the particular peak of the hill I climbed. The victory was in the climb itself. In the person climbing it. In the people who climbed it with him.

I thought, maybe, that I did know why I was here. It was why I wanted to write, after all. To write stories that mattered.

It was easiest, then, to shake my head no. Still overwhelmingly difficult, with all the knowledge there in that cup. Knowledge that could possibly show me how to fix everything, sure. But also knowledge of all the wrongs that would exist, too. Of futures I might not be able to steer this world away from. Of a dead end of everything that I would always refuse to believe could happen.

It would show me all the possibilities, maybe. It might show me all of the lives. But that cup would also show me all of the deaths.

Urd cackled again. She, too, didn't say anything, but her eyes said it all. Her laugh said it all.

Verdandi nodded as well. I couldn't tell if it was the proud nod of a mother, or the conscious nod of a parent who understood their experience could never be somehow transferred to those who were younger. The accepting nod of a professor who might say to a student, you're almost there.

I looked down to see my bowl empty.

All their bowls empty. The pot holding the stew empty. The cup that had been placed before me, empty.

The audience was over. The Fates had gotten what they had brought me here for. Or hadn't. Either way, the tapestry would continue to be woven. For as long as it had time.

This place had felt timeless. Now there was a sense to it. Of a sun descending through the sky, falling to the west. Of time ticking away. Of a clock's hands spinning faster and faster.

The Fates brought me outside. Like they were setting me free. The three of them on one side of the cottage door, me on the other. There, it was Skuld, oddly enough, who said our parting words. Not Urd, with her ancient wisdom. Not Verdandi, the mother who may want more for her child, with the lessons she might want to still impart.

"We wanted to meet you, Finn," Skuld finally said. Her face still hidden by her hair, so that I just saw one spring-like iris, the curve of one side of her lips. Her voice young and tantalizing and somewhat wistful, as her words drifted past me, and into the great forest. "Sometimes, even we have to know."

Then the Fates shut the door.

And left me there, trembling.

Because the fear had returned. Had slammed back into me. Had hit me the way a speeding locomotive might thunder along the tracks and smack into a car abandoned there.

Because if the Fates wanted to meet me, if they had to see me, if there was something they felt like they wanted to know, something they felt like they *had* to know; if the cosmic forces which touched upon and bound not just my universe, but *all* universes together wanted to meet me because they were concerned...

If the Fates were that worried, well, so was I.

CHAPTER FORTY

I walked down the path, away from the cottage. In those moments the forest changed around me. Subtly, so I didn't understand what was happening at first, but after just a couple of steps saw and felt it all and understood. Understood why I had felt a little chill earlier, why I had heard a burbling stream then, why I had scented pine among the hardwoods around the cottage.

I stopped, and glanced back behind me. The cottage was gone. The Fates were gone. Yggdrasil, the looming many-rooted tree looming over everything, was gone.

In its place was the side of a mountain, climbing above me. Not just any mountain, but one I knew well. Knew because it was in the Adirondacks. Knew because this mountain held Fenrir's den.

If I was scared before, I was terrified now. Because not only were the Fates worried, but they had actually intervened. They had stolen me as I had rode out of New Orleans and placed me here, directly in front of the cave. They had saved me the hours I didn't have, the hours I would have lost on Skidblandir.

They had given me a precious few moments. Minutes, seconds

maybe. A precious few moments I had to save the universe. Or the seconds I had to lose it all.

I raced to the cavern, my feet pounding the old trail, the satchel bouncing on my hip. Raced from the sunlight into the shadowed entrance to the cave. To the door there, with all the runes of protection. With Algiz, the upside-down peace symbol at the corners. With the pointed D of Thurisaz surrounding the outside of the door itself. With Fehu, the stick figure symbol in the center.

The door was open. Had been opened. And remained that way. The symbols of protection empty. The runes silent.

I kept running. My feet pounded over rock now, the dark rock of a dark cavern. The lights were not lit above me, when they always had been on before. I ran, feet pounding stone, ran to the elevator deep inside the cave. Never had I run harder. I didn't feel the cold air on my chest, even if I was still shirtless. I didn't feel the satchel bouncing on my hip. I didn't see the puffs of my breath, entering that icy chill of Fenrir's den, even if I was still miles above it.

All I saw was the elevator. I ran to it and pushed the button. The doors opened, slowly in the way of all elevators, and I squeezed through the doors before they had finished their motion. Squeezed through them and pushed the button for down, the only button of the two in the elevator, pushed that button over and over, wanting to scream at the machine to *hurry*.

Elevators, though, never hurried. Never, even when the world depended on it. The doors binged open, then began their slow shutting. With me dancing there, pushing the button, over and over.

Then the doors finally shut.

The elevator began to sink through the earth. Sink with that little tugging motion you feel in the pit of your stomach, in your weight getting just a bit lighter for a moment. It dropped, farther and farther, and for once felt like it picked up speed, with me there stamping my feet, telling it to hurry. It raced down, and I could feel, in the way we all feel the distance of a thing we've travelled many times, that I was nearing the bottom.

I couldn't picture what was happening down there. What was going to happen. What Emma-mae was doing down there.

The wall of weapons flashed through my mind. The collection. I realized now that while my first thought had been a collection, it hadn't been that so much as a search.

A search for something that might end a god's life. That might end all the lives. That might be strong enough to bring the Ragnarok of Ragnaroks.

I knew why she was doing this. I knew why, and I could even hear her reasoning it to me, again and again. Her, Hode, Vidar, they all had the same variation of the theme. They all had hinted to me, or told me, that if enough time passed I would feel the same. I could feel it in all of them, the assurance, that given enough time, I would be like them.

Time… did I have enough? I hoped I did. I hoped I had just a moment. I hoped Emma-mae would give me one. Just a second, just a second to stand in front of her and say…

What? How can someone be pulled out of the blackest of abysses? How can someone be pulled from the deepest of pits? How could I get the moment, how could I even stop her, hold her back from destroying all the worlds?

The elevator began to slow. I felt it, in the gathering of the weight in my feet. The slight push of gravity, pushing me against the floor. The shifting of my body, and the slight bump of the satchel against my hip. I had a moment before the doors opened, and no real plan.

Just hope. All I had was me. Me, and Skidblandir, though there wasn't enough time to create something that might help. Not with the gentle stop of the elevator. The dinging of the bells, the doors opening before me now, the slow slide apart, like curtains opening to the final act of a play.

I had me. The satchel. The book.

And, at that bump of the satchel, I had the pen.

Gungnir.

I grabbed it from the satchel. It was what I had. It was all I had, the hard golden casing of the pen both barely warm, and subtly cool. Hard, temperate, the casing both the pen and the spear. The points of both never missing their mark.

Ding.

The curtain of the elevator doors parted.

The first thing revealed was the white-tiled hospital floor. Just a thin white sliver of tile leading away from the elevator and down the hallway. A narrow section of white tiles between the gap of the opening doors, with a thick streak of red slashing from left to right across the gap.

The doors opened fully. The streak widened to the left. Where Rivers lay, the thickly muscled silent guard, in two pieces. Cleaved in two, so that his top half was completely separate from his bottom. With all the things leaking from both halves, the pink twining tissue of his intestines, with severed white bone, with burnt edges of torn skin and with thick globs of dark red and that giant puddle thickly spreading across the floor.

He was face down, thank the gods. I didn't want to see his face. I didn't want to notice his hand there, outstretched, still twitching.

The dread overwhelmed me. I couldn't help it; I closed my eyes. Even with the urgent need and worry and fear driving me. Even with the world, with *all the worlds* about to end.

No one should see something like that and not react. No person should see something like that and not take a moment. Feel the sorrow for the death and the pain of the dead. Feel the rage behind whoever had done something like this. Wonder about that person, how someone could do something like this to another. Wonder how someone they knew, connected with, loved, could do this thing.

Wonder about that deep pit that person was in. If there was a way to reach that person, that deep. And pull them out of that blackness.

Oh gods, I had to move. I had to make it. I took off running, trying not to breathe in the coppery scent of blood. The ugly scent of bowels released. The fetid smell of death.

I ran past Rivers, my feet spattering the streak of blood, the reach of red from one side of the hallway to the other. Tiny drops of it flung from my feet as I ran, the hall seeming to dim before me. The white lights seeming not to be so bright anymore, as if I ran towards darkness, towards the shadowed door of the operations center.

The feeling of dread grew. It swelled with every slap of my shoes against the hard tiles of the floor. It grew large enough I breathed it in, I took in the deep dread with every breath so that my chest was full of it, full of the fear, so full I couldn't breathe it all back out, it just kept getting larger and larger until it felt like my lungs were too full, my chest too tight with it…

I swung open the shadowed door of the operations center. The place was wrecked, lit only by what lights remained. A tiny light over the kitchen counter, by the coffee pot. The light of the refrigerator holding the beakers and vials. One of the computer displays under the window looking into Fenrir's cavern, one of the computers not smashed and broken, its pale green light tiny in the blackness.

Sounds came from the cavern. Grunts and clatters. The raking of claws on stone. A deep whuffing. The heavy breathing of a woman fighting a god.

Sounds I heard, but couldn't put together. My eyes took too long to adjust. Too long before I saw Berley in a chair by the round table. His form barely lit by the light of the laboratory refrigerator.

His body was in a chair. His feet still tucked a bit under the round white table with his magazines on it, sitting there with a cup of coffee before him, one hand on the table, on top of one of the science fiction magazines there. *Clarkesworld*. The other hand over a gaping hole in his chest, like he had been punched with the ball of something, a ball round and edged on either side.

The hole was large and round. The edges on either side had dug into his chest, had broken bone there. The wound was edged and blackened, as if by some great electrical force, like lightning. Berley's head hung back from his chair. His eyes were open behind his glasses. His mouth was half-open.

Dammit.

I blinked the shadows before me into some kind of objects. There was the door to the cave, the rubber-sealed door, half open. A chill wind blew from the crack, and the shadows in the caverns moved and twisted. There were screams and deep whuffs of exertion. There was rustling a great furred body over stone, there were the chinks and sparks of something hard and metal striking stone.

The sparks lit the forms, briefly. Lit the form of Emma-mae, dark and shadowed. Lit the great big form of the wolf, dancing, snarling, snapping. And then there was a great spark, a great two-handed swing by Emma-mae, and the wolf twisting and falling backwards with the largest of pained howls.

A roar of real pain. A roar of rage. A bellow, a howl that ended in a last gasp of a beast-like breath.

CHAPTER FORTY-ONE

I rushed into the darkness. The pen still in hand. Noticing, as I ran in, the pen growing longer, thicker. The pen thickening into a shaft, the point of it elongating, twisting, sharpening. The point sharpening until it blurred, until it shimmered a bit, a golden shimmer in the dark blackness of the cave.

It was a big cavern, with the computer banks and machines keeping Fenrir alive to the left. It was a dark cave, going back further than I knew. The spear lit what was in front of me, the tip of it glowing so I could make out the shapes.

The great wolf, to my left. Resting on top of the machines that had once kept him alive. Computers and machines destroyed now. Destroyed during the fight, or broken under the weight of the beast.

Did he live? I thought he must. Otherwise the world would be ending. Ending right now, in this moment. Ragnarok would sweep us all up, as the great serpent inside the Earth began its twisting and writhing.

There, deep in the blackness, I caught a second shimmer. A thin thread of it. Stretching back from the haunch of Fenrir's rear leg to deep in the cave. A thin thread that glowed, and something I knew would dance a bit with figures, with runes, if I had the time to sit there and let my eyes fully adjust to it.

Something that was the thinnest of threads, holding back the greatest of powers.

Finally, my eyes fully adjusted. Seeing Emma-mae there. Facing the form of the wolf. Standing so that they were a triangle. The wolf. Emma-mae. And the thread leading back to the wall.

My chest was already so tight, it couldn't handle any more fear. Any more dread. And yet, here and now, it seemed like that was all I could breathe in. It was everything, this moment, this *now*, where it was Emma-mae and me and the fate of the world.

I know. I should be thinking of saving the world. Of saving the worlds. Yet, all I could think about was saving the girl.

It was that moment for me. That moment where I just wanted to hold onto her. Hold onto Emma-mae and let the dark forces rush over us both, hold her until the tidal wave ripped through us, hold onto her no matter what dark waters tore at her, until the two of us were safe and whole. Until we had a moment where we could have another, where those moments would turn into seconds, then minutes, then hours, then years.

Emma-mae was holding one of the things I had seen on her wall. One part of her collection, the first piece I had seen and noticed. The bronzed scepter. The rod with the ball on it, a ball with two prongs, a pair of sharp metal wings spreading out on either side.

My mind raced through all the myths I had read about. The tales I had read both as a kid, walking back from the library, and as the Chronicler. All the different stories about all the different gods and powers. Of the different weapons, of those created to help the gods, and those made to challenge them.

Vajra.

That was it. That was the name. It was a sacred Hindu weapon, an indestructible object made from the bones of a sage. An invincible weapon made of universal connection and higher truths, made of the primordial stuff of the cosmos, cosmic creation forces like I had just tapped into myself, in my battle for New Orleans.

I grew very afraid. Of the weapon. Of what it meant. Of this moment, and what might come of it.

"Emma," I said. Trying.

Her eyes remained shadowed. I remembered them from the diner. Lively and sparkling green. Her lips twitched, like back then, just not in a smile.

I tried again. "Emma-mae." My voice croaked a bit. Croaked with how this was going. With the saddest of knowledge. With staring at someone you thought about sharing a world with, with sitting and comparing pancakes and hash until the end of your days, and understanding that world could never be.

Emma-mae did smile then. The same smile as back in the diner. A smile full of joy and excitement. Of interest. Of that first moment when you meet someone you find attractive, that you had an interest in, and seeing in their eyes they felt the same.

I just wanted a moment. I unstrapped the satchel from my neck. Held my arms out, with Gungnir to my left. Tossed the satchel aside, as if mirroring her actions from a time long ago.

It was like she could see every thought of mine. Much like I thought I could read her. Maybe we both could. After all, we were much the same. Much the same, except for one tiny thing.

I had a little hope.

And Emma-mae didn't. The world had taken it from her. She had experienced the greatest of evils, she had walked them, lived them. Those scars had never healed for her, they ached restless over her soul, and only widened through the years. The stabbing pain, over and over, for decades, centuries, it had stolen the light from her world.

And this was her way of evening the score.

The smallest of differences, the greatest of gaps.

I stepped forward. Closer. Slowly. Gungnir in my left hand. The hand closest to the wolf. Holding the spear out from me, shielding Fenrir from Emma-mae.

The spear shimmered there. Golden. A small light in such a large darkness.

A small moment at the end of the world.

Emma-mae's face turned with me. I couldn't see her eyes, as much as I tried to direct the glow of the spear. I couldn't see the sparkling in them, all I saw were dark orbs with darker irises. All I saw was the sadness, always there. The understanding, in the tiny set of her jaw, the planes of her face, the tiny trail of water and salt down the side of her cheek.

She was here, now. Within moments of her goal. Within moments, and with me. With me between her and the wolf..

"I had hoped you would still be in New Orleans," she finally said. "That you wouldn't have to see…" her free hand moved in the air. "This."

I knew that had been her plan. Maybe not all of it. She had started that party in New Orleans with the idea of drawing everyone's eye that way. All the gods, all the powers, saints like X. Everyone was there, thinking of the Ragnarok there, of the storm and New Orleans, when the real ending of everything was happening thousands of miles away.

"I don't think the universe works that way," I said. Thinking of the Fates. Of the powers that touched and stretched through all the universes. Of the things that bound us all together, that touched all of life. Of beginnings and endings, of terrible sadness and the smallest joys, of pancakes and hash, of fear and hope.

"No," Emma-mae agreed. Her tone soft, and full of sorrow, if not regret.

I had so much I wanted to say, and yet here and now nothing came. Nothing could possibly come. I looked on Emma-mae, looked on a woman the world had created. Looked on a woman that terrible things had happened to. A woman who had seen a way to get her vengeance on them all. Vengeance on all the gods, for allowing this world to exist. For allowing all the worlds to exist, for allowing all the pain of everything, for allowing the cries and suffering through all the universes.

A tidal wave built over the both of us. I could feel it, swelling with all the pain and rage, with all the sufferance and sense of vengeance. I could feel the tidal wave behind me. Feel the dark wave crashing down over everything. Feel the terrible force of the blackness just like back in Sendai. Felt it and gripped the spear of Gungnir hard, like I was gripping the hand of a girl. Felt it and begged the universe for a moment, for a second, for just a chance.

I felt the ride about to end.

Felt it, and knew what was about to happen. Felt it and saw it, in Emma-mae's lean forward. Shifting the balls of her feet. As if to kick her horse into a final gallop.

I couldn't say anything to stop her. I couldn't offer Emma-mae the one thing I had, she didn't. I couldn't shine a light bright enough in the dark pit she had lived in, for so long. A pit that had only gotten deeper, and darker, through the centuries.

All I could say was, "It's not too late."

Silly words, but they were all I had. All that came to mind. My words urgent, loud. Begging Emma-mae for a moment more. For just a precious second more to talk with her. To share things like dreams, to put my arm around her and help her carry her burden. To climb down into the pit with her and help her find a way out.

To, perhaps, share something like hope.

Silly words. Silly thoughts. Because she was never going to give me that second. That chance.

"Finn," she finally said, in a moment that seemed like it lasted forever between us. A moment of the tidal wave rushing down. A moment I wanted to hold on to, for the rest of my life, because I didn't want what happen next to happen. "It's been too late, for too long."

She leapt.

I hesitated.

Emma-mae didn't.

She was already swinging Vajra by the time I jumped forward. Her arm had swung up and around and was crashing down when I moved forward, holding Gungnir in front of me, trying to shield the wolf. The sceptre flashed through the shadows, little arcs coming along the wings, blue arcs like lightning.

A scream broke from me. Trying to pull everything back. Seeing what was happening before it happened. Knowing and wanting to stop the knowing of it. Trying to stop the hand of the clock swinging forward that next second.

I had been trying to shield the wolf from Emma-mae.

Turned out, I was shielding the wrong thing.

I had misunderstood Emma-mae. Maybe from the very beginning. Maybe from the moment she had told me all things must die.

I had been trying to protect Fenrir. Protect the wolf from the last blow that might end him. When Emma-mae hadn't been swinging at that at all.

Time moved from that forever moment to the next one.

Gungnir pierced Emma-mae's chest. A little to the left of her center. The sharp, shimmering blade—the point which always struck true—easily punched through her chest, her heart, through Emma-mae and out her back.

In that same moment Vajra came down. The invincible scepter.

The sharp edges of universal, cosmic truth. The edges of one wing flashing brightly as Vajra severed Gleipnir. As cosmic truth and power shattered the runes binding the thread, binding the wolf, binding the endings of all the worlds together.

There was a brilliant flash, colors of which I could name, and couldn't. The flash came with a clap of thunder, of a rumble resonating under the stormiest of cloud banks, of the crackling of the thickest of trees, of a reverberation under the deepest roots of the tallest mountains.

There was the brief, oddest scent of fish. Other sensations, so odd when I recall them. Scents and smells and sights and feels. The powerful muscles of a bear, stretching up along the tree, raking its bark. The grinding roots of rock, far below me. The briefest brush of a beard across my face.

The rumbles continued, until they didn't. They were followed by the absence of sound, like the light steps of a cat. A chill spread through the cold cavern, a chilly sense of loss, of power gone. I found a tiny dusting of water on my cheeks. Maybe the spittle of a bird.

Maybe tears.

Those moments will remain etched in my memory. I'll remember them all. I'll feel and hear and see them all. Just like I'll always remember Emma-mae letting out a little gasp. The quickest of *ohs*. The brief exhalation of a sigh, of a release, of a burden gone. Something full of wonder and surprise, of excitement the sharpest of pains.

Like I said, I'll remember that moment forever. Remember holding the spear, feeling it pierce her heart. Feeling Emma-mae feel it, too. Hearing the Vajra clatter to the stone. Feeling the weight of her body on the spear, and dropping Gungnir to catch her, seeing the spear turn back into a pen even as I caught her in my arms.

And held her there.

Her body shuddered then.

Emma-mae was so heavy in my arms. Heavy and hot and wet. Heavy and bleeding.

Blood was everywhere. Her blood ran everywhere, all over us both, hot and warm and slick. I pulled her to me, saying the words *no, no, no,* over and over again. Holding Emma to me and feeling the hole in her back. Trying to stop the flow of blood by holding her tightly in my arms, tight like I would never let go. Saying no over and over and over again.

Her lips were next to my ear. They were soft and warm, just like her breath, and through everything, all my pain and hurt and loss, I felt them lightly kiss me there. Right in front of my ear, right on the temple.

I leaned back, just a bit. My arms still tight around her. Seeing Emma's eyes, clear now. Clear of anger and rage and pain. Clear of the dark cloud she had carried for so long. As if her ride had come to an end, an end she had searched for and found, something she had looked to for a long, long time.

She hadn't killed the wolf. She hadn't ever meant to kill the wolf. She had only meant to end the rest of the worlds. The endings of all the endings. To end what Odin had started.

She had finished her ride. Of what purpose, I did not know. And, like that my understanding, my whisper was broken. "*Why?*"

Her eyes were so clear then. They would always be, in my memory. They flashed like brilliant emeralds, even there in that black cave.

Her smile was so soft. Soft like the kiss against my temple. The warm skin of her lips lightly pressed there. The slow breath, warm against my ear.

She reached both hands out and gripped the sides of my head. Holding me there, and staring at me for a moment that went on forever. I saw the light start to leave her there. The eyes twinkle a little less. The smile slowly retreat.

Still, though, she pulled me close to her. Pulled me back to her. Pulled my head down so that it nestled next to her. To hold me there, with her mouth again next to my ear. To hold me there for another long-feeling moment, with her breath there stirring my hair, wanting to tell me one last thing. Her last breath, her last words, the barest of whispers. "Chin up, Finn. It is always darkest before the dawn."

And then Emma died.

CHAPTER FORTY-TWO

I couldn't tell you how long I held her. How long that moment was. I can only tell you I held her there with the scent of jasmine fading around me, with the chill of the rocky cavern floor soaking into my knees. I can only tell you I held her long into the darkness, until some glimmer of light revealed her to me, until my eyes adjusted to the darkness and I saw the woman who had given her life for this end, for this end and *me*.

I can only keep saying these moments felt like they lasted forever. Certainly this moment, here and now, was timeless. With me holding Emma and smelling the last of her jasmine. With me holding her and feeling her warmth trickle away into the darkness surrounding me. With me staring at her eyes, trying to see some spark remaining there.

It was a timeless moment. And it would forever stay that way, for me.

Not just because Emma had died. Not because the world still spun, that Fenrir had lived. Not because I had saved the world, or worlds.

The moment lasted forever because I sat there, thinking of how much I had missed. Thinking that I called myself a writer, that I sat back and observed the world. That I saw things, felt things. And yet I had missed it all.

The laugh was bitter. Short. I had written a story about walking an alien world, about a little girl realizing that world hadn't been alien at all, but her own. My only published story, published over a decade ago, and yet it still came back to haunt me. It still came back to let me know I hadn't seen the world I had been walking in. I called myself an observer, a writer, and yet everything, from the very beginning, had been in front of me.

Emma had been in front of me. From the very beginning. Not from meeting her at the diner, no, but a time much longer ago than that. I thought about her, about a nurse long ago. About what Emma had just whispered in my ear, and what that nurse had told me, with her eyes of sad ivy staring at me over her mask. Telling me to *chin up*, that better days were ahead. Taking care of me back then, even as I raged and swung my weak arm, even as I had beat on her back then.

My breath escaped me in a long nooooooo. It dropped and trailed away, as the recognition hit me. As the wondering followed. As it all twisted in me and became something almost too great for me to recognize.

It was a denial. Just like the ones I had cried out over Emma, in that timeless moment of her dying in my arms. Me holding her like I would never let her go. Me holding her there, as she told me to chin up, as she told me in her last breath about how it's always darkest before the dawn.

That was the second no that escaped me. Not a long one. A short recognition, as the past few days rolled through my mind. Starting with Emma, in the diner. Starting with her warning about there being a real power in threes.

Starting with the Rule of Three.

I shook my head. There was just too much. Too much, in too short a time. Too much information for me to parse through. Too much for me to accept.

And yet, I did. I tried to make sense of it. The way I told myself that I observed and wrote down everything I saw. The way I tried to weave the right story from everything I had lived and learned and experienced.

The way things ought to be. The things that mattered.

The fact I tried to evade, but seemed real enough, is that Emma had known me long before sitting across from me in the diner. Maybe a century or more into her ride of vengeance she must have happened along *Reagen's Journey.* I guess she had read it, and it had stuck with her in some way.

There was our night. Emma and Huck. All the drinking. All the talk, about how she had felt there was hope in the story, hope that no matter what world we walked in, a shifting perspective might open up something new. Something different from the alien world we found ourselves in. Something that, no matter how dark it seemed, no matter how deep a pit we found ourselves, there was a chance we could find our way out.

Had Emma, even then, meant to end all the worlds? Had she known about Gleipnir and all the Ragnaroks tied together, had she seen the overwhelming darkness rising in the world, the great blackness coming, the shadows of all the evils of all the worlds opening its mouth, ready to swallow us?

I thought, maybe, Emma had.

And I thought, again maybe, she had read my story. She had found a different perspective on how to fix it. On how to end the darkness. Of finding a dawn bright enough to survive the night. And had gone about trying to find that dawn. Trying to find that light.

And stamping me with the awareness of what she was doing, of the world stamping that knowledge into me, three times.

Gaia had said those words first. Not exactly in the same way. But I remembered standing there, the Earth goddess wincing with pain as the other gods fought to end her, have their justice, their vengeance. She had winced, again and again, but still offered me food and drink, even her favorite donut, chocolate with sprinkles.

You have to hope, as the shadows swallow everything, when that day comes, that light you find is bright enough.

At the time I thought she had been talking about the world. About not diminishing the effort of those who walked in it. Of how hard the world was, and letting the small victories be worth something. Of the meaning of putting a dollar in a bucket, even if that dollar might not help. Even if that dollar isn't enough. Even if it might not help. Even if it went to some CEO instead of a person with real need.

But Gaia had been talking about not diminishing the act. About how tough the world was, and that perhaps any act, no matter how small, should count for something. That it wasn't so much the receiving of the gift that mattered as much as the giving of it.

That was hope.

Hope was in the doing. In the offering. Not in the amount received. It was in the effort, and not the reward. It was in the working, the having little, but still offering a hand up for those around you who might need it.

Tears glistened in my eyes, looking at the woman in my arms. A woman who had carried no hope for the longest time, who had only rode with a sense of justice for those who had received none, who had rode with vengeance in a world empty of compassion, for a long, long time.

Who had carried that sense of vengeance, that rage of wanting justice, that lack of hope. Who had perhaps read my story, and had a shift of perspective.

Had Emma steered the wolf to me? Had she gotten Berley to read that particular story? I would likely never know.

I just knew she had found me first. She had found me and somehow watched me grow. She had found me and given me a scent, a trail, and even if she hadn't had hope for the world, she had some hope for *me*.

That even if she hadn't had that kind of hope, she believed I did. A hope large enough to save some of the world. A hope possibly large enough to save all of it.

How could a person survive that kind of realization? To know that someone believed that much in them? To know how much Emma had hated what the world had become, what the gods had become, what humanity had become, that she had somehow seen all of the opposite of that in someone like me.

I had no answer. I would never have an answer, even if I had been warned. Even if the Fates had told me, in the end. Told me for the second time, even as I missed it.

That the darker the soil a seed is planted in, the brighter it can grow.

The world had gotten dark. It had lost compassion. It had lost the little things, the tiny efforts, one person made for the other. The pat of a shoulder, the clasp of a hand, the smile from stranger to stranger, walking down the street.

It had lost all that, and gotten darker. Gods ignored humans, just as humans ignored each other. Just as they walked around with their faces in their phones, ignoring someone lying on the ground next to them, back against a wall, an empty hand out under an empty sky. Gods ignored humans, humans ignored each other, and the world was spiraling faster and faster from there.

Darker and darker.

But Emma had darkened it further. It wasn't enough for her to find a bright light, she wanted to find the brightest of lights. The brightest of dawns.

How dark could Ragnarok be, if it was just the end of one world? Not dark enough. Not for what Emma wanted.

It had to be a real ending. An ending of everything, everything. The darkest of endings where nothing in any universe survived. Where all that was left was the black absence of everything.

Then, and only then, could Emma possibly find the dawn she was looking for. The dim light in universes and universes of the blackest shadows. The illumination of a tiny piece of hope to stand against the overwhelming darkness. Then Emma could find something—*someone*, a light possibly bright enough to be seen.

She had done this.

All of it.

Maybe the world had been sliding into darkness anyway. Maybe all Emma had done was hasten it, with her collection of gods. With her threatening the ending of everything.

Or maybe Emma had found the light she had been looking for, and set all this up. Maybe she had put all her chips in. Maybe she had created the blackest of nights, and stood there in the end, looking at me facing her, looking for the slimmest sliver of a sun cresting the horizon.

It was unbelievable.

Not just because I was here, now. Not because of everything I was putting together. It was unbelievable, only because she had believed in me that much. Because she had read something of mine, something short and small and full of words I had hoped would have led to me being a best-selling writer, but instead had led to this me, here today.

Here, today, with Emma. With Emma gone, in my arms. With her eyes open and staring sightless above me.

I had always wanted to write something that mattered. But at this cost? I didn't think someone like Emma was worth this. I wasn't sure I was.

But, I had to try now. Because if a woman like Emma could believe in me that much, then I would, too. I would try to hold that candle of light against any dark wind blowing against me. I would shelter it and fan it and keep it going. I would be that sun on the horizon.

I would dawn each day with her in mind.

I sat there for the longest time, full of so much pain and sorrow. Full of so much sadness and loss. Full of grief and heartache. It burned through me, the sense of loss, that I would never know more of Emma. That I might never know more than the two of us had both loved pancakes, and hash, and for a moment we had dreamed together of years where we sat and argued about both.

I sat there and cried, and let the tears run down both my cheeks. Let the chill stone of the floor leech my warmth. Sat there with the greatest sorrow, understanding the sacrifice of Emma and her last right.

Understanding everything she had lived. Everything she had experienced. And what she had done.

I held a woman who had lost her hope. A woman who had looked at the world and saw only darkness. Who had looked at the world and saw the blackness, the shadows, flowing over everything. All the worlds. Who had looked at it and wondered where the help was. Where the easing of suffering could come from. Who had looked at the laughing gods and *raged*.

Who had looked at all that, and had found me.

Had stood me opposite that ending, those gods.

And made sure I understood that.

I understood the thread was broken now. That all the endings that had been bound up in Gleipnir had been freed. That all the smaller gods now were free to end their universes, in their own way. And I understood now that I would have to be the person who stood in the way of those gods.

I shook now. From the cold, from the fullness of the realization, I didn't know. Emma's body still felt warm to me, and I didn't want to let her go. I didn't want to ever let her go. Not because of what she meant to me, not because of the feelings between us, our love, but because of something greater. Something I could never capture the meaning of, not with a thousand books, but because I understood she had gotten, finally, what she had looked for.

I understood she had gotten what she had needed. She had rode long and hard and found it. She had the will and the determination to see the ride through. To show me that ride, so that I understood, and let me know the larger task in front of me now.

I think she had thought maybe everything tied together had been too much for the universes. That with all of the endings of all of the worlds bound together, the darkness of any one ending would always sink the others. Each universe could drag the others into the blackest of oceans, and tied together in that way, none could survive.

Separate, each ending could be dealt with. Each darkness on its own was faceable. We could overcome each, we could cut away the anchor dragging our ship down just like we overcome each little thing that happen in our own lives. It's easy enough to swallow one bitter pill, or maybe two. It's only when a hundred pills are swallowed, a thousand, that they become toxic.

I had started out my life wanting to write words that mattered. I wanted to write about the things that would help others get through a rough day, or week, or year. I tried so hard, even in the darkest of times, to hope that something better existed. I wanted to write about those things, that had us hold onto those we loved a little longer.

Like now.

Like I kept holding onto Emma.

Like she had kept holding me, back in her home.

I didn't want to let Emma down.

And I didn't want to let her go.

I stayed that way for a long, long time. With Emma in my arms. Remembering the twinkling eyes. The curve of her lips. The joy of recognition, of her soul to mine. The imagined debates over the years of pancakes and hash. I stayed until there was low whuff behind me, and a shifting of a great weight. The slow growls of a wolf in pain. In tiny huffs and chuffs, as he moved.

Not much movement. Not a lot of huffs and chuffs. Just stretching himself along the cavern behind me. Curling a bit, as a dog might, before sleep. Becoming aware of everything in his den, in that instant.

I was sure the wolf's eyes caught everything there. I was sure he understood everything that had happened as I did. Perhaps he had always understood this was how everything ended.

I sat there, listening to the little movements. Listening to the wolf, in the wolf's den. At the end of my story, at least *this* story. Tears running down my face. I had no shame of them, because I had lost something very precious. I had witnessed a sacrifice of a woman who had the strongest of wills, the greatest determination, and the largest of loves to create something *just* in this world.

I wasn't sure I could ever be worth that.

But I was sure I would try.

The world's ending was no longer all the worlds. But there were still gods, all the gods of all the myths, and some of them would want to end it still. Some of them would certainly try, and someone would have to face them. Some of them would want darkness, and someone would have to be there, shining a light.

Maybe now that all the endings were no longer tied together, other gods might help. Maybe they would no longer consider an apple an apple. Maybe they now had something to face, something they could do, now that all the endings weren't bound up into all the universes.

I could hope. I certainly would. If not for me, for Emma.

I cried. Longer. Harder. Until there were no more tears left. Until the chill of the cavern finally got to me. Until I was shivering, not with sobs, but with an icy cold.

A small light existed in the cavern, pushing back the shadows. Whether it had been called by the wolf, by his power, or something left over from the fight, I didn't know. The cave was dark, the light was small, and existed in the darkness much like the nightlight in a child's bedroom.

The wolf shifted again. Moving just a bit more. Groaning as he did so. Reaching out with a large paw and tugging me softly, close. Pulling me so that I had to let go of Emma. Dragging me into his neck and nuzzling me there, like he might a cub. His coat was warm and smelled of earth and sweat.

I sat there, being held by this large creature. By this god, who had always told me it was all or nothing. A being who could have ended all the worlds in all the universes. Who had carried that burden, who had held on until now, only by the greatest of determination and strength of will.

Had held on, and would have kept holding on, until he had chosen to send me to New Orleans. Who had told me it was *time*.

Having chosen me as a Chronicler, having given me the scent, and sending his cub off.

He had chosen me, much like Emma had, from the very beginning. Had chosen me perhaps knowing Emma had as well. Had chosen me to face his daughter, here at the end.

The warmth of the god warmed me. I felt his great breaths, through his powerful neck, into lungs as large as living rooms. I felt him there, knowing he was watching me. Quietly. Like a wolf might watch a cub follow their first sent.

It was the way of the wolf. Everything was a lesson. To the cub. Maybe even to the wolf.

I finally asked, the question loomed in my mind. It loomed until it was all I could think about. Why the wolf had chosen me over all the others. Over the billions of people on this Earth. Millions of them writers. Tens of thousands of those likely dying, much like I had been. Much like I had been before the wolf found me.

"Why me?"

Fenrir shifted again, as if uncomfortable. His throat moved as if he tried to swallow, once, twice. His whole body shifted; a low moan escaped his throat, low, reverberating with the pain of someone who had carried pain for a long, long time.

He moved his paw. There was a clattering of claws on stone, and a scratching as the wolf searched for something. Finally pulling it back from the darkness of the cave.

A satchel and book.

The flap of the satchel open, so that the book faced me. The book there, having slid just a bit out of the satchel from when I had tossed it. There was the silhouette of the tree on the spine, the swaying man, Huginn and Muninn on Yggdrasil's branches.

The light grew a bit. A small radiance of glow, revealing the teddy bear paw hanging between the pages. Hanging there, like it always did, to hold my place.

The wolf's voice was pained. I felt him gather a breath in the lowest of rumbles. I felt it through the muscles along his chest and the tautness of the muscles along his great neck, as if he was finding the strength to say what he was going to say.

Or finding the words.

"I, too, once hoped to save a girl."

Then he went quiet. His eyes almost fully closed. Slitted. Open just enough to watch me, in the way of wolves and cubs.

For the first time in forever Fenrir was unchained. I wondered if the wolf would test his freedom, if he once again would—if not frolic—go out to the fields and roll in the flowers, feel the sun. I wondered if other gods knew, and what might happen with that knowledge.

The two of us lay there in the darkness. The wolf and the cub. The both of us having a great hurt. The both of us having carried different burdens in our past, and perhaps now shouldering the same. The both of us perhaps wistful of past dreams, apprehensive of the future, and wondering what the unknown tomorrow might bring.

The two of us would worry at this, I knew. The wistfulness, the apprehension, the wonder and the fear. I had started out this new life wanting to save some, in a world I had been told had been all or nothing. That had ended up being far more all-or-nothing than I could have ever known.

Now, I wondered, thinking of the woman who had given her life for this new world, how many more I might be able to save.

Enjoy *The Chronicles of the Wolf*?

Well, me too. I loved this story, and can't wait to write more in this world. But for now, Finn and Fenrir have to take some time. Recuperate. Figure out what their next step will be.

After all, after tens of thousands of years, Fenrir is finally unchained. And after those same years, the world is, too.

So while you wait, come visit chrisjcranford.com. Discover all the other worlds I'm building. Or just reach out and say hello.

ABOUT THE AUTHOR

When Chris isn't trying to figure out how to write a bio, he spends time contemplating the fate of the universe. Probably while walking into a door jamb. He's accepted that the two go hand-in-hand.

He currently resides in Florida, though he has some Magellan in him, and loves to wander.

It is his dream to write stories that – through their telling – influence others to live a little better. Stand a little taller. Smile a little wider. Hold someone a little longer. Fiction should be the dream real life aspires to be.

Dogs are his buddies. Football is his hobby. Books are his passion.

Find out more about Chris here:

www.chrisjcranford.com

facebook.com/chrisjcranford

x.com/chrisjcranford

instagram.com/chrisjcranford

www.ingramcontent.com/pod-product-compliance
Lightning Source LLC
Chambersburg PA
CBHW030732310726

48969CB00005B/1200